Marjorie Bowen

Black Magic

e-artnow 2022

*Marjorie Bowen*
# Black Magic

**Gothic Horror Novel**

e-artnow, 2022
Contact: info@e-artnow.org

ISBN 978-80-273-4510-6

# Contents

# Part I

## The Nun

# Chapter 1

## Sunshine

In the large room of a house in a certain quiet city in Flanders, a man was gilding a devil.

The chamber looked on to the quadrangle round which the house was built; and the sun, just overhead, blazed on the vine leaves clinging to the brick and sent a reflected glow into the sombre spaces of the room.

The devil, rudely cut out of wood, rested by his three tails and his curled-back horns against the wall, and the man sat before him on a low stool.

On the table in front of the open window stood a row of knights in fantastic armour, roughly modelled in clay; beside them was a pile of vellum sheets covered with drawings in brown and green.

By the door a figure of St. Michael leant against a chair, and round his feet were painted glasses of every colour and form.

On the white-washed wall hung a winged picture representing a martyrdom; its vivid hues were the most brilliant thing in the room.

The man was dressed in brown; he had a long dark face and straight dull hair; from the roll of gold leaf on his knee he carefully and slowly gilded the devil.

The place was utterly silent, the perfect stillness enhanced by the dazzle of the blinding sun without; presently the man rose and, crossing to the window, looked out.

He could see the sparse plants bordering the neglected grass-grown paths, the house opposite with its double row of empty windows and the yellowing vine-leaves climbing up the tiled roof that cut the polished blue of the August sky.

In between these windows, that were all closed and glittering in their golden squares, busts of old and weary philosophers were set; they peered out blindly into the unfathomable sunshine, and the dry tendrils of the vine curled across their leanness.

In the centre square of grass was an ancient and broken fountain; some tall white daisies grew there, and the pure gold of their hearts was as bright as the gilding on the devil within. The silence and the blaze of the sun were one and indescribable.

The man at the window rested his elbows on the sill; it was so hot that he felt it burning through his sleeve; he had the air of one habitually alone, the unquestioning calm that comes of long silences; he was young and, in a quiet fashion, well-looking, wide in the brows and long in the jaw, with a smooth pale skin and cloudy dark eyes, his hair hung very straightly, his throat was full and beautiful.

In expression he was reserved and sombre; his lips, well shaped but pale, were resolutely set, and there was a fine curve of strength to his prominent chin.

After a time of expressionless gazing at the sun-filled garden, he turned back into the room, and stood in the centre of the floor, with his teeth set in his forefinger looking ponderingly at the half-gilded devil.

Then he took a bunch of beautifully wrought keys from his belt, and swinging them softly in his hand left the chamber.

The house was built without corridors or passages, each room opened into another and the upper ones were reached by short dark stairways against the walls; there were many apartments, each of a lordly design with the windows in the side facing the quadrangle.

As the man moved lightly from one chamber to the next his footfall displaced dust and his gaze fell on cobwebs and the new nets of spiders, that hung in some places across the very doorways.

Many curious and gorgeous objects were in those deserted rooms; carved presses full of tarnished silver, paintings of holy subjects, furniture covered with rich-hued tapestry, other pieces of arras on the walls, and in one chamber purple silk hangings worked with ladies' hair in shades of brown and gold.

One room was full of books, piled up on the floor, and in the midst of them stood a table bearing strange goblets of shells set in silver and electrum.

Passing these things without a glance the young man mounted to the upper storey and unlocked a door whose rusty lock took his utmost strength to turn. It was a store-room he entered — lit by low long windows looking on the street and carefully shrouded by linen drawn across them; the chamber was chokingly full of dust and a sickly musty smell.

About the floor lay bales of stuff, scarlet, blue and green, painted tiles, old lanterns, clothes, priests' garments, wonderfully worked, glasses and little rusty iron coffers.

Before one of these the young man went on his knees and unlocked it.

It contained a number of bits of glass cut to represent gems; he selected two of an equal size and a clear green colour, then, with the same gravity and silence with which he had come, he returned to the workshop. When he saw the devil, half bright gold, half bald wood, he frowned, then set the green glass in the thing's hollow eye-sockets.

At the twinkling effect of light and life produced by this his frown relaxed; he stood for a while contemplating his handiwork, then washed his brushes and put away his paints and gold leaf.

By now the sun had changed and was shining full into the room casting hot shadows of the vine leaves over the little clay knights, and dazzling in St. Michael's wet red robe.

For the second time the young man left the room, now to go into the hall and open the door that gave upon the street.

He looked on to an empty market-place surrounded by small houses falling into decay, beyond them the double towers of the Cathedral flying upwards across the gold and blue.

Not long ago the town had been besieged and this part of it devastated; now new quarters had been built and this left neglected.

Grass grew between the cobbles, and there was no soul in sight.

The young man shaded his eyes and gazed across the dazzling dreariness; the shadow of his slack, slim figure was cast into the square of sun thrown across the hall through the open door.

Under the iron bell that hung against the lintel stood a basket of bread, a can of milk and some meat wrapped in a linen cloth; the youth took these in and closed the door.

He traversed a large dining-room, finely furnished, a small ante-chamber, came out into the arcaded end of the courtyard, entered the house by a low door next the pump and so into his workshop again.

There he proceeded to prepare his food; on the wide tiled hearth stood a tripod and an iron pot; he lit a fire under this, filled the pot with water and put the meat in; then he took a great book down off a shelf and bent over it, huddled up on a stool in the corner where the shade still lingered.

It was a book filled with drawings of strange and horrible things, and close writing embellished with blood-red capitals. As the young man read, his face grew hot and flushed where it rested on his hand, and the heavy volume fell cumbrous either side his knee; not once did he look up or change his twisted position, but with parted lips and absorbed eyes pored over the black lettering.

The sun sank the other side of the house, so that the garden and room were alike in shadow, and the air became cooler; still the young man made no movement.

The flames leapt on the hearth and the meat seethed in the pot unheeded.

Outside the vine leaves curled against the brick, and the stone faces looked down at the broken fountain, the struggling grass and the tall white daisies; still the young man, bending lower, his heated cheek pressed into his palm, his hair touching the page, bent over the great tome on his knee.

Not the devil with his green eyes staring before him, not St. Michael in his red robe by the door, not the martyr in the bright winged picture were more still than he, crouched upon his wooden stool.

Then, without prelude or warning, the heavy clang of a bell woke the silence into trembling echoes.

The young man dropped the book and sprang to his feet; red and white chased across his face, he stood panting, bewildered, with one hand on his heart, and dazed eyes.

Again the bell sounded.

It could only be that which hung at the front door; not for years had one rung it; he picked up the book, put it back on the shelf, and stood irresolute.

For a third time the iron clang, insistent, impatient, rang through the quiet.

The young man frowned, pushed back the hair from his hot forehead and went, with a light and cautious step, across the courtyard, through the dark dining-chamber into the hall.

Here for a second he hesitated, then drew back the bolt and opened the door.

Two men stood without.

One was most gorgeously attired, the other wore a dark cloak and carried his hat in his hand. "You cannot want me," said the youth, surveying them. "And there is no one else here." His voice fell full and low, of a soft quality, but the tone was sombre and cold.

The splendidly-dressed stranger answered —"If you are Master Dirk Renswoude, we are most desirous to see and speak with you."

The young man opened the door a little wider. "I am Dirk Renswoude, but I know neither of you!"

"I did not think so," the other answered. "Still, we have a matter to ask you of. I am Balthasar of Courtrai and this is my friend, whom you may call Theirry, born of Dendermonde."

"Balthasar of Courtrai!" repeated the youth softly; he stood aside and motioned them to enter. When they had passed into the hall he carefully bolted the door; then turned to them with a grave absorbed manner.

"Will you follow me?" he said, and went before them to his workroom.

The sun had left chamber and garden now, but the air was golden warm with it, and a sense of great heat still lay over the grass and vines seen through the open window.

Dirk Renswoude moved St. Michael from the chair and tossed a pile of parchments off a stool. He offered these seats to his guests, who accepted them in silence.

"You must needs wait till the supper is prepared," he said, and with that placed himself on the stool by the pot, and, while he stirred it with an iron spoon, openly studied the two men.

Balthasar of Courtrai was gorgeous; his age might be perhaps twenty-six or seven; he was of a large make, florid in the face with a high red colour and blunt features; his brows were straight and over fair, his eyes deep blue and expressionless; his heavy yellow hair was cut low on his forehead and fell straightly on to his neck.

He wore a flat orange hat, slashed and cut, fastened by purple cords to the shoulder of a gold doublet that opened on a shirt of fine lawn; his sleeves were enormous, fantastic, puffed and gathered; round his waist was a linked belt into which were thrust numerous daggers and a short sword.

His breeches, of a most vivid blue, were beruffled with knots and tassels, his riding-boots, that came to his knees, stained with the summer dust, showed a small foot decorated with gilt spurs. He sat with one hand on his hip, and in the other held his leathern gloves.

Such the picture, Master Dirk Renswoude, considering him coldly, formed of Balthasar of Courtrai.

His companion was younger; dressed sombrely in black and violet, but as well-looking as a man may be; he was neither dark nor fair, but of a clear brown hue, and his eyes were hazel, swift and brilliant; his mouth was set smilingly, yet the whole face expressed reserve and some disdain; he had laid his hat on the floor beside him, and with an interested glance was observing the room.

But Balthasar of Courtrai returned Master Dirk Renswoude's steady gaze.

"You have heard of me?" he said suddenly.

"Yes," was the instant answer.

"Then, belike, you know what I am here for?"

"No," said Master Dirk, frowning.

Balthasar glanced at his companion, who gave no heed to either of them, but stared at the half-gilded devil with interest and some wonder; seeing this, Balthasar answered for himself, in a manner half defiant and wholly arrogant.

"My father is Margrave of East Flanders, and the Emperor knighted me when I was fifteen. Now I am tired of Courtrai, of the castle, of my father. I have taken the road."

Master Dirk lifted the iron pot from the fire to the hearth.

"The road to — where?" he asked.

Balthasar made a large gesture with his right hand.

"To Cologne, perhaps to Rome, to Constantinople . . . to Turkey or Hungary."

"Knight errant," said Master Dirk.

Balthasar tossed his fine head.

"By the Rood, no. I have ambitions."

Master Dirk laughed.

"And your friend?" he asked.

"A wandering scholar," smiled Balthasar. "Also weary of the town of Courtrai. He dreams of fame."

Theirry looked round at this.

"I am going to the Universities," he said quietly. "To Paris, Basle, Padua — you have heard of them?"

The youth's cloudy eyes gleamed.

"Ah, I have heard of them," he replied upon a quick breath.

"I have a great desire for learning," said Theirry.

Balthasar made an impatient movement that shook the tassels and ribbons on his sleeves. "God help us, yes! And I for other things."

Master Dirk was moving about setting the supper. He placed the little clay knights on the window-sill, and flung, without any ado, drawings, paints and brushes on to the floor.

Silence fell on them; the young host's bearing did not encourage comment, and the atmosphere of the room was languid and remote, not conducive to talk.

Master Dirk, composed and aloof, opened a press in the wall, and took thence a fine cloth that he laid smoothly on the rough table; then he set on it earthenware dishes and plates, drinking-glasses painted in bright colours, and forks with agate handles.

They were well served for food, even though it might not be the princely fare the Margrave's son was used to; honey in a silver jar, shining apples lying among their leaves, wheaten cakes in a plaited basket, grapes on a gold salver, lettuces and radishes fragrantly wet; these Master Dirk brought from the press and set on the table. Then he helped his guests to meat, and Balthasar spoke.

"You live strangely here — so much alone."

"I have no desire for company. I work and take pleasure in it. They buy my work, pictures, carvings, sculptures for churches — very readily."

"You are a good craftsman," said Theirry. "Who taught you?"

"Old Master Lukas, born of Ghent, and taught in Italy. When he died he left me this house and all it holds."

Again their speech sank into silence; Balthasar ate heavily, but with elegance; Dirk, seated next the window, rested his chin on his palm and stared out at the bright yet fading blue of the sky, at the row of closed windows opposite, and the daisies waving round the broken fountain; he ate very little. Theirry, placed opposite, was of the same mind and, paying little heed to

Balthasar, who seemed not to interest him in the least, kept curious eyes on Dirk's strange, grave face.

After a while the Margrave's son asked shamelessly for wine, and the youth rose languidly and brought it; tall bottles, white, red and yellow in wicker cases, and an amber-hued beer such as the peasants drank.

The placing of these before Balthasar seemed to rouse him from his apathy.

"Why have you come here?" he demanded.

Balthasar laughed easily.

"I am married," he said as a prelude, and lifted his glass in a large, well-made hand. At that Master Dirk frowned.

"So are many men."

Balthasar surveyed the tilting wine through half-closed eyes.

"It is about my wife, Master, that I am here now."

Dirk Renswoude leant forward in his chair.

"I know of your wife."

"Tell me of her," said Balthasar of Courtrai. "I have come here for that."

Dirk slightly smiled.

"Should I know more than you?"

The Margrave's son flushed.

"What you do know? — tell me."

Dirk's smile deepened.

"She was one Ursula, daughter of the Lord of Rooselaare, she was sent to the convent of the White Sisters in this town."

"So you know it all," said Balthasar. "Well, what else?"

"What else? I must tell you a familiar tale."

"Certes, more so to you than to me."

"Then, since you wish it, here is your story, sir."

Dirk spoke in an indifferent voice well suited to the peace of the chamber; he looked at neither of his listeners, but always out of the window.

"She was educated for a nun and, I think, desired to become one of the Order of the White Sisters. But when she was fifteen her brother died and she became her father's heiress. So many entered the lists for her hand — they contracted her to you."

Balthasar pulled at the orange tassels on his sleeve.

"Without my wish or consent," he said.

The young man took no heed.

"They sent a guard to bring her back to Rooselaare, but because they were fearful of the danger of journey, and that she might be captured by one of the pretenders to her fortunes, they married her fast and securely, by proxy, to you. At this the maid, who wished most heartily, I take it, to become a nun, fell ill of grief, and in her despair she confided her misery to the Abbess."

Balthasar's eyes flickered and hardened behind their fair lashes.

"I tell you a tale," said Dirk, "that I believe you know, but since you have come to hear me speak on this matter, I relate what has come to me — of it. This Ursula was heiress to great wealth, and in her love to the Sisters, and her dislike to this marriage, she promised them all her worldly goods, when she should come into possession of them, if they would connive at saving her from her father and her husband. So the nuns, tempted by greed, spread the report that she had died in her illness, and, being clever women, they blinded all. There was a false funeral, and Ursula was kept secret in the convent among the novices. All this matter was put into writing and attested by the nuns, that there might be no doubt of the truth of it when the maid came into her heritage. And the news went to her home that she was dead."

"And I was glad of it," said Balthasar. "For then I loved another woman and was in no need for money."

"Peace, shameless," said Theirry, but Dirk Renswoude laughed softly.

"She took the final, the irrevocable vows, and lived for three years among the nuns. And the life became bitter and utterly unendurable to her, and she dared not make herself known to her father because of the deeds the nuns held, promising them her lands. So, as the life became more and more horrible to her, she wrote, in her extremity, and found means to send, a letter to her husband."

"I have it here." Balthasar touched his breast. "She said she had sworn herself to me before she had vowed herself to God — told me of her deceit," he laughed, "and asked me to come and rescue her."

Dirk crossed his hands, that were long and beautiful, upon the table.

"You did not come and you did not answer."

The Margrave's son glanced at Theirry, as he had a habit of doing, as if he reluctantly desired his assistance or encouragement; but again he obtained nothing and answered for himself, after the slightest pause.

"No, I did not come. Her father had taken another wife and had a son to inherit. And I," he lowered his eyes moodily, "I was thinking of another woman. She had lied, my wife, to God, I think. Well, let her take her punishment, I said."

"She did not wait beyond some months for your answer," said Master Dirk. "Master Lukas, born of Ghent, was employed in the chapel of the convent, and she, who had to wait on him, told him her story. And when he had finished the chapel she fled with him here — to this house. And again she wrote to her husband, speaking of the old man who had befriended her and telling him of her abode. And again he did not answer. That was five years ago."

"And the nuns made no search for her?" asked Theirry.

"They knew now that the girl was no heiress, and they were afraid that the tale might get blown abroad. Then there was war."

"Ay, had it not been for that I might have come," said Balthasar. "But I was much occupied with fighting."

"The convent was burnt and the sisters fled," continued Dirk. "And the maid lived here, learning many crafts from Master Lukas. He had no apprentices but us."

Balthasar leant back in his chair.

"That much I learnt. And that the old man, dying, left his place to you, and — what more of this Ursula?"

The young man gave him a slow, full glance.

"Strangely late you inquire after her, Balthasar of Courtrai."

The Knight turned his head away, half sullenly.

"A man must know how he is encumbered. No one save I is aware of her existence . . . yet she is my wife."

Dusk, hot and golden, had fallen on the chamber. The half-gilded devil gleamed dully; above his violet vestment Theirry's handsome face showed with a half smile on the curved lips; the Knight was a little ill at ease, a little sullen, but glowingly massive, gorgeous and finely coloured.

The young sculptor rested his smooth pale face on his palm; cloudy eyes and cloudy hair were hardly discernible in the twilight, but the line of the resolute chin was clear cut.

"She died four years ago," he said. "And her grave is in the garden . . . where those white daisies grow."

## Chapter 2

## The Students

"Dead," repeated Balthasar; he pushed back his chair and then laughed. "Why — so is my difficulty solved — I am free of that, Theirry."

His companion frowned.

"Do you take it so? I think it is pitiful — the fool was so young." He turned to Dirk. "Of what did she die?"

The sculptor sighed, as if weary of the subject.

"I know not. She was happy here, yet she died."

Balthasar rose.

"Why did you bury her within the house?" he asked half uneasily.

"It was in time of war," answered Dirk. "We did what we could — and she, I think, had wished it."

The young Knight leant a little way from the open window and looked at the daisies; they gleamed hard and white through the deepening twilight, and he could imagine that they were growing from the heart, from the eyes and lips of the wife whom he had never seen.

He wished her grave was not there; he wished she had not appealed to him; he was angry with her that she had died and shamed him; yet this same death was a vast relief to him. Dirk got softly to his feet and laid his hand on Balthasar's fantastic sleeve.

"We buried her deep enough," he said. "She does not rise."

The Knight turned with a little start and crossed himself.

"God grant that she sleep in peace," he cried.

"Amen," said Theirry gravely.

Dirk took a lantern from the wall and lit it from the coals still smouldering on the hearth.

"Now you know all I know of this matter," he remarked. "I thought that some day you might come. I have kept for you her ring — your ring —"

Balthasar interrupted.

"I want none of it," he said hastily.

Dirk lifted the lantern; its fluttering flame flushed the twilight with gold.

"Will you please to sleep here to-night?" he asked. The Knight, with his back to the window, assented, in defiance of a secret dislike to the place.

"Follow me," commanded Dirk, then to the other, "I shall be back anon."

"Good rest," nodded Balthasar. "To-morrow we will get horses in the town and start for Cologne."

"Good even," said Theirry.

The Knight went after his host through the silent rooms, up a twisting staircase into a low chamber looking on to the quadrangle.

It contained a wooden bedstead covered with a scarlet quilt, a table, and some richly carved chairs; Dirk lit the candles standing on the table, bade his guest a curt good-night and returned to the workroom.

He opened the door of this softly and looked in before he entered.

By the window stood Theirry striving to catch the last light on the pages of a little book he held.

His tall, graceful figure was shadowed by his sombre garments, but the fine oval of his face was just discernible above the white pages of the volume.

Dirk pushed the door wide and stepped in softly.

"You love reading?" he said, and his eyes shone. Theirry started, and thrust the book into the bosom of his doublet.

"Ay — and you?" he asked tentatively.

Dirk set the lantern among the disordered supper things.

"Master Lukas left me his manuscripts among his other goods," he answered. "Being much alone — I have — read them."

In the lantern light, that the air breathed from the garden fanned into a flickering glow, the two young men looked at each other.

An extraordinary expression, like a guilty excitement, came into the eyes of each.

"Ah!" said Dirk, and drew back a little. "Being much alone," whispered Theirry, "with — a dead maid in the house — how have you spent your time?"

Dirk crouched away against the wall; his hair hung lankly over his pallid face. "You — you — pitied her?" he breathed.

Theirry shuddered.

"Balthasar sickens me — yea, though he be my friend."

"You would have come?" questioned Dirk. "When she sent to you?"

"I should have seen no other thing to do," answered Theirry. "What manner of a maid was she?"

"I did think her fair," said Dirk slowly. "She had yellow hair — you may see her likeness in that picture on the wall. But now it is too dark."

Theirry came round the table.

"You also follow knowledge?" he inquired eagerly.

But Dirk answered almost roughly.

"Why should I confide in you? I know nothing of you."

"There is a tie in kindred pursuits," replied the scholar more quietly.

Dirk caught up the lantern.

"You are not aware of the nature of my studies," he cried, and his eyes shone wrathfully. "Come to bed. I am weary of talking."

Theirry bent his head.

"This is a fair place for silences," he said.

As if gloomily angry, yet disdaining the expression of it, Dirk conducted him to a chamber close to that where Balthasar lay, and left him, without speech, nor did Theirry solicit any word of him.

Dirk did not return to the workroom, but went into the garden and paced to and fro under the stars that burnt fiercely and seemed to hang very low over the dark line of the house.

His walk was hasty, his steps uneven, he bit, with an air of absorbed distraction, his lip, his finger, the ends of his straight hair, and now and then he looked with tumultuous eyes up at the heavens, down at the ground and wildly about him.

It was well into the night when he at last returned into the house, and, taking a candle in his hand, went stealthily up to Balthasar's chamber.

With a delicate touch he unfastened the door, and very lightly entered.

Shielding the candle flame with his hand he went up to the bed.

The young Knight lay heavily asleep; his yellow hair was tumbled over his flushed face and about the pillow; his arms hung slackly outside the red coverlet; on the floor were his brilliant clothes, his sword, his belt, his purse.

Where his shirt fell open at the throat a narrow blue cord showed a charm attached.

Dirk stood still, leaning forward a little, looking at the sleeper, and expressions of contempt, of startled anger, of confusion, of reflection passed across his haggard features.

Balthasar did not stir in his deep sleep; neither the light held above him nor the intense gaze of the young man's dark eyes served to wake him, and after a while Dirk left him and passed to the chamber opposite.

There lay Theirry, fully dressed, on his low couch. Dirk set the candle on the table and came on tiptoe to his side.

The scholar's fair face was resting on his hand, his chin up-tilted, his full lips a little apart; his lashes lay so lightly on his cheek it seemed he must be glancing from under them; his hair, dark, yet shining, was heaped round his temples.

Dirk, staring down at him, breathed furiously, and the colour flooded his face, receded, and sprang up again.

Then retreating to the table he sank on to the rush-bottomed chair, and put his hands over his eyes; the candle flame leapt in unison with his uneven breaths.

Looking round, after a while, with a wild glance, he gave a long, distraught sigh, and Theirry moved in his sleep.

At this the watcher sat expectant.

Theirry stirred again, turned, and rose on his elbow with a start.

Seeing the light and the young man sitting by it, staring at him with brilliant eyes, he set his feet to the ground.

Before he could speak Dirk put his finger on his lips.

"Hush," he whispered, "Balthasar is asleep." Theirry, startled, frowned.

"What do you want with me?"

For answer the young sculptor moaned, and dropped his head into the curve of his arm.

"You are strange," said Theirry.

Dirk glanced up.

"Will you take me with you to Padua — to Basle?" he said. "I have money and some learning." "You are free to go as I," answered Theirry, but awakened interest shone in his eyes. "I would go with you," insisted Dirk intensely. "Will you take me?"

Theirry rose from the bed uneasily.

"I have had no companion all my life." He said. "The man whom I would take into must be of rare quality —"

He came to the other side of the table and across the frail gleam of the candle looked at Dirk. Their eyes met and instantly sank, as if each were afraid of what the other might reveal. "I have studied somewhat," said Dirk hoarsely. "You also — I think, in the same science —" The silent awe of comprehension fell upon them, then Theirry spoke.

"So few understand — can it be possible — — that you —?"

Dirk rose.

"I have done something."

Theirry paled, but his hazel eyes were bright as flame.

"How much?" then he broke off —"God help us —"

"Ah! — do you use that name?" cried Dirk, and showed his teeth

The other, with cold fingers, clutched at the back of the rush-bottomed chair.

"So I is true — you deal with — you — ah, you —"

"What was that book you were reading?" asked Dirk sharply.

Theirry suddenly laughed.

"What is your study, that you desire to perfect at Basle, at Padua?" he counter-questioned There was a pause; then Dirk crushed the candle out with his open palm, and answered on a half sob of excitement —

"Black magic — black magic!"

# Chapter 3

## The Experiment

"I guessed it," said Theirry under his breath, "when I entered the house."

"And you?" came Dirk's voice.

"I — I also."

There was silence; then Dirk groped his way to the door.

"Come after me," he whispered. "There is a light downstairs."

Theirry had no words to answer; his throat was hot, his lips dry with excitement, he felt his temples pulsating and his brow damp.

Cautiously they crept down the stairs and into the workroom, where the lantern cast long pale rays of light across the hot dark.

Dirk set the window as wide as it would go and crouched into the chair under it; his face was flushed, his hair tumbled, his brown clothes dishevelled.

"Tell me about yourself," he said.

Theirry leant against the wall, for he felt his limbs trembling.

"What do you want to know?" he asked, half desperately; "I can do very little."

Dirk set his elbows on the table and his chin in his hand; his half-veiled gleaming eyes held Theirry's fascinated, reluctant gaze.

"I have had no chance to learn," he whispered. "Master Lukas had some books — not enough — — but what one might do —!"

"I came upon old writings," said Theirry slowly. "I thought one might be great — that way, so I fled from Courtrai."

Dirk rose and beckoned.

"I will work a spell to-night. You shall see."

He took up the lantern and Theirry followed him; they traversed the chamber and entered another; in the centre of that Dirk stopped, and gave the light into the cold hand of his companion.

"Here we shall be secret," he murmured, and raised, with some difficulty, a trap-door in the floor. Theirry peered into the blackness revealed below.

"Have you done this before?" he asked fearfully.

"This spell? No."

Dirk was descending the stairs into the dark.

"God will never forgive," muttered Theirry, hanging back.

"Are you afraid?" asked Dirk wildly.

Theirry set his lips.

"No. No."

He stepped on to the ladder, and holding the light above his head, followed.

They found themselves in a large vault entirely below the surface of the ground, so that air was attained only from the trap-door that they had left open behind them.

Floor and walls were paved with smooth stones, the air was thick and intolerably hot; the roof only a few inches above Theirry's head.

In one corner stood a tall dark mirror, resting against the wall; beside it were a pile of books and an iron brazier full of ashes.

Dirk took the lantern from Theirry and hung it to a nail on the wall.

"I have been studying," he whispered, "how to raise spirits and see into the future — I think I begin to feel my way;" his great eyes suddenly unclosed and flashed over his companion. "Have you the courage?"

"Yes," said Theirry hoarsely. "For what else have I left my home if not for this?" "It is strange we should have met," shuddered Dirk.

Their guilty eyes glanced away from each other; Dirk took a piece of white chalk from his pocket and began drawing circles, one within the other on the centre of the floor.

He marked them with strange signs and figures that he drew carefully and exactly.

Theirry stayed by the lantern, his handsome face drawn and pale, his eyes intent on the other's movements.

The upper part of the vault was in darkness; shadows like a bat's wings swept either side of the lantern that cast a sickly yellow light on the floor, and the slender figure of Dirk on one knee amid his chalk circles.

When he had completed them he rose, took one of the books from the corner and opened it. "Do you know this?" With a delicate forefinger he beckoned Theirry, who came and read over his shoulder.

"I have tried it. It has never succeeded."

"To-night it may," whispered Dirk.

He shook the ashes out of the brazier and filled it with charcoal that he took from a pile near. This he lit and placed before the mirror.

"The future — we must know the future," he said, as if to himself.

"They will not come," said Theirry, wiping his damp forehead. "I — heard them once — but they never came."

"Did you tempt them enough?" breathed Dirk. "If you have Mandrake they will do anything."

"I had none."

"Nor I — still one can force them against their will — though it is — terrible."

The thin blue smoke from the charcoal was filling the vault; they felt their heads throbbing, their nostrils dry.

Dirk stepped into the chalk circles holding the book.

In a slow, unsteady voice he commenced to read.

As Theirry caught the words of the blasphemous and horrible invocation he shook and shuddered, biting his tongue to keep back the instinctive prayer that rose to his lips.

But Dirk gained courage as he read; he drew himself erect; his eyes flashed, his cheeks burnt crimson; the smoke had cleared from the brazier, the charcoal glowed red and clear; the air grew hotter; it seemed as if a cloak of lead had been flung over their heads.

At last Dirk stopped.

"Put out the lantern," he muttered.

Theirry opened it and stifled the flame.

There was now only the light of the burning charcoal that threw a ghastly hue over the dark surface of the mirror.

Theirry drew a long sighing breath; Dirk, swaying on his feet, began speaking again in a strange and heavy tongue.

Then he was silent.

Faint muttering noises grew out of the darkness, indistinct sounds of howling, sobbing. "They come," breathed Theirry.

Dirk repeated the invocation.

The air shuddered with moanings.

"A — ah!" cried Dirk.

Into the dim glow of the brazier a creature was crawling, the size of a dog, the shape of a man, of a hideous colour of mottled black; it made a wretched crying noise, and moved slowly as if in pain.

Theirry gave a great sob, and pressed his face against the wall.

But Dirk snarled at it across the dark.

"So you have come. Show us the future. I have the power over you. You know that."

The thin flames leapt suddenly high, a sound of broken wailings came through the air; something ran round the brazier; the surface of the mirror was troubled as if dark water ran over it; then suddenly was flashed on it a faint yet bright image of a woman, crowned, and with yellow hair; as she faded, a semblance of one wearing a tiara appeared but blurred and faint. "More," cried Dirk passionately. "Show us more —"

The mirror brightened, revealing depths of cloudy sky; against them rose the dark line of a gallows tree.

Theirry stepped forward.

"Ah, God!" he shrieked, and crossed himself. With a sharp sound the mirror cracked and fell asunder; a howl of terror arose, and dark shapes leapt into the air to be absorbed in it and disappear.

Dirk staggered out of the circle and caught hold of Theirry.

"You have broken the spell!" he gibbered. "You have broken the spell!"

An icy stillness had suddenly fallen; the brazier flickered rapidly out, and even the coals were soon black and dead; the two stood in absolute darkness.

"They have gone!" whispered Theirry; he wrenched himself free from Dirk's clutch and fumbled his way to the ladder.

Finding this by reason of the faint patch of light overhead, he climbed up through the trap-door, his body heaving with long-drawn breaths.

Dirk, light-footed and lithe, followed him, and dropped the flap.

"The charm was not strong enough," he said through his teeth. "And you —"

Theirry broke in.

"I could not help myself — I — I — saw them."

He sank on a chair by the open window and dropped his brow into his hand.

The room was full of a soft starlight, far away and infinitely sweet; the vines and grasses made a quivering sound in the night wind and tapped against the lattice.

Dirk moved into the workshop and came back with the candle and a great green glass of wine. He held up the light so that he could see the scholar's beautiful agonised face, and with his other hand gave him the goblet.

Theirry looked up and drank silently.

When he had finished, the colour was back in his cheeks.

Dirk took the glass from him and set it beside the candle on the window-sill.

"What did you see — in the mirror?" he asked.

"I do not know," answered Theirry wildly. "A woman's face —"

"Ay," broke in Dirk. "Now, what was she to us? And a figure like — the Pope?"

He smiled derisively.

"I saw that," said Theirry. "But what should they do with holy things? — and then I saw —" Dirk swung round on him; each white despite the candle-light.

"Nay — there, was no more after that!"

"There was," insisted Theirry. "A stormy sky and a gallows tree —" His voice fell hollowly. Dirk strode across the room into the trailing shadows.

"The foul little imps!" he said passionately. "They deceived us!"

Theirry rose in his place.

"Will you continue these studies?" he questioned.

The other gave him a quick look over his shoulder.

"Do you think of turning aside?"

"Nay, nay," answered Theirry. "But one may keep knowledge this side of things blasphemous and unholy."

Dirk laughed hoarsely.

"I have no fear of God!" he said in a thick voice. "But you — you are afraid of Sathanas. Well, go your way. Each man to his master. Mine will give me many things — look to it yours does the like by you —"

He opened the door, and was leaving, when Theirry came after him and caught him by the robe.

"Listen to me. I am not afraid. Nay, why did I leave Courtrai?"

With resolute starry eyes Dirk gazed up at Theirry (who was near a head taller), and his proud mouth curled a little.

"I may not disregard the fate that sent me here," continued Theirry. "Will you come with me? I can be loyal."

His words were earnest, his face eager; still Dirk vas mute.

"I have hated men, not loved them, all my life — most wonderfully am I drawn to thee —"

"Oh!" cried Dirk, and gave a little quivering laugh.

"Together might we do much, and it is ill work studying alone."

The younger man put out his hand.

"If I come, will you swear a pact with me of friendship?"

"We will be as brothers," said Theirry gravely. "Sharing good and ill."

"Keeping our secret?" whispered Dirk —"allowing none to come between us?"

"Yea."

"You are a-tune to me," said Dirk. "So be it. I will come with you to Basle."

He raised his strange face; in the hollowed eyes, in the full colourless lips, were a resolution and a strength that held and commanded the other.

"We may be great," he said.

Theirry took his hand; the red candle-light was being subdued and vanquished by a glimmering grey that overspread the stars; the dawn was peering in at the window.

"Can you sleep?" asked Theirry.

Dirk withdrew his hand.

"At least I can feign it — Balthasar must not guess — get you to bed — never forget to-night and what you swore."

With a soft gliding step he gained the door, opened it noiselessly, and departed.

Theirry stood for a while, listening to the slight sound of the retreating footfall, then he pressed his hands to his forehead and turned to the window.

A pale pure flush of saffron stained the sky above the roof-line; there were no clouds, and the breeze had dropped again.

In the vast and awful stillness, Theirry, feeling marked, set apart and defiled with blasphemy, yet elated also, in a wild and wicked manner, tiptoed up to his chamber.

Each creaking board he stepped on, each shadow that seemed to change as he passed it, caused his blood to tingle guiltily; when he had gained his room he bolted the door and flung himself along his tumbled couch, holding his fingers to his lips, and with strained eyes gazing at the window. So he lay through long hours of sunshine in a half-swoon of sleep.

## Chapter 4

## The Departure

He was at length fully aroused by the sound of loud and cheerful singing.

"My heart's a nun within my breast
So cold is she, so cloistered cold" . . .

Theirry sat up, conscious of a burning, aching head and a room flooded with sunshine.

"To her my sins are all confest —
So wise is she, so wise and old —
So I blow off my loves like the thistledown"

A burst of laughter interrupted the song; Theirry knew now that it was Balthasar's voice, and he rose from the couch with a sense of haste and discomfiture.

What hour was it?

The day was of a drowsing heat; the glare of the sun had taken all colour out of the walls opposite, the grass and vines; they all blazed together, a shimmer of gold.

"So I blow off my loves like the thistledown
And ride from the gates of Courtrai town" . . .

Theirry descended.

He found Balthasar in the workshop; there were the remains of a meal on the table, and the Knight, red and fresh as a rose, was polishing up his sword handle, singing the while, as if in pleased expression of his own thoughts.

In the corner sat Dirk, drawn into himself and gilding the devil.

Theirry was conscious of a great dislike to Balthasar; ghosts nor devils, nor the thought of them had troubled his repose; there was annoyance in the fact that he had slept well, eaten well, and was now singing in sheer careless gaiety of heart; yet what other side of life should a mere animal like Balthasar know?

Dirk looked up, then quickly down again; Theirry sank on a stool by the table.

Balthasar turned to him.

"Are you sick?" he asked, wide-eyed.

The scholar's dishevelled appearance, haggard eyes, tumbled locks and peevish gathering of the brows, justified his comment, but Theirry turned an angry eye on him.

"Something sick," he answered curtly. Balthasar glanced from him to Dirk's back, bending over his work.

"There is much companionship to be got from learned men, truly!" he remarked; his blue eyes and white teeth flashed in a half amusement; he put one foot on a chair and balanced his glittering sword across his knee; Theirry averted a bitter gaze from his young splendour, but Balthasar laughed and broke into his song again.

"My heart's a nun within my breast,
So proud is she, so hard and proud,
Absolving me, she gives me rest" . . .

"We part ways here," said Theirry.

"So soon?" asked the Knight, then sang indifferently —

"So I blow off my loves like the thistledown.
And ride through the gates of Courtrai town." . . .

Theirry glanced now at his bright face, smooth yellow hair and gorgeous vestments. "Ay," he said. "I go to Basle."

"And I to Frankfort; still, we might have kept company a little longer."

"I have other plans," said Theirry shortly.

Balthasar smiled good-humouredly.

"You are not wont to be so evil-tempered," he remarked.

Then he looked from one to the other; silent both and unresponsive.

"I will even take my leave;" he laid the great glittering sword across the table.

Dirk turned on his stool with the roll of gilding in his hand.

At his cold gaze, that seemed to hold something of enmity and an unfriendly knowledge, Balthasar's dazzlingly fresh face flushed deeper in the cheeks.

"Since I have been so manifestly unwelcome," he said, "I will pay for what I have had of you." Dirk rose.

"You mistake," he answered. "I have been pleased to see you for many reasons, Balthasar of Courtrai."

The young Knight thrust his hands into his linked belt and eyed the speaker.

"You condemn me," he said defiantly. "Well, Theirry is more to your mind —"

He opened his purse of curiously cut and coloured leather, and taking from it four gold coins laid them on the corner of the table.

"So you may buy masses for the soul of Ursula of Rooselaare." He indicated the money with a swaggering gesture.

"Think you her soul is lost?" queried Dirk.

"A choired saint is glad of prayers," returned Balthasar. "But you are in an ill mood, master, so good-bye to you and God send you sweeter manners when next we meet."

He moved to the door, vivid blue and gold and purple; without looking back he flung on his orange hat.

Theirry roused himself and turned with a reluctant interest.

"You are going to Frankfort?" he asked.

"Ay," Balthasar nodded pleasantly. "I shall see in the town to the hire of a horse and man — — mine own beast being lamed, as you know, Theirry."

The scholar rose.

"Why do you go to Frankfort?" he asked. He spoke with no object, in a half-sick envy of the Knight's gaiety and light-heartedness, but Balthasar coloured for the second time.

"All men go to Frankfort," he answered. "Is not the Emperor there?"

Theirry lifted his shoulders.

"'Tis no matter of mine."

"Nay," said Balthasar, who appeared to have been both disturbed and confused by the question, "no more than it is my affair to ask you — why go you to Basle?"

The scholar's eyes gleamed behind his thick lashes.

"It is very clear why I go to Basle. To study medicine and philosophy."

They quitted the room, leaving Dirk looking covertly after them, and were proceeding through the dusty, neglected rooms.

"I do not like the place," said Balthasar. "Nor yet the youth. But he has served my purpose." And now they were in the hall.

"We shall meet again," said Theirry, opening the door.

The Knight turned his bright face.

"Like enough," he answered easily. "Farewell." With that and a smile he was swinging off across the cobbles, tightening his sword straps.

Against the sun-dried, decayed houses, across the grass-grown square his vivid garments flashed and his voice came over his shoulder through the hot blue air —

"So I blew off my loves like the thistledown And rode through the gates of Courtrai town."

Theirry watched him disappear round the angle of the houses, then bolted the door and returned to the workroom.

Dirk was standing very much as he had left him, half resting against the table with the roll of gilding in his white fingers.

"What do you know of that man?" he asked as Theirry entered. "Where did you meet him?"

"Balthasar?"

"Yea."

Theirry frowned.

"At his father's house. I taught his sister music. There was, in a manner, some friendship between us . . . we both wearied of Courtrai . . . so it came we were together. I never loved him." Dirk returned quietly to the now completely gilded devil.

"Know you anything of the woman he spoke of?" he asked.

"Did he speak of one?"

Dirk looked over his shoulder.

"Yea," he said; 'besides, I was thinking of another woman.' "They were his words." Theirry sat down; he felt faint and weak.

"I know not. There were so many. As we travelled together he made his prayers to one Ysabeau, but he was secret about her — never his way."

"Ysabeau," repeated Dirk. "A common name."

"Ay," said Theirry indifferently.

Dirk suddenly raised his hand, and pointed out of the window at the daisies and the broken fountain.

"What had he done if she had been living?" he asked, then without waiting for a reply he began swiftly on another subject.

"I have finished my work. I wished to leave it complete — it was for the church of St. Bavon, but I shall not give it them. Now, we can start when you will."

Theirry looked up.

"What of your house and goods?" he asked.

"I have thought of that. There are some valuables, some money; these we can take — I shall lock up the house."

"It will fall into decay."

"I care not." With a clear flame of eagerness alight in his eyes he flashed a full glance at Theirry, and, seeing the young scholar pale and drooping, disappointment clouded his face. "Do you commence so slackly?" he demanded. "Are you not eager to be abroad?" "Yea," answered Theirry. "But —"

Dirk stamped his foot.

"We do not begin with 'buts'!" he cried passionately. "If you have no heart for the enterprise —"

Theirry half smiled.

"Give me some food, I pray you," he said. "For I ate but little yesterday."

Dirk glanced at him.

"I forgot," he answered, and set about rearranging the remains of the meal he and Balthasar had shared in silence.

Theirry sat very still; the door into the next room was open as he had left it on his return, and he could see the line of the trap-door; he felt a great desire to raise it, to descend into the vault and gaze at the cracked mirror, the brazier of dead coals and the mystic circles on the floor. Looking up, his eyes met Dirk's, and without words his thought was understood.

"Leave it alone now," said the sculptor softly. "Let us not speak of it before we reach Basle."

At these words Theirry felt a great relief; the idea of discussing, even with the youth who so fascinated him, the horrible, alluring thing that was an intimate of his thoughts but a stranger to his lips, had filled him with uneasiness and dread. While he ate the food put before him, Dirk picked up the four gold coins Balthasar had left and looked at them curiously.

"Masses for her soul!" he cried. "Did he think that I would enter a church and bargain with a priest for that!"

He laughed, and flung the money out of the window at the nodding daisies.

Theirry gave him a startled glance.

"Why, till now I had thought that you felt tenderly towards the maid."

Dirk laughed.

"Not I. I have never cared for women."

"Nor I," said Theirry simply; he leant back in his chair and his dreamy eyes were grave. "When young they are ornaments, it is true, but pleasant only if you flatter them, when they are overlooked they become dangerous — and a woman who is not young is absorbed in little concerns that are no matter to any but herself."

The smile, still lingering on Dirk's face, deepened derisively, it seemed.

"Oh, my fine philosopher!" he mocked. "Are you well fed now, and preaching again?"

He leant against the wall by the window, and the intense sunlight made his dull brown hair glitter here and there; he folded his arms and looked at Theirry narrowly.

"I warrant your mother was a fair woman," he said. "I do not remember her. They say she had the loveliest face in Flanders, though she was only a clerk's wife," answered the young man. "I can believe it," said Dirk.

Theirry glanced at him, a little bewildered; the youth had such abrupt changes of manner, such voice and eyes unfathomable, such a pale, fragile appearance, yet such a spirit of tempered courage.

"I marvel at you," he said. "You will not always be unknown."

"No," answered Dirk. "I have never meant that I should be soon forgotten."

Then he was beside Theirry, with a strip of parchment in his hand.

"I have made a list of what we have in the place of value — but I care not to sell them here." "Why?" questioned Theirry.

Dirk frowned.

"I want no one over the threshold. I have a reputation — not one for holiness," his strange face relaxed into a smile.

Theirry glanced at the list.

"Certes! How might one carry that even to the next town? Without a horse it were impossible." Silver ware, glass, pictures, raiment, were marked on the strip of parchment.

Dirk bit his finger.

"We will not sell these things Master Lukas left to me," he said suddenly. "Only a few. Such as the silver and the red copper wrought in Italy."

Theirry lifted his grave eyes.

"I will carry those into the town if you give me a merchant's name."

Dirk mentioned one instantly, and where his house might be found.

"A Jew, but a secretive and wealthy man," he added. "I carved a staircase in his mansion." Theirry rose; the ache in his head and the horror in his heart had ceased together; the sense of coming excitement crept through his veins.

"There is much here that is worthless," said Dirk, "and many things dangerous to reveal, yet a few of those that are neither might bring a fair sum — come, and I will show you."

Theirry followed him through the dusty, sunny chambers to the store-rooms on the upper floor. Here Dirk brought treasures from a press in the wall; candlesticks, girdles with enamel links, carved cups, crystal goblets.

Selecting the finest of these he put them in a coffer, locked it and gave the key to Theirry. "There should be the worth of some gulden there," he said, red in the face from stooping, and essayed to lift the coffer but failed.

Theirry, something amazed, raised it at once.

"'Tis not heavy," he said.

"Nay," answered Dirk, "but I am not strong," and his eyes were angry.

Theirry was brought by this to give him some closer personal scrutiny than as yet he had. "How old are you" he asked.

"Twenty-five," Dirk answered curly.

"Certes!" Theirry's hazel eyes flew wide. "I had said eighteen."

Dirk swung on his heel.

"Oh, get you gone," he said roughly, "and be not over long — for I would be away from this place at once — do you hear? — at once."

They left the room together.

"You have endured this for years," said Theirry curiously. "And suddenly you count the hours to your departure."

Dirk ran lightly ahead down the stairs, and his laugh came low and pleasant.

"Untouched, the wood will lie for ever," he answered, "but set it alight and it will flame to the end."

## Chapter 5

## Comrades

They had been a week on the road and now were nearing the borders of Flanders. The company of the other had become precious to each; though Theirry was grave and undemonstrative, Dirk, changeable, and quick of temper; today, however, the silence of mutual discontent was upon them.

Open disagreement had happened once before, at the beginning of their enterprise, when the young sculptor resolutely refused, foolishly it seemed to Theirry, to sell his house and furniture, or even to deliver at the church of St. Bavon the figures of St. Michael and the Devil, though the piece was finished.

Instead, he had turned the key on his possessions, leaving them the prey of dust, spiders and rats, and often Theirry would think uneasily of the shut-up house in the deserted square, and how the merciless sunlight must be streaming over the empty workroom and the daisies growing upon the grave of Balthasar's wife.

Nevertheless, he was in thrall to the attraction of Dirk Renswoude; never in his life had he been so at ease with any one, never before felt his aims and ambitions understood and shared by another.

He knew nothing of his companion's history nor did he care to question it; he fancied that Dirk was of noble birth; it seemed in his blood to live gently and softly; at the hostel where they rested, it was he who always insisted upon the best of accommodation, a chamber to himself, fine food and humble service.

This nicety of his it was that caused the coolness between them now.

At the little town they had just left a fair was in holding, and the few inns were full; lodging had been offered them in a barn with some merchants' clerks, and this Theirry would have accepted gladly, but Dirk had refused peremptorily, to the accompaniment of much jeering from those who found this daintiness amusing in a poor traveller on foot.

After an altercation between the landlord and Theirry, a haughty silence of flashing eyes and red cheeks from Dirk, they had turned away through the gay fair, wound across the town and out on to the high road.

This led up a steep, mountainous incline; they were carrying their possessions in bundles on their backs, and when they reached the top of the hill they turned off from the road on to the meadows that bordered it, and sank on the grass exhausted.

Theirry, though coldly angry with the whim that had brought them here to sleep under the trees, could not but admit it was an exquisite place.

The evening sun overspread it all with a soft yet sparkling veil of light; the fields of long grass that spread to right and left were more golden than green; close by was a grove of pine-trees, whose tall red trunks shone delicately; above them, piled up rocks starred with white flowers mounted against the pale blue sky, beneath them the hillside sloped to the valley where lay the little town.

The streets of it were built up and down the slopes of the hill, and Theirry could see the white line of them and the irregular shapes and colours of the roofs; the church spire sprang from the midst like a spear head, strong and delicate, and here and there pennons fluttered; they could see the Emperor's flag stirring slowly above the round tourelles of the city gate.

Theirry found the prospect very pleasant; he delighted in the long flowering grass that, as he lay stretched out, with his face resting in his hand, brushed against his cheek; in the clear-cut grey rocks and the hardy yet frail-looking white flowers growing on the face of them; in the up-springing lines of the pine-trees and the deep green of their heavy foliage, intensified by the fading blue beyond. Then, as his weariness was eased, he glanced over his shoulder at Dirk;

not being passionate by nature, and controlled by habit, his tempers showed themselves in a mere coldness, not sullenness, the resort of the fretful.

Dirk sat apart, resting his back against the foremost of the pine-trees; he was wrapped in a dark red cloak, his pale profile turned towards the town lying below; the evening air just stirred the heavy, smooth locks on his uncovered head; he was sitting very still.

The cause of the quarrel had ceased to be any matter to Theirry; indeed he could not but admit it preferable to lie here than to herd with noisy beer-drinking clerks in a close barn, but recollection of the haughty spirit Dirk had discovered held him estranged still.

Yet his companion occupied his thoughts; his wonderful skill in those matters he himself was most desirous of fathoming, the strange way in which they had met, and the pleasure of having a companion — so different from Balthasar — of a kindred mind, however whimsical his manner.

At this point in his reflections Dirk turned his head.

"You are angry with me," he said.

Theirry answered calmly.

"You were foolish."

Dirk frowned and flushed.

"Certes! — a fine comrade!" his voice was vehement.

"Did you not swear fellowship with me? How do you fulfil that compact by being wrathful the first time our wills clash?"

Theirry turned on his elbow and gazed across the flowering grass.

"I am not wrathful," he smiled. "And you have had many whims . . . none of them have I opposed."

Dirk answered angrily.

"You make me out a fantastical fellow — it is not true."

Theirry sat up and gazed at the lazy sunset slowly enveloping the distant town and the hills beyond in crimson light.

"It is true you are as nice as a girl," he answered. "Many a time I would have slept by the kitchen hearth — ay, and have done, but you must always lie soft as a prince."

Dirk was scarlet from brow to chin.

"Well, if I choose," he said defiantly. "If I choose, as long as I have money in my pocket, to live gently . . . "

"Have I interfered?" interrupted Theirry. "You are of a lordly birth, belike."

"Yea, I am of a great family," flashed Dirk. "Ill did they treat me. No more of them . . . are you still angry with me?"

He rose; the red cloak slipped from his shoulders to the ground; he stood with his hand on his hip, looking down at Theirry.

"Come," he said gravely. "We must not quarrel, my comrade, my one friend . . . when shall we find another with such aims as ours . . . we are bound to each other, are we not? Certes! you swore it."

Theirry lifted his beautiful face.

"I do like you greatly," he answered. "And in no wise blame you because you are weakly and used to luxury. Others have found me over gentle."

Dirk looked at him out of the corners of his eyes.

"Then I am pardoned?"

Theirry smiled.

"Nay, I do regret my evil humour. The sun was fierce and the bundles heavy to drag up the hill."

Dirk sank down upon the grass beside him. "Truly I am wearied to death!"

Theirry considered him; panting a little, Dirk stretched himself his full length on the blowing grass. The young scholar, used and indifferent to his own great beauty, was deadened to the effect of it in others, and to any eye Dirk could be no more than well-looking; but Theirry was conscious of the charm of his slender make, his feet and hands of feminine delicacy, his fair, full throat, and pale, curved mouth, even the prominent jaw and square chin that marred the symmetry of the face were potent to attract in their suggestion of strength and the power to command.

His near presence, too, was fragrant; he breathed a faint atmosphere of essences and was exquisite in his clothes.

As Theirry studied him, he spoke.

"My heart! it is sweet here — oh, sweet!"

Faint airs wafted from the pine, and the wild flowers hidden in the woods below them stole through the grass; a glowing purple haze began to obscure the valley, and where it melted into the sky the first stars shone, pale as the moon. Overhead the dome of heaven was still blue, and in the tops of the pines was a continuous whispering of the perfumed boughs one to another. "Now wish yourself back in the town among their drinking and swearing," said Dirk. "Nay," smiled Theirry. "I am content." The faint purple colour slowly spread over everything; the towers of the town became dark, and little sharp lights twinkled in them.

Dirk drew a great breath.

"What will you do with your life?" he asked.

Theirry started.

"In what manner?"

"Why, if we succeed — in any way — if we obtain great power . . . what would you do with it?" Theirry felt his brain spin at the question; he gazed across the world that was softly receding into darkness and his blood tingled.

"I would be great," he whispered. "Like Flaccus Alcuin, like Abelard — like St. Bernard."

"And I would be greater than any of these — as great as the Master we serve can make his followers."

Theirry shuddered.

"These I speak of were great, serving God."

Dirk looked up quickly.

"How know you that? Many of these holy men owe their position to strange means. I, at least, would not be content to live and die in woollens when I could command the means to clothe me in golden silks."

The beautiful darkness now encompassed them; below them the lights of the town, above them the stars, and here, in the meadow land, the night breeze in the long grass and in the deep boughs of pine.

"I am but a neophyte," said Theirry after a pause. "Very little have I practised of these things. I had a book of necromancy and learnt a little there . . . but . . . "

"Why do you pause?" demanded Dirk.

"One may not do these things," answered Theirry slowly, "without — great blasphemy —"

Dirk laughed.

"I care nothing for all the angels and all the saints . . . "

"Ah, peace!" cried Theirry, and he put his hand to his brow growing damp with terror.

The other was silent a while, but Theirry could hear his quick breathing rising from the grass. At length he spoke in a quiet voice.

"I desire vast wealth, huge power. I would see nations at my footstool . . . ah! . . . but I have a boundless ambition . . . " He sat up, suddenly and softly, and laid his hand on Theirr's arm. "If they . . . the evil ones . . . offered you that, would you not take it?"

Theirry shuddered.

"You would! you would!" cried Dirk. "And pay your soul for it — gladly."

The scholar made no answer, but reclined motionless, gazing over the human lights in the valley to the stars beyond them; Dirk continued —

"See what a liking I have for you that I tell you this — that I give you the secret of my power to come . . . "

"'Tis my secret also," answered Theirry hastily. "I have done enough to bring the everlasting wrath of the Church upon me."

"The Church," repeated Dirk musingly; he was of a daring that knew not the word fear, and at this moment his thoughts put into words would have made his companion shudder indeed.

Gradually, by ones and twos, the lights in the town were extinguished and the valley was in darkness.

Theirry folded up his cloak as a pillow for his head and lay down in the scented grass; as he fell into a half sleep the great sweetness of the place was present to his mind, torturing him.

He knew by the pictures he had seen that Paradise was like this, remote and infinitely peaceful. Meadows and valleys spreading beneath a tranquil sky . . . he knew it was desirable and that he longed for it, yet he must meddle with matters that repelled him, even as they drew him, with their horror.

He fell into heavy dreams, moaning in his sleep.

Dirk rose from beside him and walked up and down in the dark; the dew was falling, his head uncovered; he stooped, felt for his mantle, found it and wrapped it about him, pacing to and fro with calm eyes defying the dark.

Then finally he lay down under the pines and slept, to awake suddenly and find himself in a sitting posture.

The dawn was breaking, the landscape lay in mists of purple under a green sky, pellucid and pale as water; the pines shot up against it black, clear cut, and whispering still in their upper branches.

Dirk rose and tiptoed across the wet grass to Theirry, looking at him asleep for the second time.

The scholar lay motionless, with his head flung hack on his violet cloak; Dirk looked down at the beautiful sleeping face with a wild and terrible expression on his own.

Like wine poured into a cup, light began to fill the valley and the hollows in the hills; faint mystic clouds gathered and spread over the horizon. Dirk shudderingly drew his mantle closer; Theirry sighed and woke.

Dirk gave him a distracted glance and turned away so rapidly and softly that Theirry, with the ugly shapes of dreams still riding his brain, cried out —"Is that you, Dirk?" and sprang to his feet. Dirk stayed his steps half-way to the pines. "What is the matter?" he asked in an odd voice. Theirry pushed the hair away from his forehead. "I know not — nothing."

The air seemed suddenly to become colder; the hills that on all sides bounded their vision rose up stark from grey mists; an indescribable tension made itself felt, like a pause in stillness.

Dirk stepped back to Theirry and caught his arm; they stood motionless, in an attitude of expectancy.

A roll of thunder pealed from the brightening sky and faded slowly into silence; they were looking along the hills with straining eyes.

On the furthest peak appeared a gigantic black horseman outlined against the ghostly light; he carried a banner in his hand; it was the colour of blood and the colour of night; for a moment he sat his horse, motionless, facing towards the east; then the low thunder pealed again; he raised the banner, shook it above his head, and galloped down the hillside.

Before he reached the valley he had disappeared, and at that instant the sun rose above the horizon and sparkled across the country.

Theirry hid his face in his sleeve and trembled terribly; but Dirk gazed over his bent head with undaunted eyes.

# Chapter 6

## The Lady

Through the blunt-pointed arches that gave on to the sunny gardens a thin stream of students issued from the lecture-room.

Behind the castellated roof of the university the mountains appeared, snow cold against the sun-lit sky; at the bottom of the gently sloping garden lay the town of Basle with the broad blue Rhine flowing between the glittering houses.

The students came in twos and threes and little groups, laughing together over the doctor who had been lecturing them, over some point in their studies that had roused their amusement, or merely because it was a relief after being confined for hours in the dark hall.

The long straight robes, dark shades of purple, blue and violet, fluttered behind them in the summer wind as they gradually dispersed to right and left among the trees.

Theirry, walking with two others, looked about him for Dirk, who had not attended the lecture. "We are going up the river," said one of his companions. "We have a fair sailing boat — it will be pleasant, by Ovid!"

"Will you come?" asked the other.

Theirry shook his head.

"Nay, I cannot."

They both laughed.

"See how he is given to meditation! He will be a great man, certes!"

"I have a matter that commands my time," said Theirry.

"Dear lover of rhetoric! Hark to him — he will even sit in the shade and muse!"

"'Tis cooler," smiled Theirry.

They came to a pathway bordered with laurels and dark glossy plants, and from a seat amid them Dirk rose at their approach.

He was distinguished from the others by the greater richness of his dress; his robe, very voluminous and heavy, was of brown silk; he wore a gold chain twisted round his flat black cap, and his shirt was of fine lawn, laced and embroidered.

The two students doffed their hats in half-mocking recognition of the exquisite air of aloofness that was his habitual manner.

He gave them a steady look out of half-closed eyes.

"Hast learnt much today?" he asked.

"Aristotle is not comprehended in an afternoon," answered the student, smiling. "And I was at the back — Master Joris of Thuringia yawned and yawned, and fell off his stool asleep! The Doctor was bitter!"

"It was amusing," said the other. "Yet he was not asleep, but swooned from the heat. Mass! but it was hot! Where were you?"

"Improving my Latin in the library. This after-noon I have put the story of Tereus and Philomena into the vulgar tongue."

"Give you good even." The two linked arms. "We know a joyful inn up the river." As they disappeared Dirk turned sharply to Theirry.

"Did they ask your company?"

"Yea."

Dirk frowned.

"You should have gone.

"I had no mind to it. They are foolish."

"Ay, but we are beginning to be remarked for closeness in our habits. It would not be pleasant should they — suspect."

"'Tis not possible," said Theirry hastily.

36

"It must not be," was the firm answer. "But be not churlish or over reserved."

"I wish for no company but thine," replied Theirry. "What have I in common with these idlers?"

Dirk gave him a bright tender look.

"We need not stay here over long," he answered. "I do think we know all this school can teach us."

Theirry put back the laurel bough that swung between them.

"Where would you go?" he asked; it was noticeable how in all things he had begun to defer to the younger man.

"Paris! Padua!" flashed Dirk. "Would you consider that? One might attain a reputation, and then — or one might lecture — — in any large town — Cologne, Strasbourg."

"Meanwhile —?"

"Meanwhile I progress," was the whispered answer. "I have essayed — some things. Will you come to my chamber to-night?"

"Ay — secretly?"

Dirk nodded; his grave young face under the student's flat hat was slightly flushed; he laid his hand on Theirry's arm.

"I have something to tell you. Here it is scarcely wise to speak. There is one who hates me — — Joris of Thuringia. Now, good-bye."

"

His great eyes lit with a look of strong affection that was flashed back in Theirry's glance; they clasped hands and parted.

Theirry looked after the brown, silk-clad figure, as it moved rapidly towards the university, then he took his own way, out of the gardens on to the hill-side, away from the town.

With his hands clasped behind his back, and his handsome head bent, he followed aimlessly a little path, and as he wound his way through the trees wild day-dreams stirred his blood.

He was on the eve of putting himself in possession of immense power; these evil spirits whom he would force to serve him could give him anything in the world — anything in the world!

The phantasmagoria of golden visions that arose to blind and intoxicate him, the horror of the means employed, dread of the unthinkable end to come, were not to be put into any words.

He sat down at length on a fallen tree trunk and gazed with rapt eyes down the silent forest path.

He did not know where he was; certainly he had come farther than ever before, or else taken a strange turn, for through the pine-stems he could perceive castle walls, the gates rising from the piled-up rocks, and it was unknown to him.

Presently he rose and walked on, because his galloping thoughts would not allow his body to rest, and still giving no heed to the way, he wandered out of the forest into a green valley shaded by thick trees.

Down the centre ran a stream, and the grass, of a deep green colour, was thickly sown with daisies white as the snow shining on the far-off mountains.

Here and there down the edge of the stream grew young poplar trees, and their flat gold leaves fluttered like a gipsy's sequins, even in the breezeless air.

Theirry, absorbed and withdrawn into himself, walked by the side of the water; he was unconscious of the shadowed hush and quiet of the valley, of the voices of birds falling softly from the peace of the trees, and the marvellous sunlight on the mountains, the castle, rising beyond its circle of shade up into the crystal blue; before his eyes danced thrones and crowns, gold and painted silks, glimpses of princely dwellings and little winged, creeping fiends that offered him these things.

Presently a human sound forced itself on his senses, insistently, even through his abstraction. The sound of weeping, sobbing.

He started, gazed about him with dazed eyes, like a blind man recovering sight, and discerned a lady upon the other side of the stream, seated on the grass, her head bowed in her right hand. Theirry paused, frowned, and hesitated.

The lady, warned of something, glanced up and sprang to her feet; he saw now that she held a dead bird in her left hand; her face was flushed with weeping, her long yellow hair disordered about her brow; she gazed at him with wet grey eyes, and Theirry felt it imperative to speak.

"You are troubled?" he asked, then flushed, thinking she might term it insolence.

But she answered simply and at once.

"About him I am" — she held the little brown bird out on her palm; "he was on the small poplar tree — and singing — he held his head up so" — she lifted her long throat —"and I could see his heart beating behind the feathers — I listened to him, oh! with pleasure" — fresh tears started to the eyes that she turned on Theirry —"then my miserable cat that had followed me leapt on him — and slew him. Oh, I chased them, but when I got him back he was dead."

Theirry was extraordinarily moved by this homely tragedy; it could not have occurred to him that there was matter for tears in such a common thing; but as the lady told the story, holding out, as if secure of his sympathy, the poor little ruffled body, he felt that it was both pitiful and monstrous. "You may chastise the cat," he said, for he saw the elegant soft animal rubbing itself against the stem of the poplar.

"I have beaten her," she confessed.

"You can hang her," said Theirry, thinking to console still more.

But the lady flushed up.

"She is an agreeable cat," she answered. "She cannot help her nature. Oh, it would be an odious cruelty to hang her! — see, she does not understand!"

Theirry, rebuked, was at a loss; he stood looking at the lady, feeling helpless and useless.

She wiped her eyes with a silk handkerchief, and stood in a piteous meek silence, holding her dead bird in a trembling hand.

"If you buried it —" suggested Theirry desperately. "I do think it would have wished to be buried here —"

To his joy she brightened a little.

"You think so?" she asked wistfully.

"Certes!" he reassured her eagerly. "See, I have a knife — I will make a pleasant grave."

She stepped to the edge of the stream as near as she could to him, and because she came unconsciously, with no thought for anything save the bird in her hand, Theirry thrilled with a great pleasure, as should a wild deer come fearlessly.

"I cannot cross — the water is too wide," she said. "But will you take him and make his grave?"

She went on one knee among the sorrel leaves and daisies. Theirry had a swift picture of her as she leant forward, stretching her arm towards him over the stream that divided them. He had seen fair women in Courtrai, he saw in her the most admired points of these, glass grey eyes, small features, an arched red mouth, white skin and yellow hair; she was no more beautiful than many ladies who had left him cold, but he found himself anxious to please her, and he had so far never tried to win a woman's favour.

Her pale red dress rippled about her on the grass; her curls and her veil were blown back from her face; Theirry knelt and held out his hand.

Over mid-stream their fingers touched; he took the bird, and she drew back hastily.

As he, still on his knees, looked at her, he saw that she was no longer unconscious; she stood erect as if commanding herself not to fly, and (as she was very slender) he likened her to the pale crimson pistil of a lily which has yellow on the head — her hair, he told himself.

"I am vexed to trouble you" — she spoke haltingly. There were so many things he wished to say in answer to this that he said nothing, but took his knife from his belt and cut a little square of turf.

"You are a clerk from the college?" she asked.

"Ay," he answered, and wished fiercely he could have given himself a finer name. "There are many learned men there," she said courteously.

He would not have believed it possible to find in himself such care over a trivial thing as he now took over this little bird's grave, for he knew she watched him with judgment in her eyes.

The unholy day-dreams that had vexed and enthralled him were completely forgotten in this new feeling.

The lines of a verse he had not noticed when he read it came back to him, beating in his head.

"Pleasant is she of a fair white favour,
Sweet her caress as the ripe grape's flavour.
And her lips are like the rose in their savour.
Seeing her my pulses quicken.
I turn from common things and sicken.
For the quiet wood where the May buds thicken.
Hearing her my breath is taken,
My bold heart bowed and shaken,
And I from sloth at last awaken."

He dug into the soft brown earth with the point of his knife, lined the grave with leaves, and picked up the little bird.

For a moment he held it in his hand as she had done.

And he dared not look at her.

Then he laid it in the ground and replaced the grass and daisies.

When he raised his head, his face flushed from stooping, he saw that she was no longer watching him, but she had turned sideways and was gazing at the distant woods.

He had leisure now to mark the details of her appearance.

Though slender she was of a full make and tall; her brows were very arched and darker than her hair, her mouth dipped at the corners and was firmly set; she seemed of a grave manner and very modest in her bearing.

Theirry rose from his knees; she turned. "I thank you," she said; then, on a quick breath —"do you often come here?"

He answered foolishly.

"Nay — never before — I did not know the place."

"That is my home yonder," said the lady.

"Yours?" and he pointed to the castle walls.

"Yea. I am an orphan, and the Emperor's ward."

She looked at the point of her shoe showing beneath her pale crimson robe. "What town do you come from?" she asked.

"Courtrai."

"I know no town save Frankfort."

A silence fell between them; the wicked grey cat walked in a stately manner along the edge of the stream.

"I shall lose her," said the lady. "Good even, gentle clerk. My name is Jacobea of Martzburg. Perhaps I shall see you again."

He had never felt more desirous of speaking, never less capable; he murmured — —"I do hope it," and coloured burningly at his awkwardness.

She gave him a half look, a flash from grave grey eyes, instantly veiled, and with an unsmiling mouth bade him again, "Good even."

Then she was gone after the cat.

He saw her hasten down the side of the stream, her dress bending the grasses and leaves; he saw her stoop and snatch up the creature, and, holding it in her arms, take the path towards those lordly gates. He hoped she might look back and see that he gazed after her, but she did not turn her head, and when the last flutter of pale red had disappeared he moved reluctantly from the place.

The sky was gay with sunset; as he walked through the wood, bars of orange light fell athwart the straight pine trunks and made a glitter on his path; he thought neither of those things that had occupied him when he had passed through these trees before, nor of the lady he had left; in his mind reigned a golden confusion, in which everything was unformed and exquisite; he had no wish and no ability to reduce this to definite schemes, hopes or fears, but walked on, enwrapped with fancies.

On the slopes that adjoined the garden of the college Theirry came upon a little group of students lying on the grass.

Just beyond them the others were standing; Dirk noticeable by his rich dress and elegant bearing, and another youth whom Theirry knew for Joris of Thuringia.

A glance told him there were words between them; even from where he stood he could see Dirk was white and taut, Tons hot and flushed.

He crossed the grass swiftly; he knew that it was their policy to avoid quarrels in the college. "Sirs, what is this?" he asked.

The students looked at him; some seemed amused, some excited; his heart gave a sick throb as he saw that their glances were both unfriendly and doubtful.

One gave him half-scornful information.

"Thy friend was caught with an unholy forbidden book, though he denies it; he cast it into the river sooner than allow us a sight of it, and now he is bitter with Joris' commentary thereon." Dirk saw Theirry, and turned his pale face towards him.

"This churl insulted me," he said; "yea, laid hands on me."

A burst of half angry, half good-humoured laughter came from Joris.

"I cannot get the little youth to fight — by Christus his Mother! he is afraid because I could break his neck between my finger and thumb!"

Dirk flashed burning eyes over him.

"I am not afraid, never could I fear such as thee; but neither my profession nor my degree permit me to brawl — be silent and begone."

The tone could not fail to rouse the other.

"Who art thou," he shouted —"to speak as if thou wert a noble's son? I did but touch thy arm to get the book —"

The rest joined in.

"Certes, he did no more, and what was the book?"

Dirk held himself very proudly.

"I will no more be questioned than I will be touched."

"Fine words for a paltry Flemish knave!" jeered one of the students.

"Words I can make good," flashed Dirk, and turned towards the college.

Joris was springing after him when Theirry caught his arm.

"'Tis but a peevish youth," he said.

The other shook himself free and stared after the bright figure in silk.

"He called me 'son of a Thuringian thief.'" he muttered.

A laugh rose from the group.

"How knew he that? — from the unholy book?"

Joris frowned heavily; his wrath flared in another direction.

"Ya! Silence! Son of a British swineherd, thou, red face!"

The group seethed into fisticuffs; Theirry followed Dirk across the gardens.

# Chapter 7

## Spells

Theirry found Dirk as he was passing under the arched colonnade.

"Prudence!" he quoted. "Where is your prudence now?"

Dirk turned quickly.

"I had to put on a bold front. Certes, I hate that knave. But let him go now. Come with me." Theirry followed him through the college, up the dark stairway into his chamber.

It was a low arched room, looking on to the garden, barely furnished, and containing only the bed, a chair and some books on a shelf.

Dirk opened the window on the sun-flushed twilight.

"The students are jealous of me because of my reputation with the doctors," he said, smiling. "One told me today I was the most learned youth in the college. And how long have we been here? But ten months."

Theirry was silent; the triumph in his companion's voice could find no echo in his heart; neither in his legitimate studies nor in his secret experiments had he been as successful as Dirk, who in ancient and modern lore, in languages, algebra, theology, oratory had far outshone all competitors, and who had progressed dangerously in forbidden things.

Theirry shook off the feeling of jealousy that possessed him, and spoke on another subject. "Dirk, I saw a lady today — such a lady!"

In their constant, close and tender companionship neither had ever failed in sympathy, therefore it was with surprise that Theirry saw Dirk perceptibly harden.

"A lady!" he repeated, and turned from the window so that the shadows of the room were over his face.

Theirry must have a listener, must loosen his tongue on the subject of his delicate adventure, so he proceeded.

"Ay —'twas in the valley — a valley, I mean — which I had never seen before. Oh, Dirk!" he was leaning against the end of the bed, gazing across the dusk. "'Twas a lady so sweet — she had —"

Dirk interrupted him.

"Certes!" he cried angrily; "she had grey eyes belike, and yellow hair — have they not always yellow hair? — and a mincing mouth and a manner of glancing sideways, and cunning words, I'll warrant me —"

"Why, she had all this," answered Theirry, bewildered. "But she was pleasant, had you but seen her, Dirk."

The youth sneered.

"Who is she — thy lady?"

"Jacobea of Martzburg." He took obvious pleasure in saying her name. "She is a great lady and gracious."

"Out on ye!" exclaimed Dirk passionately. "What is she to us? Have we not other matters to think of? I did not think ye so weak as to come chanting the praises of the first thing that smiles on ye!"

Theirry was angered.

"'Tis not the first time — and what have I said of her?"

"Oh enough — ye have lost your heart to her, I doubt not — and what use will ye be-a love-sick knave!"

"Nay," answered Theirry hotly. "You have no warrant for this speech. How should I love the lady, seeing her once? I did but say she was fair and gentle."

"'Tis the first woman you have spoken of to me — in that voice — did ye not say —'such a lady'?"

Theirry felt the blood stinging his cheeks.

"Could you have seen her," he repeated.

"Ay, had I seen her I could tell you how much paint she wore, how tight her lace was —"
Theirry interrupted.

"I'll hear no more — art a peevish youth, knowing nothing of women; she was one of God's
roses, pink and white, and we not fit to kiss her little shoes — ay, that's pure truth." Dirk
stamped his foot passionately.

"Little shoes! If you come home to me to rave of her little shoes, and her pink and white,
you may bide alone for me. Speak no more of her."

Theirry was silent a while; he could not afford to lose Dirk's companionship or to have him
in an ill temper, nor did he in any way wish to jeopardise the good understanding between
them, so he quelled the anger that rose in him at the youth's unreasonableness, and answered
quietly ——"On what matter did you wish to see me?"

Dirk struggled for a moment with a heaving breast and closed his teeth over a rebellious lip,
then he crossed the room and opened the door of an inner chamber.

He had obtained permission to use this apartment for his studies; the key of it he carried
always with him, and only he and Theirry had ever entered it.

In silence, lighting a lamp, and placing it on the windowsill, he beckoned Theirry to follow
him.

It was a dismal room; piled against the walls were the books Dirk had brought with him,
and on the open hearth some dead charred sticks lay scattered.

"See," said Dirk; he drew from a dark corner a roughly carved wooden figure some few inches
high. "I wrought this today — and if I know the spells aright there is one will pay for his
insolence."

Theirry took the figure in his hand.

"'Tis Joris of Thuringia."

Dirk nodded sombrely.

The room was thick with unhealthy odours, and a close stagnant smoke seemed to hang
round the roof; the lamp cast a pulsating yellow light over the dreariness and threw strange
shaped shadows from the jars and bottles standing about the floor.

"What is this Joris to you?" asked Theirry curiously.

Dirk was unrolling a manuscript inscribed in Persian.

"Nothing. I would see what skill I have."

The old evil excitement seized Theirry; they had tried spells before, on cattle and dogs, but
without success; his blood tingled at the thought of an enchantment potent to confound enemies. "Light the fire," commanded Dirk.

Theirry set the image by the lamp, and poured a thick yellow fluid from one of the bottles
over the dead sticks.

Then he flung on a handful of grey powder.

A close dun-coloured vapour rose, and a sickly smell filled the room; then the sticks burst
suddenly into a tall and beautiful flame that sprang noiselessly up the chimney and cast a clear
and unnatural glow round the chamber.

Theirry drew three circles round the fire, and marked the outer one with characters taken
from the manuscripts Dirk held.

Dirk was looking at him as he knelt in the splendid glow of the flames, and his own heavy
brows were frowning.

"Was she beautiful?" he asked abruptly.

Theirry took this as an atonement for the late ill temper, and answered pleasantly ——"Why,
she was beautiful, Dirk."

"And fair?"

"Certes, yellow hair."

"No more of her," said the youth in a kind of fierce mournfulness. "The legend is finished?"
"Yea." Theirry rose from his knees. "And now?"

Dirk was anointing the little image of the student on the breast, the eyes and mouth with a liquid poured from a purple phial; then he set it within the circle round the flame.

"'Tis carved of ash plucked from a churchyard," he said. "And the ingredients of the fire are correct. Now if this fails, Zerdusht lies."

He stepped up to the fire and addressed an invocation in Persian to the soaring flame, then retreated to Theirry's side.

The whole room was glowing in the clear red light cast by the unholy fire; the cobweb-hung rafters, the gaunt walls, the books and jars on the bare floor were all distinctly visible, and the two could see each other, red, from head to foot.

"Look," said Dirk, with a slow smile.

The image lying in the magic circle and almost touching the flames (though not burnt or even scorched), was beginning to writhe and twist on its back like a creature in pain.

"Ah!" Dirk showed his teeth. "The Magian spell has worked."

A sensation of giddiness seized Theirry; he heard something beating loud and fast in his ear, it seemed, but he knew it was his heart that thumped so, up and down.

The figure, horribly like Joris with its flat hat and student's robe, was struggling to its feet and emitting little moans of agony.

"It cannot get out," breathed Theirry.

"Nay," whispered Dirk, "wherefore did ye draw the circle?"

The flame was a column of pure fire, and it cast a glow of gold on the thing imprisoned in the ring Theirry had made; Dirk watched in an eager way, with neither fear nor compunction, but Theirry felt a wave of sickness mount to his brain.

The creature was making useless endeavours to escape from the fiery glare; it groaned and fell on its face, twisted on its back and made frantic attempts to cross the line that imprisoned it. "Let it out," whispered Theirry faintly.

But Dirk was elate with success.

"Ye are mad," he retorted. "The spell works bravely."

On the end of his words came a sound that caused both to wince; even in the lurid light Dirk saw his companion pale.

It was the bell of the college chapel ringing the students to the vespers.

"I had forgotten," muttered Dirk. "We must go — it would be noticed."

"We cannot put the fire out," cried Theirry.

"Nay, we must leave it — it must burn out," answered Dirk hurriedly.

The creature, after rushing round the circle in an attempt to escape had fallen, as if exhausted with its agony, and lay quivering.

"We will leave him, too," said Dirk unpleasantly.

But Theirry had a tearing memory of a lady kneeling among green grasses and bending towards him with a dead bird in her hand — tears for it on her cheeks — a dead bird, and this —

He stooped and snatched up the creature; it shrieked dismally as he touched it, and he felt the quick flame burn his fingers.

Instantly the fire had sunk into ashes, and he held in his hand a mere morsel of charred wood. With a sound of disgust he flung this on the ground.

"Should have let it burn," said Dirk, with the lamp held aloft to show him the way across the now dark chamber. "Perchance we cannot relight it, and I have not finished with the ugly knave."

They stepped into the outer chamber and Dirk locked the door; Theirry gasped to feel the fresher air in his nostrils, and a sense of terror clouded his brain; but Dirk was in high spirits; his eyes narrowed with excitement, his pale lips set in a hard fashion.

They descended into the hall.

It was a close and sultry evening; through the blunt arches of the window, dark purple clouds could be seen, lying heavily across the horizon; the clang of the vesper bell came persistently and with a jarring note; though the sun had set it was still light, which had a curious effect of strangeness after the dark chambers upstairs.

Without a word to each other, but side by side, the two students passed into the ante-chamber that led into the chapel.

And there they stopped.

The pale rays of a candle dispersed the gathering dark and revealed a group of men standing together and conversing in whispers.

"Why do they not enter the church?" breathed Theirry, with a curious sensation at his heart. "Something has happened."

Some of the students turned and saw them; they were forced to come forward; Dirk was silent and smiling.

"Have you heard?" asked one; all were sober and subdued.

"A horrible thing," said another. "Joris of Thuringia is struck with a strange illness. Certes! he fell down amongst us as if in the grip of hell fire."

The speaker crossed himself; Theirry could not answer, he felt that they were all looking at him suspiciously, accusingly, and he trembled.

"We carried him up to his chamber," said another. "He shrieked and tore at his flesh, imploring us to keep the flames off. The priest is with him now — God guard us from unholy things." "Why do you say that?" demanded Theirry fiercely. "Belike his disease was but natural." A look passed round the students. "I know not," one muttered. "It was strange."

Dirk, still smiling and silent, turned into the chapel; Theirry and the others, hushing their surmises, followed.

There were candles on the altar, six feet high, and a confusion of the senses came over Theirry, in which he saw them as white angels with flaming haloes coming grievingly for his destruction. A wave of fear and sorrow rushed over him; he sank on his knees on the stone floor and fixed his eyes on the priest, whose chasuble was gleaming gold through the dimness of the incense-filled chapel. The blasphemy and mortal sin of what he had done sickened and frightened him; was not his being here the most horrible blasphemy of all? — he had no right; he had made false confessions to the priest, he had received absolution on lies; daily he had come here worshipping God with his lips and Satan with his heart. A groan broke from him, he bowed his beautiful face in his hands and his shoulders shook. He thought of Joris of Thuringia writhing in the agony caused by their unhallowed spells, of the eager devils crowding to their service — and far away, in a blinding white mist, he seemed to see the arc of the saints and angels looking down on him while he fell away further, further, into unfathomable depths of darkness. With an uncontrollable movement of agony he looked up, and his starting eyes fell on the figure of Dirk kneeling in front of him. The youth's calm both horrified and soothed him; there he knelt, who had but a little while before been playing with devils, with a face as unmoved as a sculptured saint, with a placid brow, quiet eyes and hands folded on his breviary.

He seemed to feel Theirry's intense gaze, for he looked swiftly round and a look of caution, of warning shot under his white lids.

Theirry's glance fell; his companions were singing with uplifted faces, but he could not join them; the pillars with their foliated capitals oppressed him by their shadow, the saints glowing in mosaic on the drums of the arches frightened him with the unforgiving look in their long eyes.

"Laudate, pueri Dominum.

Laudate nomen Domini.

Sit nomen Domini benedictum, Ex hoc nunc et usque in saecuium.

A Solis ortu usque ad occasum Laudabile nomen Domini."

The fresh young voices rose lustily.; the church was full of incense and music; Theirry rose with the hymn ringing in his head and left the chapel.

The singers cast curious glances at him as he passed, and when he reached the door he heard a patter of feet behind him and turned to see Dirk at his elbow.

"I have done with it," he said hoarsely.

Dirk's eyes were flaming.

"Do you want to make public confession?" he demanded, breathing hard. "Remember, it is our lives to pay, if they discover."

Theirry shuddered.

"I cannot pray. I cannot stay in the church. For days I have felt the blessing scorch me."

"Come upstairs," said Dirk.

As they went down the long hall they met one who was a friend of Joris of Thuringia. Dirk stopped.

"Hast come from the sick man?"

"Yea."

"He is mending?"

Theirry stared with wild eyes, waiting the answer.

"I know not," said the youth. "He lies in a swoon and pants for breath."

He passed on, something abruptly.

"Did ye hear that?" whispered Theirry. "If he should die!"

They went up to Dirk's bare little chamber; the clouds had completely overspread the sky, and neither moon nor stars were visible.

Dirk lit the lamp, and Theirry sank on to the bed with his hands clasped between his knees.

"I cannot go on," he said. "It is too horrible."

"Art afraid?" asked Dirk quietly.

"Yea, I am afraid."

"So am not I," answered Dirk composedly.

"I cannot stay here," breathed Theirry, with agonised brows.

Dirk bit hisforefinger.

"Nay, for we have but little money and know all these pedants can teach us. 'Tis time we began to lay the corner-stones of our fortune."

Theirry rose, twisting his fingers together.

"Talk not to me of fortunes. I have set my soul in deadly peril. I cannot pray, I cannot take the names of holy things upon my lips."

"Is this your courage?" said Dirk softly. "Is this your ambition, your loyalty to me? Would you run whining to a priest with a secret that is mine as well as yours? Is this, O noble youth, what all your dreams have faded to?"

Theirry groaned.

"I know not. I know not."

Dirk came slowly nearer.

"Is this to be the end of comradeship — our league?"

He took the other's slack hand in his, and as he seldom offered or suffered a touch, Theirry thrilled at it as a great mark of affection, and at the feel of the smooth, cool fingers, the fascination, the temptation that this youth stood for stirred his pulses; still he could not forget the stern angel he thought he had seep upon the altar, and the way his tongue had refused to move when he had striven to pray.

"Belike, I have gone too far to turn back," he panted, with questioning eyes.

Dirk dropped his hand.

"Be of me or not with me," he said coldly. "Surely I can stand alone."

"Nay," answered Theirry. "Certes, I love thee, Dirk, as I have never cared for any do I care for thee . . . "

Dirk stepped back and looked at him out of half-closed eyes.

"Well, do not stop to palter with talk of priests. Certainly I will be faithful to you unto death and damnation, and be you true to me."

Theirry made a movement to answer, but a sudden and violent knock on the door checked him. They looked at each other, and the same swift thoughts came to each; the students had suspected, had come to take them by surprise — and the consequences —

For a second Dirk shook with suppressed wrath.

"Curse the Magian spell!" he muttered. "Curse Zerdusht and his foul brews, for we are trapped and undone!"

Theirry sprang up and tried the inner door.

"'Tis secure," he said; he was now quite calm. "I have the key." Dirk laid his hand on his breast, then snatched a couple of volumes from the shelf and flung them on the table. The knock was repeated.

"Unbolt the door," said Theirry; he seated himself at the table and opened one of the volumes.

Dirk slipped the bolt, the door sprang back and a number of students, headed by a monk bearing a crucifix, surged into the room.

"What do you want?" demanded Dirk, fronting them quietly. "You interrupt our studies." The priest answered sternly —

"There are strange and horrible accusations against you, my son, that you must disprove."

Theirry slowly closed his book and slowly rose; all the terror and remorse of a few moments ago had changed into wrath and defiance, and the glow his animal courage sent through his body at the prospect of an encounter; he saw the eager, excited faces of his fellow-students, crowding in the doorway, the hard and unforgiving countenance of the monk, and he felt unaccountably justified in his own eyes; he did not see his antagonists standing for Good, and himself for Evil, he saw mere men whose evident enmity roused his own.

"What accusations?" asked Dirk; his demeanour appeared to have changed as completely as Theirry's had done; he had lost his assured calm; his defiant bearing was maintained by an obvious effort, and his lips twitched with agitation.

The students murmured and forced further into the room; the monk answered — —"Ye are suspected of procuring the dire illness of Joris of Thuringia by spells."

"It is a lie," said Dirk faintly, and without conviction, but Theirry replied boldly — —"Upon what do you base this charge, father?"

The monk was ready.

"Upon your strange and close behaviour — the two of you, upon our ignorance of whence you came — upon the suddenness of the youth's illness after words passed between him and Master Dirk."

"Ay," put in one of the students eagerly. "And he lapped water like a dog."

"I have seen a light here well into the night," said another.

"And why left they before the vespers were finished?" demanded a third.

Theirry smiled; he felt that they were discovered, but fear was far from him.

"These are childish accusations," he answered. "Get you gone to find a better."

Dirk, who had retreated behind the table, spoke now. "Ye smirch us with wanton words," he said pantingly. "It is a lie."

"Will you swear to that?" asked the monk quickly.

Theirry interposed.

"Search the chamber, my father — I warrant you have already been peering through mine."

"Yea."

"And you found —?"

"Nothing."

"Then are you not content?" cried Dirk.

The murmur of the students swelled into an angry cry.

"Nay — can ye not spirit away your implements if ye be wizards?"

"Great skill do you credit us with," smiled Theirry. "But on nothing you can prove nothing." Although he knew that he could never allay their suspicions, it occurred to him that it might be possible to prevent the discovery of what the locked room held, and in that case, though they might have to leave the college, their lives would be safe; he snatched up the lantern and held it aloft.

"See you anything here?"

They stared round the bare walls with eager, straining eyes; one came to the table and turned over the volumes there.

"Seneca!" he flung them down with disappointment; the priest advanced and gazed about him; Dirk stood silent and scornful, Theirry was bold to defy them all.

"I see no holy thing," said the monk. "Neither Virgin, nor saint, nor prie-Dieu, nor holy water." Dirk's eyes flashed fiercely.

"Here is my breviary;" he pointed to it on the table.

One of the students cried —

"Where is the key? To the inner chamber!"

There were three or four of them about the door; Dirk, turning to see them striving with the handle, went ghastly pale and could not speak, but Theirry broke out into great wrath. "The room is disused. No affair of mine or Dirk. We know nothing of it."

"Will you swear?" asked the priest.

"Certes — I will swear."

But the student struggling with the door cried out —

"Dirk Renswoude asked for this room for his studies! I do know it, and he had the key." Dirk gave a great start.

"Nay, nay," he said hurriedly, "I have no key."

"Search, my sons," said the priest.

Their blood was up; some ten or twelve had crowded into the chamber; they hurled the books off the shelf, scattered the garments out of the coffer, pulled the quilt off the bed and turned up the mattress.

Finding nothing they turned on Dirk.

"He has the key about him!"

All eyes were fixed now on the youth, who stood a little in front of Theirry, he continuing to hold the lamp scornfully aloft to aid them in their search.

The light rested on Dirk's shoulders, causing the bright silk to glitter, and flickered in his short waving hair; there was no trace of colour in his face, his brows were raised and gathered into a hard frown.

"Have you the key of that chamber?" demanded the priest.

Dirk tried to speak, but could not find his voice; he moved his head stiffly in denial. "But answer," insisted the monk.

"What should it avail me if I swore?" The words seemed wrenched from him. "Would ye believe me?" His eyes were bright with hate of all of them.

"Swear on this." The monk proffered the crucifix.

Dirk did not touch it.

"I have no key," he said.

"There is your answer," flashed Theirry, and set the lamp on the table.

The foremost student laughed.

"Search him," he cried. "His garments — belike he has the key in his breast."

Again Dirk gave a great start; the table was between him and his enemies, it was the only protection he had; Theirry, knowing that he must have the key upon him, saw the end and was prepared to fight it finely.

"What are ye going to do now?" he challenged.

For answer one of them leant across the table and seized Dirk by the arm, swinging him easily into the centre of the room, another caught his mantle.

A yell of "Search him!" rose from the others.

Dirk bent his head in a curious manner, snatched the key from inside his shirt and flung it on the floor; instantly they let go of him to pick it up, and he staggered back beside Theirry. "Do not let them touch me," he said. "Do not let them touch me."

"Art a coward?" answered Theirry angrily. "Now we are utterly lost. . . . "

He thrust Dirk away as if he would abandon him; but that youth caught hold of him in desperation.

"Do not leave me — they will tear me to pieces." The students were rushing through the unlocked door shouting for lights; the priest caught up the lamp and followed them; the two were left in darkness.

"Ye are a fool," said Theirry. "With some cunning the key might have been saved . . . "

A horrid shout arose from those in the inner room as they discovered the remains of the incantations . . .

Theirry sprang to the window, Dirk after him. "Theirry, gentle Theirry, take me also — can see I am helpless! A — ah! I am small and pitiful, Theirry!"

Theirry had one leg over the window-sill.

"Come, then, in the fiend's name," he answered. A hoarse shout told them the students had found the little image of Joris; those still on the stair-way saw them at the window. "The warlocks escape!"

Theirry helped Dirk on to the window-ledge; the night air blew hot on their faces and they felt warm rain falling on them; there was no light anywhere.

The students were yelling in a thick fury as they discovered the unholy unguents and implements. They turned suddenly and dashed to the window. Theirry swung himself by his hands, then let go.

With a shock that jarred every nerve in his body he landed on the balcony of the room beneath. "Jump!" he called up to Dirk, who still crouched on the window-sill.

"Ah, soul of mine! Ah, I cannot!" Dirk stared through the darkness in a wild endeavour to discern Theirry.

"I am holding out my arms! Jump!"

The students had knocked over the lamp and it had checked them for the moment; but Dirk, looking back, saw the room flaring with fresh lights and seething figures pushing up to the window.

He closed his eyes and leapt in the darkness; the distance was not great; Theirry half caught him; he half staggered against the balcony.

A torch was thrust out of the window above them; frenzied faces looked down.

Theirry pushed Dirk roughly through the window before them, which opened on to the library, and followed.

"Now — for our lives," he said.

They ran down the dark length of the chamber and gained the stairs; the students, having guessed their design, were after them — they could hear the clatter of feet on the upper landing. How many stairs, how many before they reach the hall!

Dirk tripped and fell, Theirry dragged him up; a breathless youth overtook them; Theirry, panting, turned and struck him backwards sprawling. So they reached the hall, fled along it and out into the dark garden.

A minute after, the pursuers bearing lights, and half delirious with wrath and terror, surged out of the college doors.

Theirry caught Dirk's arm and they ran; across the thick grass, crashing through the bushes, trampling down the roses, blindly through the dark till the shouts and the lights grew fainter behind them and they could feel the trunks of trees impeding them and so knew that they must have reached the forest.

Then Theirry let go of Dirk, who sank down by his side and lay sobbing in the grass.

## Chapter 8


## The Castle

Theirry spoke angrily through the dark.

"Little fool, we are safe enough. They think the Devil has carried us off. Be silent." Dirk gasped from where he lay.

"Am not afraid. But spent . . . they have gone?"

"Ay," said Theirry, peering about him; there was no trace of light anywhere in the murky dark nor any sound; he put his hand out and touched the wet trunk of a tree, resting his shoulder against this (for he also was exhausted) he considered, angrily, the situation.

"Have you any money?" he asked.

"Not one white piece."

Theirry felt in his own pockets. Nothing.

Their plight was pitiable; their belongings were in the college, Probably by now being burnt with a sprinkling of holy water — they were still close to those who would kill them upon sight, with no means of escape; daylight must discover them if they lingered, and how to be gone before daylight?

If they tried to wander in this dark likely enough they would but find themselves at the college gates; Theirry cursed softly.

"Little avail our enchantments now," he commented bitterly.

It was raining heavily, drumming on the leaves above them, splashing from the boughs and dripping on the grass; Dirk raised himself feebly.

"Cannot we get shelter?" he asked peevishly. "I am all bruised, shaken and wet — wet — " "Likely enough," responded Theirry grimly. "But unless the charms you know, Zerdusht's incantations and Magian spells, can avail to spirit us away we must even stay where we are." "Ah, my manuscripts, my phials and bottles!" cried Dirk. "I left them all!" "They will burn them," said Theirry. "Plague blast and blight the thieving, spying knaves!" answered Dirk fiercely.

He got on to his feet and supported himself the other side of the tree.

"Certes, curse them all!" said Theirry, "if it anything helps."

He felt anger and hate towards the priest and his followers who had hounded him from the college; no remorse stung him now, their action had swung him violently back into his old mood of defiance and hard-heartedness; his one thought was neither repentance nor shame, but a hot desire to triumph over his enemies and outwit their pursuit.

"My ankle," moaned Dirk. "Ah! I cannot stand . . . "

Theirry turned to where the voice came out of the blackness.

"Deafen me not with thy complaints, weakling," he said fiercely. "Hast behaved in a cowardly fashion to-night."

Dirk was silent before a new phase of Theirry's character; he saw that his hold on his companion had been weakened by his display of fear, his easy surrender of the key. "Moans make neither comfort nor aid," added Theirry.

Dirk's voice came softly.

"Had you been sick I had not been so harsh, and surely I am sick . . . when I breathe my heart hurts and my foot is full of pain."

Theirry softened.

"Because I love you, Dirk, I will, if you complain no more, say nought of your ill behaviour." He put out his hand round the tree and touched the wet silk mantle; despite the heat Dirk was shivering.

"What shall we do?" he asked, and strove to keep his teeth from chattering. "If we might journey to Frankfort —"

"Why Frankfort?"

"Certes, I know an old witch there who was friendly to Master Lukas, and she would receive us, surely."

"We cannot reach Frankfort or any place without money . . . how dark it is!"

"Ugh! How it rains! I am wet to the skin . . . and my ankle . . . "

Theirry set his teeth.

"We will get there in spite of them. Are we so easily daunted?"

"A light!" whispered Dirk. "A light!"

Theirry stared about him and saw in one part of the universal darkness a small light with a misty halo about it, slowly coming nearer.

"A traveller," said Theirry. "Now shall he see us or no?"

"Belike he would show us on our way," whispered Dirk.

"If he be not from the college."

"Nay, he rides."

They could hear now, through the monotonous noise of the rain, the sound of a horse slowly, cautiously advancing; the light swung and flickered in a changing oval that revealed faintly a man holding it and a horseman whose bridle he caught with the other hand.

They came at a walking pace, for the path was unequal and slippery, and the illumination afforded by the lantern feeble at best.

"I will accost him," said Theirry.

"If he demand who we are?"

"Half the truth then — we have left the college because of a fight."

The horseman and his attendant were now quite close; the light showed the overgrown path they came upon, the wet foliage either side and the slanting silver rain; Theirry stepped out before them.

"Sir," he said, "know you of any habitation other than the town of Basle?"

The rider was wrapped in a mantle to his chin and wore a pointed felt hat; he looked sharply under this at his questioner.

"My own," he said, and halted his horse. "A third of a league from here."

At first he had seemed fearful of robbers, for his hand had sought the knife in his belt; but now he took it away and stared curiously, attracted by the student's dress and the obvious beauty of the young man who was looking straight at him with dark, challenging eyes.

"We should be indebted for your hospitality — even the shelter of your barns," said Theirry. The horseman's glance travelled to Dirk, shivering in his silk.

"Clerks from the college?" he questioned.

"Yea," answered Theirry. "We were. But I sorely wounded one in a fight and fled. My comrade chose to follow me."

The stranger touched up his horse.

"Certes, you may come with me. I wot there is room enow."

Theirry caught Dirk by the arm.

"Sir, we are thankful," he answered.

The light held by the servant showed a muddy, twisting path, the shining wet trunks, the glistening leaves either side, the great brown horse, steaming and passive, with his bright scarlet trappings and his rider muffled in a mantle to the chin; Dirk looked at man and horse quickly in silence; Theirry spoke.

"It is an ill night to be abroad."

"I have been in the town," answered the stranger, "buying silks for my lady. And you — so you killed a man?"

"He is not dead," answered Theirry. "But we shall never return to the college."

The horseman had a soft and curiously pleasing voice; he spoke as if he cared nothing what he said or how he was answered.

"Where will you go?" he asked.

"To Frankfort," said Theirry.

"The Emperor is there now, though he leaves for Rome within the year, they say," remarked the horseman, "and the Empress. Have you seen the Empress?"

Theirry put back the boughs that trailed across the path.

"No," he said.

"Of what town are you?"

"Courtrai."

"The Empress was there a year ago and you did not see her? One of the wonders of the world, they say, the Empress."

"I have heard of her," said Dirk, speaking for the first time. "But, sir, we go not to Frankfort to see the Empress."

"Likely ye do not," answered the horseman, and was silent.

They cleared the wood and were crossing a sloping space of grass, the rain full in their faces; then they again struck a well-worn path, now leading upwards among scattered rocks.

As they must wait for the horse to get a foothold on the slippery stones, for the servant to go ahead and cast the lantern light across the blackness, their progress was slow, but neither of the three spoke until they halted before a gate in a high wall that appeared to rise up, suddenly before them, out of the night.

The servant handed the lantern to his master and clanged the bell that hung beside the gate. Theirry could see by the massive size of the buttresses that flanked the entrance that it was a large castle the night concealed from him; the dwelling, certainly, of some great noble. The gates were opened by two men carrying lights. The horseman rode through, the two students at his heels.

"Tell my lady," said he to one of the men, "that I bring two who desire her hospitality;" he turned and spoke over his shoulder to Theirry, "I am the steward here, my lady is very gentle-hearted."

They crossed a courtyard and found themselves before the square door of the donjon.

Dirk looked at Theirry, but he kept his eyes lowered and was markedly silent; their guide dismounted, gave the reins to one of the varlets who hung about the door, and commanded them to follow him.

The door opened straight on to a large chamber the entire size of the donjon; it was lit by torches stuck into the wall and fastened by iron clamps; a number of men stood or sat about, some in a livery of bright golden-coloured and blue cloth, others in armour or hunting attire; one or two were pilgrims with the cockle-shells round their hats.

The steward passed through this company, who saluted him with but little attention to his companions, and ascended a flight of stairs set in the wall at the far end; these were steep, damp and gloomy, ill lit by a lamp placed in the niche of the one narrow deep-set window; Dirk shuddered in his soaked clothes; the steward was unfastening his mantle; it left trails of wet on the cold stone steps; Theirry marked it, he knew not why.

At the top of the stairs they paused on a small stone landing.

"Who is your lady?" asked Theirry.

"Jacobea of Martzburg, the Emperor's ward," answered the steward. He had taken off his mantle and his hat, and showed himself to be young and dark, plainly dressed in a suit of deep rose colour, with high boots, spurred, and a short sword in his belt.

As he opened the door Dirk whispered to Theirry, "It is the lady — ye met today?" "To-day!" breathed Theirry. "Yea, it is the lady."

They entered by a little door and stepped into an immense chamber; the great size of the place was emphasised by the bareness of it and the dim shifting light that fell from the circles of candles hanging from the roof; facing them, in the opposite wall, was a high arched window, faintly seen in the shadows, to the left a huge fire-place with a domed top meeting the wooden supports of the lofty beamed roof, beside this a small door stood open on a flight of steps and beyond were two windows, deep set and furnished with stone seats.

The brick walls were hung with tapestries of a dull purple and gold colour, the beams of the ceiling painted; at the far end was a table, and in the centre of the hearth lay a slender white boarhound, asleep.

So vast was the chamber and so filled with shadows that it seemed as if empty save for the dog; but Theirry, after a second discerned the figures of two ladies in the furthest window-seat. The steward crossed to them and the students followed.

One lady sat back in the niched seat, her feet on the stone ledge, her arm along the window-sill; she wore a brown dress shot with gold thread, and behind her and along the seat hung and lay draperies of blue and purple; on her lap rested a small grey cat, asleep.

The other lady sat along the floor on cushions of crimson and yellow; her green dress was twisted tight about her feet and she stitched a scarlet lily on a piece of red samite.

"This is the chatelaine," said the steward; the lady in the window-seat turned her head; it was Jacobea of Martzburg, as Theirry had known since his eyes first rested on her. "And this is my wife, Sybilla."

Both women looked at the strangers.

"These are your guests until tomorrow, my lady," said the steward.

Jacobea leant forward.

"Oh!" she exclaimed, and flushed faintly. "Why, you are welcome."

Theirry found it hard to speak; he cursed the chance that had made him beholden to her hospitality.

"We are leaving the college," he answered, not looking at her. "And for to-night could find no shelter."

"Meeting them I brought them here," added the steward.

"You did well, Sebastian, surely," answered Jacobea. "Will it please you sit, sirs?"

It seemed that she would leave it at that, with neither question nor comment, but Sybilla, the steward's wife, looked up smiling from her embroidery.

"Now wherefore left you the college, on foot on a wet night?" she said.

"I killed a man — or nearly," answered Theirry curtly.

Jacobea looked at her steward.

"Are they not wet, Sebastian?"

"I am well enough," said Theirry quickly; he unclasped his mantle. "Certes, under this I am dry."

"That am not I!" cried Dirk.

At the sound of his voice both women looked at him; he stood apart from the others and his great eyes were fixed on Jacobea.

"The rain has cut me to the skin," he said, and Theirry crimsoned for shame at his complaining tone.

"It is true," answered Jacobea courteously. "Sebastian, will you not take the gentle clerk to a chamber — we have enough empty, I wot — and give him another habit?"

"Mine are too large," said the steward in his indifferent voice.

"The youth will fall with an ague," remarked his wife. "Give him something, Sebastian, I warrant he will not quarrel about the fit."

Sebastian turned to the open door beside the fireplace.

"Follow him, fair sir," said Jacobea gently; Dirk bent his head and ascended the stairs after the steward.

The chatelaine pulled a red bell-rope that hung close to her, and a page in the gold and blue livery came after a while; she gave him instructions in a low voice; he picked up Theirry's wet mantle, set him a carved chair and left.

Theirry seated himself; he was alone with the two women and they were silent, not looking at him; a sense of distraction, of uneasiness was over him — he wished that he was anywhere but here, sitting a dumb suppliant in this woman's presence.

Furtively he observed her — her clinging gown, her little velvet shoes beneath the hem of it, her long white hands resting on the soft grey fur of the cat on her knee, her yellow hair, knotted on her neck, and her lovely, meek face.

Then he noticed the steward's wife, Sybilla; she was pale, of a type not greatly admired or belauded, but gorgeous, perhaps, to the taste of some; her russet red hair was splendid in its gleam through the gold net that confined it; her mouth was a beautiful shape and colour, but her brows were too thick, her skin too pale and her blue eyes over bright and hard.

Theirry's glance came back to Jacobea; his pride rose that she did not speak to him, but sat there idle as if she had forgotten him; words rose to his lips, but he checked them and was mute, flushing now and then as she moved in her place and still did not speak.

Presently the steward returned and took his place on a chair between Theirry and his wife, for no reason save that it happened to be there, it seemed.

He played with the tagged laces on his sleeves and said nothing.

The mysterious atmosphere of the place stole over Theirry with a sense of the portentous; he felt that something was brooding over these quiet people who did not speak to each other, something intangible yet horrible; he clasped his hands together and stared at Jacobea.

Sebastian spoke at last.

"You go to Frankfort?"

"Yea," answered Theirry.

"We also, soon, do we not, Sebastian?" said Jacobea.

"You will go to the court," said Theirry.

"I am the Emperor's ward," she answered.

Again there was silence; only the sound of the silk drawn through the samite as Sybilla stitched the red lily; her husband was watching her; Theirry glancing at him saw his face fully for the first time, and was half startled.

It was a passionate face, in marked contrast with his voice; a dark face with a high arched nose and long black eyes; a strange face.

"How quiet the castle is to-night," said Jacobea; her voice seemed to faint beneath the weight of the stillness.

"There is noise enough below," answered Sebastian, "but we cannot hear it."

The page returned, carrying a salver bearing tall glasses of wine, which he offered to Theirry, then to the steward.

Theirry felt the green glass cold to his fingers and shuddered; was that sense of something awful impending only matter of his own mind, stored of late with terrible images?

What was the matter with these people . . . Jacobea had seemed so different this afternoon . . . he tasted the wine; it burnt and stung his lips, his tongue, and sent the blood to his face.

"It still rains," said Jacobea; she put her hand out of the open window and brought it back wet. "But it is hot," said Sybilla.

Once more the heavy silence; the page took back the glasses and left the room.

Then the door beside the fire-place was pushed open and Dirk entered softly into the mute company.

# Chapter 9

## Sebastian

He wore a flame-coloured mantle that hung about him in heavy folds, and under that a tight yellow doublet; his hair drooped smoothly, there was a bright colour in his face, and his eyes sparkled.

"Ye are merry," he mocked, glancing round him. "Will you that I play or sing?" He looked, in his direct burning way at Jacobea, and she answered hastily —

"Certes, with all my heart — the air is hot — and thick — to-night."

Dirk laughed, and Theirry stared at him bewildered, so utterly had his demeanour changed; he was gay now, radiant; he leant against the wall in the centre of them and glanced from one silent face to another.

"I can play rarely," he smiled.

Jacobea took an instrument from among the cushions in the window-seat; it was red, with a heart-shaped body, a long neck and three strings.

"You can play this?" she asked in a half-frightened manner.

"Ay." Dirk came forward and took it. "I will sing you a fine tune, surely."

Theirry was something of a musician himself, but he had never heard that Dirk had any such skill; he said nothing, however; a sense of helplessness was upon him; the atmosphere of gloom and horror that he felt held him chained and gagged.

Dirk returned to his place against the wall; Sybilla had dropped the red lily on to her lap; they were all looking at him.

"I will sing you the tune of a foolish lady," he smiled.

His shadow was heavy on the wall behind him; the dark purple hues of the tapestry threw into brilliant relief the flame hues of his robe and the clear pale colour of his strange face; he held the instrument across his knees and commenced playing on it with the long bow Jacobea had given him; an irregular quick melody arose, harsh and jeering.

After he had played a while he began to sing, but in a chant under his breath, so that the quality of his voice was not heard.

He sang strange meaningless words at first; the four listening sat very still; only Sybilla had picked up her sewing, and her fingers rose and fell steadily as the bodkin glittered over the red lily.

Theirry hid his face in his hands; he hated the place, the woman quietly sewing, the dark-faced man beside him; he even hated the image of Jacobea, that he saw, as clearly as if he looked at her, brightly before him.

Dirk broke into a little doggerel rhyme, every word of which was hard and clear.

"The turkis in my fine spun hair Was brought to me from Barbarie.

My pointed shield is rouge and vair, Where mullets three shine royallie.

Now if he guessed.

He need not wait in poor estate, But on his breast

Wear all my state and be my mate.

For sick for very love am I.

My heart is weak to kiss his cheek; But he is low, and I am high.

I cannot speak, for I am weak."

Jacobea put the cat among the cushions and rose; she had a curious set smile on her lips. "Do you call that the rhyme of a foolish lady?" she asked.

"Ay, for if she had offered her love, surely it had not been refused," answered Dirk, dragging the bow across the strings.

"You think so?" said Jacobea in a shrinking tone.

54

"Mark you, she was a rich lady," smiled Dirk, "and fair enough, and young and gentle, and he was poor; so I think, if she had not been so foolish, she might have been his second wife."

At these words Theirry looked up; he saw Jacobea standing in a bewildered fashion, as if she knew not whether to go or stay, and in her eyes an unmistakable look of amazement and horror.

"The rhyme said nothing of the first wife," remarked Sybilla, without looking up from the red lily.

"The rhyme says very little," answered Dirk. "It is an old story — the squire had a wife, but if the lady had told her love belike he had found himself a widower."

Jacobea touched the steward's wife on the shoulder.

"Dear heart," she said, "I am weary — very weary with doing nought. And it is late — and the place strange — to-night — at least" — she gave a trembling smile —"I feel it — strange — so — good even."

Sybilla rose, Jacobea's lips touched her on the forehead.

The steward watched them; Jacobea, the taller of the two, stooping to kiss his wife. Theirry got to his feet; the chatelaine raised her head and looked towards him.

"To-morrow I will bid you God speed, sirs;" her blue eyes glanced aside at Dirk, who had moved to the door by the fire-placer and held it open for her; she looked back at Theirry, then round in silence and coloured swiftly.

Sybilla glanced at the sand clock against the wall.

"Yea, it is near midnight. I will come with you." She put her arm round Jacobea's waist, and smiled backwards over her shoulder at Theirry; so they went, the sound of their garments on the stairs making a faint soft noise; the little cat rose from her cushions, stretched herself, and followed them.

Sebastian picked up the red silk lily that his wife had flung down on the cushions; the candles were guttering to the iron sockets, making the light in the chamber still dimmer, the corners still more deeply obscured with waving shadows.

"You know your chamber," said the steward to Dirk. "You will find me here in the morning. Good-night."

He took a bunch of keys from his belt and swung them in his hand.

"Good-night," said Theirry heavily.

Dirk smiled, and threw himself into the vacated window-seat.

The steward crossed the room to the door by which they had entered; he did not look back, though both were watching him; the door closed after him violently, and they were alone in the vast darkening hall.

"This is fine hospitality," sneered Dirk. "Is there none to light us to our chamber?" Theirry walked to and fro with an irregular agitated step.

"What was that song of yours?" he asked. "What did you mean? What ails this place and these people? She never looked at me."

Dirk pulled at the strings of the instrument he still held; they emitted little wailing sounds.

"She is pretty, your chatelaine," he said. "I did not think to see her so soon. You love her — or you might love her."

His bright eyes glanced across the shadowy space between them.

"Ye mock and sneer at me," answered Theirry hotly, "because she is a great dame. I do not love her, and yet —"

"And yet —?" goaded Dirk.

"If our arts can do anything for us — could they not — if I wished it — some day — get this lady for me?"

He paused, his hand to his pale brow.

"You shall never have her," said Dirk, biting his under lip.

Theirry turned on him violently.

"You cannot tell. Of what use to serve Evil for nought?"

"Ye have done with remorse belike?" mocked Dirk. "Ye have ceased to long for priests and holy water?"

"Ay," said Theirry recklessly, "I shall not falter again — I will take these means — any means —"

"To attain — her?" Dirk got up from the window-seat and rose to his full height.

Theirry gave him a sick look.

"I will not bandy taunts with you. I must sleep a little."

"They have given us the first chamber ye come to, ascending those stairs," answered Dirk quietly. "There is a lamp, and the door is set open. Good-night."

"You will not come?" asked Theirry sullenly.

"Nay. I will sleep here."

"Why? You are strange to-night."

Dirk smiled unpleasantly.

"There is a reason. A good reason. Get to bed." Theirry left him without an answer, and closed the door upon him.

When he had gone, and there was no longer a sound of his footstep, a rustle of the arras to tell he had been, a great change swept over Dirk's face; a look of agony, of distraction contorted his proud features, he paced softly here and there, twisting his hands together and lifting his eyes blindly to the painted ceiling.

Half the candles had flickered out; the others smoked and flared in the sockets; the rain dripping on the window-sill without made an insistent sound.

Dirk paused before the vast bare hearth.

"He shall never have her," he said in a low, steady voice as if he saw and argued with some personage facing him. "No. You will prevent it. Have I not served you well? Ever since I left the convent? Did you not promise me great power — as the black letters of the forbidden books swam before my eyes; did I not hear you whispering, whispering?"

He turned about as though following a movement in the person he spoke to, and shivered.

"I will keep my comrade. Do you hear me? Did you send me here to prevent it? — they seemed to know you were at my elbow to-night — hush! — one comes!"

He fell back against the wall, his finger on his lips, his o her hand clutching the arras behind him.

"Hush!" he repeated.

The door at the far end of the chamber was slowly opened; a man stepped in and cautiously closed it; a little cry of triumph rose to Dirk's lips, but he repressed it and gave a glance into the pulsating shadows as if he communicated with some mysterious companion.

It was Sebastian who had entered; he looked swiftly round, and seeing Dirk, came towards him.

In the steward's hand was a little cresset lamp; the clear, heart-shaped flame illuminated his dark face and his pink habit; his eyes looked over this light in a burning way at Dirk. "So — you are not abed?" he said.

There was more than the aimless comment in his tone, an expectation, an excitement. "You came to find me," answered Dirk. "Why?"

Sebastian set the lamp on a little bracket by the window he put his hand to his neck, loosening his doublet, and looked away.

"It is very hot," he said in a low voice. "I cannot rest. I feel to-night as I have never felt — I think the cause is with you — what you said has distracted me." he turned his head. "Who are you? What did you mean?" "You know," answered Dirk, "what I am-a poor student from Basle college. And in your heart you know what I meant."

Sebastian stared at him a moment.

"God! But how could you discern — even if it be true? — you, a stranger. But now I think of it, belike there is reason in it — certes, she has shown me favour."

Dirk smiled.

"'Tis a rich lady, her husband would be a noble, think of it."

"What ye put into me!" cried Sebastian in a distracted voice. "That I should talk thus to a prating boy! But the thought clings and burns — and surely ye are wise."

Dirk, still leaning against the wall, smoothed the arras with delicate fingers.

"Surely I am wise. Well skilled in difficult sciences am I, and quick to see — and understand — — take this for your hospitality, sir steward — watch your mistress."

Sebastian put his hand to his head.

"I have a wife."

Dirk laughed.

"Will she live for ever?"

Sebastian looked at him and stammered, as if some sudden sight of terror seared his eyes. "There — there is witchcraft in this — your meaning —"

"Think of it!" flashed Dirk. "Remember it! Ye get no more from me."

The steward stood quite still, gazing at him.

"I think that I have lost my wits to-night," he said in a low voice. "I do not know what I came down to you for — nor whence come these strange thoughts."

Dirk nodded his head; a small, slow smile trembled on the corners of his lips.

"Perchance I shall see you in Frankfort, sir steward."

Sebastian caught at the words with eagerness.

"Yea — I go there with — my lady —" He stopped blankly.

"As yet," said Dirk, "I know neither my dwelling there nor the name I shall assume. But you — — if I need to I shall find you at the Emperor's court?"

"Yea," answered Sebastian; then, reluctantly, "What should you want with me?"

"Will it not be you who may need me?" smiled Dirk. "I, who have to-night put thoughts into your brain that you will not forget?"

Sebastian turned about quickly, and caught up the cresset lamp.

"I will see you before you go," he whispered, horror in his face. "Yea, on the morrow I shall desire more speech with you."

Like a man afraid, in terror of himself, filled with a dread of his companion, Sebastian, the pure flame of the lamp quivering with the shaking of his hand, crossed the long chamber and left by the door through which he had entered.

Dirk gave a half-suppressed shiver of excitement; the candles had mostly burnt out; the hall seemed monstrous in the gusty, straggling light. He crept to the window; the rain had ceased, and he looked out on a hot starless darkness, disturbed by no sound.

He shivered again, closed the window and flung himself along the cushions in the niched seat. Lying there, where Jacobea had sat, he thought of her; she was more present to his mind than all the crowded incidents of the past day; his afternoon passed in the sunny library, his evening before the beautiful witch fire, the wild escape into the night, the flight through the wet forest, the sombre arrival at the castle, were but flitting backgrounds to the slim figure of the chatelaine.

Certainly she had a potent personality; she was exquisite, a thing shut away in sweet fragrancy. He thought of her as an ivory pyx filled with red flowers; there were her trembling passionate emotions, her modest secrets, that she guarded delicately.

It was his intention to tear open this tabernacle to wrench from her her treasures and scatter them among blood and ruin; he meant to bring her to utter destruction; not her body, perhaps, but her soul.

And this because she had interfered with the one being on earth he cared about — Theirry; not because he hated her for herself.

"How beautiful she is!" he said aloud, almost tenderly.

The last candle fluttered up and sank out; Dirk, lying luxuriously among the cushions, looked into the complete blackness with half-closed eyes.

"How beautiful!" he repeated; he felt he could have loved her himself; he thought of her now, lying in her white bed, her hair unbound; he wished himself kneeling beside her, caressing those yellow locks; a desire possessed him to touch her curls, her soft cheek, to have her hand in his and hear her laugh surely she was a sweet thing, made to be loved.

Yet the power that had brought him here to-night had made plain that if he did not take the chance of her destruction set in his way, she would win Theirry from him for ever.

He had made the first move; in the dark face of Sebastian the steward he had seen the beginning of — — the end.

But thinking of her he felt the tears come to his eyes; suddenly he fell into weary weeping, thinking of her, and sobbed sadly, face downwards, on the cushion.

Her yellow hair, mostly he thought of that, her long, fine, soft, yellow hair, and how, before the end, it would be trailing in the dust of despair and humiliation.

Presently he laughed at himself for his tears, and drying them, fell asleep; and awoke from blank dreamlessness to hear his name ringing in his ears. He sat up in the window-seat.

His eyes were hot with his late tears; the misty blue light of dawn that he found about him hurt them; he shrank from this light that came in a clear shaft through the arched window, and, crouching away from it, saw Theirry standing close to him, Theirry, fully dressed and pale, looking at him earnestly.

"Dirk, we must go now. I cannot stay any longer in this place."

Dirk, leaning his head against the cushions, said nothing, impressed anew with his friend's beauty. How fine and fair a thing Theirry's face was in the colourless early light; in hue and line splendid, in expression wild and pained.

"I could not sleep much," continued Theirry. "I do not want to see them — her — again — not like this — get up, Dirk — why did you not come to bed? I wanted your company — things were haunting me."

"Mostly her face?" breathed Dirk.

"Ay," said Theirry sombrely. "Mostly her face."

Dirk was silent again; was not her loveliness the counterpart of his friend's? — he imagined them together — close — touching hands, lips — and as he pictured this he grew paler.

"The castle is open, there are varlets abroad," cried Theirry. "Let us go — supposing — oh, my heart! supposing one came from the college to look for us!"

Dirk considered; he reflected that he had no desire to meet Sebastian again; he had said all he wished to.

"Let us go," he assented; his one regret was that he should not see again the delicate face crowned with the yellow hair.

He rose from the seat and shook out his borrowed flame-coloured mantle, then he closed his tired eyes as he stood, for a very exquisite sensation rushed over him; nothing had come between him and his friend; Theirry of his own choice had roused him — wanting him — they were to go forth together alone.

# Chapter 10

## The Saint

They were wandering through the forest in an endeavour to find the high road; the sun, nearly at its full strength, dazzled through the pines and traced figures of gold on the path they followed.

Theirry was silent; they were hungry, without money or any hope of procuring any, fatigued with the rough walking through the heat, and also, it seemed, lost; these facts were ever present to his mind; also, every step was taking him further away from Jacobea of Martzburg, and he longed to see her again, to make her notice him, speak to him; yet of his own desire he had left her castle ungraciously; these things held him bitterly silent.

But Dirk, though he was pale and weary, kept a light joyous heart; he had trust in the master he was serving.

"We shall be helped yet," he said. "Were we not hopeless last night when one came and gave us shelter?"

Theirry did not answer.

The forest grew up the base of the mountain chain, and after a while, walking steadily, they came out upon a gorge some landslip had torn, uprooting trees and hurling aside rocks; over this bare space harshly cleared, water rippled and dripped, finding its way through fern-grown rocks and boulders until it fell into a little stream that ran across the open space of grass and was lost in the shadow of the trees.

By the side of it, on the pleasant stretch of grass, a small white horse was browsing, and a man sat near, on one of the uprooted pines.

The two students paused and contemplated him; he was a monk in a blue-grey habit; his face was infinitely sweet; with his hands clasped in his lap and his head a little raised he gazed with large, peaceful eyes through the shifting fir boughs to the blue sky beyond them.

"Of what use he!" said Theirry bitterly; since the Church had hurled him out the Devil was gaining such sure possession of his soul that he loathed all things holy.

"Nay," said Dirk, with a little smile. "We will speak to him."

The monk, hearing their voices, looked round and fixed on them a calm smiling gaze. "Dominus det nobis suam pacem," he said.

Dirk replied instantly.

"Et vitam aeternam. Amen."

"We have missed our way," said Theirry curtly.

The monk rose and stood in a courteous, humble position.

"Can you put us on the high road, my father?" asked Dirk.

"Surely!" The monk glanced at the weary face of his questioner. "I am myself travelling from town to town, my son. And know this country well. Will you not rest a while?"

"Ay." Dirk came down the slope and flung himself along the grass; Theirry, half sullen, followed.

"Ye are both weary and in lack of food," said the monk gently. "Praise be to the angels that I have wherewithal to aid ye."

He opened one of the leather bags resting against the fallen tree, took out a loaf, a knife and a cup, cut the bread and gave them a portion each, then filled the cup from the clear dripping water.

They disdained thanks for such miserable fare and ate in silence.

Theirry, when he had finished, asked for the remainder of the loaf and devoured that; Dirk was satisfied with his allowance, but he drank greedily of the beautiful water.

"Ye have come from Basle?" asked the monk.

Dirk nodded.

"And we go to Frankfort."

"A long way," said the monk cheerfully. "And on foot, but a pleasant journey, certes." "Who are you, my father?" asked Theirry abruptly. "I saw you in Courtrai, surely."

"I am Ambrose of Menthon," answered the monk. "And I have preached in Courtrai. To the glory of God."

Both students knew the name of Saint Ambrose.

Theirry flushed uneasily.

"What do you here, father?" he asked. "I thought you were in Rome."

"I have returned," replied the saint humbly. "It came to me that I could serve Christus" — he crossed himself — "better here. If God His angel will it I desire to build a monastery up yonder — — above the snow."

He pointed through the trees towards the mountains; his eyes, that were blue-grey, the colour of his habit, sparkled softly.

"A house to God His glory," he murmured. "In the whiteness of the snows. That is my intent." "How will you attain it, holy sir?" questioned Theirry.

Saint Ambrose did not seem to notice the mocking tone.

"I have," he said, "already considerable moneys. I beg in the great castles, and they are generous to God His poor servant. We, my brethren and I, have sold some land. I return to them now with much gold. Deo gratias."

As he spoke there was such a pure sweetness in his fair face that Theirry turned away abashed, but Dirk, lying on his side and pulling up the grass, answered —

"Are you not afraid of robbers, my father?"

The saint smiled.

"Nay; God His money is sacred even unto the evildoer. Surely I fear nothing."

"There is much wickedness in the heart of man," said Dirk. And he also smiled.

"Judge with charity," answered Ambrose of Menthon. "There is also much goodness. You speak, my son, with seeming bitterness which showeth a soul not yet at peace. The wages of the world are worthless, but God giveth immortality."

He rose and began fastening the saddle bags on the pony; as his back was turned Theirry and Dirk exchanged a quick look.

Dirk rose from the grass and spoke.

"May we, my father, come with you, as we know not the way?"

"Surely!" The saint looked at them, his eyes fixed half yearningly on Theirry's beautiful face. "Ye are most welcome to my poor company."

The little procession started through the pine forest; Ambrose of Menthon, erect, spare, walking lightly with untroubled face and leading the white pony, burdened with the saddle bags containing the gold; Theirry, sombre, silent, striding beside him, and Dirk, a little behind, in his flame-coloured mantle, his eyes bright in a weary face.

Saint Ambrose spoke, beautifully, on common things; he spoke of birds, of St. Hieronymus and his writings, of Jovinian and his enemy Ambrose of Milan, of Rufinus and Pelagius the Briton, of Vigilantius and violets, with which flowers, he said, the first court of Paradise was paved.

Dirk answered with a learning, both sacred and profane, that surprised the monk; he knew all these writers, all the fathers of the Church and many others, he quoted from them in different tongues; he knew Pagan philosophies and the history of the old world; he argued theology like a priest and touched on geometry, mathematics, astrology.

"Ye have a vast knowledge," said Saint Ambrose, amazed; and in his heart Theirry was jealous.

And so they came, towards evening, on to the road and saw in a valley beneath them a little town.

All three halted.

The Angelus was ringing, the sound came sweetly up the valley.

Saint Ambrose sank on his knees and bowed his head; the students fell back among the trees. "Well?" whispered Dirk.

"It is our chance," frowned Theirry in the same tone. "I have been thinking of it all day —"

"I also; there is much money . . . "

"We could get it without . . . blood?"

"Surely, but if need be even that."

Their eyes met; in the pleasant green shade they saw each other's excited faces.

"It is God His money," murmured Theirry.

"What matter for that, if the Devil be stronger?"

"Hush! the Angelus ends."

"Now — we join him."

They sank on their knees, to rise as the saint got to his feet and glanced about him; at the edge of the wood they joined him and looked down at the town below.

"Now we can find our way," said Dirk in a firm, suddenly changed voice.

Ambrose of Menthon considered him over the little white pony.

"Will you not bear me company into the town?" he asked wistfully; he did not notice that Theirry had slipped behind him.

Dirk's eyes flashed a signal to his companion. "We will into the town," he said, "but without thy company, Sir Saint, now!"

Theirry flung his mantle from behind and twisted it tightly over the monk's head and face, causing him to stagger backwards; Dirk rushed, seized his thin hands, and strapped them together with the leather belt he had just loosened from his waist, and between them they dragged him into the trees.

"My ears are weary of thy tedious talk," said Theirry viciously, "my eyes of thy sickly face." They took the straps from the pony and bound their victim to a tree; it was an easy matter, for he made no resistance and no sound came from under the mantle twisted over his face.

"There is much evil in the heart of man," mocked Dirk. "And much folly, oh, guileless, in the hearts of saints!"

Having seen to it that he was securely fastened the two returned to the pony and examined their plunder.

In one bag there were parchments, books, and a knotted rope, in the other numerous little linen sacks of varying sizes.

These they turned out upon the grass and swiftly unfastened the strings.

Gold — each one filled with gold, fine, shining coins with the head of the Emperor glittering on them.

Dirk retied the sacks and replaced them in the saddle bags; neither of them had seen so much gold together before; because of it they were silent and a little trembling.

Theirry, as he heard the good yellow money chink together, felt his last qualms go; for the first time since he had entered into league with the spirits of evil he had plain evidence it was a fine thing to have the Devil on his side. A stupefying pleasure and exaltation came over him, he did not doubt that Satan had sent this saintly man their way, and he was grateful; to find himself possessed of this amount of money was a greater delight than any he had known, even a more delightful thing than seeing Jacobea of Martzburg lean across the stream towards him.

As they reloaded the pony, managing as best they might without the straps, Dirk fell to laughing.

"I will get my mantle," said Theirry; he went up to Ambrose of Menthon, telling himself he was not afraid of meeting the saint's eyes, and unwound the heavy mantle from his head. The saint sank together like the dead.

Dirk still laughed, mounted on the white pony, flourishing a stick.

"The fellow has swooned," said Theirry, bewildered.

"Well," answered Dirk over his shoulder, "you can bring the straps, which we need, surely." Theirry unfastened the monk and laid his slack body on the grass; as he did so he saw that the grey habit was stained with blood, there was wet blood, too, on the straps.

"Now what is this?" he cried, and bent over the unconscious man to see where he was wounded.

His searching hand came upon cold iron under the rough robe; Ambrose of Menthon wore a girdle lined with sharp points, that at every movement must have been torture, and that, at their brutal binding of him, had entered his flesh with an agony unbearable.

"Make haste!" cried Dirk.

Theirry straightened his back and looked down at the sweet face of Saint Ambrose; he wished that their victim had cried out or moaned, his silence being a hard thing to think of — and he must have been in a pain.

"Be quick!" urged Dirk.

Theirry joined him.

"What shall we do with — that man?" he said awkwardly; his blood was burning, leaping.

"'Tis a case for the angels, not for us," answered Dirk. "But if ye feel tenderly (and certainly he was pleasant to us) we can tell, in the town, that we found him. 'Deo gratias,'" he mocked the saintly, low calm voice, but Theirry did not laugh.

A splendid yellow sunset was shimmering in their eyes as they came slowly down into the valley and passed through the white street of the little town.

They visited the hostel, fed the white pony there and recounted how they had seen a monk in the wood they had just traversed, whether unconscious in prayer or for want of breath they had not the leisure to examine.

Then they went on their way, eschewing, by common consent this time, the accommodation of the homely inn, and taking with them a basket of the best food the town afforded.

Clearing the scattered cottages they gained the heights again and paused on the grassy borders of a mighty wood that spread either side the high road.

There they spread a banquet very different from the saint's poor repast; they had yellow wine, red wine, baked meats, cakes, jellies, a heron and a basket of grapes, all bought with the gold Ambrose of Menthon had toiled to collect to build God's house amid the snows.

Arranging these things on the soft grass they sat in the pleasant shade, luxuriously, and laughed at each other over their food.

The heavens were perfectly clear, there was no cloud in all the great dome of sky, and, reflecting on the night before, and how they had stood shivering in the wet, they laughed the more.

Then were they penniless, with neither hope nor prospect and in danger of pursuit. Now they were on the high road with more gold in their possession than they had ever seen before, with a horse to carry their burdens, and good food and delicate wine before them.

Their master had proved worth serving. They toasted him in the wine bought with God His money and made merry over it; they did not mention Ambrose of Menthon.

Dirk was supremely happy; everything about him was a keen delight, the fragrant perfume of the pine woods, the dark purple depths of them, the bright green grass, the sky changing into a richer colour as the sun faded, the mountain peaks tinged with pearly rose, the whole beautiful, silent prospect and his comrade looking at him with a smile on his fair face. A troop of white mountain goats driven by a shepherd boy went past, they were the only living things they saw.

Dirk watched them going towards the town, then he said —

"The chatelaine . . . Jacobea of Martzburg —" he broke off. "Do you remember, the first night we met, what we saw in the mirror? A woman, was it not? Her face — have you forgotten it?" "Nay," answered Theirry, suddenly sombre.

Dirk turned to look at him closely.

"It was not Jacobea, was it?"

"It was utterly different," said Theirry. "No, she was not Jacobea."

He propped a musing face on his hand and stared down at the grass.

Dirk did not speak again, and after a while of silence Theirry slept.

With a start he woke, but lay without moving, his eyes closed; some one was singing, and it was so beautiful that he feared to move lest it should be in his dreams only that he heard it. A woman's voice, and she sang loud and clearly, in a passion of joyous gaiety; her notes mounted like birds flying up a mountain, then sank like snowflakes softly descending.

After a while the wordless song died away and Theirry sat up, quivering, in a maze of joy. "Who is that?" he called, his eager eyes searching the twilight.

No one . . . nothing but the insignificant figure of Dirk, who sat at the edge of the wood gazing at the stars.

"I dreamt it," said Theirry bitterly, and cursed his waking.

# Chapter 11

## The Witch

In a back street of the city of Frankfort stood an old one-storied house, placed a little apart from the others, and surrounded by a beautiful garden.

Here lived Nathalie, a woman more than suspected of being a witch, but of such outward quiet and secretive ways that there never had been the slightest excuse for even those most convinced of her real character to interfere with her.

She was from the East — Syria, Egypt or Persia; no one could remember her first coming to Frankfort, nor how she had become possessed of the house where she dwelt; her means of livelihood were also a mystery. It was guessed that she made complexion washes and dyes supplied secretly to the great court ladies; it was believed that she sold love potions, perhaps worse; it was known that in some way she made money, for though generally clothed in rags, she had been seen wearing very splendid garments and rich jewels.

Also, it was rumoured by those living near that strange sounds of revelry had on occasion arisen from her high-walled garden, as if a great banquet were given, and dark-robed guests had been seen to enter her narrow door.

That garden was empty now and a great stillness lay over the witch's house; the hot mid-summer sun glowed in the rose bushes that surrounded it; red roses all of them, and large and beautiful.

The windows of the great room at the back of the house had their shutters closed so that only a few squares of light fell through the lattice-work, and the room was in shadow.

It was a barely furnished chamber, with an open tiled hearth on which stood a number of bronze and copper bowls and drinking vessels. In the low window-seat were cushions of rich Eastern embroidery, hanging on the walls, hideous distorted masks made of wood and painted fantastically, some short curved swords, and a parchment calendar.

Before this stood Dirk, marking with a red pencil a day in the row of dates.

This done he stepped back, stared at the calendar and frowned, sucking the red pencil.

He was attired in a grave suit of black, and wearing a sober cap that almost concealed his hair; he held himself very erect, and the firm set of his mouth emphasised the prominent jaw and chin.

As he stood there, deep in thought, Theirry entered, nodded at him and crossed to the window; he also was dressed in dull straight garments, but they could not obscure the glowing brown beauty of his face.

Dirk looked at him with eyes that sparkled affection.

"I am making a name in Frankfort," he said.

"Ay," answered Theirry, not returning his glance. "I have heard you spoken of by those who have attended your lectures — they said your doctrines touched infidelity."

"Nevertheless they come," smiled Dirk. "I do not play for a safe reputation . . . otherwise should I be here? — living in a place of evil name?"

"I do not think," replied Theirry, "that any go so far as to guess the real nature of your studies, nor what it is you pursue." And he also smiled, but grimly.

"Every man in Frankfort is not priest-beridden," said Dirk quickly. "They would not meddle with me just because I do not preach the laws of the Church. I teach my scholars rhetoric, logic and philosophy . . . they are well pleased."

"I have heard it," answered Theirry, looking out of the window at the red roses dazzling in the sunshine; Dirk could not guess how it rankled with his friend that he obtained no pupils, that no one cared to listen to his teaching; that while Dirk was becoming famous as the professor of rhetoric at Frankfort college, he remained utterly unknown.

"To-day I disclosed to them Procopius," said Dirk, "and propounded a hundred proposition out of Priscianus — should improve their Latin — there were some nobles from the Court. One submitted that my teaching was heretical — asked if I was a Gnostic or an Arian — aaid I should be condemned by the Council of Saragossa — as Avila was, and for as good reasons . . . "

"Meanwhile . . . "

Dirk interrupted.

"Meanwhile — we know almost all the wise woman can teach us, and are on the eve of great power . . . "

Theirry pushed wider the shutters so that the strong sunlight fell over the knee of his dark gown.

"You perhaps," he said heavily. "Not I — the spirits will not listen to me . . . only with great difficulty can I compel them . . . well I wot that I am bound to evil, but I wot also that it doth little for me."

At this complaint a look of apprehension came into Dirk's eyes.

"My fortune is your fortune," he said.

"Nay," answered Theirry, half fiercely, "it is not . . . you have been successful . . . so have not I . . . old Nathalie loves you — she cares nothing for me — you have already a name in Frankfort — I have none, nor money either . . . Saint Ambrose's gold is gone, and I live on your charity."

While he was speaking Dirk gazed at him with a strengthening expression of trouble and dismay; with large distracted eyes full of tenderness, while his cheeks paled and his mouth quivered.

"No — no." He spoke in protest, but his distress was too deep and too genuine to allow of much speech.

"I am going away from here," said Theirry firmly.

Dirk gasped as if he had been wounded.

"From Frankfort?" he ejaculated.

"Nay . . . from this place."

There was a little silence while the last traces of light and colour seemed to be drained from Dirk's face.

"You do not mean that," he said at length. "After we have been . . . Oh, after all of it — you cannot mean . . . "

Theirry turned and faced the room.

"You need not fear that I shall break the bond that unites us," he cried. "I have gone too far yea, and still I hope to attain by the Devil's aid my desires. But I will not stay here." "Where will you go?"

Theirry's hazel eyes again sought the crimson roses in the witch's garden.

"To-day as I wandered outside the walls I met a hawking party. Jacobea of Martzburg was among them."

"They had been in Frankfort many weeks, and so had she, yet this was the first time that he had mentioned her name."

"Oh!" cried Dirk.

"She knew me," continued Theirry; "and spoke to me. She asked, out of her graciousness, if I had aught to do in Frankfort . . . thinking, I wot, I looked not like it." He blushed and smiled. "Then she offered me a post at Court. Her cousin is Chamberlain to the Queen — nay, Empress, I should say — and he will take me as his secretary. I shall accept."

Dirk was miserably, hopelessly silent; all the radiance, the triumph that had adorned him when Theirry eutered were utterly quenched; he stood like one under the lash, with agonised eyes. "Are you not glad?" asked Theirry, with a swell in his voice. "I shall be near her . . . "

"Is that a vast consideration?" said Dirk faintly. "That you should be near her?"

"Did you think that I had forgotten her because I spoke not?" answered Theirry. "Also there are chances that by your arts I may strengthen —"

Through the heavy golden shadows of the room Dirk moved slowly towards the window where Theirry stood.

"I shall lose you," he said.

Theirry was half startled by the note in his voice.

"Nay . . . shall I not come here . . . often? Are you not my comrade?"

"So you speak," answered Dirk, his brow drawn, his lips pale even for one of his pallor. "But you leave me . . . You choose another path from mine." He wrung his frail hands together. "I had not thought of this."

"It need not grieve you that I go," answered Theirry, half sullen, half wondering. "I wot I am pledged deeply enough to thy Master." His eyes flashed wildly. "Is there not sin on my soul? — — Have I not awakened in the night to see Saint Ambrose smile at me? Am I not outside the Church and in league with Hell?"

"Hush! hush!" warned Dirk.

Theirry flung himself into the window-seat, his elbows on his knees, his palms pressed into his cheeks; the sunlight fell through the open window behind him and shone richly in his dark brown hair.

Dirk leant against the wall and stared down at him; in his poor pale face were yearning and tenderness beyond expression.

At last Theirry rose and turned to the door.

"Are you going?" questioned Dirk fearfully.

"Yea."

Dirk braced himself.

"Do not go," he said. "There is everything before us if we stay together . . . if you . . . " His words choked him, and he was silent.

"All your reasoning cannot stay me," answered Theirry, his hand on the door. "She smiled at me and I saw her yellow hair . . . and I am stifled here and useless."

He opened the door and went out.

Dirk sank on the brilliant gold cushions and twisted his fingers together; through the half-closed shutters he could see that marvellous blaze of red roses and their sharp green leaves, the garden wall and the blue August sky; he could hear a bird singing, far away and pleasantly, and after a while he heard Theirry sing, too, as he moved about in an upper chamber. Dirk had not known him sing before, and now, as the little wordless song fell on his ears, he winced and writhed.

"He sings because he is going away."

He sprang up and crossed to the calendar; a year ago today he and Theirry had first met; he had marked the day with red — and now —

Presently Theirry entered again; he was no longer singing, and he had his things in a bundle on his back.

"I will come tomorrow and take leave of Nathalie," he said; "or perhaps this evening. But I must see the Chamberlain now."

Dirk nodded; he was still standing by the calendar, and for the second time Theirry passed out. "Oh! oh!" whispered Dirk. "He is gone — gone — — gone — gone."

He remained motionless, picturing the Court Theirry would join, picturing Jacobea of Martzburg; the other influences that would be brought to bear on his companion —

Then he crept to the window and pushed the shutter wide, so that half the dark room was flooded with gold.

The great burning roses nodded in unison, heavy bees humming among them. Dirk leant from the window and flung out his arms with sudden passion.

"Satan! Satan!" he shrieked. "Give him back to me! Everything else you have promised me for that! Do you hear me! Satan! Satan!"

His voice died away in a great sob; he rested his throbbing head against the hot mullions and put his hand over his eyes; red of the roses and gold of the sunshine of the Eastern cushions blended in one before him; he sank back into the window-seat, and heard some one speak his name.

Lifting his sick gaze, he saw the witch standing in the centre of the floor, looking at him.

Dirk gave a great sigh, hunched up his shoulders, and smoothed his cuffs; then he said, very quietly, looking sideways at the witch —

"Theirry has gone."

Nathalie, the witch, seated herself on a little stool that was all inlaid with mother-o'-pearl, folded her hands in her lap and smiled.

She was not an old nor an ugly woman, but of a pale, insignificant appearance, with shining, blank-looking eyes set in wrinkles, a narrow face and dull black hair, threaded now with flat gold coins; she stooped a little, and had marvellously delicate hands.

"I knew he would go," she answered in a small voice.

"With scant farewell, with little excuse, with small preparation, with no regret, he has gone," said Dirk. "To the Court — at the bidding of a lady. You know her, for I have spoken of our meeting with her when we were driven forth from Basle." He closed his eyes, as if he made a great effort at control. "I think he is on the verge of loving her." He unclosed his eyes, full, blazing. "This must be prevented."

The witch shook her head.

"If you are wise, let him go." She fixed her glimmering glance on Dirk's smooth pale face. "He is neither good nor evil; his heart sayeth one thing, his passions another — let him go. His courage is not equal to his desires. He would be great — by any means — yet he is afraid — let him go. He thinks to serve the Devil while it lurks still in his heart: 'At last I will repent — in time I will repent!' — let him go. He will never be great, or even successful, for he is confused in his aims, hesitating, passionate and changeable; therefore, you who can have the world — — let him go."

"All this I know," answered Dirk, his fingers clutching the gold cushions. "But I want him back."

"He will come. He has gone too far to stay away."

"I want him to return for ever," cried Dirk. "He is my comrade — he must be with me always — — he must have none in his thoughts save me."

Nathalie frowned.

"This is folly. The day you came here to me with words of Master Lukas, I saw that you were to be everything — he nothing; I saw that the world would ring with your name, and that he would die unknown." She rose vehemently. "I say, let him go! He will be but a clog, a drag on your progress. He is jealous of you; he is not over skilful . . . what can you say for him save that he is pleasant to gaze upon?"

Dirk slipped from the cushions and walked slowly up and down the room; a slow, beautiful smile rested on his lips, and his eyes were gentle.

"What can I say for him? 'Tis said in three words — I love him."

He folded his arms on his breast, and lifted his head.

"How little you know of me, Nathalie! Though you have taught me all your wisdom, what do you know of me save that I was Master Lukas's apprentice boy?"

"Ye came from mystery — as you should come," smiled the witch.

And now Dirk seemed to smile through agony.

"It is a mystery — methinks to tell it would be to be blasted as I stand; it seems so long ago — so strange — so horrible . . . well, well!" — he put his hand to his forehead and took a turn about the room —"as I sat in Master Lukas's empty house, painting, carving, reading forbidden books, I was not afraid; it seemed to me I had no soul . . . so why fear for that which was lost before I was born? 'The Devil has put me here,' said I, 'and I will serve him . . . he shall make me his archetype on earth . . . and I waited for his signal to bid me forth. Men talked of Antichrist! What if I am he?' . . . so I thought."

"And so you shall be," breathed the witch.

Dirk's great eyes glowed above his smiling lips.

"Could any but a demon have such thoughts? . . . then Theirry came, and I saw in his face that he did what I did — knew what I knew; and — and" — his voice faltered —"I mind me how I went and watched him as he slept — and then I thought after all I was no demon, for I was aware that I loved him. I had terrible thoughts — if I love, I have a soul, and if I have a soul it is damned — but he shall go with me — — if I came from hell I shall return to hell, and he shall go with me — if I am damned, he shall be damned and go hand in hand with me into the pit!"

The smile faded from his face, and an intense, ardent expression took its place; he seemed almost in an ecstasy.

"She may make fight with me for his soul — if he love her she might draw him to heaven — with her yellow hair! Did I not long for yellow locks when I saw my bridal? . . . I have forgotten what I spoke of — I would say that she does not love him . . . "

"Yet she may," said the witch; "for he is gay and beautiful."

Dirk slowly turned his darkening eyes on Nathalie.

"She must not."

The witch fondled her fingers.

"We can control many things — not love nor hate."

Dirk pressed a swelling bosom.

"Her heart is in the hand of another man — and that man is her steward, ambitious, poor and married."

He came up to the witch, and, slight as he was, beside the withered Eastern woman, he appeared marvellously fresh, glowing, and even splendid.

"Do you understand me?" he said.

The witch blinked her shining eyes. "I understand that there is little need of witchcraft or of black magic here."

"No," said Dirk. "Her own love shall be her poison . . . she herself shall give him back to me."

Nathalie moved, the little coins shaking in her hair. "Dirk, Dirk, why do you make such a point of this man's return?" she said, between reproach and yearning. She fondled the cold, passive and smiling youth with her tiny hands. "You are going to be great;" she mouthed the words greedily. "I may never have done much, but you have the key to many things. You will have the world for your footstool yet — let him go."

Dirk still smiled.

"No," he answered quietly.

The witch shrugged her shoulders and turned away.

"After all," she said in a half whine, "I am only the servant now. You know words that can compel me and all my kind to obey you. So let it be; bring your Theirry back."

Dirk's smile deepened.

"I shall not ask your aid. Alone I can manage this matter. Ay, even if it jeopardise my chance of greatness, I will have my comrade back."

"It will not be difficult," nodded the witch. "A silly maid's influence against thine!" she laughed.

"There is another will seek to detain him at the Court," said Dirk reflectively. "His old-time friend, the Margrave's son, Balthasar of Courtrai, who shines about the Emperor. I saw him not long ago — he also is my enemy."

"Well, the Devil will play them all into thy hands," smiled the witch.

Dirk turned an absent look on her and she crept away.

It grew to the hour of sunset; the red light of it trembled marvellously in the red roses and filled the low, dark chamber with a sombre crimson glow.

Dirk stood by the window biting his forefinger, revolving schemes in which Jacobea, her steward, Sybilla and Theirry were to be entangled as flies in a web; desperate devilry and despairing human love mingled grotesquely, giving rise to thoughts dark and hideous.

The clear peal of a bell roused him, and he started with remembrances of when last this sound through an empty house had broken on his thoughts — of how he had gone and found Theirry without his door.

Then he left the room and sought the witch; she had disappeared; he did not doubt that the summons was for her; not infrequently did she have hasty and secret visitors, but as she came not he crossed the dark passage and himself opened the door on to the slip of garden that divided the house from the cobbled street — opened it on a woman in a green hood and mantle, who stood well within the shadow of the porch.

"Whom would you see?" he asked cautiously.

The stranger answered in a low voice.

"You. Are you not the young doctor who lectures publicly on — many things? Constantine they call you.

"Yea," said Dirk; "I am he."

"I heard you today. I would speak to you."

She wore a mask that as completely concealed her face as her cloak concealed her figure. Dirk's keen eyes could discover nothing of her person.

"Let me in," she said in an insistent, yet anxious voice.

Dirk held the door wide, and she stepped into the passage, breathing quickly.

"Follow after me," smiled Dirk; he decided that the lady was Jacobea of Martzburg.

# Chapter 12

## Ysabeau

Dirk and the lady entered the room he had just quitted; he set a chair for her near the window and waited for her to speak, but kept his eyes the while on her shrouded figure.

She wore a mask such as he had often seen on ladies; fantastic Italian taste had fashioned them in the likeness of a plague-stricken countenance, flecked green and yellow, and more lively fancy had nicknamed them "melons" from their similarity to an unripe melon skin; these masks, oval-shaped, with a slit for the mouth and eyes, and extending from the brow to the chin, were an effective concealment of every feature, and high favourites among ladies.

For the rest, the stranger's hood was pulled well forward so that not a lock of hair was visible, and her mantle was gathered close at her throat; it was of fine green cloth edged with miniver; she wore thick gauntlets so that not an inch of her skin was visible.

"You are well disguised," said Dirk at last, as she made no sign of speaking. "What is your business with me?"

He began to think that she could not be Jacobea since she gave no indication of revealing herself; also, he fancied that she was too short.

"Is there any one to overhear us or interrupt?" the lady spoke at last, her voice muffled a little by the mask.

"None," answered Dirk half impatiently. "I beg that you tell me who you are."

"Certes, that can wait;" her eyes sparkled through their holes in contrast with the ghastly painted wood that made her face immovable. "But I will tell you who you are, sir." "You know?" said Dirk coldly.

It seemed as if she smiled.

"The student named Dirk Renswoude who was driven forth from Basle University for practising the black arts."

For the first time in his life Dirk was taken aback, and hopelessly disconcerted; he had not believed it possible for any to discover the past life of the learned doctor Constantine; he went red and white, and could say nothing in either defence or denial.

"It was only about three months ago," continued the lady. "And both students and many other in the town of Basle would still know you, certes."

A rush of anger against his unknown accuser nerved Dirk.

"By what means have you discovered this?" he demanded. "Basle is far enough from Frankfort, I wot . . . and how many know . . . and what is the price of your silence, dame?"

The lady lifted her head.

"I like you," she said quietly. "You take it well. No one knows save I. I have made cautious inquiries about you, and pieced together your story with my own wit."

"My story!" flashed Dirk. "Certes! Ye know nought of me beyond Basle."

"No," she assented. "But it is enough. Joris of Thuringia died."

"Ah!" ejaculated Dirk.

The lady sat very still, observing him.

"So I hold your life, sir," she said.

Dirk, goaded, turned on her impetuously.

"Ye are Jacobea of Martzburg —"

"No" — she started at the name. "But I know her —"

"She told you this tale —"

Again the lady answered —

"No."

"She is from Basle," cried Dirk.

"Believe me," replied the stranger earnestly, "she knows nothing of you — I alone in Frankfort hold your secret, and I can help you to keep it . . . it were easy to spread a report of Dirk Renswoude's death."

Dirk bit his finger, his lip, glared out at the profusion of roses, at the darkening sky, then at the quiet figure in the hideous speckled mask; if she chose to speak he would have, at the best of it, to fly Frankfort, and that did not suit his schemes.

"Another youth lives here," said the lady. "I think he also fled from Basle."

Dirk's face grew pale and cunning; he was quick to see that she did not know Theirry was compromised.

"He was here — now he has gone to Court — he was at Basle, but innocent, he came with me out of friendship. He is silly and fond."

"I have to do with you," answered the lady. "Ye have a great, a terrible skill, evil spirits league with you . . . your spells killed a man —" She stopped.

"Poor fool," said Dirk sombrely.

The stranger rose; her calm and self-possession had suddenly given way to fierce only half-repressed passion; she clasped her hands and trembled as she stood.

"Well," she cried thickly. "You could do that again — a softer, more subtle way?" "For you?" he whispered.

"For me," she answered, and sank into the window-seat, pulling at her gloves mechanically.

A silence, while the dying red sunlight fell over the Eastern cushions and over her dark mantle and outside the red roses shook and whispered in the witch's garden.

"I cannot help you if you tell me nothing," said Dirk at length in a grim manner.

"I will tell you this," answered she passionately. "There is a man I hate, a man in my way — I do not talk wildly; that man must go, and if you will be the means —"

"You will be in my power as I am now in yours," thought Dirk, completing the broken sentence.

The lady looked out at the roses.

"I cannot convey to you what nights of horror and days of bitterness, what resolutions formed and resolutions broken — what hate, and what — love have gone to form the impulse that brought me here today — nor does it concern ye; certes enough I am resolved, and if your spells can aid me —" She turned her head sharply. "I will pay you very well."

"You have told me nothing," repeated Dirk. "And though I can discover what you are and who is your enemy, it were better that you told me with your own lips."

She seemed, now, in an ill-concealed agitation.

"Not today will I speak. I will come again. I know this place . . . meanwhile, certes, your secret is safe with me — think over what I have said."

She rose as if to take a hasty departure; but Dirk was in her way.

"Nay," he said firmly. "At least show your face — — how shall I know you again? And what confidence have you in me if you will not take off your mask? I say you shall."

She trembled between a sigh and a laugh.

"Perhaps my face is not worth gazing at," she answered on a breath.

"I wot ye are a fair woman," replied Dirk, who heard the consciousness of it in her alluring voice.

Still she hesitated.

"Know ye many about the Court?" she asked.

"Nay. I have not concerned myself with the Court."

"Well, then — and since I must trust you — and like you" — her voice rose and fell —"look at me and remember me."

She loosened her cloak, flung back the hood and quickly unfastening the mask, snatched it off. The disguise flung aside, she was revealed to the shoulders, clearly in the warm twilight.

Dirk's first impression was, that this was beauty that swept from his mind all other beauty he had ever beheld; his second, that it was the same face he and Theirry had seen in the mirror. "Oh!" he cried. "Well?" said the lady, the hideous mask in her band.

Now she was disclosed, it was as if another presence had entered the dusky chamber, so difficult was it to associate this brilliance with the cloaked figure of a few moments since.

Certainly she was of a great beauty, smiting into breathlessness, a beauty not to be realised until beheld; Dirk would not have believed that a woman could be so fair.

If Jacobea's hair was yellow, this lady's locks were pale, pure glittering gold, and her eyes a deep, soft, violet hue; the throwing back of her cloak revealed her round slender throat, and the glimmer of a rich bodice.

The smile faded from her lips, and her gorgeous loveliness became grave, almost tragic. "You do not know me?" she asked.

"No," answered Dirk; he could not tell her that he had seen her before in his devil's mirror.

"But you will recognise me again?"

Dirk laughed quietly.

"You were not made to be forgotten. Strange with such a face ye should have need of witchcraft!"

The lady replaced the mottled mask, that looked the more horrible after that glimpse of gleaming beauty, and drew her mantle over her shoulders.

"I shall come to you or send to you, sir. Think on what I have said, and on what I know."

She was obscured again, hidden in her green cloak. Dirk proffered no question, made no comment, but preceded her down the dark passage and opened the door; she passed out; her footstep was light on the path; Dirk watched her walk rapidly down the street then closed the door and bolted it. After a pause of breathless confusion and heart-heating excitement, he ran to the back of the house and out into the garden.

It was just light enough for the huge dusky roses to be visible as they nodded on their trailing bushes; Dirk ran between them until he reached a gaunt stone statue half concealed by laurels; in front of this were flags irregularly placed; in the centre of one was an iron ring; Dirk, pulling at this, disclosed a trap door that opened at his effort, and revealed a flight of steps; he descended from the soft pure evening and the red roses into the witch's kitchen, closing the stone above him.

The underground chamber was large and lit by lamps hanging from the roof, revealing smooth stone walls and damp floor; in one side a gaping blackness showed where a passage twisted to the outer air; on another was a huge alchemist's fireplace; before this sat the witch, about her a quantity of glass vessels, retorts and pots of various shapes.

Either side this fireplace hung a human body, black and withered, swinging from rusted ropes and crowned with wreaths of green and purple blotched leaves.

On a table set against the wall was a brass head that glimmered in the feeble light. Dirk crossed the floor with his youthful step and touched Nathalie on the shoulder. "One came to see me," he said breathlessly. "A marvellous lady."

"I know," murmured the witch. "And was it to play into thy hands?"

The air was thick and tainted with unwholesome smells; Dirk leant against the wall and stared down the chamber, his hand to his brow.

"She threatened me," he said, "and for a moment I was afraid; for, certes, I do not wish to leave Frankfort . . . but she wished me to serve her — which I will do — for a price." "Who is she?" blinked the witch.

"That I am come to discover," frowned Dirk. "And who it is she spoke of — also somewhat of Jacobea of Martzburg" — he coughed, for the foul atmosphere had entered his nostrils. "Give me the globe."

The witch handed him a ball of a dark muddy colour, which he placed on the floor, flinging himself beside it; Nathalie drew a pentagon round the globe and pronounced some words in a low tone; a slight tremor shook the ground, though it was solid earth they stood on, and the globe turned a pale, luminous, blue tint.

Dirk pushed back the damp hair from his eyes, and, resting his face in his hands, his elbows on the ground, he stared into the depths of the crystal, the colour of which brightened until it glowed a ball of azure fire.

"I see nothing," he said angrily.

The witch repeated her incantations; she leant forward, the yellow coins glistening on her pale forehead.

Rays of light began to sparkle from the globe. "Show me something of the lady who came here today," commanded Dirk.

They waited.

"Do ye see anything?" breathed the witch.

"Yea — very faintly."

He gazed for a while in silence.

"I see a man," he said at last. "The spells are wrong . . . I see nothing of the lady —"

"Watch, though," cried the witch. "What is he like?"

"I cannot see distinctly . . . he is on horseback . . . he wears armour . . . now I can see his face — he is young, dark — he has black hair —"

"Do ye know him?"

"Nay — I have never seen him before." Dirk did not lift his eyes from the globe. "He is evidently a knight . . . he is magnificent but cold . . . ah!"

His exclamation was at the change in the ball; slowly it faded into a faint blue, then became again dark and muddy.

He flung it angrily out of the pentagon.

"What has that told me?" he cried. "What is this man?"

"Question Zerdusht," said the witch, pointing to the brass head. "Maybe he will speak tonight."

She flung a handful of spices on to the slow-burning fire, and a faint smoke rose, filling the chamber.

Dirk crossed to the brass head and surveyed it with eager hollow eyes.

"The dead men dance," smiled the witch. "Certes, he will speak to-night."

Dirk turned his wild gaze to where the corpses hung. Their shrivelled limbs twisted and jerked at the end of their chain, and the horrid lurid colour of their poisonous wreaths gleamed through the smoke and shook with the nodding of their faceless heads.

"Zerdusht, Zerdusht," murmured Dirk. "In the name of Satan, his legions, speak to thy servant, show or tell him something of the woman who came here today on an evil errand."

A heavy stillness fell with the ending of the words; the smoke became thick and dense, then suddenly cleared.

At that instant the lamps were extinguished and the fire fell into ashes.

"Something comes," whispered the witch.

Through the dark could be heard the dance of the dead men and the grind of their bones against the ropes.

Dirk stood motionless, his straining eyes fixed before him.

Presently a pale light spread over the end of the chamber, and in it appeared the figure of a young knight; his black hair fell from under his helmet, his face was composed and somewhat haughty, his dark eyes fearless and cold.

"'Tis he I saw in the crystal!" cried Dirk, and as be spoke the light and the figure disappeared. Dirk beat his breast.

"Zerdusht! ye mock me! I asked ye of this woman! I know not the man."

The brass head suddenly glowed out of the darkness as if a light shone behind it; the lids twitched, opened, and glittering red eyeballs stared at Dirk, who shouted in triumph. He fell on his knees.

"A year ago today I saw a woman in the mirror; today she came to me . . . who is she? . . . Zerdusht — her name?"

The brass lips moved and spoke.

"Ysabeau."

What did this tell him?

"Who was the knight ye have shown me?" he cried.

"Her husband," answered the head.

"Who is the man she seeks my aid to . . . to . . . who is it of whom she spoke to me?" The flaming eyeballs rolled.

"Her husband."

Dirk gave a start.

"Make haste," came the witch's voice through the swimming blackness. "The light fades." "Who is she?"

"The Empress of the West," said the brass head. A cry broke from Dirk and the witch; Dirk shrieked another question.

"She wishes to put another in the Emperor's place?"

"Yea;" the light was growing fainter; the eyelids flickered over the red eyes.

"Whom?" cried Dirk. Faint, yet distinct came the answer —

"The Lord of Ursula of Rooselaare, Balthasar of Courtrai."

The lids fell and the jaws clicked, the light sank into nothingness, and the lamps sprang again into dismal flame that disclosed the black bodies of the dead men, hanging slackly with their wreaths touching their chests, the witch crouching by the hearth —

And in the centre of the floor Dirk, smiling horribly.

# Chapter 13

## The Snaring of Jacobea

The great forest was so silent, so lonely, the aisles of a vast church could have been no more sanctified by holy stillness.

Even the summer wind that trembled in the upper boughs of the huge trees had not penetrated their thick branches and intertwined leaves, so that the grass and flowers were standing erect, untroubled by a breath of air, and the sun, that dazzled without on the town of Frankfort did not touch the glowing green gloom of the forest.

Seated low on the grass by a wayside shrine that held a little figure of the Madonna, Nathalie the witch, hunched together in a brown cloak, looked keenly into the depths of cool shade between the tree trunks.

She was watching the distant figure of a lady tremble into sight among the leaves of the undergrowth.

A lady who walked hesitatingly and fearfully; as she drew near, the witch could see that the long yellow dress she held up was torn and soiled, and that her hair hung disarranged on her shoulders; breathing in a quick, fatigued manner she came towards the shrine, but seeing the witch she stopped abruptly and her grey eyes darkened with apprehension.

"'What is amiss with Jacobea of Martzburg," asked the witch in her expressionless way, "that she walks the forest disarrayed and alone?"

"I am lost," answered Jacobea, shrinking. "How do you know me?"

"By your face," said Nathalie. "How is it you are lost?"

"Will you tell me the way to Frankfort?" asked Jacobea wearily. "I have walked since noon. I was accompanying the Empress from the tournament and my horse broke away with me — I slipped from the saddle. Now I have lost him."

Nathalie smiled faintly.

"I know not where I am," said Jacobea, still with that look of apprehension in her sweet eyes. "Will you set me on my path?"

She glanced at the shrine, then at the witch, and put her hand to her forehead; dazed, she seemed, and bewildered.

"Of what are you afraid?" asked Nathalie.

"Oh, why should I be afraid!" answered Jacobea, with a start. "But — why, it is very lonely here and I must get home."

"Let me tell your fortune," said the witch, slowly rising. "You have a curious fortune, and I will reveal it without gold or silver."

"No!" Jacobea's voice was agitated. "I have no credence in those things. I will pay you to show me the way out of the forest."

But the witch had crossed softly to her side, and, to her manifest shrinking terror, caught hold of her hand.

"What do you imagine you hold in your palm?" she smiled.

Jacobea endeavoured to draw her hand away, the near presence of the woman quickened her unnamed terror.

"Lands and castles," said the witch, while her fingers tightened on the striving wrist. "Gold and loneliness —"

"You know me," answered Jacobea, in anger. "There is no magic in this . . . let me go!" The witch dropped the lady's hand and smoothed her own together.

"I do not need the lines in your palm to tell me your fortune," she said sharply. "I know more of you than you would care to hear, Jacobea of Martzburg."

The lady turned away and stepped quickly but aimlessly down the shaded glade.

Nathalie, dragging her brown cloak, came lightly after.

"You cannot escape," she said. "You may walk in and out the trees until you die of weariness, yet never find your way to Frankfort."

She laid her small thin fingers on the soft velvet of Jacobea's yellow sleeve and blinked up into her startled eyes.

"Who are you?" cried the lady, with a touch of desperation in her faint voice. "And what do you want with me?"

The witch licked her pale lips.

"Come with me and I will show you."

Jacobea shuddered.

"No, I will not."

"You cannot find your way alone," nodded the witch.

The lady hesitated; she looked around her at the motionless aisles of trees, the silent glades, she looked up at the arching boughs and clustering leaves concealing the sky.

"Indeed I will nay you well if you will guide me out of this," she entreated.

"Come with me now," answered Nathalie, "and afterwards I will set you on your way."

"To what end should I go with you?" exclaimed Jacobea. "I know you not, and, God help me, I mistrust you."

The witch shot a scornful glance over the lady's tall figure, supple with the strength of youth. "What evil could I do you?" she asked.

Jacobea considered her intently; indeed she was small, seemed frail also; Jacobea's white fingers could have crushed the life out of her lean throat.

Still she was reluctant.

"To what end?" she repeated.

Nathalie did not answer, but turned into a grass-grown path that twisted through the trees, and Jacobea, afraid of the loneliness, followed her slowly.

As they went through the forest, the green, still forest, with no flower to vary the clinging creepers and great blossomless plants, with no sound of bird or insect to mingle with their light tread and the sweep of their garments on the ground, Jacobea was aware that her senses were being dulled and drugged with the silence and the strangeness; she felt no longer afraid or curious. After a while they came upon a pool lying in a hollow and grown about with thick, dark ferns; the sunless waters were black and dull, on the surface of them floated some dead leaves and the vivid unwholesome green of a tangled weed.

A young man in a plain dark dress was seated on the opposite bank.

On his knees was an open book, and his long straight hair hung either side of his face and brushed the yellow page.

Behind him stood the shattered trunk of a blasted tree, grown with fan-shaped fungi of brilliant scarlet and blotched purple and orange that glowed gorgeously in the universal cold soft greenness.

"Oh me!" murmured Jacobea.

The young man lifted his eyes from the book and looked at her across the black water.

Jacobea would have fled, would have flung herself into the forest with no thought but that of escape from those eyes gazing at her over the pages of that ancient volume; but the witch's loathsome little hands closed on hers with a marvellous strength and drew her, shuddering, round the edge of the pond.

The youth shut the book, stretched his slender limbs, and, half turning on his side, lay and watched.

Jacobea's noble and lovely figure, clothed in a thick soft velvet of a luminous yellow hue; her blonde hair, straying on her shoulders and mingling with the glowing tint of her gown; her grave and sweet face, lit and guarded by grey eyes, soft and frightened, made a fair picture against the sombre background of the dark wood.

A picture marred only by the insignificant and drab-coloured figure of the little witch who held her hand and dragged her through the dank grass.

"Do you remember me?" asked the youth.

Jacobea turned her head away.

"Let go of her, Nathalie," continued the youth impatiently; he rested his elbow on the closed book and propped his chin on his hand; his eyes rested eagerly and admiringly on the lady's shuddering fairness.

"She will run," said Nathalie, but she loosened her hold.

Jacobea did not stir; she shook the hand Nathalie had held and caressed it with the other. The young man put back his heavy hair.

"Do you know me?"

She slowly turned her face, pearl pale above the glowing colour of her dress.

"Yes, you came to my castle for shelter once."

Dirk did not lower his intense, ardent gaze.

"Well, how did I reward your courtesy? I told you something."

She would not answer.

"I told you something," repeated Dirk. "And you have not forgotten it."

"Let me go," she said. "I do not know who you are nor what you mean. Let me go."

She turned as if to move away, but sank instead on to one of the moss-covered boulders that edged the pond and clasped her fingers over the shining locks straying across her bosom. "You have never been the same since that time you sheltered me," said Dirk.

She stiffened with dread and pride.

"Ye are some evil thing," she said; her glance was fierce for the passive witch. "Why was I brought here?"

"Because it was my wish," answered Dirk gravely. "Your horse does not often carry you away, Jacobea of Martzburg, and leave you in a trackless forest."

The lady started at his knowledge.

"That also was my will," said Dirk.

"Your will!" she echoed.

Dirk smiled, with an ugly show of his teeth.

"Belike the horse was bewitched — have ye not heard of such a thing?"

"Santa Maria!" she cried.

Dirk sat up and clasped his long fingers round his knees.

"You have given a youth I know a post at Court," he said. "Why?"

Jacobea shivered and could not move; she looked drearily at the black water and the damp masses of fern, then with a slow horror at the figure of the young man seated under the blasted tree.

"I do not know," she answered weakly, "I never disliked him."

"As ye did me," added Dirk.

"Maybe I had no cause to love you," she returned, goaded. "Why did you ever come to my castle? why did I ever see you?"

She put her cold hand over her eyes.

"No matter for that," mocked Dirk. "So ye liked my comrade Theirry?"

She answered as if forced against her will. "Well enough I liked him. Was he not pleasured to encounter me again, and since he was doing nought — I — but why do you question me? Can it be that you are jealous?"

The young man pulled his heavy brows together.

"Am I a silly maid to be jealous? Meddle not with things ye cannot measure, it had been better for you had you never seen my comrade's fair face — ay, and for me also," and he frowned.

"Surely he is free to do as he may list," returned Jacobea. "If he choose to come to Court." "If ye choose to tempt him," answered Dirk. "But enough of that."

He rose and leant against the tree; above his slender shoulder rose the jagged tongue of grey wood and the smooth colour of the clustering fungi, and beyond that the forest sank into immense depths of still gloom.

Jacobea strove desperately with her dull dread and terror, but it seemed to her as if a sickly vapour was rising from the black pool that chilled her blood to horror; she could not escape Dirk's steady eyes that were like bright stones in his smooth face.

"Come here," he said.

Jacobea made no movement to obey until the witch clutched her arm, when she shook off the clinging fingers and approached the spot where Dirk waited.

"I think you have bewitched me," she said drearily.

"Not I, another has done that," he answered. "Certes, ye are slow in mating, Jacobea of Martzburg."

A little shuddering breath stirred her parted lips; she looked to right and left, saw nothing but the enclosing forest, and turned her frightened eyes on Dirk.

"I know some little magic," he continued. "Shall I show you the man you would wish to make Lord of Martzburg?"

"There is no one," she said feebly.

"You lie," he answered. "As I could prove."

"As you cannot prove," she returned, clasping her hands together.

Dirk smiled.

"Why, you are a fair thing and a gentle, but you have rebellious thoughts, thoughts ye would blush to whisper at the confessional grate."

She moved her lips, but did not speak.

"Why did your steward come with ye to Frankfort?" asked Dirk. "And his wife stay as chatelaine of Martzburg? It had been more fitting had he remained. What reward will he receive for his services as your henchman at the Court?"

Jacobea drew her handkerchief from her girdle and pressed it to her lips.

"What reward do you imagine I should offer?" she answered very slowly.

"I cannot tell," said Dirk, with a hot force behind every word. "For I do not know if you are a fool or no, but this I know, the man waits a word from you —"

"Stop!" said Jacobea.

But Dirk continued ruthlessly —

"He waits, I tell you —"

"Oh God, for what?" she cried.

"For you to say —'you think me fair, Sebastian, you know me rich and all my life shall prove me loving, and only a red-browed woman in Martzburg Castle prevents you coming from my footstool to my side' — said you that, he would take horse tomorrow for Martzburg and return a free man."

The handkerchief fell from Jacobea's fingers and fluttered on the dark ferns.

"You are a fiend," she said in a sick voice. "You cannot be human to so touch my heart, and you are wrong, I dare to tell you in the name of God that you are wrong — those evil thoughts have never come to me."

"In the name of the Devil I am right," smiled Dirk.

"The Devil! Ye are one of his agents!" she cried in a trembling defiance. "Or how could you guess what I scarcely knew until ye came that baleful night? — what he never knew till then — ah, I swear it, be never dreamt that I — never dreamt what my favour meant, but now — his — eyes — I cannot mistake them."

"He is a dutiful servant," said Dirk, "he waits for his mistress to speak."

Jacobea sank to her knees on the grass.

"I entreat you to forbear," she whispered. "Whoever you are, whatever your object I ask your mercy. I am very unhappy — do not goad me — drive me further."

Dirk stepped forward and caught her drooping shoulders in his firm hands.

"Pious fool!" he cried. "How long do you think you can endure this? how long do you think he will remain the servant when he knows he might be the master?"

She averted her agonised face.

"Then it was from you he learned it, you —"

Dirk interrupted hotly —

"He knows, remember that! he knows and he waits. Already he hates the woman who keeps him dumb; it were very easily done — one look, some few words — ye would not find him slow of understanding." He loosened his grasp on her and Jacobea fell forward and clasped his feet.

"I implore you take back this wickedness, I am weak; since my first sight of you I have been striving against your influence that is killing me; man or demon, I beseech you, let me be!"

She raised her face, the slow, bitter tears forced out of her sweet, worn eyes; her hair fell like golden embroidery over the yellow gown, and her fingers fluttered on her unhappy bosom. Dirk considered her curiously and coldly.

"I am neither man nor demon," he said. "But this I tell you, as surely as he is more to you than your own soul, so surely are you lost."

"Lost! lost!" she repeated, and half raised herself.

"Certes, therefore get the price of your soul," he mocked. "What is the woman to you? A coldhearted jade, as good dead now as fifty years hence — what is one sin the more? I tell you while you set that man's image up in your heart before that of God ye are lost already."

"I am so lonely," she whispered piteously. "Had I one friend —" She paused, as though some one came into her mind with the words, and Dirk, intently watching her, suddenly flushed and glowed with anger.

He stepped back and clapped his hands.

"I promised you a sight of your lover," he said. "Now let him speak for himself." Jacobea turned her head sharply.

A few feet away from her stood Sebastian, holding back the heavy boughs and looking at her.

She gave a shriek and swiftly rose; Dirk and the witch had disappeared; if they had slipped into the undergrowth and were yet near they gave no answer when she wildly called to them; the vast forest seemed utterly empty save for the silent figure of Sebastian.

Not doubting now that Dirk was some evil being whom her own wicked thoughts had evoked, believing that the appearance of her steward was some phantom sent for her undoing, she, unfortunate, distracted with misery and terror, turned with a shuddering relief to the oblivion of the still pool.

Hastening with trembling feet through the clinging weeds and ferns, she climbed down the damp bank and would have cast herself into the dull water, when she heard his voice calling her — a human voice.

She paused, lending a fearful ear to the sound while the water rippled from her foot. "It is I," he called. "My lady, it is I."

This was Sebastian himself, no delusion nor ghost but her living steward, as she had seen him this morning in his brown riding-habit, wearing her gold and blue colours round his hat. She mastered her terror and confusion.

"Indeed, you frightened me," — a lie rose to save her. "I thought it some robber — I did not know you."

Fear of his personal aid gave her strength to move away from the water and gain the level ground.

"I have been searching for you," said Sebastian. "We came upon your horse on the high road and then upon your gloves in the grass, so, as no rider could come among these trees, on foot I sought for you. I am glad that you are safe."

This calm and carefully ordered speech gave her time to gather courage; she fumbled at her bosom, drew forth a crucifix and clutched it to her lips with a murmur of passionate prayers.

He could not but notice this; he must perceive her soiled torn dress, her wild face, her white exhaustion, but he gave no sign of it.

"It was a fortunate chance that sent me here," he said gravely. "The wood is so vast —" "Ay, so vast," she answered. "Know you the way out, Sebastian?"

She tried to nerve herself to look at him, but her glance was lifted only to fall instantly again.

"You must forgive me," she said, struggling with a fainting voice. "I have walked very far, I am so weary — I must rest a while."

But she did not sit, nor did he urge that she should.

"Have you met no one?" he asked.

She hesitated; if he had encountered neither the woman nor the young man, then they were indeed wizards or of some unearthly race — she could not bring herself to speak of them.

"No," she answered at length.

"We have a long way to walk," said the steward.

Jacobea felt his look upon her, and grasped her crucifix until the sharp edges of it cut her palm. "Do you know the way?" she repeated dully.

"Ay," he answered now. "But it is far."

She gathered up her long skirt and shook off the withered leaves that clung to it. "Will you lead the way?" she said.

He turned and moved ahead of her down the narrow path by which he had come; as she followed him she heard his foot fall soft on the thick grass and the swishing sound of the straying boughs as he held them back for her to pass, till she found the silence so unendurable that she nerved herself to break it; but several times she gathered her strength in vain for the effort, and when at last some foolish words had come to her lips, he suddenly looked back over his shoulder and checked her speech.

"'Tis strange that your horse should have gone mad in such a manner," he said.

"But ye found him?" she faltered.

"Ay, a man found him, exhausted and trembling like a thing bewitched."

Her heart gave a great leap — had he used that word by chance —

She could not answer.

"Ye were not hurt, my lady, when ye were thrown?" said the steward.

"No," said Jacobea, "no."

Silence again; no bird nor butterfly disturbed the sombre stillness of the wood, no breeze stirred the thick leaves that surrounded them; gradually the path widened until it brought them into a great space grown with ferns and overarched with trees.

Then Sebastian paused.

"It is a long way yet," he said. "Will you rest a while?"

"No," she replied vehemently. "Let us get on — — where are the others? surely we must meet some one soon!"

"I do not know that any came this way," he answered, and cast his brooding glance over the "trembling weariness of her figure.

"Ye must rest, certes, it is folly to persist," he added, with some authority.

She seated herself, lifting the hand that held the crucifix to her bosom.

"How full of shadows it is here," she said. "It is difficult to fancy the shining of the sun on the tops of these darkened trees."

"I do not love forests," answered Sebastian. As he stood his profile was towards her; and she must mark again the face that she knew so bitterly well, his thin dark cheek, his heavy-lidded eyes, his contained mouth.

Gazing down into the clusters of ferns at his feet, he spoke —

"I think I must return to Martzburg," he said.

She braced herself, making a gesture with her hand as if she would ward off his words. "You know that you are free to do what you will, Sebastian."

He took off his right glove slowly and looked at his hand.

"Is it not better that I should go?"

He challenged her with a full sideways glance.

"I do not know," she said desperately, "why you put this to me, here and now."

"I do not often see you alone."

He was not a man of winning manners or of easy speech; his words came stiffly, yet with a purpose in them that chilled her with a deeper sense of dread.

She opened her hand to stare down at the crucifix in her palm.

"You can leave Frankfort when you wish — why not?" she said.

He faced her quickly.

"But I may come back?"

It seemed to Jacobea that he echoed Dirk's words; the crucifix slipped through her trembling fingers on to the grass.

"What do you mean? Oh, Sebastian, what do you mean?" The words were forced from her, but uttered under her breath; she added instantly, in a more courageous voice, "Go and come as you list, are you not free?"

He saw the crucifix at her feet and picked it up, but she drew back as he came near and held out her hand.

He put the crucifix into it, frowning, his eyes dark and bright with excitement.

"Do you recall the two students who were housed that night in Martzburg?" he asked. "Yes," she said. "Is not one now at Court?"

"I would mean the other — the boy," answered Sebastian.

She averted her face and drooped until the ends of her hair touched her knees.

"I met him again today," continued the steward, with a curious lift in his voice, "here, in this forest, while searching for you. He spoke to me."

Certainly the Devil was enmeshing her, surely he had brought her to this pass, sent Sebastian, of all men, to find her in her weariness and loneliness.

And Sebastian knew — knew also that she knew — outspoken words between them could be hardly more intolerable shame than this.

"He is cunning beyond most," said the steward.

Jacobea lifted her head.

"He is an enchanter — a wizard, do not listen to him, do not speak to him — as you value your soul, Sebastian, do not think of him."

"As I value some other things," he answered grimly, "I must both listen to him and consider what he says."

She rose.

"We will go on our way. I cannot talk with you now, Sebastian."

But he stood in her path.

"Let me journey to Martzburg," he said thickly; "one word — I shall understand you."

She glanced and saw him extraordinarily keen and moved; he was lord of Martzburg could he but get her to pledge herself; in his eagerness, however, he forgot advice. "Tell her," said Dirk, "you have adored her for years in secret." This escaped his keenness, for though his wife was nothing to him compared with his ambition, he had no tenderness for Jacobea. Had he remembered to feign it he might have triumphed and now; but though her gentle heart believed he held her dear, that he did not say so made firmness possible for her.

"You shall stay in Frankfort," she said, with sudden strength.

"Sybilla asks my return," he said, gazing at her passionately. "Do we not understand each other without words?"

"The fiend has bewitched you also," she answered fearfully. "You know too much — — you guess too much — and yet I tell you nothing, and I, I also am bewitched, for I cannot reply to you as I should."

"I have been silent long," he said. "But I have dared to think — had I been free — as I can be free —"

The crucifix was forgotten in her hand.

"We do evil to talk like this," she said, half fainting.

"You will bid me go to Martzburg," he insisted, and took her long cold fingers.

She raised her eyes to the boughs above her.

"No, no!" then, "God have compassion on me!" she said.

The thick foliage stirred — Jacobea felt as if the bars of a cage were being broken about her — — she turned her head and a little colour flushed her cheek.

Through the silvery stems of the larches came some knights and a page boy, members of the party left to search for her.

She moved towards them; she hailed them almost gaily; none, save Sebastian, saw her as they turned towards Frankfort raise the crucifix and press her lips to it.

# Chapter 14

## The Snaring of Theirry

Dirk and the witch kept company until they reached the gates of Frankfort.

There the young man took his own way through the busy town, and Nathalie slipped aside into the more retired streets; many of the passers-by saluted Dirk, some halted to speak with him; the brilliant young doctor of rhetoric, with a reputation made fascinating by an air of mystery, was a desired acquaintance among the people of Frankfort. He returned their greetings pleasantly yet absently; he was thinking of Jacobea of Martzburg, whom he had left behind in the great forest, and considering what chances there might be, either for Theirry or Sybilla the steward's wife.

He passed the tall red front of the college, where the quiet trees tapped their leaves against the arched windows, turned over the narrow curved bridge that spanned the steadily flowing waters of the Main, and came to the thick walls surrounding the Emperor's castle.

There for a moment he paused and looked thoughtfully up at the Imperial flag that fluttered softly against the evening sky.

When he passed on it was with a cheerful step and whistling a little tune under his breath; a few moments brought him to the long street where the witch lived, a few more to her gate, and then his face lit and changed wonderfully, for ahead of him was Theirry.

Flushed and panting, he ran to his friend's side and touched him on the arm.

Theirry turned, his hand on the latch; his greeting was hurried, half shamefaced.

"My master and most of the Court were at the tourney today," he said. "I thought it safe to come."

Dirk withdrew his hand, and his eyes narrowed.

"Ah! —ye are beginning to be circumspect how ye visit here."

"You word it unkindly," answered Theirry hastily. "Let us enter the house, where we can talk at ease."

They passed into the witch's dwelling, and to the room at the back that looked into the garden of red roses.

The windows were set wide, and the scented softness of the evening filled the half-darkened chamber; Dirk lit a little lamp that had a green glass, and by the faint flame of it gazed long and lingeringly at Theirry.

He found his friend richly dressed in black and crimson, wearing an enamel chain round his bonnet, and a laced shirt showing at his bosom; he found the glowing, bright charm of his face disturbed by some embarrassment or confusion, the beautiful mouth uneasily set, the level brows slightly frowning.

"Oh, Theirry!" he cried in a half-mournful yearning. "Come back to me — come back."

"I am very well at Court," was the quick answer. "My master is gentle and my tasks easy."

Dirk seated himself at the table; he watched the other intently and rested his pale cheek on his hand.

"Very clearly can I see ye are well, and very well at Court — seldom do ye leave it." "I find it difficult to get here often," said Theirry.

He crossed to the window and looked out, as if the room oppressed him, and he thought the prospect of the roses pleasanter than the shadows and lamplight within.

"Ye find it difficult," said Dirk, "because your desires chain you to the Court. I think ye are a faithless friend."

"That am not I — ye know more of me than any man — I care more for ye than for any man —" "Or woman?" added Dirk dryly.

An impatient colour came into Theirry's cheeks; he looked resolutely at the red roses.

"That is unworthy in you, Dirk — is it disloyal to you to know a lady — to — to — admire a lady, to strive to serve and please a lady?"

He turned his charming face, and, in his effort to conciliate, his voice was gentle and winning.

"Truly she is the sweetest of her kind, Dirk; if you knew her — evil is abashed before her —"

"Then it is as well I do not know her," Dirk retorted grimly. "Strangely ye talk — you and I know we are not saints — but belike ye would reform — belike a second time ye have repented." Theirry seemed in some agitation.

"No, no — have I not gone too far? Do I not still hope to gain something — perhaps everything?" He paused, then added in a low voice, "But I wish I had never laid hands on the monk. I wish I had not touched God His money — and when I see her I cannot prevent my heart from smarting at the thought of what I am."

"How often do you see her?" asked Dirk quietly.

"But seldom," answered Theirry sadly. "And it is better — what could I ever be to her?" Dirk smiled sombrely.

"That is true. Yet you would waste your life dallying round the places where you may sometimes see her face."

Theirry bit his lip.

"Oh, you think me a fool — to falter, to regret — — but what have my sins ever done for me? There are many honest men better placed than I — and without the prospect of hell to blast their souls."

Dirk looked at him with lowering eyes.

"You had been content had you not met this lady."

"Enough of her," answered Theirry wearily. "You make too much of it. I do not think I love her; but one who is fallen must view such sweetness, such gentle purity with sorrow — yea, with yearning."

Dirk clasped his hand on the edge of the table.

"Maybe she is neither so pure nor so gentle as you think. Certes! she is but as other women, as one day ye may see."

Theirry turned from the window half in protest, half in excuse.

"Cannot you understand how one may hold a fair thing dear — how one might worship — — even — love?"

"Yes," answered Dirk, and his great eyes were bright and misty. "But if I — loved" — he spoke the word beautifully, and rose as he uttered it —"I would so grapple his — her soul to mine that we should be together to all eternity; nor devil nor angel should divide us. But — but there is no need to talk of that — there are other matters to deal with."

"Would I had never seen the evil books or never seen her face," said Theirry restlessly. "So at least I had been undivided in my thoughts."

He came to the table and looked at Dirk across the sickly, struggling flame of the lamp; in his hazel eyes was an expression of appeal, the call of the weak to the strong, and the other held out his hands impulsively.

"Ah, I am a fool to trouble with ye, my friend," he said, and his voice broke with tenderness. "For ye are headstrong and unstable, and care not for me one jot, I warrant me — yet — yet you may do what you will with this silly heart of mine."

There was a grace, a wistful affection in his face, in his words, in his gesture of outstretched hands that instantly moved Theirry, ever quick to respond. He took the young doctor's slender fingers in a warm clasp; they were very quickly withdrawn. Dirk had a notable dislike to a touch, but his deep eyes smiled.

"I have somewhat to tell you," he said, "at which your impatience will be pleased."

He went lightly to a press in the wall and brought forth a mighty candlestick of red copper, branched and engraved three half-burnt candles remained in the sockets; he lit these, and the room was filled with a brighter and pleasanter light.

Setting the candlestick on the table, where it glowed over Theirry's splendid presence, he returned to the cupboard and took out a tall bottle of yellow wine and two glasses with milk-white lines about the rims.

Theirry seated himself at the table, pulled off his gloves and smoothed his hair back from his face.           .

"Have you seen the Empress?" asked Dirk, pouring out the wine.

"Yea," answered Theirry, without interest.

"She is very beautiful?"

"Certes! — — but of a cloying sweetness — there is no touch of nobility in her."

Dirk held the wine out across the table and seated himself.

"I have heard she is ambitious," he said.

"Ay, she gives the Emperor no rest; for ever urging him to Rome, to be crowned by the Pope as Emperor of the West — but he better loves the North, and has no spirit to rule in Italy."

"The nobles chafe at his inaction?" asked Dirk. "'Tis not idle questioning."

"Mostly, I think — do we not all have golden dreams of Rome? Balthasar — ye mind him, he is Margrave of East Flanders now, since his father was killed at the boar hunt — and powerful, he is mad to cross the Alps — he has great influence with the Emperor. Indeed, I think he loves him."

Dirk set down the untasted wine.

"Balthasar loves the Emperor!" he cried.

"Certes! yes — why not? The Margrave was always affectionate, and the Emperor is lovable." A second time Dirk raised the glass, and now drained it.

"Here is good matter for plots," he said, elegantly wiping his lips. "Here is occasion for you and me to make our profit. Said ye the Devil was a bad master? — listen to this."

Theirry moved the candlestick; the gold light dazzled in his eyes.

"What can Emperor or Empress be to us?" he asked, a half-bewildered fear darkening his brows.

"She has been here," said Dirk. "The Lady Ysabeau."

Theirry stared intently; a quick breath stirred his parted lips; his cheeks glowed with excited colour.

"She knows," continued Dirk, "that I, Doctor Constantine of Frankfort College, and you, meek secretary to her Chamberlain, are the two students chased from Basle University."

Theirry gave a little sound of pain, and drew back in the huge carved chair.

"So," said Dirk slowly, "she has it in her power to ruin us — at least in Frankfort." "How can I hold up my head at Court again!" exclaimed Theirry bitterly.

Dirk noted the utterly selfish thought; he did not mention how he had shielded Theirry from suspicion.

"There is more in it than that," he answered quietly. "Did she choose she might have us burnt in the market place — Joris of Thuringia died of his illness that night."

"Oh!" cried Theirry, blenching.

"But she will not choose," said Dirk calmly. "She needs me — us — that threat is but her means of forcing obedience; she came secretly to my lectures — she had heard somewhat — she discovered more."

Theirry filled his glass.

"She needs us?" he repeated falteringly.

"Cannot ye guess in what way?"

Theirry drank, set down the half-emptied glass, and looked at the floor with troubled eyes that evaded the other's bright eyes.

"How can I tell?" he asked, as if reluctant to speak at all.

Dirk repressed a movement of impatience.

"Come, you know. Shall I speak plainly?"

"Certes! — yes," answered Theirry, still with averted face.

"There is a man in her way."

Theirry looked up now; his eyes showed pale in his flushed face.

"Who must die as Joris of Thuringia died?" he asked.

"Yes."

Theirry moistened his lips.

"Am I to help you?"

"Are we not one — inseparable? The reward will be magnificent."

Theirry put his hand to a damp brow.

"Who is the man?"

"Hush!" whispered Dirk, peering through the halo of the candle-flame. "It is the Emperor."

With a violent movement, Theirry pushed back his chair and rose.

"Her husband! I will not do it, Dirk!"

"I do not think ye have a choice," was the cold answer. "Ye gave yourself unto the Devil and unto me — and you shall serve us both."

"I will not do it," repeated Theirry in a shuddering voice.

Dirk's eyes glimmered wrathfully.

"Take care how you say that. There are two already — what of the monk? I do not think you can turn back."

Theirry showed a desperate face.

"Why have ye drawn me into this? Ye are deeper in devils' arts than I."

"That is a strange thing to say," answered Dirk, very pale, his lips quivering. "You swore comradeship with me — together we were to pursue success — fame — power — you knew the means — ay, you knew by whose aid we were to rise, you shared with me the labours, the disgrace that fell on both of us. Together we worked the spells that slew Joris of Thuringia — — together we stole God His gold from the monk; now — — ay, and now when I tell you our chance has come — this is your manner of thanking me!"

"A chance! — to help a woman in a secret murder?"

Theirry spoke sullenly.

"Ye never thought our way would be the way of saintship — ye were not so nice that time ye bound Ambrose of Menthon to the tree."

"How often must you remind me of that?" cried Theirry fiercely. "I had not done it but for you."

"Well, say the same of this; if you be weak, I am strong enough for two."

Theirry pulled at the crimson tassels on his slashed sleeves.

"It is not that I am afraid," he said, flushing.

"Certes! you are afraid," mocked Dirk. "Afraid of God, of justice, maybe of man — but I tell you that these things are nought to us." He paused, lifted his eyes and lowered them again. "Our destiny is not of our shaping — we take the weapons laid to our hands and use them as we are bid. Life and death shall both serve us to our appointed end."

Theirry came to the other side of the table and gazed, fearfully, across at him.

"Who are you?" he questioned softly.

Dirk did not answer; an expression of dread and despair withered all the life in his features; the extraordinary look in his suddenly dimmed eyes sent a chill to Theirry's heart.

"Ah!" he cried, stepping back with manifest loathing.

Dirk put his hand over his eyes and moaned.

"Do you hate me, Theirry? Do you hate me?"

"I — I do not know." He could not explain his own sudden revulsion as he saw the change in Dirk's face; he paced to and fro in a tumult.

Dark had closed in upon them and now blackness lay beyond the window and the half-open door; shadows obscured the corners of the long chamber; all the light, the red gleam of the candles, the green glow of the lamp, shone over the table and the slight figure of Dirk.

As Theirry stopped to gaze at him anew, Dirk suddenly lowered his white hand, and his eyes, blinking above his long fingers, held Theirry in a keen glance.

"This will make us more powerful than the Empress or the Emperor," he said. "Leave your thoughts of me and ponder on that."

He withdrew his hand and revealed lips as pale as his cheeks.

"What does that mean?" cried Theirry. "I am distracted."

"

"We shall go to Rome," replied Dirk; there was a lulling quality of temptation in his tone. "And you shall have your desires."

"My desires!" echoed Theirry wildly. "I have trod an unholy path, pursuing the phantom of —— my desires! Do you still promise me I shall one day grasp it?"

"Surely — money — and power and pleasure, these things wait you in Rome when Ysabeau shall have placed the imperial diadem on Balthasar's brow. These things — and" — it seemed as if Dirk's voice broke —"even Jacobea of Martzburg," he added slowly.

"Can one win a saint by means of devilry?" cried Theirry.

"She is only a woman," said Dirk wearily. "But, since you hesitate, and falter, I will absolve you from this league with me — go your way, serve your saint, renounce your sins — and see what God will give you."

Theirry crossed the room with unequal steps.

"No — I cannot — I will not forego even the hope of what you offer me." His great eyes glittered with excitement; the hot blood darkened his cheek. "And I pledged myself to you and your master. Do not think me cowardly because I paused — who is the Emperor?" He spoke hoarsely. "Nothing to you or to me . . . As you say, Joris of Thuringia died."

"Now you speak like my comrade at Basle," cried Dirk joyfully. "Now I see again the spirit that roused me to swear friendship with you the night we first met. Now I — ah, Theirry, we will be very faithful to one another, will we not?"

"I have no choice."

"Swear it," cried Dirk.

"I swear it," said Theirry.

He went to the window, pushed it wider open and gazed out into the moonless night. Dirk clasped and unclasped his hands on the table, murmuring —

"I have won him back — won him back!"

Theirry spoke, without turning his head.

"What do you mean to do next?"

"I shall see the Empress again," answered Dirk.

"At present — be very secret — that is all — there is no need to speak of it."

Now it was he that was anxious to evade the subject; his eyes, bright under the drooping lids, marked the vehement, desperate eagerness of Theirry's flushing face, and he smiled to see it.

"Your absence may be noticed at the palace," he said softly. "You must return. How you can help me I will let you know."

But Theirry stood irresolute.

"It seems I have no will when you command me," he said, half in protest. "I come and go as you bid me — you stir my cold blood, and then will not give me satisfaction."

"You know all that I do," returned Dirk. He rose and raised the copper candlestick in both hands. "I am very weary. I will light you to the door."

"Where have you been today?" asked Theirry.

"Did you see the Court returning from the tourney?"

The candle-flames, flaring with the movement, cast a rich glow over Dirk's pallid face. "No — why do you ask?" he said.

"I know not." Theirry's crimson doublet sparkled in its silk threads as his breast rose with the irregular breaths; he walked heavily to the door, gathering up his black mantle over his arm. "When may I come again?" he asked.

"When you will," answered Dirk. He entered the passage and held up the heavy candlestick, so that a great circle of light was cast on the darkness. "Ye are pledged to me whether ye come or no — are ye not?"

"Certes! I do think so," said Theirry. He hesitated.

"Good-night," whispered Dirk.

Theirry went down the passage.

"Good-night."

He found the door and unlatched it; a soft but powerful breath of air fluttered the candle-flames almost on to Dirk's face; he turned back into the room and shut himself in, leaving darkness behind him. Theirry stepped into the street and drew the latch; a few stars were out, but the night was cloudy. He leant against the side of the house; he felt excited, confused, impatient; Dirk's abrupt dismissal rankled, he was half ashamed of the power exercised over him by his frail comrade, half bewildered by the allurement of the reward that promised to be so near now.

Rome — splendour, power — Jacobea of Martzburg — and only one stranger between him and this consummation; he wondered why he had ever hesitated, ever been horrified; his antic-ipations became so brilliant that they mounted like winged spirits to the clouds, catching him up with them; he could scarcely breathe in the close atmosphere of excitement; a thousand questions to which he might have demanded answer of Dirk occurred to him and stung with impatience his elated heart.

On a quick impulse he turned to the door and tried the handle.

To his surprise he found it bolted from within; he wondered both at Dirk's caution and his softness of tread, for he had heard no sound.

It was not yet late, but he did not desire to attract attention by knocking.

Full of his resolution to speak further with Dirk, he passed round the house and entered the garden with the object of gaining admittance by the low windows of the room where they had been conversing.

But the light had gone from the chamber, and the windows were closed.

With an exclamation of impatience Theirry stepped back among the rose bushes and looked up.

Dirk's bedchamber was also in darkness; black and silent the witch's dwelling showed against the still but stormy sky. Theirry felt a chill run to his heart — where had the youth gone so instantly, so silently? Who had noiselessly bolted door and windows?

Then suddenly a light flashed across his vision; it appeared in the window of a room built out from the house at the side — a room that Theirry had always imagined was used only as a store-place for Nathalie's drugs and herbs; he did not remember that he had ever entered it or ever seen a light there before.

His curiosity was stirred; Dirk had spoken of weariness — perhaps this was the witch herself. He waited for the light to disappear, but it continued to glow, like a steady star across the darkness of the rose garden.

The heavy scent of the half-seen blooms filled the gusty wind that began to arise; great fragments of cloud sped above the dark roof-line of the house; Theirry crept nearer the light.

It had crossed his mind many times that Dirk and Nathalie held secrets they kept from him, and the doubt had often set him raging inwardly, as well he knew the witch despised him as a useless novice in the black arts; old suspicions returned to him as, advancing warily, he drew near the light and crouched against the wall of the house. A light curtain was pulled across the window, but carelessly, and drawn slightly awry to avoid the light set in the window-seat.

Theirry, holding his breath, looked in.

He saw an oval room hung with Syrian tapestries of scarlet and yellow, and paved with black and white marble; the air was thick with the blue vapour of some perfume burning in a copper brazier, and lit by lamps suspended from the wall, their light glowing from behind screens of a pure pink silk. The end of the apartment was hidden by a violet velvet curtain embroidered with grapes and swans; near this a low couch covered with scarlet draperies and purple cushions was placed, and close to this a table, set with a white cloth bearing moons and stars worked in blue.

Across this cloth a thick chain of amber beads was flung; a single tall glass edged with gold and a silver dish of apples stood together in the centre of the table.

As there was no one in the room to attract his attention, Theirry had leisure to remark these details.

He noticed, also, that the light close to him in the window-seat was the copper candlestick he had seen, not long since, in Dirk's hands.

With a certain angry jealousy at being, as he considered, duped, he waited for his friend's appearance.

Mystery and horror both had he seen at the witch's house, yet nothing ever disclosed to him helped him now to read the meaning of this room he peered into.

As he gazed, his brows contracted in wonderment; he saw the violet curtain gently shaken, then drawn slightly apart in the middle.

Theirry almost betrayed himself by a cry of surprise. A long, slender woman's hand and arm slipped between the folds of the velvet; a delicate foot appeared; the curtain trembled, the aperture widened, and the figure of a girl was revealed in dusky shadow.

She was tall, and wore a long robe of yellow sendal that she held up over her bosom with her left hand. She might have just come forth from the bath, for her shoulders, arms and feet were bare, and the lines of her limbs noticeable through the thin silk.

Her head and face were wrapped in a silver gauze. She stood quite still, half withdrawn behind the curtain, only the finely shaped white arm that held it back fully revealed.

Her appearance impressed Theirry with unnameable dread and terror; he remained rigid at the window gazing at her, not able, if he would, to fly. Through the veil that concealed her face he could see restless dark eyes and the line of dark hair; he thought that she must see him, that she looked at him even as he looked at her, but he could not stir.

Slowly she came forward into the room; her feet were noiseless on the stone floor, but as she moved Theirry heard a curious dragging sound he could not explain.

She took up the amber beads from the table and put them down again; on her left hand was a silver ring set with a flat red stone; supporting her drapery with her other hand, she looked at this ornament, moved her finger so that the crimson jewel flashed, then shook her hand, angrily it seemed.

As the ring was large it fell and rolled across the floor. Theirry saw it sparkling under the edge of one of the hangings.

The woman looked after it, then straight at the window, and the pale watcher could have shrieked in horror.

Again she moved, and again Theirry heard that noise as of something being trailed across the floor.

She was drawing nearer the window; as she approached she half turned, and Theirry saw flat green and dull wings of wrinkled skin folded on her back; the tips of them touched the floor — — these had made the dragging sound he had heard.

With a tortured cry wrung from him he flung up his hand to shut out the dreadful thing. She heard him, stopped and gave a shriek of dread and anguish; the lights were instantly extinguished, the room was in absolute darkness.

Theirry turned and rushed across the garden. He thought the rose bushes catching on his garments were hands seeking to detain him; he thought that he heard a window open and a flapping of wings in the air above him.

He cried out to the God on whom he had turned his back —

"Christus have mercy!" And so he stumbled to the gate and out into the quiet street of Frankfort.

# Chapter 15

## Melchoir of Brabant

The last chant of the monks died away.

The Sabbath service was ended and the Court rose from its place in the Emperor's chapel, but Jacobea remained on her knees and tried to pray.

The Empress, very fair and childishly sweet, drooping under the weight of her jewelled garments even with three pages to lift her train, raised her brows to see her lady remaining and gave her a little smile as she passed.

The Emperor, dark, reserved, devout and plainly habited, followed with his eyes still on his breviary; he was leaning on the arm of Balthasar of Courtrai; the sun falling slantwise through the high coloured windows made the fair locks and golden clothes of the Margrave one glitter in a dazzling brightness.

Jacobea could not bring her thoughts to dwell on holy things; her hands were clasped on her prie-Dieu, her open book was before her, but her eyes wandered from the altar to the crowd passing down the aisle.

Among the faces that went by she could not but mark the beautiful countenance of Theirry the secretary to the Queen's Chamberlain; she noticed him, as she always did, for his obvious calm handsomeness, today she noticed further that he looked grieved, distraught and pale. Wondering at this she observed him so intently that his long hazel eyes glanced aside and met hers in an intense gaze, grave and sad.

She thought there was a question or an appeal — some meaning in his look, and she turned her slender neck and stared after him, so that two ladies following smiled at each other.

Theirry kept his eyes fixed on her until he left the C chapel, and a slow colour crept into his cheek.

When the last courtier had glittered away out of the low arched door, Jacobea bent her head and rested her cheek against the top of the high prie-Dieu; her yellow hair, falling from under her close linen cap, hung in a shimmering line over her tight blue velvet gown, her hands were interlaced beside her cheek, and her long skirt rippled over her feet on to the stone pavement.

Could her prayers have been shaped into words they would have been such as these —

"Oh Mary, Empress of Heaven, oh saints and angels, defend me from the Devil and my own wicked heart, shelter me in my weakness and arm me to victory!"

Incense still lingered in the air; it stole pleasantly to her nostrils; she raised her eyes timidly to the red light on the altar, then rose from her knees clasping her breviary to her bosom, and turning she saw Theirry standing inside the door watching her.

She knew that he was waiting to speak to her, and, she knew not why, it gave her a sense of comfort and pleasure.

Slowly she came down the aisle towards him, and as she approached, smiled. He took a step into the church; there was no answering smile on his face.

"Teach me to pray, I beseech you," he said ardently. "Let me kneel beside you —" She looked at him in a troubled way.

"I? — alas!" she answered. "You do not know me."

"I know that if any one could lead a soul upwards it would be you."

Jacobea shook her head sadly.

"Scarcely can I pray for myself," she answered. "I am weak, unhappy and alone. Sir, whatever your trouble you must not come to me for aid."

His dark eyes flashed softly.

"You — unhappy? I have ever thought of you as gay and careless as the roses."

She gazed on him wistfully.

"Once I was. That day I saw you first — do you remember, sir? I often recall it because it seemed — that after that I changed —" She shuddered, and her grey eyes grew wet and mournful. "It was your friend."

Theirry's face hardened.

"My friend?"

She leant against the chapel wall and gazed passionately at the Chamberlain's secretary. "Who is he? Surely you must know somewhat of him."

"My friend —" repeated Theirry.

"The young scholar," she said quickly and fearfully, "he — he is in Frankfort now." "You have seen him?"

She bowed her head. "What does he want with me? He will not let me be in peace — he pursues me with horrible thoughts — he hates me, he will undo my soul —"

She stopped, catching close to her the ivory-covered book and shivering.

"I think," she said after a second, "he is an evil thing."

"When did you meet him?" asked Theirry in a low fearful voice.

Jacobea told him of the encounter in the forest; he marked that it was the day of the great tourney, the day when he had last seen Dirk; he remembered certain matters he had uttered concerning Jacobea.

"If he has been tampering with you," he cried wrathfully, "if he dares —"

"Then you know somewhat of him?" she interrupted in a half horror.

"Ay, to my shame I do," he answered. "I know him for what he is; if you value your peace, your soul — do not heed him."

She drew away.

"But you — you — Are you in league with him?"

Theirry groaned and set his teeth.

"He holds me in a mesh of temptation — he lures me into great wickedness."

Jacobea moved still further back; shrinking from him into the gloom of the chapel. "Oh!" she said. "Who — who is he?"

Theirry lowered his eyes and frowned.

"You must not ask me." He fingered the base of the pilaster against the door.

"But he troubles me," she answered intensely. "The thought of him is like some on clinging to my garments to drag me down."

Theirry lifted his head sharply to gaze at her tall slender figure; but lifted his eyes no higher than her clasped hands that lay over the breviary below her heart.

"How can he or such as he disturb you? What temptation can you be beguiled with?"

And as he saw the delicate fingers tremble on the ivory cover, his soul was hot and sore against Dirk.

"I will not speak of what might beguile me," said Jacobea in a low Voice. "I dare not speak of it — let it go — it is great sin."

"There is sin for me also," murmured Theirry, "but the prize seems almost worth it."

He bit his finger and stared on the ground; he felt that she shuddered and heard the shiver of her silks against the chapel wall.

"Worth it, you say?" she whispered, "worth it?"

Her tone made him wince; he could fancy Dirk at her shoulder prompting her, and he lifted his head and answered strongly —

"You cannot care to know, and I dare not tell, what has put me in the power of this young scholar, nor what are the temptations with which he enmeshes me — but this you must hear" — his hand was outspread on his bosom, pressing on his heart, his hazel eyes were dilated and intense —"this — I should be his, utterly, wholly his, one with him in evil, if it were not for you and the thought of you."

She leant her whole weight against the stone wall and stared at him; a shaft of dusty sunlight played on the smooth ivory book and her long fingers; fell, too, glowingly across the blue velvet bosom of her dress; but her throat and face were in shadow.

"You are the chatelaine of Martzburg," continued Theirry in a less steady voice, "and you do not know me — it is not fit that you should — but twice you have been gentle with me, and if — and if you could so care, for your sake I would shake the clinging devils off — I would live good and humble, and scorn the tempting youth."

"What must I do to help you?" answered Jacobea. "Alas! why do you rate me so high?" Theirry came a step nearer; he touched the border of her long sleeve.

"Be what you are — that is all. Be noble, pure — ah, sweet I — that seeing you I can still believe in heaven and strive for it."

She looked at him earnestly.

"Why — you are the only one to care, that I should be noble and sweet. And it would make a difference to you?" Her questioning voice fell wistfully. "Ah, sir — were you to hear a wicked thing of me and know it true — did I become a vile, a hideous creature — would it make a difference?"

"It would — for me — make the difference between hell and paradise."

She flushed and trembled.

"Certes, you have heartened me — nay, you must not set me in a shrine — but, but — — Oh, sir, honour me and I will be worthy of it."

She raised an appealing face.

"On my knees," answered Theirry earnestly, "I will do you worship. I am no knight to wear your colours boldly — but you shall win a fairer triumph than ever graced the jousts, for I will come back to God through you and live my days a repentant man — because of you."

"Nay — each through the other," said Jacobea. "I think I too — had . . . ah, Jesu! fallen — if some one had not cared."

He paled with pain.

"What did he — that youth — tempt you with?"

"No matter," she said faintly. "It is over now — I will be equal to your thoughts of me, sir. I have no knight, nor have wished for one — but I will often think of you who have encouraged me in this my loneliness."

"Please God," he said. "We both are free of devilry — will you make that a pact with me? that I may think of you as far above it all as is the moon above the mire — will you give me leave to think you always as innocent as I would have my Saint?"

"Your worship, sir, shall make me so," she answered gravely. "Think no ill of me and I will do no ill."

He went on his knee and kissed the hem of her soft gown.

"You have saved me," he whispered, "from everlasting doom."

As he rose, Jacobea held out her hand and touched him gently on the sleeve.

"God be thanked," she said.

He bent his head and left her; she drew from her bosom the crucifix that had been her companion in the forest and kissed it reverently, her heart more at ease than since the day when first she met Dirk Renswoude.

Returning to the great hall of the palace with quick resolve to return to Martzburg or to send for Sybilla forming in her mind, she encountered the Empress walking up and down the long chamber discontentedly.

Ysabeau, who affected a fondness for Jacobea, smiled on her indolently, but Jacobea, always a little overawed by her great loveliness, and, in her soul, disliking her, would have passed on. The Empress raised her hand.

"Nay, stay and talk to your poor deserted lady," she said in her babyish voice. "The Emperor is in his chamber writing Latin prayers — on a day like this!" She kissed her hand to tile sunshine and the flowers seen through the window. "My dames are all abroad with their gallants — and I Hazard what I have been doing?"

She held her left hand behind her and laughed in Jacobea's face; seen thus in her over-gorgeous clothes, her childlike appearance and beauty giving her an air of fresh innocence, She was not unlike the little image of the Virgin often set above her altars.

"Guess!" she cried again; then, without waiting for an answer — "Catching butterflies in the garden."

She showed her hand now, and held delicately before Jacobea's eyes a white net drawn tightly together full of van-coloured butterflies.

"What is the use of them, poor souls?" asked Jacobea.

The Empress looked at her prisoners.

"Their wings are very lovely," she said greedily. "If I pulled them off would they last? Sewn on silk how they would shimmer!"

"Nay, they would fade," answered Jacobea hastily.

"Ye have tried it?" demanded the Empress.

"Nay, I could not be so cruel . . . I love such little gay creatures."

Reflection darkened Ysabeau's gorgeous eyes.

"Well, I will take the wings off and see if they lose their brightness." She surveyed the fluttering victims. "Some are purple . . . a rare shade!"

Jacobea's smooth brow gathered in a frown of distress.

"They are alive," she said, "and it is agreeable to them to live; will you not let them free?"

Ysabeau laughed; not at all babyishly now.

"You need not watch me, dame."

"Your Grace does not consider how gentle and helpless they are, indeed" — Jacobea flushed in her eagerness — "they have faces and little velvet jackets on their bodies."

Ysabeau frowned and turned away.

"It amuses you to thwart my pleasures," she answered. She suddenly flung the net at Jacobea. "Take them and begone."

The chatelaine of Martzburg, knowing something of the Empress, was surprised at this sudden yielding; looking round, however, she learnt the cause of it. The Margrave of East Flanders had entered the hall.

She caught up the rescued butterflies and left the chamber, while the Empress sank into the window-seat among the crimson cushions patterned with sprawling lions, pulled a white rose out of her belt and set her teeth in the stem of it.

"Where is Melchoir?" asked the Margrave, coming towards her; his immense size augmented by his full rich clothes gave him the air of a golden giant.

"Writing Latin prayers," she mocked. "Were you Emperor of the West, Lord Balthasar, would you do that?"

He frowned.

"I am not such a holy man as Melchoir." Ysabeau laughed.

"Were you my husband would you do that?" His fresh fair face flushed rose colour. "This is among the things I may not even fancy."

She looked out of the window; her dress was low and loosened about the shoulders, by cause of the heat, she said, but she loved to make a pageant of her beauty; red, bronze and purple silks clung about her fastened with a thick belt; her pale gold hair was woven into a great diadem of curls above her brow, and round her throat was a string of emeralds, a gift from Byzantium, her home.

Purposely she was silent, hoping Balthasar would speak; but he stood, without a word, leaning against the tapestry.

"Oh God!" she said at last, without turning her head, "I loathe Frankfort!"

His eyes glittered, but he made no answer.

"Were I a man I would not be so tame."

Now he spoke.

"Princess, you know that I am sick for Rome, but what may we do when the Emperor makes delays?"

"Melchoir should be a monk," his wife returned bitterly, "since a German township serves him when he might rule half the world." Now she gave Balthasar her lovely face, and fixed on him her violet eyes. "We of the East do not understand this diffidence. My father was an Aegean groom who took the throne by strangling the life out of his master — he ruled strongly in Ravenna, I was born in the purple, nursed in the gold — I do not fathom your northern tardiness.

"The Emperor will go to Rome," said the Margrave in a troubled voice. "He will cross the Alps this year, I think."

Her white lids drooped.

"You love Melchoir — therefore you bear with him."

He lifted his head.

"You, too, must bear with him, since he is your lord, Princess," he answered.

And the Empress repressed the words she longed to utter, and forced a smile.

"How stern you are, Margrave; if I but turn a breath against Melchoir — and, sometimes, you wrong me, forgetting that I also am your friend."

Her eyes were quick to flash over him, to mark how stiffly and awkwardly he stood and could not look at her.

"My duty to the Emperor," she said softly, "and my love, cannot blind me to his weakness now; come, Lord Balthasar, to you also it is weakness — even your loyalty must admit we lose the time. The Pope says — Come — the King of the Lombards will acknowledge my lord his suzerain — and here we stay in Frankfort waiting for the winter to cut off the Alps."

"Certes he is wrong," frowned the Margrave. "Wrong . . . if I were he — I would be Emperor in good sooth and all the world should know that I ruled in Rome . . . "

She drew a long breath.

"Strange that we, his friend and his wife, cannot persuade him; the nobles are on our side also." "Save Hugh of Rooselaare, who is ever at his ear," answered Balthasar. "He brings him to stay in Germany."

"The Lord of Rooselaare!" echoed the Empress. "His daughter was your wife?"

"I never saw her," he interrupted quickly. "And she died. Her father seems, therefore, to hate me."

"And me also, I think, though why I do not know," she smiled. "His daughter's dead, dead . . . oh, we are very sure that she is dead."

"Certes, she was as good as another;" the Margrave spoke gloomily. "Now I must wed again."

The Empress stared at him.

"I did not think you considered that."

"I must. I am the Margrave now."

Ysabeau turned her head and fixed her eyes on the palace garden.

"There is no lady worthy of your rank and at the same time free," she said.

"You have an heiress in your train, Princess — — Jacobea of Martzburg — I have thought of her." The rich colours in the Empress's gown shimmered together with her hidden trembling.

"Can you think of her? She is near as tall as you, Margrave, and not fair — oh, a gentle fool enough — but — but" — she looked over her shoulder —"am I not your lady?"

"Ay, and ever will be," he answered, lifting his bright blue eyes. "I wear your favour, I do battle for you, in the jousts you are my Queen of Love — — — I make my prayers in your name and am your servant, Princess."

"Well — you need not a wife." She bit her lips to keep them still.

"Certes," answered Balthasar wonderingly. "A knight must have a wife besides a lady — since his lady is ofttimes the spouse of another, and his highest thought is to touch her gown — but a wife is to keep his castle and do his service."

The Empress twisted her fingers in and out her girdle.

"I had rather," she cried passionately, "be wife than lady."

"Ye are both," he answered, flushing. "The Emperor's wife and my lady."

She gave him a curious glance.

"Sometimes I think you are a fool, yet maybe it is only that I am not used to the North. How you would show in Byzantium, my cold Margrave!" And she leant across the gold and red cushions towards him. "Certes, you shall have your long straight maiden. I think her heart is as chill as yours."

He moved away from her.

"Ye shall not mock me, Princess," he said fiercely. "My heart is hot enough, let me be." She laughed at him.

"

"Are you afraid of me? Why do you move away? Come back, and I will recount you the praises of Jacobea of Martzburg."

He gave her a sullen look.

"No more of her."

"And yet your heart is hot enough —"

"Not with the thought of her — God knows."

But the Empress pressed her hands together and slowly rose, looking past Balthasar at the door.

"Melchoir, we speak of you," she said.

The Margrave turned; the Emperor, velvet shod, was softly entering; he glanced gravely at his wife and smilingly at Balthasar.

"We speak of you," repeated Ysabeau, dark-eyed and flushed, "of you . . . and Rome."

Melchoir of Brabant, third of his name, austere, reserved, proud and cold, looked more like a knight h of the Church than King of Germany and Emperor of the West; he was plainly habited, his dark hair cut close, his handsome, slightly haughty face composed and stern; too earnest was he to be showily attractive yet many men adored him, among them Balthasar of Courtrai, for in himself the Emperor was both brave and lovable.

"Cannot you have done with Rome?" he asked sadly, while his large intelligent eyes rested affectionately on the Margrave. "Is Frankfort grown so distasteful?"

"Certes, no, Lord Melchoir — it is the chance! the chance!"

The Emperor sank in a weary manner on to a seat.

"Hugh of Rooselaare and I have spoken together and we have agreed, Balthasar, not to go to Rome."

The Empress stiffened and drooped her lids; the Margrave turned swiftly to face his master, and all the colour was dashed out of his fresh face.

Melchoir smiled gently.

"My friend, ye are an adventurer, and think of the glory to be gained — but I must think of my people who need me here — the land is not fit to leave. It will need many men to hold Rome; we must drain the land of knights, wring money from the poor, tax the churches — leave Germany defenceless, a prey to the Franks, and this for the empty title of Emperor."

Balthasar's breast heaved.

"Is this your decision?"

The Emperor answered gravely —

"I do not think it God His wish that I should go to Rome."

The Margrave bent his head and was silent, but Ysabeau flung her clear voice into the pause.

"In Constantinople a man such as you would not long fill a throne; ere now you had been a blinded monk and I free to choose another husband!"

The Emperor rose from his seat.

"The woman raves," he said to the pale Margrave. "Begone, Balthasar."

The German left them; when his heavy footfall had died into silence, Melchoir looked at his wife and his eyes flashed.

"God forgive my father," he said bitterly, "for tying me to this Eastern she-cat!"

The Empress crouched in the window-seat and clutched the cushions.

"I was meant for a man's mate," she cried fiercely, "for a Cæsar's wife. I would they had flung me to a foot-boy sooner than given me to thee — thou trembling woman's soul!"

"Thou hast repaid the injury," answered the Emperor sternly, "by the great unhappiness I have in thee. My life is not sweet with thee nor easy. I would thou hadst less beauty and more gentleness."

"I am gentle enough when I choose," she mocked. "Balthasar and the Court think me a loving wife."

He took a step towards her; his cheek showed pale.

"It is most true none save I know you for the thing you are — heartless, cruel, fierce and hard —"

"Leave that!" she cried passionately. "You drive me mad. I hate you, yea, you thwart me every turn —"

She came swiftly across the floor to him.

"Have you any courage — any blood in you — will you go to Rome?"

"To please your wanton ambition I will do nothing, nor will I for any reason go to Rome." Ysabeau quivered like an infuriated animal.

"I will talk no more of it," said Melchoir coldly and wearily. "Too often do we waste ourselves in such words as these."

The Greek could scarcely speak for passion; her nostrils were dilated, her lips pale and compressed.

"I am ashamed to call you lord," she said hoarsely; "humbled before every woman in the kingdom who sees her husband brave at least — while I — know you coward —"

Melchoir clenched his hands to keep them off her.

"Hark to me, my wife. I am your master and the master of this land — I will not be insulted, nay, nor flouted, by your stinging tongue. Hold me in what contempt ye will, you shall not voice it — by St. George, no! — not if I have to take the whip to hold you dumb!"

"Ho! a Christian knight!" she jeered. "I loathe your Church as I loathe you. I am not Ysabeau, but still Marozia Porphyrogentris."

"Do not remind me thy father was a stableman and a murderer," said Melchoir. "Nor that I caused thee to change a name the women of thy line had made accursed. Would I could send thee back to Ravenna! — for thou hast brought to me nought but bitterness!"

"Be careful," breathed Ysabeau. "Be careful."

"Stand out of my way," he commanded.

For answer she loosened the heavy girdle round her waist; he saw her purpose and caught her hands.

"You shall not strike me." The links of gold hung from her helpless fingers while she gazed at him with brilliant eyes. "Would you have struck me?"

"Yea — across your mouth," she answered. "Now were you a man, you would kill me."

He took the belt from her arm, releasing her. "That you should trouble me!" he said wearily.

At this she stood aside to let him pass; he turned to the door, and as he lifted the tapestry flung down her belt.

The Empress crept along the floor, snatched it up and stood still, panting.

Before the passion had left her face the hangings were stirred again.

One of her Chamberlains.

"Princess, there is a young doctor below desires to see you. Constantine, his name, of Frankfort College."

"Oh!" said Ysabeau; a guilty colour touched her whitened cheek. "I know nothing of him," she added quickly.

"Pardon, Princess, he says 'tis to decipher an old writing you have sent to him; his words are, when you see him you will remember."

The blood burnt more brightly still under the exquisite skin.

"Bring him here," she said.

But even as the Chamberlain moved aside, the slender figure of Dirk appeared in the doorway. He looked at her, smiling calmly, his scholar's cap in his hand.

"You do remember me?" he asked.

The Empress moved her head in assent.

## Chapter 16

## The Quarrel

Dirk Renswoude laid down the pen and pushed aside the parchment, and lifted heavy eyes with a sigh of weariness.

It was midday and very hot; the witch's red roses were beginning to shed their petals and disclose their yellow hearts, and the leaves of the great trees that shaded the house were curling and yellowing in the fierce sun.

From his place at the table Dirk could mark these signs of autumn without; yet by the look in his eyes it seemed that he saw neither trees nor flowers, but only some image evoked by his thoughts; presently he picked up the quill, bit the end of it, frowned and laid it down.

Then he started and looked round with some eagerness, for a light sound broke the sleepy stillness, the door opened, and before his expectant gaze Theirry appeared.

Dirk flushed and smiled.

"Well met," he said. "I have much to say to you." He rose and held out his hand. Theirry merely touched it with his fingers.

"And I am come because I also have much to say." Dirk's manner changed, the warmth died from his face, and he gave the other a keen glance.

"Speak, then." He returned to his seat, took his face between his two delicate hands, and rested his elbows on the table. "I was writing my lecture for to-night, certes, I shall be glad of a diversion."

"You will not be pleased with mine," answered Theirry his expression was grave and cold, his dress plain and careless; he frowned, lifted his eyebrows continually, and played with the buttons on his doublet.

"Be seated," said Dirk.

Theirry took the chair he proffered.

"There is no need to make an ado," he began, obviously with an effort. "I am not going on with you.."

"You are not going on?" repeated Dirk. "Well, your reasons?"

"May God forgive me what I have done," cried Theirry in great agitation; "but I will sin no more — — I have resolved it — and ye cannot tempt me."

"And all you swore — to me?" demanded Dirk; his eyes narrowed, but he remained composed. Theirry clasped his restless fingers.

"No man is bound to bargains with the Devil . . . I have been weak and wicked — but I mingle no more in your fiendish councils —"

"This is for Jacobea of Martzburg's sake."

"It is for her sake — because of her that I am here now to tell you I have done with it — done with you!"

Dirk dropped his hands on to the table.

"Theirry! Theirry!" he cried wildly and sorrowfully.

"I have measured the temptation," said Theirry; "I have thought of the gain — the loss — I have put it aside, with God's help and hers — I will not aid you in the way you asked me — nor will I see it done."

"And ye call that virtue!" cried Dirk. "Poor fool — all it amounts to is that you, alas! — love the chatelaine."

"Nay," he answered hotly. "It is that, having seen her, I would not be vile. You meditate a dastard thing — the Emperor is a noble knight."

"Ambrose of Menthon was a holy monk," retorted Dirk. "Who choked the pious words in his throat? Joris of Thuringia was an innocent youth — who sent him to a hideous death?"

"I!" cried Theirry fiercely; "but always with you to goad me on! Before the Devil sent you across my way I had never touched sin save in dim thoughts but you, with talk of friendship, lured me from an honest man's company to poison me with forbidden knowledge, to tempt me into hideous blasphemies — — and I will have no more of it!"

"Yet you vowed comradeship with me," said Dirk. "Is your loyalty of such quality?" Theirry sprang violently from his chair and paced heavily up and down the room.

"You blinded me . . . I knew not what I did . . . but now I know; when I — I — heard her speak, and heard that you had dared to try to trap her to destruction —"

Dirk interrupted with a low laugh.

"So she told you that! But I warrant that she was dumb about the nature of her temptation!"

"That is no matter," answered Theirry; "now she is free of you, as I shall be-"

"As you vowed to her you would be," added Dirk. "Well, go your way — I thought you loved me a little — but the first woman's face!"

Theirry stood still to front him.

"I cannot love that which — I fear."

Dirk went swiftly very pale.

"Do you — fear me, Theirry?" he asked wistfully.

"Ay, ye know too much of Satan's lore — more than you ever taught me," he shuddered uncontrollably; "there are things in this very house —"

"What do you mean — what do you mean?" Dirk rose in his place.

"Who is the woman?" whispered Theirry fearfully; "there is a woman here —"

"In this house there are none save Nathalie and me," answered Dirk on the defensive, his eyes dark and glowing.

"There you lie to me; the last time I was here, I turned back swiftly on leaving, but found the door bolted, the lights out, all save one — in the little chamber next to this — I watched at the window and saw a gorgeous room and a woman, a winged woman."

"You dream," answered Dirk in a low voice. "Do you think I have enough power to raise such shapes?"

"I think 'twas some love of yours from Hell — — whence you came —"

"My love is not in Hell, but on the earth," answered Dirk quietly — "yet shall we go together into the pit — as for the woman, it was a dream — there is no gorgeous chamber there." He crossed the room and flung open a little door in the wall.

"See — old Nathalie's closet — full of herbs and charms —"

Theirry peered into an ill-lit apartment fitted with shelves containing jars and bottles.

"The enchantment that could bring the woman could change the room," he muttered, unconvinced.

Dirk gave a slow, strange look.

"Was she beautiful?"

"Yea — but —"

"More beautiful than Jacobea of Martzburg?"

Theirry laughed.

"I cannot compare Satan's handmaiden with a lily from Paradise."

Dirk closed the closet door.

"Theirry," he said falteringly, "do not leave me — you are the only thing in all the universe can move me to joy or pain — I love you, utterly."

"Out on such affection that would steal my soul —"

He was turning away when Dirk laid a timid hand upon his sleeve.

"I will make you great, ay, very great . . . do not hate me —"

But Theirry gazed fearfully at the youth's curious pale face.

"I will have none of you."

"You do not know how dear I hold you," insisted Dirk in a trembling voice; "come back to me, and I will let your lady be-"

"She can scorn ye . . . defy ye . . . as I do now!"

And he flung off the slim hand from his arm and strode away down the long room. Dirk drew himself together and crouched against the wall.

"Will she? certes, I wonder, will she?" he cried. "You will have none of me, you say, you reject me; but for how long?"

"For ever," answered Theirry hoarsely.

"Or until Jacobea of Martzburg falls."

Theirry swung round.

"That leaves it still for ever."

"Maybe, however, only for a few poor weeks — your lily is very fragile, Theirry, so look to see it broken in the mud —"

"If you harm her," cried Theirry fiercely, "if you blast her with your hellish spells —" "Nay — I will not; of herself she shall come to ruin."

"When that is, I will return to you, so — farewell for ever —"

He made a passionate gesture with his hand as if he swept aside Dirk and all thoughts of him, and turned quickly towards the door.

"Wait!" Dirk called to him. "What of this that you know of me?"

Theirry paused.

"So much I owe you — that I should be silent."

"Since, if you speak, you bring to light your own history," smiled Dirk. "But — about the Emperor?"

"God helping me I will prevent that."

"How will you prevent it?" Dirk asked quietly; "would you betray me as a first offering to your outraged God?"

Theirry pressed his hand to his brow in a bewildered, troubled manner.

"No, no, not that; but I will take occasion to warn him — to warn some one of the Empress." Dirk hunched his shoulders scornfully.

"Ah, begone, ye are a foolish creature — go and put them on their guard."

Theirry flushed.

"Ay, I will," he answered hotly. "I know one honest man about the Court — Hugh of Rooselaare."

A quick change came over Dirk's face.

"The Lord of Rooselaare?" he said. "I should remember him, certes; his daughter was Balthasar's wife — Ursula."

"She was, and he is the Emperor's friend, and opposed to the schemes of Ysabeau."

Dirk returned to the table and took up one of the books lying there; mechanically he turned the pages, and his eyes were bright on Theirry's pallid face.

"Warn whom you will, say what you will; save, if ye can, Melchoir of Brabant; begone, see, I seek not to detain you. One day you shall come back to me, when yon soft saint fails, and I shall be waiting for you; till then, farewell."

"For ever farewell," answered Theirry. "I take up your challenge; I go to save the Emperor." Their eyes met; Theirry's were the first to falter; he muttered something like a malediction on himself, lifted the latch and strode away.

Dirk sank into his chair; he looked very young and slight in his plain brown silk; his brow was drawn with pain, his eyes large and grieved; he turned the books and parchments over as though he did not see them.

He had not been long alone when the door was pushed open and Nathalie crept in. "He has gone?" she whispered, "and in enmity?"

"Ay" answered Dirk slowly. "Renouncing me."

The witch came to the table, took up the youth's passive hand and fawned over it. "Let him go," she said in an insinuating voice. "He is a fool."

"Why, I have put no strain on him to stay," Dirk smiled faintly. "But he will return." "Nay," pleaded Nathialie, "forget him."

"Forget him!" repeated Dirk mournfully. "But I love him."

Nathalie stroked the still, slim fingers anxiously.

"This affection will be your ruin," she moaned.

Dirk gazed past her at the autumn sky and the overblown red roses.

"Well, if it be so," he said pantingly, "it will be his ruin also; he must go with me when I leave the world — the world! after all, Nathalie" — he turned his strange gaze on the witch —"it does not matter if she hold him here, so long as he is mine through eternity."

His cheeks flushed and quivered, the long lashes drooped over his eyes; then suddenly he smiled.

"Nathalie, he has good intentions; he hopes to save the Emperor."

The witch blinked up at him.

"But it is too late?

"Certes; I conveyed the potion to Ysabeau this morning." And Dirk's smile deepened.

# Chapter 17

## The Murder

"Balthasar," said the Emperor, in pity of his friend's sullen face, "I will send ye to Rome to make treaty with the Pope since it goes so heavily with you to stay in Frankfort."

The Margrave bit the ends of his yellow hair and made no answer.

The Empress half lay along the seat against the wall. She wore a white and silver gown; on the cushion, where her elbow rested to support her head, lay a great cluster of crimson roses.

On low stools near her sat her maidens sewing, three of them embroidering between them a strip of scarlet silk.

It was the dining hall, the table laid already with rudely magnificent covers; through the low windows, from which the tapestry was looped back, was to be seen a red sunset sky flaming over Frankfort.

"Nay, be pleasant with me," smiled the Emperor; he laid his arm affectionately round the Margrave's huge shoulders. "Certes, since I took this resolution not to go to Rome, I have nought but sour looks from all, save Hugh."

Balthasar's good-humoured face cleared.

"Ye are wrong, my Prince; but God wot, I am not angered — we can manage without Rome" — — he heroically stifled his sigh — "and who knows that ye may not change yet?" he added cheerfully. Ysabeau looked at them as they paced up and down, their arms about each other, the golden locks and the black almost touching, the gorgeous purple and red habit of the Margrave against the quiet black garments of the Emperor.

She yawned as she looked, but her eyes were very bright; slowly she rose and stretched her slender body while the red roses fell softly to the ground, but she took no heed of them, fixing her gaze on the two men; her husband seemed not to know of her presence, but the Margrave was hotly conscious of her eyes upon him, and though he would not turn his upon her, nevertheless, she marked it and, in a half-smiling way, came and leant on the table that divided them.

The sunset flashed final beams that fell in flushing rosy lines on the gold and silver goblets and dishes, struck the Empress's embroideries into points of vivid light, and shone marvellously through Balthasar's brilliant locks.

"Surely we are late to-night," said the Emperor.

"Yea," answered Balthasar; "I do not love to wait."

He stopped to pour himself a tankard of amber wine and drank it at a draught.

Ysabeau watched him, then snatched up the fallen roses and laid them on the cloth.

"Will not my lord also drink?" she asked; the fingers of her right hand were hidden in the red flowers, with her left she raised a chased flagon in which the sunlight burnt and sparkled. "As you please, Princess," answered Melchoir, and gazed towards the light indifferently. "Ye might have poured for me," murmured the Margrave in a half voice.

Her hand came from the roses and touched a horn glass bound with silver, it lingered there a moment, then rose to her bosom; Balthasar, absorbing her face, did not notice the gesture.

"Another time," she answered, "I will serve you, Balthasar of Courtrai." She filled the glass until the wine bubbled at the brim. "Give it to my lord," she said.

Balthasar laughed uneasily; their fingers touched upon the glass, and a few drops were spilled. "Take care!" cried the Empress.

Melchoir turned and took the goblet.

"Why did you say — take care?" he asked.

"Between us we upset the wine," said Ysabeau.

Melchoir drank.

"It has an ugly taste," he said.

She laughed.

"Is it the cupbearer, perchance?"

"The wine is good enough," put in Balthasar.

The Emperor drank again, then set it down.

"I say it is strange — taste it, Balthasar."

In an instant the Empress intervened.

"Nay" — she caught up the glass with a movement swifter than the Margrave's —"since I poured, the fault — if fault there be-is mine."

"Give it to me!" cried Balthasar.

But she made a quick motion aside, the glass slipped from her fingers and the wine was lost on the floor.

As Balthasar stooped to pick up the goblet, the Emperor smiled.

"I warn you of that flagon, Margrave."

The pages and varlets entered with the meats and set them on the table; they who sat at the Emperor's board came to take their places; Theirry followed his master and fixed quick eyes on the Emperor.

He knew that Melchoir had been abroad all day at the hunt and could not have long returned, hardly could their designs upon him be put in practice tonight; after the supper he meant to speak to Hugh of Rooselaare, this as an earnest of his final severance with Dirk.

As the beautiful shining crowd settled to their seats, the young secretary, whose place was behind his master's chair, took occasion to note carefully the lord who was to receive his warning.

The candles, hanging in their copper circlets, were lit, and the ruddy light shone over the company, while bright pages drew the curtains over the last sunset glow.

Theirry marked the Empress, sitting languorously and stripping a red rose of its petals; Melchoir, austere, composed, as always; Balthasar, gay and noisy; then he turned his gaze on Hugh of Rooselaare.

That noble sat close to the Emperor. Theirry had not, so far, studied his personal appearance though acquainted with his reputation; observing him intently he saw a tall, well-made man dressed with sombre elegance, a man with a strong, rather curious face framed in straight, dull brown hair.

There was something in the turn of the features, the prominent chin, dark, clear eyes, pale complexion and resolute set of the mouth that gradually teased Theirry as he gazed; the whole expression reminded him of another face, seen under different circumstances, whose he could not determine.

Suddenly the Lord of Rooselaare, becoming aware of this scrutiny, turned his singularly intent eyes in the direction of the young scholar.

At once Theirry had it, he placed the likeness. In this manner had Dirk Renswoude often looked at him.

The resemblance was unmistakable if elusive; this man's face was of necessity sterner, darker, older and more set; he was of larger make, moreover, than Dirk could ever be, his nose was heavier, his jaw more square, yet the likeness, once noticed, could not be again overlooked.

It strangely discomposed Theirry, he felt he could not take his warning to one who had Dirk's trick of the intense gaze and inscrutable set of the lips; he considered if there were not some one else — let him go straightway, he thought, to the Emperor himself.

His reflections were interrupted by a little movement near the table, a pause in the converse. All eyes were turned to Melchoir of Brabant.

He leant back in his seat and stared before him as if he saw a sight of horror at the other end of the table; he was quite pale, his mouth open, his lips strained and purplish.

The Empress sprang up from beside him and caught his arm.

"Melchoir!" she shrieked. "Jesu, he does not bear me!"

Bahthasar rose in his place.

"My lord," he said hoarsely, "Melchoir."

The Emperor moved faintly like one struggling hopelessly under water.

"Melchoir!" — the Margrave pushed back his chair and seized his friend's cold hand —"do you not hear us . . . will you not speak?"

"Balthasar" — the Emperor's voice came as if from depths of distance — "I am bewitched!" Ysabeau shrieked and beat her hands together.

Melchoir sank forward, while his face glistened with drops of agony; he gave a low crying sound and fell across the table.

With an instantaneous movement of fright and horror, the company rose from their seats and pressed towards the Emperor.

But the Margrave shouted at them —

"Stand back — would you stifle him? — he is not dead, nor, God be thanked, dying."

He lifted up the unconscious man and gazed eagerly into his face, as he did so his own blanched despite his brave words; Melchoir's eyes and cheeks had fallen hollow, a ghastly hue overspread his features, his jaw dropped and his lips were cracked, as if his breath burnt the blood.

The Empress shrieked again and again and wrung her hands; no one took any heed of her, she was that manner of woman.

Attendants, with torches and snatched-up candles, white, breathless ladies and eager men, pressed close about the Emperor's seat.

"We must take him hence," said Hugh of Rooselaare, with authority. "Help me, Margrave." He forced his way to Balthasar's side.

The Empress had fallen to her husband's feet, a gleam of white and silver against the dark trappings of the throne.

"What shall I do!" she moaned. "What shall I do!"

The Lord of Rooselaare glanced at her fiercely.

"Cease to whine and bring hither a physician and a priest," he commanded.

Ysabeau crouched away from him and her purple eyes blazed.

The Margrave and Hugh lifted the Emperor between them; there was a swaying confusion as chair and seats were pulled out, lights swung higher, and a passage forced through the bewildered crowd for the two nobles and their burden.

Some flung open the door of the winding stairway that ascended to the Emperor's bedchamber, and slowly, with difficulty, Melchoir of Brabant was borne up the narrow steps.

Ysabeau rose to her feet and watched it; Balthasar's gorgeous attire flashing in the torchlight, Hugh of Rooselaare's stern pale face, her husband's slack body and trailing white hands, the eager group that pressed about the foot of the stairs.

She put her hands on her bosom and considered a moment, then ran across the room and followed swiftly after the cumbrous procession.

It was now a quarter of an hour since the Emperor had fainted, and the hall was left — empty. Only Theirry remained, staring about him with sick eyes.

A flaring flambeau stuck against the wall cast a strong light over the disarranged table, the disordered seats, scattered cushions and the rich array of gold vessels; from without came sounds of hurrying to and fro, shouted commands, voices rising and falling, the clink of arms, the closing of doors.

Theirry crossed to the Emperor's seat where the gorgeous cushions were thrown to right and left; in Ysabeau's place lay a single red rose, half stripped of its leaves, a great cluster of red roses on the floor beside it.

This was confirmation; he did not think there was any other place in Frankfort where grew such blooms; so he was too late, Dirk might well defy him, knowing that he would be too late.

His resolution was very quickly taken: he would be utterly silent, not by a word or a look would he betray what he knew, since it would be useless. What could save the Emperor now? It was one thing to give warning of evil projected, another to reveal evil performed; besides, he told himself, the Empress and her faction would be at once in power — Dirk a high favourite.

He backed fearfully from the red roses, glowing sombrely by the empty throne.

He would be very silent, because he was afraid; softly he crept to the window-seat and stood there, motionless, his beautiful face overclouded; in an agitated manner he bit his lip and reflected eagerly on his own hopes and dangers . . . on how this affected him — and Jacobea of Martzburg.

To the man, dying miserably above, he gave no thought at all; the woman, who waited impatiently for her husband's death to put his friend in his place, he did not consider, nor did the fate of the kingship trouble him; he pictured Dirk as triumphant, potent, the close ally of the wicked Empress, and he shivered for his own treasured soul that he had just snatched from perdition; he knew he could not fight nor face Dirk triumphant, armed with success, and his outlook narrowed to the one idea —"let me get away."

"But where? Martzburg!" — would the chatelaine let him follow her? It was too near Basle; he clasped his hands over his hot brow, calling on Jacobea.

As he dallied and trembled with his fears and terrors, one entered the hall from the little door leading to the Emperor's chamber.

Hugh of Rooselaare holding a lamp.

A feverish feeling of guilt made Theirry draw back, as if what he knew might be written on his face for this man to read, this man whom he had meant to warn of a disaster already befallen.

The Lord of Rooselaare advanced to the table; he was frowning fiercely, about his mouth a dreadful look of Dirk that fascinated Theirry's gaze.

Hugh held up the lamp, glanced down and along the empty seats, then noticed the crimson flowers by Ysabeau's chair and picked them up.

As he raised his head his grey eyes caught Theirry's glance.

"Ah! the Queen's Chamberlain's scrivener," he said. "Do you chance to know how these roses came here?"

"Nay," answered Theirry hastily. "I could not know."

"They do not grow in the palace garden," remarked Hugh; he laid them on the throne and walked the length of the table, scrutinising the dishes and goblets.

In the flare of flambeaux and candles there was no need for his lamp, but he continued to hold it aloft as if he hoped it held some special power.

Suddenly he stopped, and called to Theirry in his quiet, commanding way.

The young man obeyed, unwillingly.

"Look at that," said Hugh of Rooselaare grimly.

He pointed to two small marks in the table, black holes in the wood.

"Burns," said Theirry, with pale lips, "from the candles, lord."

"Candles do not burn in such fashion." As he spoke Hugh came round the table and cast the lamp-light over the shadowed floor.

"What is that?" He bent down before the window.

Theirry saw that he motioned to a great scar in the board, as if fire had been flung and had bitten into the wood before extinguished.

The Lord of Rooselaare lifted a grim face.

"I tell you the flames that made that mark are now burning the heart and blood out of Melchoir of Brabant."

"Do not say that — do not speak so loud!" cried Theirry desperately, "it cannot be true." Hugh set his lamp upon the table.

"I am not afraid of the Eastern witch," he said sternly; "the man was my friend and she has bewitched and poisoned him; now, God hear me, and you, scrivener, mark my vow, if I do not publish this before the land."

A new hope rose in Theirry's heart; if this lord would denounce the Empress before power was hers, if her guilt could be brought home before all men — yet through no means of his own — why, she and Dirk might be defeated yet!

"Well," he said hoarsely, "make haste, lord, for when the breath is out of the Emperor it is too late . . . she will have means to silence you, and even now be careful . . . she has many champions."

Hugh of Rooselaare smiled slowly.

"You speak wisely, scrivener, and know, I think, something, hereafter I shall question you." Theirry made a gesture for silence; a heavy step sounded on the stair, and Balthasar, pallid but still magnificent, swept into the room.

A great war-sword clattered after him, he wore a gorget and carried his helmet; his blue eyes were wild in his colourless face; he gave Hugh a look of some defiance.

"Melchoir is dying," he said, his tone rough with emotion, "and I must go look after the soldiery or some adventurer will seize the town."

"Dying!" repeated Hugh. "Who is with him?"

"The Empress; they have sent for the bishop until he come none is to enter the chamber." "By whose command?"

"By order of the Empress."

"Yet I will go."

The soldier paused at the doorway.

"Well, ye were his friend, belike she will let you in."

He swung away with a chink of steel.

"Belike she will not," said Hugh. "But I can make the endeavour."

With no further glance at the shuddering young man, who held himself rigid against the wall, Hugh of Rooselaare ascended to the Emperor's chamber.

He found the ante-room crowded with courtiers and monks; the Emperor's door was closed, and before it stood two black mutes brought by the Empress from Greece.

Hugh touched a black-robed brother on the arm. "By what authority are we excluded from the Emperor's death-bed?"

Several answered him —

"The Queen! she claims to know as much of medicine as any of the physicians."

"She is in possession."

Hugh shouldered his way through them.

"Certes, I must see him — and her."

But not one stepped forward to aid or encourage; Melchoir was beyond protecting his adherents, he was no longer Emperor, but a man who might be reckoned with the dead, the Empress and Balthasar of Courtrai had already seized the governance, and who dared interfere; the great nobles even held themselves in reserve and were silent.

But Hugh of Rooselaare's blood was up, he had always held Ysabeau vile, nor had he any love for the Margrave, whose masterful hand he saw in this.

"Since none of you will stand by me," he cried, speaking aloud to the throng, "I will by myself enter, and by myself take the consequences!"

Some one answered —

"II think it is but folly, lord."

"Shall a woman hold us all at bay?" he cried. "What title has she to rule in Frankfort?"

He advanced to the door with his sword drawn and ready, and the crowd drew back neither supporting nor preventing; the slaves closed together, and made a gesture warning him to retire. He seized one by his gilt collar and swung him violently against the wall, then, while the other crouched in fear, he opened the door and strode into the Emperor's bed-chamber.

It was a low room, hung with gold and brown tapestry; the windows were shut and the air faint; the bed stood against the wall, and the heavy, dark curtains, looped back, revealed Melchoir of Brabant, lying in his clothes on the coverlet with his throat bare and his eyes staring across the room.

A silver lamp stood on a table by the window, and its faint radiance was the only light.

On the steps of the bed stood Ysabeau; over her white dress she had flung a long scarlet cloak, and her pale, bright hair had fallen on to her shoulders.

At the sight of Hugh she caught hold of the bed-hangings and gazed at him fiercely. He sheathed his sword as he came across the room.

"Princess, I must see the Emperor," he said sternly.

"He will see no man — he knows none nor can he speak," she answered, her bearing prouder and more assured than he had ever known it. "Get you gone, sir; I know not how ye forced an entry."

"You have no power to keep the nobles from their lord," he replied. "Nor will I take your bidding."

She held herself in front of her husband so that her shadow obscured his face.

"I will have you put without the doors if you so disturb the dying."

But Hugh of Rooselaare advanced to the bed. "Let me see him," he demanded, "he speaks to me!"

Indeed, he thought that he heard from the depths of the great bed a voice saying faintly — —"Hugh, Hugh!"

The Empress drew the curtain, further concealing the dying man.

"He speaks to none. Begone!"

The Lord of Rooselaare came still nearer.

"Why is there no priest here?"

"Insolent! the bishop comes."

"Meanwhile he dies, and there are monks enow without."

As he spoke Hugh sprang lightly and suddenly on to the steps, pushed aside the slight figure of the Empress and caught back the curtains.

"Melchoir!" he cried, and snatched up the Emperor by the shoulders.

"He is dead," breathed the Empress.

But Hugh continued to gaze into the distorted, hollow face, while with eager fingers he pushed back the long, damp hair.

"He is dead," repeated Ysabeau, fearing nothing now.

With a slow step she went to the table and seated herself before the silver lamp, while she uttered sigh on sigh and clasped her hands over her eyes.

Then the hot stillness began to quiver with the distant sound of numerous bells; they were holding services for the dying in every church in Frankfort.

The Emperor stirred in Hugh's arms; without opening his eyes he spoke —

"Pray for me . . . Balthasar. They did not slay me honourably —"

He raised his hands to his heart, to his lips, moaned and sank from Hugh's arm on to the pillow.

"Quia apud Dominum misericordia, et copiosa apud eum," he murmured.

"Eum redemptio," finished Hugh.

"Amen," moaned Melchoir of Brabant, and so died. For a moment the chamber was silent save for the insistent bells, then Hugh turned his white face from the dead, and Ysabeau shivered to her feet.

"Call in the others," murmured the Empress, "since he is dead."

The Lord of Rooselaare descended from the bed. "Ay, I will call in the others, thou Eastern witch, and show them the man thou hast murdered."

She stared at him a moment, her face like a mask of ivory set in the glittering hair. "Murdered?" she said at last.

"Murdered!" He fingered his sword fiercely. "And it shall be my duty to see you brought to the stake for this night's work."

She gave a shriek and ran towards the door. Before she reached it, it was flung open, and Balthasar of Courtrai sprang into the room.

"You called?" he panted, his eyes blazing on Hugh of Rooselaare.

"Yes; he is dead — Melchoir is dead, and this lord says I slew him — Balthasar, answer for me!" "Certes!" cried Hugh. "A fitting one to speak for you — your accomplice!"

With a short sound of rage the Margrave dragged out his sword and struck the speaker a blow across the breast with the flat of it.

"So ho!" he shouted, "it pleases you to lie!" He yelled to his men without, and the death-chamber was filled with a clatter of arms that drowned the mournful pealing of the bells. "Take away this lord, on my authority."

Hugh drew his sword, only to have it wrenched away. The soldiers closed round him and swept their prisoner from the chamber, while Balthasar, flushed and furious, watched him dragged off. "I always hated him," he said.

Ysabeau fell on her knees and kissed his mailed feet.

"Melchoir is dead, and I have no champion save you."

The Margrave stooped and raised her, his face burning with blushes till it was like a great rose. "Ysabeau, Ysabeau!" he stammered.

She struggled out of his arms.

"Nay, not now," she whispered in a stifled voice, "not now can I speak to you, but afterwards — my lord! my lord!"

She went to the bed and flung herself across the steps, her face hidden in her hands. Balthasar took off his helmet, crossed himself and humbly bent his great head.

Melchoir IV lay stiffly on the lily-sewn coverlet, and without the great bells tolled and the monks' chant rose.

"De Profundis . . . "

# Chapter 18

## The Pursuit of Jacobea

The chatelaine of Martzburg sat in the best guest-chamber of a wayside hostel that lay a few hours' journeying from her home. Outside the rain dripped in the trees and a cold mountain wind shook the signboard. Jacobea trimmed the lamp, drew the curtains, and began walking up and down the room; the inner silence broken only by the sound of her footfall and an occasional sharp patter as the rain fell on to the bare hearth.

So swiftly had she fled from Frankfort that its last scenes were still before her eyes like a gorgeous and disjointed pageant; the Emperor stricken down at the feast, the brief, flashing turmoil, Ysabeau's peerless face, that her own horrid thoughts coloured with a sinister expression, Balthasar of Courtrai bringing the city to his feet — Hugh of Rooselaare snatched away to a dungeon — and over it all the leaping red light of a hundred flambeaux.

She herself was free here of everything save the sound of the rain, yet she must needs think of and brood on the tumult she had left.

The quiet about her now, the distance she had put between herself and Frankfort, gave her no sense of peace or safety; she strove, indeed, with a feeling of horror, as if they from whom she had fled were about her still, menacing her in this lonely room.

Presently she passed into the little bed-chamber and took up a mirror into which she gazed long and earnestly.

"Is it a wicked face?"

She answered herself —

"No, no."

"Is it a weak face?"

"Alas!"

The wind rose higher, fluttered the lamp-flame and stirred the arras on the wall; and laying the mirror down she returned to the outer chamber. Her long hair that hung down her back was the only bright thing in the gloomy apartment where the tapestry was old and dusty, the furniture worn and faded; she wore a dark dress of embroidered purple, contrasting with her colourless face; only her yellow locks glittered as the lamplight fell on them.

The wind rose yet higher, struggled at the casement, seized and shook the curtains and whistled in the chimney.

Up and down walked Jacobea of Martzburg, clasping and unclasping her soft young hands, her grey eyes turning from right to left.

It was very cold, blowing straight from the great mountains the dark hid; she wished she had asked for a fire and that she had kept one of the women to sleep with her — it was so lonely, and the sound of the rain reminded her of that night at Martzburg when the two scholars had been given shelter. She wanted to go to the door and call some one, but a curious heaviness in her limbs began to make movement irksome; she could no longer drag her steps, and with a sigh she sank into the frayed velvet chair by the fireplace.

She tried to tell herself that she was free, that she was on her way to escape, but could not form the words on her lips, hardly the thought; her head throbbed, and a Cold sensation gripped her heart; she moved in the chair, only to feel as if held down in it; she struggled in vain to rise. "Barbara!" she whispered, and thought she was calling aloud.

A gathering duskiness seemed to overspread the chamber, and the tongue-shaped flame of the lamp showed through it distinct yet very far away; the noise of the wind and rain made one long insistent murmur and moaning.

Jacobea laughed drearily, and lifted her hands to her bosom to try to find the crucifix that hung there, but her fingers were like lead, and fell uselessly into her lap again.

Her brain whirled with memories, with anticipations and vague expectations, tinged with fear like the sensations of a dream; she felt that she was sinking into soft infolding darkness; the lamp-flame changed into a fire-pointed star that rested on a knight's helm, the sound of wind and rain became faint human cries.

She whispered, as the dying Emperor had done — —"I am bewitched."

Then the Knight, with the star glittering above his brow, came towards her and offered her a goblet.

"Sebastian!" she cried, and sat up with a face of horror; the chamber was spinning about her; she saw the Knight's long painted shield and his bare hand holding out the wine; his visor was down.

She shrieked and laughed together, and put the goblet aside.

Some one spoke out of the mystery.

"The Empress found happiness — why not you? — may not a woman die as easily as a man?"

She tried to remember her prayers, to find her crucifix; but the cold edge of the gold touched her lips, and she drank.

The hot wine scorched her throat and filled her with strength; as she sprang up the Knight's star quivered back into the lamp-flame, the vapours cleared from the room; she found herself staring at Dirk Renswoude, who stood in the centre of the room and smiled at her.

"Oh!" she cried in a bewildered way, and put her hands to her forehead.

"Well," said Dirk; he held a rich gold goblet, empty, and his was the voice she had already heard. "Why did you leave Frankfort?"

Jacobea shuddered.

"I do not know;" her eyes were blank and dull. "I think I was afraid

"Lest you might do as Ysabeau did?" asked Dirk.

"What has happened to me?" was all her answer. All sound without had ceased; the light burnt clear and steadily, casting its faint radiance over the slim outlines of the young man and the shuddering figure of the lady.

"What of your steward?" whispered Dirk.

She responded mechanically as if she spoke by rote. "I have no steward. I am going alone to Martzburg."

"What of Sebastian?" urged the youth.

Jacobea was silent; she came slowly down the chamber, guiding herself with one hand along the wall, as though she could not see; the wind stirred the arras under her fingers and ruffled her gown about her feet.

Dirk set the goblet beside the lamp the while he watched her intently with frowning eyes. "What of Sebastian?" he repeated. "Ye fled from him, but have ye ceased to think of him?" "No," said the chatelaine of Martzburg; "no, day and night — what is God, that He lets a man's face to come between me and Him?"

"The Emperor is dead," said Dirk.

"Is dead," she repeated.

"Ysabeau knows how."

"Ah!" she whispered. "I think I knew it."

"Shall the Empress be happy and you starve your heart to death?"

Jacobea sighed. "Sebastian! Sebastian!" She had the look of one walking in sleep. "What is Sybilla to you?"

"His wife," answered Jacobea in the same tone; "his wife."

"The dead do not bind the living." Jacobea laughed.

"No, no — how cold it is here; do you not feel the wind across the floor?" Her fingers wandered aimless over her bosom. "Sybilla is dead, you say?"

"Nay — Sybilla might die — so easily."

Jacobea laughed again.

"Ysabeau did it — she is young and fair," she said. "And she could do it — why not I? But I cannot bear to look on death."

Her expressionless eyes turned on Dirk still in sightless fashion.

"A word," said Dirk —"that is all your part; send him ahead to Martzburg."

Jacobea nodded aimlessly.

"Why not? — why not? — Sybilla would be in bed, lying awake, listening to the wind as I have done — — so often — and he would come up the steep, dark stairs. Oh, and she would raise her head —"

Dirk put in-

"Has the chatelaine spoken?' she would say, and he would make an end of it."

"Perhaps she would be glad to die," said Jacobea dreamily. "I have thought that I should be glad to die."

"And Sebastian?" said Dirk.

Her strangely altered face lit and changed.

"Does he care for me?" she asked piteously.

"Enough to make life and death of little moment," answered Dirk. "Has he not followed you from Frankfort?"

"Followed me?" murmured Jacobea. "I thought he had forsaken me."

"He is here."

"Here — here?" She turned, her movements still curiously blind, and the long strand of her hair shone on her dark gown as she stood with her back to the light.

"Sebastian," said Dirk softly.

He waved his little hand, and the steward appeared in the dark doorway of the inner room; he looked from one to the other swiftly, and his face was flushed and dangerous.

"Sebastian," said Jacobea; there was no change in voice nor countenance; she was erect and facing him, yet it might well be she did not see him, for there seemed no life in her eyes.

He came across the room to her, speaking as he came, but a sudden fresh gust of wind without scattered his words.

"Have you followed me?" she asked.

"Yea," he answered hoarsely, staring at her; he had not dreamed a living face could look so white as hers, no, nor dead face either. He dropped to one knee before her, and took her limp hand.

"Shall we be free to-night?" she asked gently.

"You have but to speak," he said. "So much will I do for you."

She bent forward, and with her other hand touched his tumbled hair.

"Lord of Martzburg and my lord," she said, and smiled sweetly. "Do you know how much I love you, Sebastian? why, you must ask the image of the Virgin — I have told her so often, and no one else; nay, no one else."

Sebastian sprang to his feet.

"Oh God!" he cried. "I am ashamed — ye have bewitched her — she knows not what she says." Dirk turned on him fiercely.

"Did ye not curse me when ye thought she had escaped? did I not swear to recover her for you? is she not yours? Saint Gabriel cannot save her now."

"If she had not said that," muttered Sebastian; he turned distracted eyes upon her standing with no change in her expression, the tips of her fingers resting on the table; her wide grey eyes gazing before her.

"Fool," answered Dirk; "an' she did not love you, what chance had you? I left my fortunes to help you to this prize, and I will not see you palter now — lady, speak to him."

"Ay, speak to me," cried Sebastian earnestly; "tell me if it be your wish that I, at all costs, should become your husband, tell me if it is your will that the woman in our way should go." A slow passion stirred the calm of her face; her eyes glittered.

"Yes," she said; "yes."

"Jacobea!" — he took her arm and drew her close to him — "look me in the face and repeat that to me; think if it is worth — Hell — to you and me."

She gazed up at him, then hid her face on his sleeve.

"Ay, Hell," she answered heavily; "go to Martzburg to-night; she cannot claim you when she is dead; how I have striven not to hate her — my lord, my husband." She clung to him like a sleepy child that feels itself falling into oblivion. "Now it is all over, is it not? — the unrest, the striving. Sebastian beware of the storm — it blows so loud."

He put her from him into the worn old chair. "I will come back to you — tomorrow." "To-morrow," she repeated — "when the sun is up."

The wind rushed between them and made the lamp-flame leap wildly.

"Make haste!" cried Dirk; "away — the horse is below."

But Sebastian still gazed at Jacobea.

"It is done," said Dirk impatiently, "begone."

The steward turned away.

"They are all asleep below?" he questioned.

"Nor will they wake."

Sebastian opened the door on to the dark stairway and went softly out.

"Now, it is done," repeated Dirk in a swelling whisper, "and she is lost."

He snatched up the lamp, and, holding it aloft, looked down at the drooping figure in the chair; Jacobea's head sank back against the tarnished velvet; there was a smile on her white lips, and her hands rested in her lap; even with Dirk's intent face bending over her and the full light pouring down on her, she did not look up.

"Gold hair and grey eyes — and her little feet," murmured Dirk; "one of God's own flowers — — what are you now?"

He laughed to himself and reset the lamp on the table; the lull in the storm was over, wind and rain strove together in the bare trees, and the howlings of the tempest shook the long bare room. Jacobea moved in her seat.

"Is he gone?" she asked fearfully.

"Certes, he has gone," smiled Dirk. "Would you have him daily on such an errand?" Jacobea rose swiftly and stood a moment listening to the unhappy wind.

"I thought he was here," she said under her breath. "I thought that he had come at last." "He came," said Dirk.

The chatelaine looked swiftly round at him; there was a dawning knowledge in her eyes. "Who are you?" she demanded, and her voice had lost its calm; "what has happened?" "Do you not remember me?" smiled Dirk.

Jacobea staggered back.

"Why," she stammered, "he was here, down at my feet, and we spoke — about Sybilla." "And now," said Dirk, "he has gone to free you of Sybilla — as you bid him."

The Pursuit of Jacobea

"As I bid him?"

Dirk clasped his cloak across his breast.

"At this moment he rides to Martzburg on this service of yours, and I must begone to Frankfort where my fortunes wait. For you, these words: should you meet again one Theirry, a pretty scholar, do not prate to him of God and Judgment, nor try to act the saint. Let him alone, he is no matter of yours, and maybe some woman cares for him as ye care for Sebastian, ay, and will hold him, though she have not yellow hair."

Jacobea uttered a moan of anguish.

"I bid him go," she whispered. "Did God utterly forsake me and I bid him go?"

She gave Dirk a wild look over her shoulders, huddling them to her ears, as she crouched upon the floor.

"You are the Devil!" she shrieked. "I have delivered myself unto the Devil!"

She beat her hands together, and fell towards his feet.

Dirk stepped close and peered curiously into her unconscious face.

"Why, she is not so fair," he murmured, "and grief will spoil her bloom, and 'twas only her face he loved."

He extinguished the lamp and smiled into the darkness.

"I do think God is very weak."

He drew the curtain away from the deep-set window, and the moon, riding the storm clouds like a silver armoured Amazon, cast a ghastly light over the huddled figure of Jacobea of Martzburg, and threw her shadow dark and trailing across the cold floor. Dirk left the chamber and the hostel unseen and unheard. The wind made too great a clamour for stray sounds to tell. Out in the wild, wet night he paused a moment to get his bearings; then turned towards the shed where he and Sebastian had left their horses.

The trees and the sign-board creaked and swung together; the long lances of the rain struck his face and the wind dashed his hair into his eyes, but he sang to himself under his breath with a joyous note.

The angry triumphant moon, casting her beams down the clouds, served to light the hittle wooden shed — the inn-stable — built against the rocks.

There were the chatelaine's horses asleep in their stalls, here was his own; but the place beside it where Sebastian's steed had waited was empty.

Dirk, shivering a little in the tempest, unfastened his horse, and was preparing to depart, when a near sound arrested him.

Some one was moving in the straw at the back of the shed.

Dirk listened, his hand on the bridle, till a moonbeam striking across his shoulder revealed a cloaked figure rising from the ground.

"Ah," said Dirk softly, "who is this?"

The stranger got to his feet.

"I have but taken shelter here, sir," he said, "deeming it too late to rouse the hostel —"

"Theirry!" cried Dirk, and laughed excitedly. "Now, this is strange —"

The figure came forward.

"Theirry — yes; have you followed me?" he exclaimed wildly, and his face showed drawn and wan in the silver light. "I left Frankfort to escape you; what fiend's trick has brought you here?"

Dirk softly stroked his horse's neck.

"Are you afraid of me, Theirry?" he asked mournfully. "Certes, there is no need." But Theirry cried out at him with the fierceness of one at bay —

"Begone, I want none of you nor of your kind; I know how the Emperor died, and I fled from a city where such as you come to power, ay, even as Jacobea of Martzburg did — I am come after her."

"And where think you to find her?" asked Dirk.

"By now she is at Basle."

"Are ye not afraid to go to Basle?"

Theirry trembled, and stepped back into the shadows of the shed.

"I want to save my soul; no, I am not afraid; if need be, I will confess."

Dirk laughed.

"At the shrine of Jacobea of Martzburg? Look to it she be not trampled in the mire by then."

"You lie, you malign her!" cried the other in strong agitation.

But Dirk turned on him with imperious sternness. "I did not leave Frankfort on a fool's errand — I was triumphant, at the high tide of my fortunes, my foot on Ysabeau's neck. I had good reason to have left this alone. Come with me to Martzburg and see my work, and know the saint you worship."

"To Martzburg?" Theirry's voice had terror in it.

"Certes — to Martzburg." Dirk began to lead hi horse into the open.

"Is the chatelaine there?"

"If not yet, she will be soon; take one of these horses," he added.

"I know not your meaning," answered fearfully; "but my road was to Martzburg. I mean to pray Jacobea, who left without a word to me, to give me some small place in her service."

"Belike she will," mocked Dirk.

"You shall not go alone," cried Theirry, becoming more distracted, "for no good purpose can you be pursuing her."

"I asked your company."

Impatiently and feverishly Theirry unfastened and prepared himself a mount.

"If ye have evil designs on her," he cried, "be very sure ye will be defeated, for her strength is as the strength of angels."

Dirk delicately guided his steed out of the shod; the moon had at last conquered the cloud battalions, and a clear cold light revealed the square dark shape of the hostel, the flapping sign, the bare pine-trees and the long glimmer of the road; Dirk's eyes turned to the blank window of the room where Jacobea lay, and he smiled wickedly.

"The night has cleared," he said, as Theirry, leading one of the chatelaine's horses, came out of the stable; "and we should reach Martzburg before the dawn."

# Chapter 19

## Sybilla

Sebastian paused on the steep, dark stairs and listened.

Castle Martzburg was utterly silent; he knew that there were one or two servants only within the walls, and that they slept at a distance; he knew that his cautious entry by the donjon door had made no sound, yet on every other step or so he stood still and listened.

He had procured a light; it fluttered in danger of extinction in the draughty stairway, and he had to shield it with his hand.

Once, when he stopped, he took from his belt the keys that had gained him admission and slipped them into the bosom of his doublet; hanging at his waist, they made a little jingling sound as he moved.

When he gained the great hall he opened the door as softly and slowly as if he did not know emptiness alone awaited him the other side.

He entered, and his little light only served to show the expanses of gloom.

It was very cold; he could hear the rain falling in a thin stream from the lips of the gargoyles without; he remembered that same sound on the night the two students took shelter; the night when the deed he was about to do had by a devil, in a whisper, been first put into his head.

He crossed to the hearth and set the lamp in the niche by the chimney-piece; he wished there was a fire — certainly it was cold.

The dim rays of the lamp showed the ashes on the hearth, the cushions in the window-seat, and something that, even in that dullness, shone with fiery hue.

Sebastian looked at it in a half horror: it was Sybilla's red lily, finished and glowing from a samite cushion; by the side of it slept Jacobea's little grey cat.

The steward gazing in curiously intent fashion recalled the fact that he had never conversed with his wife and never liked her; he could not tell of one sharp word between them, yet had she said she hated him he would have felt no surprise; he wondered, in case he had ever loved her, would he have been here to-night on this errand.

Lord of Martzburg! — lord of as fine a domain as any in the empire, with a chance of the imperial crown itself — nay, had he loved his wife it would have made no difference; what sorry fool even would let a woman interfere with a great destiny — Lord of Martzburg.

With little reflection on the inevitable for his wife, he fell to considering Jacobea; until to-night she had been a cipher to him — that she favoured him a mere voucher for his crime; for the procuring of this or that for him — a fact to be accepted and used; but that she should pray about him — speak as she had — that was another matter, and for the first time in his cold life he was both moved and ashamed. His thin, dark face flushed; he looked askance at the red lily and took the light from its niche.

The shadows seemed to gather and throng out of the silence, bearing down on him and urging him forward; he found the little door by the fireplace open, and ascended the steep stone stairs to his wife's room.

Here there was not even the drip of the rain or the wail of the wind to disturb the stillness; he had taken off his boots, and his silk-clad feet made no sound, but he could not hush the catch of his breath and the steady thump of his heart.

When he reached her room he paused again, and again listened.

Nothing — how could there be? Had he not come so softly even the little cat had slept on undisturbed?

He opened the door and stepped in.

It was a small, low chamber; the windows were unshrouded, and fitful moonlight played upon the floor; Sebastian looked at once towards the bed, that stood to his left; it was hung with dark arras, now drawn back from the pillows.

Sybilla was asleep; her thick, heavy hair lay outspread under her cheek; her flesh and the bedclothes were turned to one dazzling whiteness by the moon.

Worked into the coverlet, that had slipped half to the polished floor, were great wreaths of purple roses, showing dim yet gorgeous.

Her shoes stood on the bed steps; her clothes were flung over a chair; near by a crucifix hung against the wall, with her breviary on a shelf beneath.

The passing storm clouds cast luminous shadows across the chamber; but they were becoming fainter, the tempest was dying away. Sebastian put the lamp on a low coffer inside the door and advanced to the bed.

A large dusky mirror hung beside the window, and in it he could see his wife again, reflected dimly in her ivory whiteness with the dark lines of her hair and brows.

He came to the bedside so that his shadow was flung across her sleeping face.

"Sybilla," he said.

Her regular breathing did not change.

"Sybilla."

A swift cloud obscured the moon; the sickly rays of the lamp struggled with darkness. "Sybilla."

Now she stirred; he heard her fetch a sigh as one who wakens reluctantly from soft dreams. "Do you not hear me speak, Sybilla?"

From the bewildering glooms of the bed he heard her silk bed-clothes rustle and slip; the moon came forth again and revealed her sitting up, wide awake now and staring at him.

"So you have come home, Sebastian?" she said. "Why did you rouse me?"

He looked at her in silence; she shook back her hair from her eyes.

"What is it?" she asked softly.

"The Emperor died," said Sebastian.

"I know — what is that to me? Bring the light, Sebastian; I cannot see your face."

"There is no need; the Emperor had not time to pray, I would not deal so with you, therefore I woke you."

"Sebastian!"

"By my mistress's commands you must die tonight, and by my desire; I shall be Lord of Martzburg, and there is no other way —"

She moved her head, and, peering forward, tried to see his face.

"Make your peace with Heaven," he said hoarsely; "for tomorrow I must go to her a free man."

She put her hand to her long throat.

"I wondered if you would ever say this to me — I did not think so, for it did not enter my mind that she could give commands."

"Then you knew?"

Sybilla smiled.

"Before ever you did, Sebastian, and I have so thought of it, in these long days when I have been alone, it seemed that I must sew it even into my embroideries —'Jacobea loves Sebastian.'"

He gripped the bed-post.

"It is the strangest thing," said his wife, "that she should love you — you — and send you here to-night; she was a gracious maiden."

"I am not here to talk of that," answered Sebastian; "nor have we long — the dawn is not far off."

Sybilla rose, setting her long feet on the bed step.

"So I must die," she said —"must die. Certes! I have not lived so ill that I should fear to die, nor so pleasantly that I should yearn to live; it will be a poor thing in you to kill me, but no shame to me to be slain, my lord."

As she stood now against the shadowed curtains her hair caught the lamplight and flashed into red gold about her colourless face; Sebastian looked at her with hatred and some terror, but she smiled strangely at him.

"You never knew me, Sebastian, but I am very well acquainted with you, and I do scorn you so utterly that I am sorry for the chatelaine."

"She and I will manage that," answered Sebastian fiercely; "and if you seek to divert or delay me by this talk it is useless, for I am resolved, nor will I be moved."

"I do not seek to move you, nor do I ask you for my life. I have ever been dutiful, have I not?" "Do not smile at me!" he cried. "You should hate me."

She shook her head.

"Certes! I hate you not."

She moved from the bed, in the long linen garment that she wore, slim and childish to see. She took a wrap of gold-coloured silk from a chair and put it about her. The man gazed at her the while with sullen eyes.

She glanced at the crucifix.

"I have nothing to say; God knows it all. I am ready."

"I do not want your soul," he cried.

Sybilla smiled.

"I made confession yesterday. How cold it is for this time of the year! — I do not shiver for fear, my lord."

She put on her shoes, and as she stooped her brilliant hair fell and touched the patch of fading moonshine.

"Make haste," breathed Sebastian.

His wife raised her face.

"How long have we been wed?" she asked.

"Let that be."

He paled and bit his lip.

"Three years — nay, not three years. When I am dead give my embroideries to Jacobea, they are in these coffers; I have finished the red lily — I was sewing it when the two scholars came, that night she first knew — and you first knew — but I had known a long while."

Sebastian caught up the lamp.

"Be silent or speak to God," he said.

She came gently across the floor, holding the yellow silk at her breast.

"What are you going to do with me?" she whispered. "Strangle me? — nay, they would see that — — afterwards."

Sebastian went to a little door that opened beside the bed and pulled aside the arras. "That leads to the battlements," she said.

He pointed to the dark steps.

"Go up, Sybilla."

He held the lamp above his haggard face, and the light of it fell over the narrow winding stone steps; she looked at them and ascended. Sebastian followed, closing the door after him. In a few moments they were out on the donjon roof.

The vast stretch of sky was clear now and paling for the dawn; faint pale clouds clustered round the dying moon, and the scattered stars pulsed wearily.

Below them lay the dark masses of the other portions of the castle, and beside them rose the straining pole and wind-tattered banner of Jacobea of Martzburg.

Sybilla leant against the battlements, her hair fluttering over her face.

"How cold it is!" she said in a trembling voice. "Make haste, my lord."

He was shuddering, too, in the keen, insistent wind.

"Will you not pray?" he asked again.

"No," she answered, and looked at him vacantly. "If I shriek would any one hear me? — Will it be more horrible than I thought? Make haste — make haste — or I shall be afraid."

She crouched against the stone, shivering violently. Sebastian put the lamp upon the ground. "Take care it does not go out," she said, and laughed. "You would not like to find your way back in the dark — the little cat will be sorry for me."

She broke off to watch what he was doing.

A portion of the tower projected; here the wall was of a man's height, and pierced with arblast holes; through there Sybilla had often looked and seen the country below framed in the stone like a picture in a letter of an horäe, so small it seemed, and yet clear and brightly coloured.

Beneath the wall was a paving-stone, raised at will by an iron ring; when lifted it revealed a sheer open drop the entire height of the donjon, through which stones and fire could be hurled in time of siege upon the assailants in the courtyard below; but Jacobea had always shuddered at it, nor had there been occasion to open it for many years.

Sybilla saw her husband strain at the ring and bend over the hole, and stepped forward. "Must it be that way? — O Jesu! Jesu! shall I not be afraid?"

She clasped her hands and fixed her eyes on the figure of Sebastian as he raised the slab and revealed the black aperture; quickly he stepped back as stone rang on stone.

"So," he said; "I shall not touch you, and it will be swiftly over — walk across, Sybilla." She closed her eyes and drew a long breath.

"Have you not the courage?" he cried violently. "Then I must hurl you from the battlements . . . it shall not look like murder . . . "

She turned her face to the beautiful brightening sky.

"My soul is not afraid, but . . . how my body shrinks! — I do not think I can do it . . . "

He made a movement towards her; at that she gathered herself.

"No — you shall not touch me."

Across the donjon roof she walked with a firm step.

"Farewell, Sebastian; may God assoil me and thee."

She put her hands to her face and moaned as her foot touched the edge of the hole . . . no shriek nor cry disturbed the serenity of the night, she made no last effort to save herself; but disappeared silently to the blackness of her death.

Sebastian listened to the strange indefinite sound of it, and drops of terror gathered on his brow; then all was silent again save for the monotonous flap of the banner.

"Lord of Martzburg," he muttered to steady himself; "Lord of Martzburg."

He dropped the stone into place, picked up the lantern and returned down the close, cold stairs. Her room . . . on the pillow the mark where her head had lain, her clothes over the coffer; well, he hated her, no less than he had ever done; to the last she had shamed him; why had he been so long? — too long — soon some one would be stirring, and he must be far from Martzburg before they found Sybilla.

He crept from the chamber with the same unnecessary stealth he had observed in entering, and in a cautious manner descended the stairs to the great hall.

To reach the little door that had admitted him he must traverse nearly half the castle; he cursed the distance, and the grey light that crept in through every window he passed and revealed to him his own shaking hand holding the useless lamp. Martzburg, his castle soon to be, had become hateful to him; always had he found it too vast, too empty; but now he would fill it as Jacobea had never done; the knights and her kinsfolk who had ever overlooked him should be his guests and his companions.

The thoughts that chased through his brain took curious turns; Jacobea was the Emperor's ward . . . but the Emperor was dead, should he wed her secretly and how long need he wait? . . . Sybilla was often on the donjon keep, let it seem that she had fallen . . . none had seen him come, none would see him go . . . and Jacobea, strangest thing of all (he seemed to hear Sybilla saying it) that she should love him . . .

The pale glow of a dreary dawn filled the great hall as he entered it; the grey cat was still asleep, and the shining silks of the red lily shone like the hair of the strange woman who had worked it patiently into the samite. He tiptoed across the hall, descended the wider stairs and made his way to the first chamber of the donjon.

Carefully he returned the lamp to the niche where he had found it; wondering, as he extinguished it, if any would note that it had been burnt that night; carefully he drew on his great muddy boots and crept out by the little postern door into the court.

So sheltered was the castle, and situated in so peaceful a place, that when the chatelaine was not within the walls the huge outer gates that required many men to close them stood open on to the hillside; beyond them Sebastian saw his patient horse, fastened to the ring of the bell chain, and beyond him the clear grey-blue hills and trees.

His road lay open; yet he closed the door slowly behind him and hesitated. He strove with a desire to go and look at her; he knew just how she had fallen . . . when he had first come to Martzburg, the hideous hole in the battlements exercised a great fascination over him; he had often flung down stones, clods of grass, even once a book, that he might hear the hollow whistling sound and imagine a furious enemy below.

Afterwards he had noticed these things and how they struck the bottom of the shaft — lying where she would be now; he desired to see her, yet loathed the thought of it; there was his horse, there the open road, and Jacobea waiting a few miles away, yet he must linger while the accusing daylight gathered about him, while the rising sun discovered him; he must dally with the precious moments, bite the ends of his black hair, frown and stare at the round tower of the donjon the other side of which she lay.

At last he crossed the rough cobbles; skirted the keep and stood still, looking at her.

Yes — he had pictured her; yet he saw her more distinctly than he had imagined he would in this grey light. Her hair and her cloak seemed to be wrapped close about her; one hand still clung to her face; her feet showed bare and beautiful.

Sebastian crept nearer; he wanted to see her face and if her eyes were open; to be certain, also, if that dark red that lay spread on the ground was all her scattered locks . . . the light was treacherous.

He was stooping to touch her when the quick sound of an approaching horseman made him draw back and glance round.

But before he could even tell himself it were well to fly they were upon him; two horsemen, finely mounted, the foremost Dirk Renswoude, bare-headed, a rich colour in his cheek and a sparkle in his eyes; he reined up the slim brown horse.

"So — it is done?" he cried, leaning from the saddle towards Sebastian.

The steward stepped back.

"Whom have you with you?" he asked in a shaking voice.

"A friend of mine and a suitor to the chatelaine —— f which folly you and I shall cure him." Theirry pressed forward, the hoofs of his striving horse making musical clatter on the cobbles. "The steward!" he cried; "and . . . "

His voice sank; he turned burning eyes on Dirk.

" — the steward's wife that was," smiled the youth. "But, certes! you must do him worship now, he will be Lord of Martzburg."

Sebastian was staring at Sybilla.

"You tell too much," he muttered.

"Nay, my friend is one with me, and I can answer for his silence." Dirk patted the horse's neck and laughed again; laughter with a high triumphant note in it.

Theirry swung round on him in a desperate, bitter fierceness.

"Why have you brought me here? Where is the chatelaine? — by God His saints that woman has been murdered . . . "

Dirk turned in the saddle and faced him.

"Ay, and by Jacobea of Martzburg's commands."

Theirry laughed aloud.

"The lie is dead as you give it being," he answered —"nor can all your devilry make it live."

"Sebastian," said Dirk, "has not this woman come to her death by the chatelaine's commands?" He pointed to Sybilla.

"You know it, since in your presence she bade me hither," answered Sebastian heavily. Dirk's voice rose clear and musical.

"You see your piece of uprightness thought highly of her steward, and that she might endow him with her hand his wife must die —"

"Peace! peace!" cried Sebastian fiercely, and Theirry rose in his saddle.

"It is a lie!" he repeated wildly. "If 'tis not a lie God has turned His face from me, and I am lost indeed!

"If 'tis no lie," cried Dirk exultingly, "you are mine — did ye not swear it?"

"An' she be this thing you name her," answered Theirry passionately — "then the Devil is cunning indeed, and I his servant; but if you speak false I will kill you at her feet."

"And by that will I abide," smiled Dirk. "Sebastian, you shall return with us to give this news to your mistress."

"Is she not here?" cried Theirry.

Dirk pointed to the silver-plated harness.

"You ride her horse. See her arms upon his breast. Sweet fool, we left her behind in the hostel, waiting the steward's return . . . "

"All ways ye trap and deceive me," exclaimed Theirry hotly.

"Let us begone," said Sebastian; he looked at Dirk as if at his master. "Is it not time for us to begone?"

It was full daylight now, though the sun had not yet risen above the hills; the lofty walls and high towers of the huge grey castle blocked up the sky and threw into the gloom the three in their shadow.

"Hark!" said Dirk, and lifted his finger delicately. Again the sound of a horse approaching on the long white road, the rise and fall of the quick trot bitterly distinct in the hard stillness.

"Who is this?" whispered Sebastian; he caught Dirk's bridle as if he found protection in the youth's near presence, and stared towards the blank open gates.

A white horse appeared against the cold misty background of grey Country; a woman was in the saddle: Jacobea of Martzburg.

She paused, peered up at the high little windows in the donjon, then turned her gaze on the silent three.

"Now can the chatelaine speak for herself," breathed Dirk.

Theirry gave a great sigh, his eyes fixed with a painful intensity on the approaching lady, but she did not seem to see either of them.

"Sebastian," she cried, and drew rein gazing at him, "where is your wife?"

Her words rang on the cold, clear air like strokes on a bell.

"Sybilla died last night," answered the steward, "but I did nought. And you should not have come."

Jacobea shaded her brows with her gloved hand and stared past the speaker.

Theirry broke out in a trembling passion.

"In the name of the angels in whose company I ever placed you, what do you know of this that has been done?"

"What is that on the ground?" cried Jacobea. "Sybilla — he has slain Sybilla — but, sirs," — she — looked round her distractedly —"ye must not blame him — he saw my wish . . . "

"From your own lips!" cried Theirry.

"Who are you who speak?" she demanded haughtily. "I sent him to slay Sybilla . . . " She interrupted herself with a hideous shriek. "Sebastian, ye are stepping in her blood!"

And, letting go of the reins, she sank from the saddle; the steward caught her, and as she slipped from his hold to her knees her unconscious head came near to the stiff white feet of the dead.

"Her yellow hair!" cried Dirk. "Let us leave her to her steward — you and I have another way!" "May God curse her as He has me," said Theirry in an agony — "for she has slain my hope of heaven!"

"You will not leave me?" called Sebastian. "What shall I say? — what shall I do?"

"Lie and lie again!" answered Dirk with a wild air; "wed the dame and damn her people — let fly your authority and break her heart as quickly as you may —"

"Amen to that!" added Theirry.

"And now to Frankfort!" cried Dirk, exultant. They set their horses to a furious pace and galloped out of Castle Martzburg.

# Chapter 20

## Hugh of Rooselaare

Dirk took off his riding-coat and listened with a smile to the quick step of Theirry overhead; he was again in the long low chamber looking out on the witch's garden, and nothing was changed save that the roses bloomed no longer on the bare thorny bushes.

"So you have brought him back," said Nathalie, caressing the youth's soft sleeve; "pulled his saint out of her shrine and given her over to the demons."

Dirk turned his head; a beautiful look was in his eyes.

"Yea, I have brought him back," he said musingly.

"You have done a foolish thing," grumbled the witch, "he will ruin you yet; beware, for even now you hold him against his will; I marked his face as he went into his old chamber." Dirk seated himself with a sigh.

"In this matter I am not to be moved, and now some food, for I am so weary that I can scarcely think. Nathalie, the toil it has been, the rough roads, the delays, the long hours in the saddle — but it was worth it!"

The witch set the table with a rich service of ivory and silver.

"Worth leaving your fortunes at the crisis? Ye left Frankfort the day after the Emperor died, and have been away two months. Ysabeau thinks you dead."

Dirk frowned.

"No matter, tomorrow she shall know me living. Martzburg is far away and the weather delayed us, but it had to be; now I am free to work my own advancement."

He drank eagerly of the wine put before him, and began to eat.

"Ye have heard," asked Nathalie, "that Balthasar of Courtrai has been elected Emperor?" "Yea," smiled Dirk, "and is to marry Ysabeau within the year; we knew it, did we not?" "Next spring they go to Rome to receive the Imperial crown."

"I shall be with them," said Dirk. "Well, it is good to rest. What a thick fool Balthasar is!" He smiled, and his eyes sparkled.

"The Empress is a clever woman," answered the witch, "she came here once to know whither you had gone. I told her, for the jest, that you were dead. At that she must think her secret dead with you, yet she gave no sign of joy nor relief, nor any hint of what her business was."

Dirk elegantly poured out more wine

"She is never betrayed by her puppet's face — an iron-hearted fiend, the Empress." "They say, though, that she is a fool for Balthasar, a dog at his heels."

"Until she change."

"Belike you will be her next fancy," said Nathalie; "the crystals always foretell a throne for you."

Dirk laughed.

"I do not mean to share my honours with any — woman," he answered; "pile up the fire, Nathalie, certes, it is cold."

He pushed back his chair with a half sigh on his lips, and turned contented eyes on the glowing hearth Nathalie replenished.

"And none has thought evil of Melchoir's death?" he asked curiously.

The witch returned to her little stool and rubbed her hands together; the leaping firelight cast a false colour over her face.

"Ay, there was Hugh of Rooselaare."

Dirk sat up.

"The Lord of Rooselaare?"

"Certes, the night Melchoir died he flung 'Murderess!' in the Empress's face."

Dirk showed a grave, alert face.

"I never heard of that."

"Nay," answered the witch with some malice, "ye were too well engaged in parting that boy from his love — it is a pretty jest — certainly, she is a clever woman, she enlists Balthasar as her champion — he becomes enraged, furious, and Hugh is cast into the dungeons for his pains." The witch laughed softly. "He would not retract, his case swayed to and fro, but Balthasar and the Empress always hated him, he had never a chance."

Dirk rose and pressed his clasped hand to his temple.

"What do you say? never a chance?"

Nathalie stared at him.

"Why, you seem moved."

"Tell me of Hugh of Rooselaare," Dirk in an intense voice.

"He is to die to-night at sunset."

Dirk uttered a hoarse exclamation.

"Old witch!" he cried bitterly, "why tell me this before? I lose time, time."

He snatched his cloak from the wall and flung on his hat.

"What is Hugh of Rooselaare to you?" asked Nathalie, and she crept across the room and clung to the young man's garments.

He shook her off fiercely.

"He must not die — he, on the scaffold! I, as you say, I was following that boy and his love while this was happening!"

The witch fell back against the wall, while overhead the restless tread of Theirry sounded. Dirk dashed from the room and out into the quiet street.

For a second he paused; it was late afternoon, he had perhaps an hour or an hour and a half. Clenching his hands, he drew a deep breath, and turned in the direction of the palace at a steady run.

By reason of the snow clouds and the bitter cold there were few abroad to notice the slim figure running swiftly and lightly; those who were about made their way in the direction of the market-place, where the Lord of Rooselaare was presently to meet his death.

Dirk arrived at the palace one hand over his heart, stinging him with the pain of his great speed; he demanded the Empress.

None among the guards knew either him or his name, but, at his imperious insistence, 'they sent word by a page to Ysabeau that the young doctor Constantine had a desire to see her.

The boy returned, and Dirk was admitted instantly, smiling gloomily to think with what feelings Ysabeau would look on him.

So far all had been swiftly accomplished; he was conducted to her private chamber and brought face to face with her while he still panted from his running.

She stood against a high arched window that showed the heavy threatening winter clouds without; her purple, green and gold draperies shone warmly in the glitter of the fire; a tray of incense stood on the hearth after the manner of the East, and the hazy clouds of it rose before her.

Until the page had gone neither spoke, then Dirk said quickly — —"I returned to Frankfort to — day."

Ysabeau was agitated to fear by his sudden appearance.

"Where have you been?" she asked. "I thought you dead."

Dirk, pale and grave, gave her a penetrating glance.

"I have no time for speech with you now — you owe me something, do you not? Well, I am here to ask part payment."

The Empress winced.

"Well — what? I had no wish to be ungrateful, 'twas you avoided me."

She crossed to the hearth and fixed her superb eyes intently on the youth.

"Hugh of Rooselaare is to die this evening," he said.

"Yea," answered Ysabeau, and her childish loveliness darkened.

For a while Dirk was silent; he showed suddenly frail and ill; on his face was an expression of emotion, mastered and held back.

"He must not die," he said at last and lifted his eyes, shadowed with fatigue. "That is what I demand of you, his pardon, now, and at once — we have but little time."

Ysabeau surveyed him curiously and fearfully.

"You ask too much," she replied in a low voice; "do you know why this man is to die?" "For speaking the truth," he said, with a sudden sneer.

The Empress flushed, and clutched the embroidery on her bodice.

"You of all men should know why he must be silenced," she retorted bitterly. "What is your reason for asking his life?"

Dirk's mouth took on an ugly curl

"My reason is no matter — it is my will."

Ysabeau beat her foot on the edge of the Carpet.

"Have I made you so much my master?" she muttered.

The young man answered impatiently.

"You will give me his pardon, and make haste, for I must ride with it to the market-place." She answered with a lowering glance.

"I think I will not; I am not so afraid of you, and I hate this man — my secret is your secret after all."

Dirk gave a wan smile.

"I can blast you as I blasted Melchoir of Brabant, Ysabeau, and do you think I have any fear of what you can say? But" — he leaned towards her —"suppose I go with what I know to Balthasar?" The name humbled the Empress like a whip held over her.

"So, I am helpless," she muttered, loathing him.

"The pardon," insisted Dirk; "sound the bell and write me a pardon."

Still she hesitated; it was a hard thing to lose her vengeance against a dangerous enemy. "Choose another reward," she pleaded. "Of what value can this man's life be to you?"

"You seek to put me off until it be too late," cried Dirk hoarsely — he stepped forward and seized the hand-bell on the table —"now an' you show yourself obstinate, I go straight from here to Balthasar and tell him of the poisoning of Melchoir."

Instinct and desire rose in Ysabeau to defy him with everything in her possession, from her guards to her nails; she shuddered with suppressed wrath, and pressed her little clenched hands against the wall.

Her Chamberlain entered.

"Write out a pardon for the Lord of Rooselaare," commanded Dirk, "and haste, as you love your place."

When the man had gone, Ysabeau turned with an ill-concealed savagery.

"What will they think! What will Balthasar think!"

"That must be your business," said Dirk wearily.

"And Hugh himself!" flashed the Empress. The youth coloured painfully.

"Let him be sent to his castle in Flanders," he said, with averted face. "He must not remain here."

"So much you give in!" cried Ysabeau. "I do not understand you."

He responded with a wild look.

"No one will ever understand me, Ysabeau."

The Chamberlain returned, and in a shaking hand the Empress took the parchment and the reed pen, while Dirk waved the man's dismissal.

"Sign," he cried to her.

Ysabeau set the parchment on the table and looked out at the gathering clouds; the Lord of Rooselaare must have already left the prison.

She dallied with the pen; then took a little dagger from her hair and sharpened it; Dirk read her purpose in her lovely evil eyes, and snatched the lingering right hand into his own long fingers.

The Empress drew together and looked up at him bitterly and darkly, but Dirk's breath stirred the ringlets that touched her cheek, his cool grip guided her reluctant pen; she shivered with fear and defiance; she wrote her name.

Dirk flung her hand aside with a great sigh of relief.

"Do not try to foil me again, Marozia Porphyrogentris," he cried, and caught up the parchment, his hat and cloak.

She watched him leave the room; heard the heavy door close behind him, and she writhed with rage, thrusting, with an uncontrollable gesture of passion, the dagger into the table; it quivered in the wood, then broke under her hand.

With an ugly cry she ran to the window, flung it open and cast the handle out.

When it rattled on the cobbled yard Dirk was already there; he marked it fall, knew the gold and red flash, and smiled.

Showing the parchment signed by the Empress, he had commanded the swiftest horse in the stables. He cursed and shivered, waiting while the seconds fled; his slight figure and fierce face awed into silence the youngest in the courtyard as he paced up and down. At last — the horse; one of the grooms gave him a whip; he put it under his left arm and leapt to his seat; they opened the gate and watched him take the wind-swept street.

The market-place lay at the other end of the town; and the hour for the execution was close at hand — but the white horse he rode was fresh and strong.

The thick grey clouds had obscured the sunset and covered the sky; a few trembling flakes of snow fell, a bitter wind blew between the high narrow houses; here and there a light sparkling in a window emphasized the colourless cold without.

Dirk urged the steed till he rocked in the saddle; curtains were pulled aside and doors opened to see who rode by so furiously; the streets were empty — — but there would be people enough in the marketplace.

He passed the high walls of the college, galloped over the bridge that crossed the sullen waters of the Main, swept by the open doors of St. Wolfram, then had to draw rein, for the narrow Street began to be choked with people.

He pulled his hat over his eyes and flung his cloak across the lower half of his face; with one hand he dragged on the bridle, with the other waved the parchment.

"A pardon!" he cried. "A pardon! Make way!" They drew aside before the plunging steed; some answered him —

"It is no pardon — he wears not the Empress's livery."

One seized his bridle; Dirk leant from the saddle and dashed the parchment into the fellow's face, the horse snorted, and plunging cleared a way and gained the market-place.

Here the press was enormous; men, women and children were gathered close round the mounted soldiers who guarded the scaffold; the armour, yellow and blue uniforms and bright feathers of the horsemen showed vividly against the grey houses and greyer sky.

On the scaffold were two dark, graceful figures; a man kneeling, with his long throat bare, and a man standing with a double-edged sword in his hands.

"A pardon!" shrieked Dirk. "In the name of the Emperor!"

He was wedged in the crowd, who made bewildered movements but could not give place to him; the soldiers did not or would not hear.

Dirk rose desperately in his stirrups; as he did so the hat and cloak fell back and his head and shoulders were revealed clearly above the swaying mass.

Hugh of Rooselaare heard the cry; he looked across the crowd and his eyes met the eyes of Dirk Renswoude.

"A pardon!" cried Dirk hoarsely; he saw the condemned man's lips move.

The sword fell . . .

"A woman screamed," said the monk on the scaffold, "and proclaimed a pardon."

And he pointed to the commotion gathered about Dirk, while the executioner displayed to the crowd the serene head of Hugh of Rooselaare.

"Nay, it was not a woman," one of the soldiers answered the monk, "'twas this youth." Dirk forced to the foot of the scaffold.

"Let me through," he said in a terrible voice; the guard parted; and seeing the parchment in his hand, let him mount the steps.

"You bring a pardon?" whispered the monk.

"I am too late," said Dirk; he stood among the hurrying blood that stained the platform, and his face was hard.

"Dogs! was this an end for a lord of Rooselaare!" he cried, and clasped his hand on a straining breast. "Could you not have waited a little — but a few moments more?"

The snow was falling fast; it lay on Dirk's shoulders and on his smooth hair; the monk drew the parchment from his passive hand and read it in a whisper to the officer; they both looked askance at the young man.

"Give me his head," said Dirk.

The executioner had placed it at a corner of the scaffold; he left off wiping his sword and brought it forward.

Dirk watched without fear or repulsion, and took Hugh's head in his slim fair hands. "How heavy it is," he whispered.

The quick distortion of death had left the proud features; Dirk held the face close to his own, with no heed to the blood that trickled down his doublet.

Priest and captain standing apart, noticed a horrible likeness between the dead and the living, but would not speak of it.

"Churl," said Dirk, gazing into the half-closed grey eyes that resembled so his own. "He spoke — as he saw me; what did he say?"

The headsman polished the mighty blade.

"Nought to do with you, or with any," he answered, "the words had no meaning, certes."

"What were they?" whispered the youth.

"Have you come for me, Ursula?' then he said again, 'Ursula.'"

A quiver ran through Dirk's frame.

"She shall repent this, the Eastern witch!" he said wildly. "May the Devil snatch you all to bitter judgment!"

He turned to the captain, with the head held against his breast.

"What are you going to do with this?"

"His wife has asked for his head and his body that he may be buried befitting his estate."

"His wife!" echoed Dirk; then slowly, "Ay, he had a wife — and a son, sir?"

"The child is dead."

Dirk set the head down gently by the body.

"And his lands?" he asked.

"They go, sir, by favour of the Empress, to Balthasar of Courtrai, who married, as you may know, this lord's heiress, Ursula, dead now many years."

The snow had scattered the crowd; the soldiers were impatient to begone; the blood stiffened and froze about their feet; Dirk looked down at the dead man with an anguished and hopeless expression.

"Sir," said the officer, "will you return with me to the palace, and we will tell the Empress how this mischance arose, how you came too late."

"Nay," replied Dirk fiercely. "Take that good news alone."

He turned and descended the scaffold steps in a proud, gloomy manner.

One of the soldiers held his horse; he mounted in silence and rode away; they who watched saw the thick snowflakes blot out the solitary figure, and shuddered with no cause they understood.

## Chapter 21

### Betrayed

Nathalie stood at the door with a lantern in her hand.

Dirk was returning; the witch held up the light to catch a glimpse of his face, then, whispering and crying under her breath, followed into the house.

"There is blood on your shoes and on your breast," she whispered, when they reached the long chamber at the back.

Dirk flung himself on a chair and moaned; the snow lay still on his hair and his shoulders; he buried his face in the bend of his arm.

"Zerdusht and his master have forsaken us," whimpered the witch. "I could work no spells tonight, and the mirror was blank."

Dirk spoke in a muffled voice, without raising his head.

"Of what use magic to me? I should have stayed in Frankfort."

Nathalie drew his wet cloak from his shoulders. "Have I not warned you? has not the brass head warned you that the young scholar will be your ruin, bringing you to woe and misery and shame?"

Dirk rose with a sob, and turned to the fire; the one dim lamp alone dispelled the cold darkness of the room, and the thin flames on the hearth fell into ashes before their eyes.

"Look at his blood on me!" cried Dirk, "his blood! Balthasar and Ysabeau make merry with his lands, but my hate shall mean something to them yet — I should not have left Frankfort."

He rested his head against one of the supports of the chimney-piece, and Nathalie, peering into his face, saw that his eyes were wet.

"Alas! who was this man?"

"I did all I could," whispered Dirk . . . "the Empress shall burn in hell."

The sickly creeping flames illuminated his pallid face and his small hand, hanging clenched by his side.

"This is an evil day for us," moaned the witch, "the spirits will not answer, the flames will not burn . . . some horrible misfortune threatens."

Dirk turned his gaze into the half-dark room.

"Where is Theirry?"

"Gone." Nathalie rocked to and fro on her stool.

"Gone!" shivered Dirk, "gone where?"

"Soon after you left he crept from his chamber, and his face was evil — he went into the street." Dirk paced up and down with uneven steps.

"He will come back, he must come back! Ah, my heart! You say Zerdusht will not speak tonight?"

The witch moaned and trembled over the fire.

"Nay, nor will the spirits come."

Dirk shook his clenched fist in the air.

"They shall answer me."

He went to the window, opened it and looked out into blackness.

"Bring the lamp."

Nathalie obeyed; the faint light showed the hastening snowflakes, no more.

"Maybe they will listen to me, nay, as I say, they shall."

The witch followed with the swinging lamp in her hand, while they made their way in silence through the darkness and the snow, in between the bare rose bushes, over the wet, cold earth until they reached the trap-door at the end of the garden that led to the witch's kitchen. Here she paused while Dirk raised the stone.

"Surely the earth shook then," he said. "I felt it tremble beneath my feet — hush, there is a light below!"

The witch peered over his shoulder and saw a faint glow rising from the open trap, while at that moment her own lamp went suddenly out.

They stood in outer darkness.

"Will you dare descend?" muttered Nathalie. "What should I fear?" came the low, wild answer, and Dirk put his foot on the ladder . . . the witch followed . . . they found themselves in the chamber, and saw that it was lit by an immense fire, seated before which was an enormous man, with his back towards them; he was dressed in black, and at his feet lay stretched a huge black hound.

The snow dripped from the garments of the newcomers as it melted in the hot air; they stood very still.

"Good even," said Dirk in a low voice.

The stranger turned a face as black as his garments; round his neck he wore a collar of most brilliant red and purple stones.

"A cold night," he said, and again it seemed as if the earth rumbled and shook.

"You find our fire welcome," answered Dirk, but the witch crouched against the wall, muttering to herself.

"A good heat, a good heat," said the Blackamoor.

Dirk crossed the room, his arms folded on his breast, his head erect.

"What are you doing here?" he asked.

"Warming myself, warming myself."

"What have you to say to me?"

The Blackamoor drew closer to the fire.

"Ugh! how cold it is!" he said, and stuck out his leg and thrust it deep into the seething flames. Dirk drew still nearer.

"If you be what I think you, you have some reason coming here."

The black man put his other leg into the fire, and flames curled to his knees.

"I have been to the palace, I have been to the palace. I sat under the Empress's chair while she talked to a pretty youth whose name is Theirry — a-ah! it was cold in the palace, there was snow on the youth's garments, as there is blood on yours, and the Emperor was there . . . " All this while he looked into the fire, not at Dirk.

"Theirry has betrayed me," said the youth.

The Blackamoor took his legs from the fire unscorched and untouched, and the hell-hound rose and howled.

"He has betrayed you, and Ysabeau accuses you to save herself; but the devils are on your side since there is other work for you to do; flee from Frankfort, and I will see that you fulfil your destiny."

And now he glanced over his shoulder.

"The witch comes home to-night, to-night, the work here is done, take the road through Frankfort."

He stood up, and his head touched the roof; the gems on his throat gave out long rays of light . . . the fire grew dim; the Blackamoor changed into a thick column of smoke . . . that spread . . . "Hell will not forsake you, Ursula of Rooselaare."

Dirk fell back against the wall, thick vapours encompassing him; he put his hands over his face . . . When he looked up again the room was clear and lit by the beams of the dying fire; he gazed round for the witch, but Nathalie had gone.

With a thick sob in his throat he sprang up the ladder into the outer air, and rushed towards the desolate house.

Desolate indeed; empty, dark and cold it stood, the snow drifting in through the open windows, the fires extinguished on the hearths, a dead place never more to be inhabited.

Dirk leant against the door, breathing hard.

Here was a crisis of his fate; betrayed by the one whom he loved, deserted, too, it seemed, since Nathalie had disappeared . . . the Blackamoor . . . he remembered him as a vision . . . a delusion perhaps.

Oh, how cold it was! Would his accusers come for him to-night? He crept to the gate that gave on to the street and listened.

"Nathalie!" he cried forlornly.

Out of the further darkness came a distant hurry and confusion of sound.

Horses, shouting, eager feet; a populace roused, on the heels of the dealer in black magic, armed with fire and sword for the witches.

Dirk opened the gate, for the last time stepped from the witch's garden; he wondered if Theirry was with the oncoming crowd, yet he did not think so, probably he was in the palace, probably he had repented already of what he had done; but the Empress had found her chance; her accusation falling first, who would take his word against her?

He wore neither cloak nor hat, and as he waited against the open gate the thick snow covered him from head to foot; his spirit had never been afraid, was not afraid now, but his frail body shivered and shrank back as when the angry students fronted him at Basle.

He listened to the noises of the approaching people, till through these another sound, nearer and stranger, made him turn his head.

It came from the witch's house.

"Nathalie!" called Dirk in a half hope.

But the blackness rippled into fire, swift flames sprang up, a column of gold and scarlet enveloped house and garden in a curling embrace.

Dirk ran out into the road, where the glare of the fire lit the swirling snow for a trembling circle, and shading his eyes he stared at the flames that consumed his books, his magic herbs and potions, the strange things, rich and beautiful, that Nathalie had gathered in her long evil life; then he turned and ran down the street as the crowd surged in at the other end, to fall back upon one another aghast before the mighty flames that gave them mocking welcome.

Their dismayed and angry shouts came to Dirk's ears as he ran through the snow; he fled the faster, towards the eastern gate.

It was not yet shut; light of foot and swift he darted through before they could challenge him, perhaps even before the careless guards saw him.

He was a fine runner, not easily fatigued, but he had already strained his endurance to the utmost, and, after he had well cleared the city gates, his limbs failed him and he fell to a walk.

The intense darkness produced a feeling of bewilderment, almost of light-headedness; he kept looking back over his shoulder, at the distant lights of Frankfort, to assure himself that he was not unwittingly stumbling back to the gates.

Finally he stood still and listened; he must be near the river; and after a while he could distinguish the sound of its sullen flow coming faintly out of the silent dark.

Well, of what use was the river to him, or aught else; he was cold, weary, pursued and betrayed; all he had with him were some few pieces of white money and a little phial of swift and keen poison that he never failed to carry in his breast; if his master failed him he would not go alive into the flames.

But, hopeless as his case might seem, he was far from resorting to this last refuge; he remembered the Blackamoor's words, and dragged his numbed and aching limbs along. After a while he saw, glimmering ahead of him, a light.

It was neither in a house nor carried in the hand, for it shone low on the ground, lower, it seemed to Dirk, than his own feet.

He paused, listened, and proceeded cautiously for fear of the river, that must lie, he thought, very close to his left.

As he neared the light he saw it to be a lantern, that cast long rays across the clearing snow-storm; a glittering, trembling reflection beneath it told him it belonged to a boat roped to the bank.

Dirk crept towards it, went on his knees in the snow and mud, and beheld a small, empty craft, the lantern hanging at the prow.

He paused; the waters, rushing by steadily and angrily, must be flowing towards the Rhine and the town of Cologne.

He stepped into the boat that rocked while the water splashed beneath him; but with cold hands he undid the knotted rope.

The boat trembled a moment, then sped on with the current as if glad to be freed.

An oar lay in the bottom, with which for a while Dirk helped himself along, fearful lest the owners of the boat should pursue, then he let himself float down stream as he might. The water lapped about him, and the snow fell on his unprotected and already soaked figure; he stretched himself along the bottom of the boat and hid his face in the cushioned seat.

"Hugh of Rooselaare is dead and Theirry has betrayed me," he whispered into the darkness. Then he began sobbing, very bitterly.

His anguished tears, the cruel cold, the steady sound of the unseen water exhausted and numbed him till he fell into a sleep that was half a swoon, while the boat drifted towards the town.

When he awoke he was still in the open country. The snow had ceased, but lay on the ground thick and untouched to the horizon.

Dirk dragged his cramped limbs to a sitting posture and stared about him; the river was narrow, the banks flat; the boat had been caught by a clump of stiff withered reeds and the prow driven into the snowy earth.

On either side the prospect was wintry and dreary; a grey sky brooded over a white land, a pine forest showed sadly in dark mournfulness, while near by a few bare isolated trees bent under their weight of snow; the very stillness was horribly ominous.

Dirk found it ill to move, for his limbs were frozen, his clothes wet and clinging to his wincing flesh, while his eyes smarted with his late weeping, and his head was racked with giddy pains.

For a while he sat, remembering yesterday till his face hardened and darkened, and he set his pale lips and crawled painfully out of the boat.

Before him was a sweep of snow leading to the forest, and as he gazed at this with dimmed, hopeless eyes, a figure in a white monk's habit emerged from the trees.

He carried a rude wooden spade in his hand, and walked with a slow step; he was coming towards the river, and Dirk waited.

As the stranger neared he lifted his eyes, that had hitherto been cast on the ground, and Dirk recognised Saint Ambrose of Menthon.

Nevertheless Dirk did not despair; before the saint bad recognised him his part was resolved upon . . .

Ambrose of Menthon gazed with pity and horror at the forlorn little figure shivering by the reeds. It was not strange that he did not at once know him; Dirk's face was of a ghastly hue, his eyes shadowed underneath, red and swollen, his lank hair clinging close to his small head, his clothes muddy, wet and soiled, his figure bent.

"Sir," he said, and his voice was weak and sweet, "have pity on an evil thing."

He fell on his knees and clasped his hands on his breast.

"Rise up," answered the saint. "What God has given me is yours; poor soul, ye are very miserable."

"More miserable than ye wot of," said Dirk, through chattering teeth, still on his knees. "Do you not know me?"

Ambrose of Menthon looked at him closely.

"Alas!" he murmured slowly, "I know you."

Dirk beat his breast.

"Mea culpa!" he moaned. "Mea culpa!"

"Rise. Come with me," said the saint. "I will attend your wants."

The youth did not move.

"Will you solace my soul, sir?" he cried. "God must have sent you here to save my soul —
for long days I have sought you."

Saint Ambrose's face glowed

"Have ye, then, repented?"

Dirk rose slowly to his feet and stood with bent head.

"May one repent of such offences?"

"God is very merciful," breathed the saint tenderly.

"Remorse and sorrow fill my heart," murmured Dirk. "I have cast off my evil comrades,
renounced my vile gains and journeyed into the loneliness to find God His pardon . . . and it
seemed He would not hear me . . . "

"He hears all who come in grief and penitence," said the saint joyously. "And He has heard
you, for has He not sent me to find you, even in this most desolate place?"

"You feed me with hope," answered Dirk in a quivering voice, "and revive me with glad tidings
. . . may I dare, I, poor lost wretch, to be uplifted and exalted?"

"Poor youth," was the tender murmur. "Come with me."

He led the way across the thick snow, Dirk following with downcast eyes and white cheeks.
They skirted the forest and came upon a little hut, set back and sheltered among the scattered
trees.

Saint Ambrose opened the rude door.

"I am alone now," he said softly, as he entered. "I had with me a frail holy youth, who was
travelling to Paris; last night he died, I have just laid his body in the earth, his soul rests on
the bosom of the Lord."

Dirk stepped into the hut and stood meekly on the threshold, and Saint Ambrose glanced
at him wistfully.

"Maybe God has sent me this soul to tend and succour in place of that He has called home."
Dirk whispered humbly —

"If I might think so."

The saint opened an inner door.

"Your garments are wet and soiled."

A sudden colour stained Dirk's face.

"I have no others."

Ambrose of Menthon pointed to the inner chamber. "There Blaise died yester-eve; there
are his clothes, enter and put them on."

"It will be the habit of a novice?" asked Dirk softly.

"Yea."

Dirk bent and kissed the saint's fingers with ice-cold lips.

"I have dared," he whispered, "to hope that I might die wearing the garb of God His servants,
and now I dare even to hope that He shall grant my prayer."

He stepped into the inner chamber and closed the door.

# Chapter 22

## Blaise

Ambrose of Menthon and his meek and humble follower rested at Châlons, on their way to Paris.

For many weeks they had begged from door to door, sleeping in some hermit's cell or by the roadside when the severity of the bitter nights permitted, occasionally finding shelter in a wayside convent.

So patient, so courageous before hardship, so truly sad and remorseful, so grateful for the distant chance of ultimate pardon was Dirk, that the saint grew to love the penitent vagabond.

No one eager to look for it could have found any fault with his behaviour; he was gentle as a girl, obedient as a servant, rigid in his prayers (and he had a strangely complete knowledge of the offices and penances of the Church), silent and sorrowful often, taking no pleasure in anything save the saint's talk of Paradise and holy things.

Particularly he loved to hear of the dead youth Blaise, of his saintly life, of his desire to join the stern Brotherhood of the Sacred Heart, in Paris, of his fame as one beloved of God, of the convent's wish to receive him, of his great learning, of his beautiful death in the snowy evening.

To all this Dirk listened with still attention, and from Saint Ambrose's rapt and loving recital he gathered little earthly details of the subject of their speech.

Such as that he was from Flanders, of a noble family, that his immediate relatives were dead, that his years were no more than twenty, and that he was dark and pale.

For himself Dirk had little to say; he described simply his shame and remorse after he had stolen the holy gold, his gradual sickening of his companions, the long torture of his awakening soul, his attempts to find the saint, and how, finally, after he had resolved to flee his evil life and enter a convent, he had run out of Frankfort, found a boat waiting — and so drifted to Saint Ambrose's feet.

The saint, rejoicing in his penitence, suggested that he should enter the convent whither they journeyed with the tidings of the holy youth's death, and Dirk consented with humble gratitude. And so they passed through Châlons, and rested in a deserted hut overlooking the waters of the Maine.

Having finished their scanty meal they were seated together under the rough shelter; the luxury of a fire was denied their austerity; a cold wind blew in and out of the ill-built doors, and a colourless light filled the mean bare place. Dirk sat on a broken stool, reading aloud the writings of Saint Jerome.

He wore a coarse brown robe, very different from his usual attire, fastened round the waist with a rope into which was twisted a wooden rosary; his feet were encased in rude leather boots, his hands reddened with the cold, his face hollow and of a bluish pallor in which his eyes shone feverishly large and dark.

His smooth hair hung on to his shoulders; he stooped, in contrast with his usual erect carriage. Pausing on his low and gentle reading he looked across at the saint.

Ambrose of Menthon sat on a rough-hewn bench against the rougher wall; weariness, exposure, and sheer weakness of body had done their work at last; Dirk knew that for three nights he had not slept . . . he was asleep now or had swooned; his fair head fell forward on his breast, his hands hung by his side.

As Dunk became assured that his companion was unconscious, he slowly rose and set down the holy volume. He was himself half starved, cold to the heart and shuddering; he looked round the plaster walls and the meek expression of his face changed to one of scorn, derision and wicked disdain; he darted a bitter glance at the wan man, and crept towards the door.

Opening it softly, he gazed out; the scene was fair and lonely — the distant tourelles of Châlons rose clear and pointed against the winter clouds; near by the grey river flowed between its high banks, where the bare willows grew and the snow-wreaths still lay.

Dunk took shivering steps into the open and turned towards the Maine; the keen wind penetrated his poor garments and lifted the heavy hair from his thin cheeks; he beat his breast, chafed his hands and walked rapidly.

Reaching the bank he looked up and down the river; there was no one in sight, neither boat nor animal nor house to break the monotony of land, sky and water, only those distant towers of the town.

Dirk walked among the twisted willows, then came to a pause.

A little ahead of him were a black man and a black dog, both seated on the bank and gazing towards Châlons.

The youth came a little nearer.

"Good even," he said. "It is very cold."

The Blackamoor looked round.

"Are you pleased with the way you travel?" he asked, nodding his head. "And your companion?"

Dunk's face lowered.

"How much longer am I to endure it?"

"You must have patience," said the black man, "and endurance."

"I have both," answered Dirk. "Look at my hands — they are no longer soft, but red and hard; my feet are galled and wounded in rough boots — I must walk till I am sick, then pray instead of sleeping; I see no fire, and scarcely do I touch food."

The hell-hound stirred and whined among the osiers, the jewels in the Blackamoor's collar flashed richly, though there was no light to strike them.

"You will be rewarded," he said, "and revenged too — o — ho — o! it is very cold, as you say, very cold."

"What must I do?" asked Dirk.

The black man rubbed his hands together.

"You know — you know."

Dirk's pinched wan face grew intent, and eager.

"Am I to use . . . this?" He touched the breast of his rough habit.

"Yea."

"Then shall I be left defenceless." Dirk's voice shook a little. "If anything should happen — I would not, I could not — oh, Sathanas! — I could not be revealed!"

The Blackamoor rose from among the willows.

"Do you trust yourself and me?" he asked.

Dirk put his thin hand over his eyes.

"Yea, master."

"Then you know what to do. You will not see me for many years — when you have triumphed I shall come."

He turned swiftly and ran down the bank, the hound at his heels; one after another they leaped into the waters of the Maine and disappeared with an inner sound.

Dunk straightened himself and set his lips. He reentered the hut to find Ambrose of Menthon still against the wall, now indeed wearily asleep; Dirk came softly forward; slowly and cautiously he put his hand into his bosom and drew out a small green-coloured phial.

With his eyes keenly on the saint he broke the seal, then crept close.

By Saint Ambrose's side hung his rosary, every bead smooth with the constant pressure of his lips; Dunk raised the heavy crucifix attached, and poured on to it the precious drop contained in the phial.

Saint Ambrose did not wake nor move; Dunk drew away and crouched against the wall, cursing the bitter wind with fierce eyes . . .

When the saint awoke, Dirk was on the broken stool reading aloud the writings of Saint Jerome.

"Is it still light?" asked Ambrose of Menthon amazedly.

"It is the dawn," answered Dunk.

"And I have slept the night through." The saint dragged his stiff limbs from the seat and fell on his knees in a misery of prayer.

Dunk closed the book and watched him; watched his long fingers twining in the beads of his rosary, watched him kiss the crucifix, again and again; then he, too, knelt, his face hidden in his hands.

He was the first to rise.

"Master, shall we press on to Paris?" he asked humbly.

The saint lifted dazed eyes from his devotions.

"Yea," he said. "Yea."

Dunk began putting together in a bundle their few books, and the wooden platter in which they collected their broken food; this being their all.

"I dreamt last night of Paradise," said Saint Ambrose faintly, "the floor was so thick-strewn with close little flowers, red, white, and purple . . . and it was warm as Italy in May . . . " Dunk swung the bundle on to his shoulder and opened the door of the hut.

"There is no sun today," he remarked.

"How long it is since we have seen the sun!" said Saint Ambrose wistfully.

They passed out into the dreary landscape and took their slow way along the banks of the Maine.

Until midday they did not pause, scarcely spoke; then they passed through a little village, and the charitable gave them food.

That night they slept in the open, under shelter of a hedge, and Ambrose of Menthon complained of weakness; Dunk, waking in the dark, heard him praying . . . heard, too, the rattle of the wooden rosary.

When the light came and they once more recommenced their journey the saint was so feeble he was fain to lean on Dunk's shoulder.

"I think I am dying," he said; his face was flushed, his eyes burning, he smiled continuously. "Let me reach Paris," he added, "that I may tell the Brethren of Blaise . . . "

The youth supporting him wept bitterly.

Towards noon they met a woodman's cart that helped them on their way; that night they spent in the stable of an inn; the next day they descended into the valley of the Seine, and by the evening reached the gates of Paris.

As the bells over all the beautiful city were ringing to vespers they arrived at their destination, an old and magnificent convent surrounded with great gardens set near the river bank.

The winter sky had broken at last, and wreathed and motionless clouds curled back from a clear expanse of gold and scarlet, against which the houses, churches and palaces rose from out the blue mist of evening.

The straight roof of the convent, the little tower with its slow-moving bell, the bare bent fruit trees, the beds of herbs, sweet-smelling even now, the red lamp glowing in the dark doorway, showed themselves to Dirk as he entered the gate — he looked at them all intently, and bitter distant memories darkened his hollow face.

The monks were singing the Magnificat; their thin voices came clearly on the frosty air.

"Fecit potentiam in brachio suo: dispersit superbos mente cordis sui."

Ambrose of Menthon took his feeble hand from Dunk's arm and sank on his knees.

"Deposuit potentes de sede, et exaltavit humiles."

But Dirk's pale lips curled, and as he gazed at the sunset flaming beyond the convent walls, there was a haughty challenge in his brooding eyes.

"Esurientes implevit bonis, et divites dimisit manes.

Suscepit Israel puerum suum, recordatus misericordiae suae."

The saint murmured the chanted words and clasped his hands on his breast, while the sky brightened vividly above the wide waters of the Seine.

"Sicut locutus est ad patres nostros Abraham et semini ejus in saecula."

The chant faded away on the still evening, but the saint remained kneeling.

"Master," whispered Dirk, "shall we not go in to them?"

Ambrose of Menthon raised his fair face.

"I am dying," he smiled. "A keen flame licks up my blood and burns my heart to ashes —' Sustinuit anima mea in verbo ejus. '" His voice failed, he sank forward and his head fell against the grey beds of rue and fennel.

"Alas! alas!" cried Dirk; he made no attempt to bring assistance nor called aloud, but stood still, gazing with intent eyes at the unconscious man.

But when the monks came out of the chapel and turned two by two towards the convent, Dirk pulled off his worn cap.

"Divinum auxilium maneat semper nobiscum."

"Amen," said Dirk, then he ran lightly forward and flung himself before the procession. "My father!" he cried, with a sob in his voice.

The priests stopped, the "amens" still trembling on their lips.

"Ambrose of Menthon lies within your gates a dying man," said Dirk meekly and sadly.

With little exclamations of awe and grief the grey-clad figures followed him to where the saint lay.

"Ah me!" murmured Dirk. "The way has been so long, so rough, so cold."

Reverently they raised Saint Ambrose.

"He has done with his body," said an old monk, holding up the dying man.

The flushed sky faded behind them; the saint stirred and half opened his eyes.

"Blaise," he whispered. "Blaise" — he tried to point to Dirk who knelt at his feet —"he will tell you." His eyes closed again, he strove to pray; the "De profundis" trembled on his lips, he made a sudden upward gesture with his hands, smiled and died.

For a while there was silence among them, broken only by a short sob from Dunk, then the monks turned to the ragged, emaciated youth who crouched at the dead feet.

"Blaise, he said," one murmured, "it is the holy youth."

Dirk roused himself as from a silent prayer, made the sign of the cross and rose.

"Who art thou?" they asked reverently.

Dunk raised a tear-stained, weary face.

"The youth Blaise, my fathers," he answered humbly.

# Part II

## The Pope

# Chapter 1

## Cardinal Luigi Caprarola

The evening service in the Basilica of St. Peter was over; pilgrims, peasants and monks had departed; the last chant of the officiating Cardinal's train still trembled on the incense-filled air and the slim novices were putting out the lights, when a man, richly and fantastically dressed, entered the bronze doors and advanced a little way down the centre aisle.

He bent his head to the altar, then paused and looked about him with the air of a stranger. He was well used to magnificence, but this first sight of the chapel of the Vatican caused him to catch his breath. Surrounding him were near a hundred pillars, each of a different marble and carving; they supported a roof that glittered with the manifold colours of mosaic; the rich walls were broken by numerous chapels, from which issued soft gleams of purple and violet light; mysterious shrines of porphyry and cipolin, jasper and silver showed here and there be-hind red lamps. A steady glow of candles shone on a mosaic and silver arch, beyond which the high altar sparkled like one great jewel; the gold lamps on it were still alight, and it was heaped with white lilies, whose strong perfume was noticeable even through the incense.

To one side of the high altar stood a purple chair, and a purple footstool, the seat of the Cardinal, some-times of the Pontiff. This splendid and holy beauty abashed, yet inspired the stranger; he leant against one of the smooth columns and gazed at the altar.

The five aisles were crossed by various shafts of delicate trembling light that only half dispersed the lovely gloom; some of the columns were slender, some massive — the spoils from ancient palaces and temples, no two of them were alike; those in the distance took on a sea-green hue, luminous and exquisite; one or two were of deep rose red, others black or dark green, others again pure ghostly white, and all alike enveloped in soft shadows and quivering lights, violet, blue and red.

The novices were putting out the candles and preparing to close the church; their swift feet made no sound; silently the little stars about the high altar disappeared and deeper shadows fell over the aisles.

The stranger watched the white figures moving to and fro until no light remained, save the purple and scarlet lamps that cast rich rays over the gold and stained the pure lilies into colour, then he left his place and went slowly towards the door.

Already the bronze gates had been closed; only the entrance to the Vatican and one leading into a side street remained open.

Several monks issued from the chapels and left by this last; the stranger still lingered.

Down from the altar came the two novices, prostrated themselves, then proceeded along the body of the church.

They extinguished the candles in the candelabra set down the aisles, and a bejewelled darkness fell on the Basilica.

The stranger stood under a malachite and platinum shrine that blinded with the glimmer and sparkle of golden mosaic; before it burnt graduated tapers; one of the novices came towards it, and the man waiting there moved towards him.

"Sir," he said in a low voice, "may I speak to you?"

He spoke in Latin, with the accent of a scholar, and his tone was deep and pleasant.

The novice paused and looked at him, gazed intently and beheld a very splendid person, a man in the prime of life, tall above the ordinary, and, above the ordinary, gorgeous to the eyes; his face was sunburnt to a hue nearly as dark as his light bronze hair, and his Western eyes showed clearly bright and pale in contrast; in his ears hung long pearl and gold ornaments that touched his shoulders: his dress was half Eastern, of fine violet silk and embroidered leather; he carried in his belt a curved scimitar inset with turkis, by his side a short gold sword, and against his hip he held a purple cap ornamented with a plume of peacocks' feathers, and wore long gloves fretted in the palm with the use of rein and sword.

But more than these details did the stranger's face strike the novice; a face almost as perfect as the masks of the gods found in the temples; the rounded and curved features were over-full for a man, and the expression was too indifferent, troubled, almost weak, to be attractive, but taken in itself the face was noticeably beautiful.

Noting the novice's intent gaze, a flush crept into the man's dark cheek.

"I am a stranger," he said. "I want to ask you of Cardinal Caprarola. He officiated here to — day?"

"Yea," answered the novice. "What can I tell you of him? He is the greatest man in Rome — — now his Holiness is dying," he added.

"Why, I have heard of him — even in Constantinople. I think I saw him — many years ago, before I went to the East."

The novice began to extinguish the candles round the shrine.

"It may be, sir," he said. "His Eminence was a poor youth as I might be; he came from Flanders."

"It was in Courtrai I thought I saw him."

"I know not if he was ever there; he became a disciple of Saint Ambrose of Menthon when very young, and after the saint's death he joined the Convent of the Sacred Heart in Paris — you have heard that, sir?"

The stranger lowered his magnificent eyes.

"I have heard nothing — I have been away — many years; this man, Cardinal Caprarola — he is a saint also — is he not? . . . tell me more of him."

The youth paused in his task, leaving half the candles alight to cast a trembling glow over the man's gold and purple splendour; he smiled.

"Born of Dendermonde he was, sir, Louis his name, in our tongue Luigi, Blaise the name he took in the convent — he came to Rome, seven, nay, it must be eight years ago. His Holiness created him Bishop of Ostia, then of Caprarola, which last name he retains now he is Cardinal — — he is the greatest man in Rome," repeated the novice.

"And a saint?" asked the other with a wistful eagerness.

"Certes, when he was a youth he was famous for his holy austere life, now he lives in magnificence as befits a prince of the Church . . . he is very holy."

The novice put out the remaining candles, leaving only the flickering red lamp.

"There was a great service here today?" the stranger asked.

"Yea, very many pilgrims were here."

"I grieve that I was too late — think you Cardinal Caprarola would see one unknown to him?" "If the errand warranted it, sir."

From the rich shadows came a sigh.

"I seek peace — if it be anywhere it is in the hands of this servant of God — my soul is sick, will he help me heal it?"

"Yea, I do think so."

The youth turned, as he spoke, towards the little side door.

"I must close the Basilica, sir," he added.

The stranger seemed to rouse himself from depths of unhappy thoughts, and followed through the quivering gloom.

"Where should I find the Cardinal?" he asked.

"His palace lies in the Via di San Giovanni in Laterano, any will tell you the way, sir." The novice opened the door. "God be with you."

"And with you;" the stranger stepped into the open and the church door was locked behind him.

The purple after-glow still lingered over Rome; it was May and sweetly warm; as the stranger crossed the Piazza of St. Peter the breeze was like the touch of silk on his face; he walked slowly and presently hesitated, looking round the ruined temples, broken palaces and walls; there were people about, not many, mostly monks; the man glanced back at the Vatican, where the lights had begun to sparkle in the windows, then made his way, as rapidly as his scant knowledge served, across the superb and despoiled city.

He reached the Via Sacra; it was filled with a gay and splendid crowd, in chariots, on foot, and on horse, that mingled unheeding with the long processions of penitents winding in and out the throng, both here and in the Appian Way. He turned towards the Arch of Titus; the ladies laughed and stared as he passed; one took a flower from her hair and threw it after him, at which he frowned, blushed, and hastened on; he had never been equal to the admiration he roused in women, though he disliked neither them nor their admiration; he carried still on his wrist the mark of a knife left there by a Byzantine Princess who had found his face fair and his wooing cold; the laughter of the Roman ladies gave him the same feeling of hot inadequacy as when he felt that angry stab.

Passing the fountain of Meta Sudans and the remains of the Flavian Amphitheatre, he gained the Via di San Giovanni in Laterano leading to the Cælimontana Gate.

Here he drew a little apart from the crowd and looked about him; in the distance the Vatican and Castel San Angelo showed faintly against the remote Apennines; he could distinguish the banner of the Emperor hanging slackly in the warm air, the little lights in St. Peter's.

Behind him rose the Janiculum Hill set with magnificent palaces and immense gardens, beneath the city lay dark in the twilight, and the trees rising from the silent temples made a fair murmur as they shook in their tipper branches.

The stranger sighed and stepped again into the crowd, composed now of all ranks and all nationalities; he touched a young German on the shoulder.

"Which is Cardinal Caprarola's palace?"

"Sir, the first." He pointed to a gorgeous building on the slope of the hill.

The stranger caught a glimpse of marble porticoes half obscured by soft foliage.

With a "Thank you" he turned in the direction of the Palatine.

A few moments brought him to the magnificent gates of the Villa Caprarola; they stood open upon a garden of flowers just gleamingly visible in the dusk; the stranger hesitated in the entrance, fixing his gaze on the luminous white walls of the palace that showed between the boughs of citron and cypress.

This Cardinal, this Prince, who was the greatest man in Rome, which was to say in Christendom, had strangely captured his imagination; he liked to think of him as an obscure and saintly youth devoting his life to the service of God, rising by no arts or intrigues but by the pure will of his Master solely until he dominated the great Empire of the West; the stranger now at his beautiful gates had been searching for peace for many years, in many lands, and always in vain.

In Constantinople he had heard of the holy Frankish priest who was already a greater power than the old and slowly dying Pope, and it had comforted his tired heart to think that there was one man in a high place set there by God alone — one, too, of a pure life and a noble soul; if any could give him promise of salvation, if any could help him to redeem his wasted, weak life, it would be he — this Cardinal who could not know evil save as a name.

With this object he came to Rome; he wished to lay his sins and penitence at the feet of him who had been a meek and poor novice, and now by his virtues was Luigi Caprarola as mighty as the Emperor and as innocent as the angels.

Shame and awe for a while held him irresolute, how could he dare relate his miserable and horrible story to this saint? . . . but God had bidden him, and the holy were always the merciful.

He walked slowly between the dim flowers and bushes to the stately columned portico; with a thickly beating heart and a humble carriage he mounted the low wide steps and stood at the Cardinal's door, which stood open on a marble vestibule dimly lit with a soft roseate violet colour; the sound of a fountain came to his ears, and pungent aromas mingled with the perfume of the blossoms.

Two huge negroes, wearing silver collars and tiger-skins, were on guard at each column of the door, and as the new-comer set foot within the portals one of them struck the silver bell attached to his wrist.

Instantly appeared a slim and gorgeous youth, habited in black, a purple flower fastened at his throat.

The stranger took off his cap.

"This is the residence of his Eminence, Cardinal Caprarola?" he asked, and the hint of hesitation always in his manner was accentuated.

"Yea," the youth bowed gracefully; "I am his Eminence's secretary, Messer Paolo Orsini." "I do desire to see the Cardinal."

The young Roman's dark eyes flashed over the person of the speaker.

"What is your purpose, sir?"

"One neither political nor worldly;" he paused, flushed, then added, "I would confess to his Eminence; I have come from Constantinople for that — for that alone."

Paolo Orsini answered courteously.

"The Cardinal hears confession in the Basilica."

"Certes, I know, yet I would crave to see him privately, I have matters relating to my soul to put before him, surely he will not refuse me." The stranger's voice was unequal, his bearing troubled, as the secretary curiously observed; penitents anxious for their souls did not often trouble the Cardinal, but Orsini's aristocratic manner showed no surprise.

"His Eminence," he said, "is ever loath to refuse himself to the faithful; I will ask him if he will give you audience; what, sir, is your quality and your name?"

"I am unknown here," answered the other humbly; "lately have I come from Constantinople, where I held an office at the court of Basil, but by birth I am a Frank, of the Cardinal's own country."

"Sir, your name?" repeated the elegant secretary.

The stranger's beautiful face clouded.

"I have been known by many . . . but let his Eminence have the truth — I am Theirry, born of Dendermonde."

Paolo Orsini bowed again.

"I will acquaint the Cardinal," he said. "Will you await me here?"

He was gone as swiftly and silently as he had come; Theirry put his hand to a hot brow and gazed about him.

The vestibule was composed of Numidian marble toned by time to a deep orange hue; the capitals of the Byzantine columns were encrusted with gold and supported a ceiling that glittered with violet glass mosaic; gilt lamps, screened with purple or crimson silk, cast a coloured glow down the sloping walls; a double staircase sprang from the serpentine and malachite floor, and where the gold hand-rails ended a silver lion stood on a cipolin pillar, holding between his paws a dish on which burnt aromatic incense; in the space between the staircases was an alabaster fountain — the basin, raised on the backs of other silver lions, and filled with iridescent sea shells, over which the water splashed and fell, changed by the lamplight to a glimmering rose purple.

Either side the fountain were placed great bronze bowls of roses, pink and white, and their petals were scattered over the marble pavement. Against the walls ran low seats, cushioned with dark rich tapestries, and above them, at intervals, marvellous antique statues showed white in deep niches.

Theirry had seen nothing more lavishly splendid; Cardinal Caprarola was no ascetic whatever the youth Blaise may have been, and for a moment Theirry was bewildered and disappointed — — could a saint live thus?

Then he reflected; good it was to consider that God, and not the Devil, who so often used beauty and wealth for his lures, had given a man this.

He walked up and down, none to watch him but the four silent and motionless negroes; the exquisite lights, the melody of the fountain, the sweet odours that rose from the slow-curling blue vapours, the gorgeous surroundings, lulled and soothed; he felt that at last, after his changeful wanderings, his restless unhappiness, he had found his goal and his haven.

In this man's hands was redemption, this man was housed as befitted an Ambassador of the Lord of Heaven.

Paolo Orsini, in person as rare and splendid as the palace, returned.

"The Cardinal will receive you, sir," he said; if the message astonished him he did not show it; he bowed before Theirry, and preceded him up the magnificent stairs.

The first landing was entirely hung with scarlet embroidery worked with peacocks' feathers, and lit by pendent crystal lamps; at either end a silver archway led into a chamber.

The secretary, slim and black against the vivid colours, turned to the left; Theirry followed him into a long hall illuminated by bronze statues placed at intervals and holding scented flambeaux; between them were set huge porphyry bowls containing orange trees and oleanders; the walls and ceiling were of rose-hued marble inlaid with basalt, the floor of a rich mosaic.

Theirry caught his breath; the Cardinal must possess the fabled wealth of India . . .

Paolo Orsini opened a gilt door and held it wide while Theirry entered, then he bowed himself away, saying —

"His Eminence will be with you presently."

Theirry found himself in a fair-sized chamber, walls, floor and ceiling composed of ebony and mother-of-pearl.

Door and window were curtained by hangings of pale colours, on which were stitched in glittering silks stories from Ovid.

In the centre of the floor was a Persian carpet of a faint hue of mauve and pink; three jasper and silver lamps hung by silken cords from the ceiling and gave the pale glow of moonlight; an ivory chair and table raised on an ebony step stood in one corner; on the table was a sand clock, a blood-red glass filled with lilies and a gold book with lumps of turkis set in the covers; on the chair was a purple velvet cushion.

Opposite this hung a crucifix, a scarlet light burning beneath it; to this, the first holy thing Theirry had seen in the palace, he bent the knee.

Incense burnt in a gold brazier, the rich scent of it growing almost insupportable in the close confined space.

A silver footstool and a low ebony chair completed the furniture; against the wall facing the door was a gilt and painted shrine, of which the glittering wings were closed, but Theirry, turning from the crucifix, bent his head to that.

A great excitement crept into his blood, he could not feel that he was in a holy or sacred place, awaiting the coming of the saint who was to ease the burden of his sin, yet what but this feeling of relief, of righteous joy should be heating his blood now . . .

The dim blue light, the strong perfumes were confusing to the senses; his pulses throbbed, his heart leapt; it did not seem as if he could speak to the Cardinal . . . then it seemed as if he could tell him everything and leave — absolved.

Yet — and yet — what was there in the place reviving memories that had been thrust deep into his heart for years . . . a certain room in an old house in Antwerp with the August sunlight over the figure of a young man gilding a devil . . . a chamber in the college at Basle and two youths bending over a witch's fire . . . a dark wet night, and the sound of a weak voice coming to him . . . Frankfort and a garden blazing with crimson roses, other scenes, crowded, horrible . . . why did he think of them here . . . in this remote land, among strangers . . . here where he had come to purge his soul?

He began to murmur a prayer; giddiness touched him, and the blue light seemed to ripple and dim before his eyes.

He walked up and down the soft carpet clasping his hands.

All at once he paused and turned.

There was a shiver of silks, and the Cardinal stepped into the chamber.

Theirry sank on his knees and bowed his throbbing head.

The Cardinal slowly closed the door; a low rumble of thunder sounded; a great storm was gathering over the Tyrrhenian Sea.

# Chapter 2

## The Confession

"'In nomine Patris, et Filii, et Spinitus Sancti,' I give you greeting," said the Cardinal in a low grave voice; he crossed to the ivory chair and seated himself.

Theirry lifted his head and looked eagerly at the man who he hoped would be his saviour.

The Cardinal was young, of the middle height, of a full but elegant person and conveying an impression of slightness and delicacy, though he was in reality neither small nor fragile. His face was pale, by this light only dimly to be seen; he wore a robe of vivid pink and violet silk that spread about the step on which his chair was placed; his hands were very beautiful, and ornamented with a variety of costly rings; on his head was a black skull-cap, and outside it his hair showed, thick, curling and of a chestnut-red colour; his foot, very small and well shaped, encased in a gold slipper, showed beneath his gown.

He caught hold of the ivory arms of his seat and looked straight at Theirry with intense, dark eyes.

"On what matters did you wish to speak with me?" he asked.

Theirry could not find words, a choking sense of horror, of something dreadful and blasphemous beyond all words clutched at his heart . . . he stared at the young Cardinal . . . he must be going mad . . .

"The air — the incense makes me giddy, holy father," he murmured.

The Cardinal touched a bell that stood by the sand clock, and motioned to Theirry to rise. A beautiful boy in a white tunic answered the summons.

"Extinguish the incense," said the Cardinal, "and open the window, Gian . . . it is very hot, a storm gathers, does it not?"

The youth drew apart the painted curtains and unlatched the window; as the cooler air was wafted into the close chamber Theirry breathed more freely.

"The stars are all hidden, your Eminence," said Gian, looking at the night. "Certainly, it is a storm."

He raised the brazier, shook out the incense, leaving it smouldening greyly, went on one knee to the Cardinal, then withdrew backwards.

As the door closed behind him Luigi Caprarola turned to the man standing humbly before him. "Now can you speak?" he said gravely.

Theirry flushed.

"Scarcely have I the heart . . . your Eminence abashes me, I have a sickening tale to relate . . . hearing of you I thought, this holy man can give me peace, and I came half across the world to lay my troubles at your feet; but now, sir, now — I fear to speak, indeed, am scarce able, unreal and hideous it seems in this place."

"In brief, sir," said the Cardinal, "ye have changed your mind — I think ye were ever of a changeful disposition, Theirry of Dendermonde."

"How does your Eminence know that of me is, alas! true."

"I see it in your face," answered the Cardinal, "and something else I see — you are, and long have been, unhappy."

"It is my great unhappiness that has brought me before your Eminence."

Luigi Caprarola rested his elbow on the ivory chair arm and his cheek on his palm; the pale, dim light was full on his face; because of something powerful and intense that shone in his eyes Theirry did not care to look at him.

"Weary of sin and afraid of Heaven ye have come to seek absolution of me," said the Cardinal.

"Yea, if it might be granted me, if by any penitence I might obtain pardon."

Then Theirry, whose gaze was fixed on the ground as he spoke, had an extraordinary vivid impression that the Cardinal was laughing; he looked up quickly, only to behold Luigi Caprarola calm and grave.

A peal of thunder sounded, and the echoes hovered in the chamber.

"The confession must come before the absolution," said the Cardinal. "Tell me, my son, what troubles you."

Theirry shuddered.

"It involves others than myself . . . "

"The seal of the confession is sacred, and I will ask for no names. Theirry of Dendermonde, kneel here and confess."

He pointed to the ivory footstool close to his raised seat; Theirry came and humbly knelt.

The curtains fluttered in the hot wind, a flash of lightning darted in between them and mingled with the luminous colour cast by the faint lamps.

The Cardinal took up the gold book and laid it on his knee, his pink silk sleeve almost touched Theirry's lips . . . his garments gave out a strange and beautiful perfume. "Tell me of these sins of thine," he said, half under his breath.

"I must go far back," answered the penitent in a trembling voice, "for your Eminence to understand my sins — they had small beginnings."

He paused and fixed his gaze on the Cardinal's long fair fingers resting across the gold cover of the breviary.

"I was born in Dendermonde," he said at length. "My father was a clerk who taught me his learning. When he died I came to Courtrai. I was eighteen, ambitious and clever beyond other scholars of my age. I wished above everything to go to one of the colleges . . . "

He gave a hot sigh, as if he could still recall the passionate throb of that early desire.

"To gain a living I taught the arts I was acquainted with, among others I gave lessons in music to the daughter of a great lord in Courtrai . . . in this manner I came to know her brother, who was a young knight of lusty desires."

The Cardinal was listening intently; his breathing seemed hardly to stir his robe; the hand on the gilt and turkis cover was very still.

Theirry wiped his damp forehead, and continued —

"He was, as I, restless and impatient with Courtrai . . . but, unlike me, he was innocent, for I," — he moistened his lips —"I about this time began to practise — black magic."

The thunder rolled sombrely yet triumphantly round the seven hills, and the first rain dashed against the window.

"Black magic," repeated the Cardinal, "go on."

"I read forbidden books that I found in an old library in the house of a Jew whose son I taught — I tried to work spells, to raise spirits; I was very desperate to better myself, I wished to become as Alcuin, as Saint Jerome — nay, as Zerdusht himself, but I was not skilful enough. I could do little or nothing . . . "

The Cardinal moved slightly; Theirry, in an agony of old bitter memories, torn between horror and ease at uttering these things at last, continued in a low desperate voice —

"The young knight I have spoken of was in love with a mighty lady who came through Courtrai, he wished to follow her to Frankfort, she had given him hopes that she would find him service there — he asked me to bear him company, and I was glad to go. On the journey he told me of his marriage to the daughter of a neighbouring lord — and — though that is no matter here — — he knew not if she were alive or dead, but he knew of the place where she had last been known of, and we went thither — it was in the old, half-deserted town of Antwerp . . . "

"And the young knight hoped to find she was dead," interrupted the Cardinal. "Was she, I wonder?"

"All the world thought so. It is a strange story, not for my telling; we found the house, and there we met a youth, who told us of the maid's death and showed us her grave . . . "

The thunder, coming nearer, shook the palace, and Theirry hid his face in his hands. "What of this youth?" asked the Cardinal softly, "tell me of him."

"He ruined me — by night he came to me and told of his studies — black magic! black magic! . . . cast spells and raised a devil . . . in a mirror he showed me visions, I swore with him faithful friendship . . . he ruined my soul — he sold some of the goods in the house, and we went together to Basle College."

"Ye make him out your evil angel," said the Cardinal. "Who was he?"

"I know not; he was high-born, I think, dainty in ways and pleasant to look upon; my faltering soul was caught by his wiles, for he spoke of great rewards; I know not who he was, man or demon . . . I think he loved me."

There was a little silence in the chamber, then the Cardinal spoke.

"Loved you? — what makes you think he loved you?"

"Certes, he said so, and acted so . . . we went to Basle College — then, I also thought I loved him . . . he was the only thing in the world I had ever spoken to of my hopes, my desires . . . we continued our experiments . . . our researches were blasphemous, horrible, he was ever more skilful than I . . . then one day I met a lady, and then I knew myself hideous, but that very night I was drawn into the toils again . . . we cast a spell over another student — we were discovered and fled the college."

A flash of lightning pierced the blue gloom like a sword rending silk; Theirry winced and shuddered as the thunder crashed overhead.

"Does your tale end here?" demanded the Cardinal. "Alas! alas! no; I fell from worse sin to worse sin — we were poor, we met a monk, robbed him of God His moneys, and left him for dead . . . we came to Frankfort and lived in the house of an Egyptian hag, and I began to loathe the youth because the lady was ever in my thoughts, and he hated the lady bitterly because of this; he tempted me to do murder for gain, and I refused for her sake." Theirry's voice became hot and passionate. "Then I found that he was tempting her — my saint! but I had no fear that she would fall, and while she spurned him I thought I could also, ay, and I did . . . but she proved no stronger — she loved her steward, and bid him slay his wife: 'You staked on her virtue,' the Devil cried to me, 'and you've lost! lost!'"

The sobs thickened his voice, and the bitter tears gathered in his beautiful eyes.

"I was the youth's prey again, but now I hated him for his victory . . . we came back to Frankfort, and he was sweet and soft to me, while I was thinking how I might injure him as he had injured me . . . I dwelt on that picture of — her — dishonoured and undone, and I hated him, so waited my chance, and the night we reached the city I betrayed him for what he was, betrayed him to whom I had sworn friendship . . . well, half the town came howling through the snow to seize him, but we were too late, we found a flaming house . . . it burnt to ashes, he with it . . . I had had my revenge, but it brought me no peace. I left the West and went to the East, to India, Persia, to Greece, I avoided both God and the Devil, I dreaded Hell and dared not hope for Heaven, I tried to forget but could not, I tried to repent but could not. Good and evil strove for me, until the Lord had pity . . . I heard of you, and I have come to Rome to cast myself at your feet, to ask your aid to help throw myself on God His mercy."

He rose with his hands clasped on his breast and his wild eyes fixed on the white face of Luigi Caprarola; thunder and lightning together were rending the hot air; Theirry's gorgeous dress glimmered in gold and purple, his face was flushed and exalted.

"God wins, I think, this time," he said in an unsteady voice. "I have confessed my sins, I will do penance for them, and die at least in peace — God and the angels win!"

The Cardinal rose; with one hand he held to the back of the ivory chair, with the other he clasped the golden book to his breast; the light shining on his red hair showed it in filmy brightness against the wall of ebony and mother-of-pearl; his face and lips were very pale above the vivid hue of his robe, his eyes, large and dark, stared at Theirry.

Again the lightning flashed between the two, and seemed to sink into the floor at the Cardinal's feet.

He lifted his head proudly and listened to the following mighty roll; when the echoes had quivered again into hot stillness he spoke.

"The Devil and his legions win, I think," he said. "At least they have served Dirk Renswoude well."

Theirry fell back, and back, until he crouched against the gleaming wall.

"Cardinal Caprarola!" he cried fearfully. "Cardinal Caprarola, speak to me! even here I hear the fiends jibe!"

The Cardinal stepped from the ebony dais, his stiff robes making a rustling as he walked; he laughed.

"Have I learned a mien so holy my old comrade knows me not? Have I changed so, I who was dainty and pleasant to look upon, your friend and your bane?"

He paused in the centre of the room; the open window, the dark beyond it, the waving curtains, the fierce lightning made a terrific background for his haughty figure.

But Theirry moaned and whispered in his throat. "Look at me," commanded the Cardinal, "look at me well, you who betrayed me, am I not he who gilded a devil one August afternoon in a certain town in Flanders?"

Theirry drew himself up and pressed his clenched hands to his temples.

"Betrayed!" he shrieked. "It is I who am betrayed. I sought God, and have been delivered unto the Devil!"

The thunder crashed so that his words were lost in the great noise of it, the blue and forked lightning darted between them.

"You know me now?" asked the Cardinal.

Theirry slipped to his knees, crying like a child.

"Where is God? where is God?"

The Cardinal smiled.

"He is not here," he answered, "nor in any place where I have been."

An awful stillness fell after the crash of thunder; Theirry hid his face, cowering like a man who feels his back bared to the lash.

"Cannot you look at me?" asked the Cardinal in a half-mournful scorn; "after all these years am I to meet you — thus? At my feet!"

Theirry sprang up, his features mask-like in their unnatural distortion and lifeless hue.

"You do well to taunt me," he answered, "for I am an accursed fool, I have been seeking for what does not exist — God! — ay, now I know that there is no God and no Heaven, therefore what matter for my soul . . . what matter for any of it since the Devil owns us all!"

The storm was renewed with the ending of his speech, and he saw through the open window the vineyards and gardens of the Janiculum Hill blue for many seconds beneath the black sky.

"Your soul!" cried the Cardinal, as before. "Always have you thought too much, and not enough, of that; you served too many masters and not one faithfully; had you been a stronger man you had stayed with your fallen saint, not spurned her, and then avenged her by my betrayal."

He crossed to the window and closed it, the while the lightning picked him out in a fierce flash, and waited until the after-crash had rocked to silence, his eyes all the while not leaving the shrinking, horror-stricken figure of Theirry.

"Well, it is all a long while ago," he said. "And I and you have changed."

"How did you escape that night?" asked Theirry hoarsely; hardly could he believe that this man was Dirk Renswoude, yet his straining eyes traced in the altered older face the once familiar features.

As the Cardinal moved slowly across the gleaming chamber Theirry marked with a horrible fascination the likeness of the haughty priest to the poor student in black magic.

The straight dark hair was now curled, bleached and stained a deep red colour, after the manner of the women of the East; eyes and brows were the same as they had ever been, the first as bright and keen, the last as straight and heavy; his clear skin showed less pallor, his mouth seemed fuller and more firmly set, the upper lip heavily shaded with a dark down, the chin less prominent, but the line of the jaw was as strong and clear as ever; a handsomer face than it had been, a remarkable face, with an expression composed and imperious, with eyes to tremble before.

"I thought you burnt," faltered Theirry.

"The master I serve is powerful," smiled the Cardinal. "He saved me then and set me where I am now, the greatest man in Rome — so great a man that did you wish a second time to betray me you might shout the truth in the streets and find no one to believe you."

The lightning darted in vain at the closed window, and the thunder rolled more faintly in the distance.

"Betray you!" cried Theirry, wild-eyed. "No, I bow the knee to the greatest thing I have met, and kiss your hand, your Eminence!"

The Cardinal turned and looked at him over his shoulder.

"I never broke my vows," he said softly, "the vows of comradeship I made to you; just now you said you thought I loved you, then, I mean, in the old days . . . " — he paused and his delicate hand crept over his heart —"well, I . . . loved you . . . and it ruined me, as the devils promised. Last night I was warned that you would come today and that you would be my bane . . . well, I do not care since you are come, for, sir, I love you still."

"Dirk!" cried Theirry.

The Cardinal gazed on him with ardent eyes.

"Do you suppose it matters to me that you are weak, foolish, or that you betrayed me? You are the one thing in all the world I care for . . . Love! what was your love when you left her at Sebastian's feet? — had she been my lady I had stayed and laughed at all of it . . . "

"It is not the Devil who has taught you to be so faithful," said Theirry.

For the first time a look of trouble, almost of despair, came into the Cardinal's eyes; he turned his head away.

"You shame me," continued Theirry; "I have no constancy in me; thinking of my own soul, almost have I forgotten Jacobea of Martzburg — and yet —"

"And yet you loved her."

"Maybe I did — it is long ago."

A bitter little smile curved the Cardinal's lips.

"Is that the way men care for women?" he said. "Certes, not in that manner had I wooed and remembered, had I been a — a — lover."

"Strange that we, meeting here like this, should talk of love!" cried Theirry, his heart heaving, his eyes dilating, "strange that I, driven round the world by fear of God, that I, coming here to one of God's own saints, should find myself in the Devil's net again; come, he has done much for you, what will he do for me?"

The Cardinal smiled sadly.

"Neither God nor Devil will do anything for you, for you are not single-hearted, neither constant to good nor evil; but I — will risk everything to serve your desires."

Theirry laughed.

"Heaven has cast the world away and we are mad! You, you famous as a holy man — did you murder the young Blaise? I will back to India, to the East, and die an idol-worshipper. See yonder crucifix, it hangs upon your walls, but the Christ does not rise to smite you; you handle the Holy Mysteries in the Church and no angel slays you on the altar steps — — let me away from Rome!"

He turned to the gilt door, but the Cardinal caught his sleeve.

"Stay," he said, "stay, and all I promised you in the old days shall come true — do you doubt me? Look about you, see what I have won for myself . . . "

Theirry's beautiful face was flushed and wild. "Nay, let me go . . . "

The last rumble of the thunder crossed their speech.

"Stay, and I will make you Emperor."

"Oh devil!" cried Theirry, "can you do that?"

"We will rule the world between us; yea, I will make you Emperor, if you will stay in Rome and serve me; I will snatch the diadem from Balthasar's head and cast his Empress out as I ever meant to do, and you shall bear the sceptre of the Cæsars, oh, my friend, my friend!"

He held out his right hand as he spoke; Theirry caught it, crushed the fingers in his hot grasp and kissed the brilliant rings; the Cardinal flushed and dropped his lids over sparkling eyes.

"You will stay?" he breathed.

"Yea, my sweet fiend, I am yours, and wholly yours; lo! were not rewards such as these better worth crossing the world for than a pardon from God?"

He laughed and staggered back against the wall, his look dazed and reckless; the Cardinal withdrew his hand and crossed to the ivory seat.

"Now, farewell," he said, "the audience has been over-long; I know where to find you, and in a while I shall send for you; farewell, oh Theirry of Dendermonde!"

He spoke the name with a great tenderness, and his eyes grew soft and misty.

Theirry drew himself together.

"Farewell, oh disciple of Sathanas! I, your humble follower, shall look for fulfilment of your promises."

The Cardinal touched the bell; when the fair youth appeared, he bade him see Theirry from the palace.

Without another word they parted, Theirry with the look of madness on him . . .

When Luigi Caprarola was alone he put his hand over his eyes and swayed backwards as if about to fall, while his breath came in tearing pants . . . with an effort he steadied himself, and, clenching his hands now over his heart, paced up and down the room, his Cardinal's robe trailing after him, his golden rosary glittering against his knee.

As he struggled for control the gilt door was opened and Paolo Orsini bowed himself into his presence.

"Your Eminence will forgive me," he began.

The Cardinal pressed his handkerchief to his lips.

"Well, Orsini?"

"A messenger has just come from the Vatican, my lord —"

"Ah! — his Holiness?"

"Was found dead in his sleep an hour ago, your Eminence."

The Cardinal paled and fixed his burning eyes on the secretary.

"Thank you, Orsini; I thought he would not last the spring; well, we must watch the Conclave." He moved his handkerchief from his mouth and twisted it in his fingers.

The secretary was taking his dismissal, when the Cardinal recalled him.

"Orsini, it is desirable we should have an audience with the Empress, she has many creatures in the Church who must be brought to heel; write to her, Orsini."

"I will, my lord."

The young man withdrew, and Luigi Caprarola stood very still, staring at the gleaming walls of his gorgeous cabinet.

# Chapter 3

## The Empress

Ysabeau, wife of Balthasar of Courtrai and Empress of the West, waited in the porphyry cabinet of Cardinal Caprarola.

It was but little after midday, and the sun streaming through the scarlet and violet colours of the arched window, threw a rich and burning glow over the gilt furniture and the beautiful figure of the woman; she wore a dress of an orange hue; her hair was bound round the temples with a chaplet of linked plates of gold and hung below it in fantastic loops; wrapped about her was a purple mantle embroidered with ornaments in green glass; she sat on a low chair by the window and rested her chin on her hand. Her superb eyes were grave and thoughtful; she did not move from her reflective attitude during the time the haughty priest kept her waiting.

When at last he entered with a shimmer and ripple of purple silks, she rose and bent her head. "It pleases you to make me attendant on your pleasure, my lord," she said.

Cardinal Caprarola gave her calm greeting.

"My time is not my own," he added. "God His service comes first, lady."

The Empress returned to her seat.

"Have I come here to discuss God with your Eminence?" she asked, and her fair mouth was scornful. "This text was stolen from someone who worked hard to get it to you."

The Cardinal crossed to the far end of the cabinet and slowly took his place in his carved gold chair.

"It is of ourselves we will speak," he said, smiling. "Certes, your Grace will have expected that."

"Nay," she answered. "What is there we have in common, Cardinal Caprarola?"

"Ambition," said his Eminence, "which is known alike to saint and sinner."

Ysabeau looked at him swiftly; he was smiling with lips and eyes, sitting back with an air of ease and power that discomposed her; she had never liked him.

"If your talk be of policy, my lord, it is to the Emperor you should go."

"I think you have as much influence in Rome as your husband, my daughter."

There was a dazzling glitter of coloured light as the Empress moved her jewelled hands. "It is our influence you wish, my lord — certes, a matter for the Emperor."

His large keen eyes never left her face.

"Yea, you understand me."

"Your Eminence desires our support in the Conclave now sitting," she continued haughtily.

"But have you ever shown so much duty to us, that we should wish to see you in St. Peter's seat?" She thought herself justified in speaking thus to a man whose greatness had always galled her, for she saw in this appeal for her help an amazing confession of weakness on his part. But Luigi Caprarola remained entirely composed.

"You have your creatures in the Church," he said, "and you intend one of them to wear the Tiara — there are sixteen Cardinals in the Conclave, and I, perhaps, have half of them. Your Grace, you must see that your faction does not interfere with what these priests desire — my election namely."

"Must?" she repeated, her violet eyes dilating. "Your Eminence has some reputation as a holy man — and you suggest the corruption of the Conclave."

The Cardinal leant forward in his chair.

"I do not play for a saintly fame," he said, "and as for a corrupted Conclave — your Grace should know corruption, seeing that your art, and your art alone, achieved the election of Balthasar to the German throne."

Ysabeau stared at him mutely; he gave a soft laugh.

"You are a clever woman," he continued. "Your husband is the first King of the Germans to hold the Empery of the West for ten years and keep his heel on the home lands as well; but even your wits will scarcely suffice now; Bohemia revolts, and Basil stretches greedy fingers from Ravenna, and to keep the throne secure you desire a man in the Vatican who is Balthasar's creature."

The Empress rose and placed her hand on the gilded ribbing of the window-frame.

"Your Eminence shows some understanding," she flashed, pale beneath her paint; "we gained the West, and we will keep the West, so you see, my lord, why my influence will be against you, not with you, in the Conclave."

The Cardinal laid his hand lightly over his heart.

"Your Grace speaks boldly — you think me your enemy?"

"You declare yourself hostile, my lord."

"Nay, I may be a good friend to you — in St. Peter's."

She smiled.

"The Conclave have not declared their decision yet, your Eminence; you are a great prince, but the Imperial party have some power."

The Cardinal sat erect, and his intense eyes quelled her despite herself.

"Some power — which I ask you to exert in my behalf."

She looked away, though angry with herself that his gaze overawed her.

"You have declared your ambition, my lord; your talents and your wealth we know — you are too powerful already for us to tolerate you as master in Rome."

"Again you speak boldly," smiled the Cardinal. "Perhaps too boldly — I think you will yet help me to the Tiara."

Ysabeau gave a quick glance at his pale, handsome face framed in the red hair.

"Do you seek to bribe me, my lord?" She remembered the vast riches of this man and their own empty treasury.

"Nay," said Luigi Caprarola, still smiling. "I threaten."

"Threaten!" At once she was tempestuous, panting, furious; the jewels on her breast sparkled with her hastened breathing.

"I threaten that I will make you an outcast in the streets unless you serve me well."

She was the tiger-cat now, ready to turn at bay, Marozia Porphyrogentris of Byzantium.

"I know that of you," said the Cardinal, "that once revealed, would make the Emperor hurl you from his side."

She sucked in her breath and waited. "Melchoir of Brabant died by poison and by witchcraft."

"All the world knows that" — her eyes were long and evil; "he was bewitched by a young doctor of Frankfort College who perished for the deed."

The Cardinal looked down at the hand on his lap.

"Yea, that young doctor brewed the potion — you administered it."

Ysabeau took a step forward into the room. "You lie . . . I am not afraid of you — you lie most utterly . . . "

Luigi Caprarola sprang to his feet.

"Silence, woman! speak not so to me! It is the truth, and I can prove it!"

She bent and crouched; the plates of gold on her hair shook with her trembling.

"You cannot prove it" — the words were forced from her quivering throat; "who are you that you should dare this — should know this?"

The Cardinal still stood and dominated her.

"Do you recall a youth who was scrivener to your Chamberlain and friend of the young doctor of rhetoric — Theirry his name, born of Dendermonde?"

"Yea, he is now dead or in the East . . . "

"He is alive, and in Rome. He served you well once, Empress, when he came to betray his friend, and you were quick to seize the chance — it suited him then to truckle to you . . . I think he was afraid of you . . . he is not now; he knows, and if I bid him he will speak."

"And what is his bare word against my oath and the Emperor's love?"

"I am behind his word — I and all the power of the Church."

Ysabeau answered swiftly.

"I am not of a nation easily cowed, my lord, nor are the people of our blood readily trapped — I can tear your reputed saintship to rags by spreading abroad this tale of how you tried to bargain with me for the Popedom."

The Cardinal smiled in a way she did not care to see.

"But first I say to the Emperor — your wife slew your friend that she might be your wife, your friend Melchoir of Brabant — you loved him better than you loved the woman — will you not avenge him now?"

The Empress pressed her clenched hands against her heart and, with an effort, raised her eyes to her accuser's masterful face.

"My lord's love against it all," she said hoarsely. "He knows Melchoir's murderer perished in Frank-fort in the flames, he knows that I am innocent, and he will laugh at you — weave what tissue of falsehoods you will, sir, I do defy you, and will do no bargaining to set you in the Vatican."

The Cardinal rested his finger-tips on the arm of the chair, and looked down at them with a deepening smile.

"You speak," he answered, "as one whom I can admire — it requires great courage to put the front you do on guilt — but I have certain knowledge of what I say; come, I will prove to you that you cannot deceive me — you came first to the house of a certain witch in Frankfort on a day in August, a youth opened the door and took you into a room at the back that looked on to a garden growing dark red roses; you wore, that day, a speckled green mask and a green gown edged with fur."

He raised his eyes and looked at her; she moved back against the wall, and outspread her hands either side her on the gleaming porphyry.

"You threatened the youth as I threaten you now — you knew that he had been driven from Basle College for witchcraft, even as I know you compassed the death of your first husband, and you asked him to help you, even as I ask you to help me now."

"Oh!" cried the Empress; she brought her hands to her lips. "How can you know this?"

The Cardinal reseated himself in his gold chair and marked with brilliant, merciless eyes the woman struggling to make a stand against him.

"Hugh of Rooselaare died," he said with sudden venom —"died basely for justly accusing you, and so shall you die — basely — unless you aid me in the Conclave."

He watched her very curiously; he wondered how soon he would utterly break her courage, what new turn her defiance would take; he almost expected to see her at his feet.

For a few seconds she was silent; then she came a step nearer; the veins stood out on her forehead and neck; she held her hands by her side — they were very tightly clenched, but her beautiful eyes were undaunted.

"Cardinal Caprarola," she said, "you ask me to use my influence to bring about your election to the Popedom — knowing you as I know you now I cannot fail to see you are a man who would stop at nought . . . if I help you I shall help my husband's enemy — once you are in the Vatican, how long will you tolerate him in Rome? You will be no man's creature, and, I think, no man's ally — what chance shall we have in Rome once you are master? Sylvester was old and meek, he let Balthasar hold the reins — will you do that?"

"Nay," smiled the Cardinal. "I shall be no puppet Pope."

"I knew it," answered the Empress with a deep breath; "will you swear to keep my husband in his place?"

"That will not I," said Luigi Caprarola. "If it please me I will hurl him down and set one of my own followers up. I have no love for Balthasar of Courtrai."

Ysabeau's face hardened with hate.

"But you think he can help you to the Tiara —"

"Through you, lady —you can tell him I am his friend, his ally, what you will —or you may directly influence the Cardinals, I care not, so the thing be done; what I shall do if it be not done, I have said."

The Empress twisted her fingers together and suddenly laughed.

"You wish me to deceive my lord to his ruin, you wish me to place his enemy over him — now, when we are harassed, here and in Germany, you wish me to do a thing that may bring his fortunes to the dust — — why, you are not so cunning, my lord, if you think you can make me the instrument of Balthasar's down-fall!"

The Cardinal looked at her with curiosity.

"Nevertheless your Grace will do it — sooner than let me say what I can say."

She held up her head and smiled in his face. "Then you are wrong; neither threats nor bribery can make me do this thing —say what you will to the Emperor, I am secure in his good affections; blight my fame and turn him against me if you can, I am not so mean a woman that fear can make me betray the fortunes of my husband and my son."

The Cardinal lowered his eyes; he was very pale.

"You dare death," he said, "a shameful death —if my accusation be proved —as proved it shall be."

The Empress looked at him over her shoulder. "Dare death!" she cried. "You say I have dared Hell for —him! —shall I be afraid, then, of paltry death?"

Luigi Caprarola's breast heaved beneath the vivid silk of his robe.

"Of what are you afraid?" he asked.

"Of nothing save evil to my lord."

The Cardinal's lids drooped; he moistened his lips.

"This is your answer?"

"Yea, your Eminence; all the power I possess shall go to prevent you mounting the throne you covet so —and now, seeing you have that answer I will leave, my courtiers grow weary in your halls."

She moved to the door, her limbs trembling beneath her, her brow cold, her hands chilled and moist, and her heart shivering in her body, yet with a regal demeanour curbing and controlling her fear.

As she opened it the Cardinal turned his head. "Give me a little longer, your Grace," he said softly. "I have yet something to say."

She reclosed the door and stood with her back against it.

"Well, my lord?"

"You boast you are afraid of nothing —certes, I wonder —you defy me boldly and something foolishly in this matter of your guilt; will you be so bold in the matter of your innocence?"

He leant forward in his chair to gaze at her; she waited silently, with challenging eyes.

"You are very loyal to your husband, you will not endanger your son's possible heritage; these things, you tell me, are more to you than shame or death; your lord is Emperor of the West, your son King of the Romans —well, well —you are too proud —"

"Nay," she flashed, "I am not too proud for the wife of Balthasar of Courtrai and the mother of a line of Emperors —we are the founders of our house, and it shall be great to rule the world."

The Cardinal was pale and scornful, his narrowed eyes and curving mouth expressed bitterness —and passion.

"Here is the weapon shall bring you to your knees," he said, "and make your boasting die upon your lips —you are not the wife of Balthasar, and the only heritage your son will ever have is the shame and weariness of the outcast."

She gathered her strength to meet this wild enormity. "Not his wife . . . why, you rave . . . we were married before all Frankfort . . . not Balthasar's wife!"

The Cardinal rose; his head was held very erect; he looked down on her with an intense gaze. "Your lord was wed before."

"Yea, I know . . . what of it?"

"This — Ursula of Rooselaare lives!"

Ysabeau gave a miserable little cry and turned about as if she would fall; she steadied herself with a great effort and faced the Cardinal desperately.

"She died in a convent at Flanders — this is not the truth —"

"Did I not speak truth before?" he demanded. "In the matter of Melchoir."

A cry was wrung from the Empress.

"Ursula of Rooselaare died in Antwerp," she repeated wildly —"in the convent of the White Sisters."

"She did not, and Balthasar knows she did not — he thinks she died thereafter, he thinks he saw her grave, but he would find it empty — she lives, she is in Rome, and she is his wife, his Empress, before God and man."

"How do you know this?" She made a last pitiful attempt to brave him, but the terrible Cardinal had broken her strength; the horror of the thing he said had chilled her blood and choked her heart-beats.

"The youth who helped you once, the doctor Constantine . . . from him Balthasar obtained the news of his wife's death, for Ursula and he were apprenticed to the same old master — ask Balthasar if this be not so — well, the youth lied, for purposes of his own; the maid lived then, and is living now, and if I choose it she will speak."

"It is not possible," shuddered the Empress; "no — you wish to drive me mad, and so you torture me — why did not this woman speak before?"

The Cardinal smiled.

"She did not love her husband as you do, lady, and so preferred her liberty; you should be grateful."

"Alive, you say," whispered Ysabeau, unheeding, "and in Rome? But none would know her, she could not prove she was — his — Ursula of Rooselaare."

"She has his ring," answered Luigi Caprarola, "and her wedding deeds, signed by him and by the priest — there are those at Rooselaare who know her, albeit it is near twenty years since she was there; also she hath the deposition of old Master Lukas that she was a supposed nun when she came to him, and in reality the wife of Balthasar of Courtrai; she can prove no one lies buried in the garden of Master Lukas's house, and she can bring forward sisters of the Order to which she belonged to show she did not die on her wedding day — this and further proof can she show."

The Empress bowed her head on her breast and put her hand over her eyes.

"She came to you — sir, with . . . this tale?"

"That is for me to say or not as I will."

"She must be silenced! By Christus His Mother she must be silent!"

"Secure me the casting vote in the Conclave and she will never speak."

"I have said. I . . . cannot, for his sake, for my son's sake —"

"Then I will bring forth Ursula of Rooselaare, and she shall prove herself the Emperor's wife — then instantly must you leave him, or both of you will be excommunicated — your alternative will be to stay and be his ruin or go to obscurity, never seeing his face again; your son will no longer be King of the Romans, but a nameless wanderer — spurned and pitied by those who should be his subjects — and another woman will sit by Balthasar's side on the throne of the West!"

The Empress set her shoulders against the door.

"And if my lord be loyal to me as I to him — to me and to my son —"

"Then will he be hounded from his throne, cast out by the Church and avoided by men; will not Lombardy be glad to turn against him and Bohemia?"

For a little while she was silent, and the Cardinal also as he looked at her, then she raised her eyes to meet his; steadily now she kept them at the level of his gaze, and her base, bold blood served her well in the manner of her speech.

"Lord Cardinal," she said, "you have won; before you, as before the world, I stand Balthasar's wife, nor can you fright me from that proud station by telling of — this impostor; yet, I am afraid of you; I dare not come to an issue with you, Luigi Caprarola, and to buy your silence on these matters I will secure your election — and afterwards you and my lord shall see who is the stronger."

She opened the door, motioning him to silence.

"My lord, no more," she cried. "Believe me, I can be faithful to my word when I am afraid to break it . . . and be you silent about this woman Ursula." The Cardinal came from his seat towards her.

"We part as enemies," he answered, "but I kiss the hem of your gown, Empress, for you are brave as you are beautiful."

He gracefully lifted the purple robe to his lips.

"And above all things do I admire a constant woman;" his voice was strangely soft. Her face, cold, imperial beneath the shining gold and glittering hair, did not change. "But, alas, you hate me!" he suddenly laughed, raising his eyes to her.

"To-day I cannot speak further with you, sir."

She moved away, steadying her steps with difficulty; the two chamberlains in the ante-chamber rose as she stepped out of the cabinet.

"Benedictus, my daughter," smiled the Cardinal, and closed the door.

His face was flushed and bright with triumph; there was a curious expression in his eyes; he went to the window and looked out on purple Rome.

"How she loves him still!" he said aloud; "yet — — why do I wonder? — is he not as fair a man as —"

He broke off, then added reflectively, "Also, she is beautiful."

His long fingers felt among his silk robes; he drew forth a little mirror and gazed at his handsome face with the darkened upper lip and tonsured head.

As he looked he smiled, then presently laughed.

# Chapter 4

## The Dancer in Orange

Theirry walked slowly through the gorgeous ruins of Imperial Rome; it was something after noon and glowingly hot; the Tiber curled in and about the stone houses and broken palaces like a bronze and golden serpent, so smooth and glittering it was.

He followed the river until it wound round the base of Mount Aventine; and there he paused and looked up at the Emperor's palace, set splendidly on the hill.

Above the dazzling marble floated the German standard, vivid against the vivid sky, and Frankish guards were gathered thick about the magnificent portals.

The noble summit of Soracté dominated the distance and the city; over the far-off Campagna quivered a dancing vapour of heat; the little boats on the Tiber rested lazily in their clear reflections, and their coloured sails drooped languidly.

Theirry marked with a vacant gaze the few passersby; the mongrel crowd of Rome — Slav, Frank, Jew or Greek, with here and there a Roman noble in a chariot, or a German knight on horseback.

He was not considering them, but Cardinal Caprarola.

Several days now he had been in the city, but there had come no message from the Cardinal; a dozen times he had gone over every word, every little incident of his strange interview in the palace on the Palatine with a wild desire to assure himself of its truth; had he not been promised the Imperial crown? — impossible that seemed, yet no more impossible than that Dirk Renswoude should have become a Prince of the Church and the greatest man in Rome.

He could not think of those two as the same; different forms of the same devil, but not actually the same man, the same flesh and blood . . . black magic! . . . it was a terrible thing and a wonderful; if he had served the fiend better what might it not have done for him, what might not it still do? Neither could he understand Dirk's affection or tenderness; even after the betrayal his one-time comrade was faithful to those long-ago vows..

He looked at the Golden Palace on the Aventine — Emperor of the West!

Balthasar reigned there now . . . well, why not he? . . . with the Devil as an ally . . . and there was no God.

His beautiful face grew sombre with thought; he walked thoughtfully round the base of the hill, remarked by those coming and going from the palace for his splendid appearance and rich Eastern dress.

A little Byzantine chariot, gilt, with azure curtains and drawn by a white horse, came towards him; the occupant was a lady in a green dress; the grooms ran either side the horse's head to assist it up the hill; the chariot passed Theirry at a walking pace.
"

The lady was unveiled, and the sun was full on her face.

It was Jacobea of Martzburg.

She did not see him; her car continued its slow way towards the palace, and Theirry stood staring after it.

He had last seen her ten years, and more, ago, in her steward's arms in the courtyard of Castle Martzburg; beyond them Sebastian's wife . . .

He wondered if she had married the steward, and smiled to think that he had once considered her a saint; ten years ago, and he had not yet learnt his lesson; many men had he met and none holy, many women and none saintly, and yet he had been fool enough to come to Rome because he believed God was triumphant in the person of Luigi Caprarola . . .

A fool's reward had been his; Heaven's envoy had proved the Devil incarnate, and he had been mocked with the sight of the woman for whose sake he had made pitiful attempts to be cleansouled; the woman who had, for another man's love, defied the angels and taken her fate into her own hands.

For another man's sake! — this the bitterest thought of all bitter thoughts yet — and yet — he did not know if he had ever loved her, or only the sweet purity she was a false symbol of — he was sure of nothing. This way and that his mind went, ever hesitating, ever restless — his heart was ready as water to take the colour of what passed it, and his soul was as a straw before the breath of good and evil.

The sound of cymbals and laughter roused him from his agitated thoughts.

He looked along the road that wound by the Tiber and saw a little crowd approaching, evidently following a troupe of jugglers or mountebanks.

As they came nearer to where he loitered, Theirry, ever easily attracted by any passing excitement or attraction, could not choose but give them a half-sullen attention.

The centre of the group was a girl in an orange gown, they who followed her the mere usual citizens of Rome, some courtiers of the Emperor's, soldiers, merchants' clerks, and the rabble of children, lazy mongrel foreigners and Franks.

The dancer stopped and spread a scarlet carpet on the roadway; the crowd gathered about it in a circle, and Theirry drew up with the rest, interested by what interested them — the two facts, namely, that marked the girl as different from her kind.

Firstly, she affected the unusual modesty or coquetry of a black mask that completely covered her face, and, secondly, she was attended only by an enormous and hideous ape.

She wore a short robe in the antique style, girdled under her bosom, and fastened on her shoulders with clasps of gold; gilt sandals, closely laced, concealed her feet and ankles; round her bust and arms was twisted a gauze scarf of the same hue as her gown, a deep, bright orange, and her hair, which was a dark red gold, was gathered on the top of her head in a cluster of curls, and bound with a violet fillet.

Although the mask concealed her charms of face, it was obvious that she was young, and probably Greek; her figure was tall, full, and splendidly graceful; she held a pair of brass cymbals and struck them with a stormy joyousness above her proud head.

The ape, wearing a collar of bright red stones and a long blue jacket trimmed with spangles, curled himself on the corner of the carpet and went to sleep.

The girl began dancing; she had no music save her cymbals, and needed none.

Her movements were quick, passionate, triumphant; she clashed the brass high in the air and leapt to meet the fierce sound; her gold-shod feet twinkled like jewels, the clinging skirt showed the beautiful lines of her limbs, and the gauze floating back revealed her fair white arms and shoulders. Suddenly she lowered the cymbals, struck them together before her breast, and looked from right to left. Theirry caught the gleam of her dark eyes through the holes in her mask.

For a while she crouched together, panting, then drew herself erect, and let her hands fall apart. The burning sun shone in her hair, in the metal hems of her robe, in her sandals, and changed the cymbals into discs of fire.

She began to sing; her voice was deep and glorious, though muffled by the mask.

Slowly she moved round the red carpet, and the words of her song fell clearly on the hot air.
"If Love were all!
His perfect servant I would be.
Kissing where his foot might fall, Doing him homage on a lowly knee.
If Love were all!
If Love were all!
And no such thing as Pride nor Empery, Nor, God, nor sins or great or small, If Love were all!

She passed Theirry, so close, her fluttering robe touched his slack hand; he looked at her curiously, for he thought he knew her voice; he had heard many women sing, in streets and in palaces, and, somewhere, this one.

"If Love were all!

But Love is weak.

And Hate oft giveth him a fall.

And Wisdom smites him on the cheek, If Love were all!

If Love were all!

I had lived glad and meek, Nor heard Ambition call And Valour speak.

If Love were all!

The song ended as it had begun on a clash of cymbals; the dancer swung round, stamped her foot and called fiercely to the ape, who leapt up and began running round the crowd, offering a shell and making an ugly jabbering noise.

Theirry flung the hideous thing a silver bezant and moved away; he was thinking, not of the dancer with the unknown memory in her voice, but of the lady in the gilt chariot behind the azure curtains how little she had changed!

A burst of laughter made him look round; he saw a quick picture: the girl's orange dress flashing in the strong sunlight, the ape on her shoulder hurling the contents of the shell in the air, which glittered for a second with silver pieces, and the jesting crowd closing round both.

He passed on moodily into the centre of the town; in the unrest and agitation of his thoughts he had determined to seek Cardinal Caprarola, since the Cardinal gave no sign of sending for him.

even of remembering him; but today it was useless to journey to the Palace on the Palatine, for the Conclave sat in the Vatican, and the Cardinal would be of their number.

The streets, the wine shops, the public squares were full of a mixed and excited mob; the adherents of the Emperor, who wished to see a German pontiff, and they who were ardent Romans or Churchmen came, here and there, to open brawls; the endless processions that crossed and recrossed from the various monasteries and churches were interrupted by the lawless jeers of the Frankish inhabitants, who, under a strong Emperor and a weak Pope, had begun to assume the bearing of conquerors.

Theirry left them all, too concerned, as always, in his own small affairs to have any interest in larger issues; he turned into the Via Sacra, and there, under the splendid but broken arch of Constantine, he saw again the dancing girl and her ape.

She looked at him intently; of that he could have no doubt, despite her mask, and, as he turned his hesitating steps towards the Palatine, she rose and followed him.

As he ascended the narrow grey road that wound above the city, he kept looking over his shoulder, and she was always there, following, with the ape on her shoulder.

They passed scattered huts, monasteries, decaying temples and villas, and came out on to the deserted stretches of the upper Palatine, where the fragmentary glories of another world lay under the cypress and olive trees.

Here Theirry paused, and again looked, half fearfully, for the bright figure of the dancer.

She stood not far from him, leaning against a slender shaft of marble, the sole remaining column of a temple to some heathen god; behind it a blue-green grove of cypress arose, and behind them the city lay wrapt in the sparkling mist of noonday, through which, at intervals, gleamed the dusky waters of the Tiber.

The mighty walls showed brown and dark against the houses they enclosed, and the dusty vineyards scorched in the sun that blazed on the lantern of St. Peter and the angel on Castel del' Angelo.

The stillness of great heat was over city and ruins, noiseless butterflies fluttered over the shattered marble, and pale narcissi quivered in the deep grass; the sky, a bronze gold over the city and about the mountainous horizon, was overhead a deep and burning blue; a colour that seemed reflected in the clusters of violets that grew about the fallen masonry.

Theirry flung himself on a low marble seat that stood in the shade of a cypress, and his blood-red robe was vivid even in the shadow; he looked at the veiled city at his feet, and at the dancing girl resting against the time-stained, moss-grown column.

She loosened the cymbals from her hands and flung them on the ground; the ape jumped from her shoulder and caught them up.

Again she sang her passionate little song.

"If Love were all!

His faithful servant I would be.

Kissing where his foot might fall, Doing him homage on a lowly knee.

If Love were all!"

As she sang, another and very different scene was suddenly brought to Theirry's mind; he remembered a night when he had slept on the edge of a pine forest, in Germany — many years ago — and had suddenly awoke — nay, he had dreamt he heard singing, and a woman's singing ... if it were not so mad a thought he would have said — this woman's singing.

He turned bitter, dark eyes towards her — why had she followed him?

Swiftly and lightly she came across the grass, glittering from head to foot in the sunlight, and paused before him.

"Certes, you should be in Rome today," she said. "The Conclave come to their decision this afternoon; do you wish to hear it announced from the Vatican?"

"Nay," smiled Theirry. "I would rather see you dance."

Her answer was mocking.

"You care nothing for my dancing — I would wager to stir any man in Rome sooner than you!" Theirry flushed.

"Why did you follow me?" he asked in a half-indifferent dislike.

She seated herself on the other end of his marble bench.

"My reasons are better than my dancing, and would, could I speak them, have more effect on you."

The light hot wind ruffled back the gauze from her beautiful arms and shoulders; her bright hair and masked face were in shadow, but her gold-sandalled foot, which rested lightly on the wild, sweet violets, blazed in the sunshine.

Theirry looked at her foot as he answered —

"I am a stranger to Rome and know not its customs, but if you are what you seem you can have no serious reason in following me."

The dancing girl laughed.

"A stranger! then that is why you are the only man in Rome not waiting eagerly to know who the new Pope will be."

"It is curious for a wandering minstrel to have such interest in holy matters," said Theirry.

She leant towards him across the length of the bench, and the perfume of her orange garments mingled with the odour of the violets.

"Take me for something other than I appear," she replied, in a mournful and passionate voice. "In being here I risk an unthinkable fate — I stake the proudest hopes ... the fairest fortune ... " "Who are you?" cried Theirry. "Why are you masked?"

She drew back instantly, and her tone changed to scorn again.

"When there are many pilgrims in Rome the monks bid us poor fools wear masks, lest, with our silly faces, we lure souls away from God."

Theirry stared at the proud city beneath him. "Could I find God," he said bitterly, "no fair face should beguile me away — but God is bound and helpless, I think, at the Devil's chair." The dancer crushed her bright foot down on the violets.

"I cannot imagine," she said intensely, "how a man can spend his life looking for God and saving his own soul — is not the world beautiful enough to outweigh heaven?"

Theirry was silent.

The dancing girl laughed softly.

"Are you thinking of — her?" she asked.

He turned with a start.

"Thinking of whom?" he demanded.

"The lady in the Byzantine chariot — Jacobea of Martzburg."

He sprang up.

"Who are you, and what do you know of me?"

"This, at least — that you have not forgotten her! — — Yet you would be Emperor, too, would you not?"

"

Theirry drew back from her stretched along the marble seat, until his crimson robe touched the dark trunks of the cypress trees.

"Ye are some witch," he said.

"I come from Thessaly, where we have skill in magic," she answered.

And now she sat erect, her yellow dress casting a glowing reflection into the marble.

"And I tell you this," she added passionately. "If you would be Emperor, let that woman be-she will do nought for you — let her go! — this is a warning, Theirry of Dendermonde!"

His face flushed, his eyes sparkled.

"Have I a chance of wearing the Imperial crown?" he cried. "May I — I, rule the West? — Tell me that, witch!"

She whistled the ape to her side.

"I am no witch — but I can warn you to think no more of Jacobea of Martzburg." He answered hotly.

"I love not to hear her name on your tongue; she is nothing to me; I need not your warning."

The dancer rose.

"For your own sake forget her, Theirry of Dendermonde, and you may be indeed Emperor of the West and Cæsar of the Romans."

The gold gleaming on her robe, her sandals, in her hair, confused and dazzled him, the hideous ape gave him a pang of terror.

"How came you by your knowledge?" he asked, and clutched the cypress trunk.

"I read your fortune in your eyes," she answered. "We in Thessaly have skill in these things, as I have said . . . Look at the city beneath us — is it not worth much to reign in it?"

The gold vapour that lay about the distant hills seemed to be resolving into heavy, menacing clouds.

Theirry, following the direction of her slender pointing finger, gazed at the city and saw the clouds beyond.

"A storm gathers," he said, and knew not why he shivered suddenly until his pearl earrings tinkled on the collar round his neck.

The dancer laughed, wildly and musically.

"Come with me to the Piazza of St. Peter," she said, "and you shall hear strange words." With that she caught hold of his blood-red garments and drew him towards the city.

The perfume from her dress and her hair stole into his nostrils; the hem of her tunic made a delicate sound as it struck her sandals, the violet ribbon in her fillet touched his face . . . he hated the black, expressionless mask; he had strange thoughts under her touch, but he came silently.

As they went down the road that wound through the glorious desolation Theirry heard the sound of pattering feet, and looked over his shoulder.

It was the ape who followed them; he walked on his hind legs . . . how tall he was! — Theirry had not thought him so large, nor of such a human semblance.

The dancer was silent, and Theirry could not speak; when they entered the city gates the dun-coloured clouds had swallowed up the gold vapour and half covered the sky; as they crossed the Tiber and neared the Vatican the last beams of the sun disappeared under the shadow of the oncoming storm.

Enormous crowds were gathered in the Piazza of St. Peter; it seemed as if all Rome had assembled there; many faces were turned towards the sky, and the sudden gloom that had overspread the city seemed to infect the people, for they were mostly silent, even sombre.

The enormous and terrible ape cleared an easy way for himself through the crowd, and Theirry and the dancing girl followed until they had pushed through the press of people and found themselves under the windows of the Vatican.

The heavy, ominous clouds gathered and deepened like a pall over the city; black, threatening shapes rolled up from behind the Janiculum Hill, and the air became fiery with the sense of impending tempest.

Suspense, excitement and the overawing aspect of the sky kept the crowd in a whispering stillness.

Theirry heard the dancing girl laugh; she was thrust up close against him in the press, and, although tall, was almost smothered by a number of Frankish soldiers pressing together in front of her.

"I cannot see," she said —"not even the window —"

He, with an instinct to assist her, and an impulse to use his strength, caught her round the waist and lifted her up.

For a second her breast touched his; he felt her heart beating violently behind her thin robe, and an extraordinary sensation took possession of him.

Occasioned by the touch of her, the sense of her in his arms, there was communicated, as if from her heart to his, a high and rapturous passion; it was the most terrible and the most splendid feeling he had ever known, at once an agony and a delight such as he had never dreamed of before; unconsciously he gave an exclamation and loosened his hold. She slipped to the ground with a stifled and miserable cry.

"Let me alone," he said wildly. "Let me alone

"Who are you?" he whispered excitedly, and tried to catch hold of her again; but the great ape came between them, and the seething crowd roughly pushed him.

Cardinal Maria Orsini had stepped out on to one of the balconies of the Vatican; he looked over the expectant crowd, then up at the black and angry sky, and seemed for a moment to hesitate.

When he spoke his words fell into a great stillness.

"The Sacred College has elected a successor to St. Peter in the person of Louis of Den-dermonde, Abbot of the Brethren of the Sacred Heart in Paris, Bishop of Ostia and Cardinal Caprarola, who will ascend the Papal throne under the name of Michael II."

He finished; the cries of triumph from the Romans, the yells of rage from the Franks were drowned in a sudden and awful peal of thunder; the lightning darted across the black heavens and fell on the Vatican and Castel San' Angelo. The clouds were rent in two behind the temple of Mars the Avenger, and a thunderbolt fell with a hideous crash into the Forum of Augustus.

Theirry, whipped with terror, turned with the frightened crowd to flee . . . he heard the dancing girl laugh, and tried to snatch at her orange garments, but she swept by him and was lost in the surge.

Rome quivered under the onslaught of the thunder, and the lightning alone lit the murky, hot gloom.

"The reign of Antichrist has begun!" shrieked Theirry, and laughed insanely.

# Chapter 5

## The Pope

The chamber in the Vatican was so dimly, richly lit with jewelled and deep-coloured lamps that at first Theirry thought himself alone.

He looked round and saw silver walls hung with tapestries of violet and gold; pillars with columns of sea-green marble and capitals of shining mosaic supported a roof encrusted with jasper and jade; the floor, of Numidian marble, was spread with Indian silk carpets; here and there stood crystal bowls of roses, white and crimson, fainting in the close, sweet air.

At the far end of the room was a dais hung with brocade in which flowers and animals shone in gold and silver on a purple ground; gilt steps, carved and painted, led up to a throne on the dais, and Theirry, as his eyes became used to the wine-coloured gloom, saw that some one sat there; some one so splendidly robed and so still that it seemed more like one of the images Theirry had seen worshipped in Constantinople than a human being.

He shivered.

Presently he could discern intense eyes looking at him out of a dazzle of dark gold and shimmering shadowed colours.

Michael II moved in his seat.

"Again do you not know me?" he asked in a low tone.

"You sent for me," said Theirry; to himself his voice sounded hoarse and unnatural. "At last —"

"At last?"

"I have been waiting — you have been Pope thirty days, and never have you given me a sign."

"Is thirty days so long?"

Theirry came nearer the enthroned being.

"You have done nothing for me — you spoke of favours."

Silver, gold and purple shook together as Michael II turned in his gorgeous chair.

"Favours!" he echoed. "You are the only man in Christendom who would stand in my presence; the Emperor kneels to kiss my foot."

"The Emperor does not know," shuddered Theirry; "but I do — and knowing, I cannot kneel to you . . . Ah, God! — how can you dare it?"

The Pope's soft voice came from the shadows. "Your moods change — first this, then that; what humour are you in now, Theirry of Dendermonde; would you still be Emperor?"

Theirry put his hand to his brow.

"Yea, you know it — why do you torture me with suspense, with waiting? If Evil is to be my master, let me serve him . . . and be rewarded."

Michael II answered swiftly.

"I was not the one to be faithless to our friendship, nor shall I now shrink from serving you, at any cost — be you but true."

"In what way can I be false?" asked Theirry bitterly. "I, a thing at your mercy?"

The Pope held back the blossom-strewn brocade so that he could see the other's face. "I ask of you to let Jacobea of Martzburg be."

Theirry flushed.

"How ye have always hated her! . . . since I came to Rome I have seen her the once."

The Pope's smooth pale face showed a stain of red from the dim beams of one of the splendid lamps; Theirry observed it as he leant forward.

"She did not marry her steward," he said.

The Pope's eyes narrowed.

"Ye have been at the pains to discover that?"

Theirry laughed mournfully.

"You have won! you, sitting where you sit now, can afford to mock at me; at my love, at my hope — both of which I placed once at stake on — her — and lost! . . . and lost! Ten years ago — but having again seen her, sometimes I must think of her, and that she was not vile after all, but only trapped by you, as I have been . . . Sebastian went to Palestine, and she has gone unwed."

The Pope gave a quick sigh and bit his lip.

"I will make you Emperor," he said. "But that woman shall not be your Empress." Again Theirry laughed.

"Did I love her even, which I do not — I would put her gladly aside to sit on the Imperial throne! — Come, I have dallied long enough on the brink of devilry — let me sin grandly now, and be grandly paid!"

Michael II gave so quick a breath the jewels on his breast scattered coloured light.

"Come nearer to me," he commanded, "and take my hand — as you used to, in Frankfort . . . I am always Dirk to you — you who never cared for me, hated me, I think — oh, the traitors our hearts are, neither God nor devil is so fierce to fight!"

Theirry approached the gold steps; the Pope leant down and gave him his cool white hand, heavy with gemmed rings, and looked intently into his eyes.

"When they announced your election — how the storm smote the city," whispered Theirry fearfully; "were you not daunted?"

The Pope withdrew his hand.

"I was not in the Conclave," he said in a strange tone. "I lay sick in my villa — as for the storm —"

"It has not lifted since," breathed Theirry; "day and night have the clouds hung over Rome — is not there, after all, a God?"

"Silence!" cried the Pope in a troubled voice.

"You would be Emperor of the West, would you not? — let us speak of that."

Theirry leant against the arm of the throne and stared with an awful fascination into the other's face.

"Ay, let us speak of that," he answered wildly; "can all your devilries accomplish it? It is common talk in Rome that you secured your election by Frankish influence because you vowed to league with Balthasar — they say you are his ally —"

The dark intense eyes of Michael II glittered and glowed.

"Nevertheless I will cast him down and set you in his place — he comes today to ask my aid against Lombardy and Bohemia; and therefore have I sent for you that you may overhear this audience, and see how I mate and checkmate an Emperor for your sake."

As he spoke, he pointed to the other end of the room where hung a sombre and rich curtain. "Conceal yourself — behind that tapestry — and listen carefully to what I say, and you will understand how I may humble Balthasar and shake him from his throne."

Theirry, not joyous nor triumphant, but agitated and trembling with a horrible excitement, crept across the room and passed silently behind the arras.

As the long folds shook into place again the Pope touched a bell.

Paolo Orsini entered.

"Admit the Emperor."

The secretary withdrew; there was a soft sound in the ante-chamber, the voices of priests.

Michael II put his hand to his heart and fetched two or three quick panting breaths; his full lips curved to a strange smile, and a stranger thought was behind it; a thought that, if expressed, would not have been understood even by Theirry of Dendermonde, who of all men knew most of his Holiness.

This it was —

"Did ever lady meet her lord like this before, or like this use him to advance her love!"

A heavy tread sounded without, and the Emperor advanced into the splendid glooms of the audience-chamber.

He was bare-headed, and at sight of the awe-inspiring figure, went on his knees at the foot of the dais.

Michael II looked at him in silence; the silver door was closed, and they were alone, save for the unseen listener behind the arras.

At last the Pope said slowly —

"Arise, my son."

The Emperor stood erect, showing his magnificent height and bearing; he wore bronze-hued armour, scaled like a dragon's breast, the high gold Imperial buskins, and an immense scarlet mantle that flowed behind him; his thick yellow hair hung in heavy curls on to his shoulders, and his enormous sword made a clatter against his armour as he moved.

Theirry, cautiously drawing aside the curtain to observe, dug his nails into his palms with bitter envy.

Behold the man who had once been his companion — little more than his equal, and now — an Emperor!

"You desired an audience of us," said the Pope. "And some tedium may be spared, for we can well guess what you have to say."

A look of relief came into Balthasar's great blue eyes; he was no politician; the Empress, whose wits alone had kept him ten years on a throne, had trembled for this audience.

"Your Holiness knows that it is my humble desire to form a firm alliance between Rome and Germany. I have ruled both long enough to prove myself neither weak nor false, I have ever been a faithful servant of Holy Church —"

The Pope interrupted.

"And now you would ask her help against your rebellious subjects?"

"Yea, your Holiness."

Michael II smiled.

"On what right does your Grace presume when you ask us to aid you in steadying a trembling throne?"

Balthasar flushed, and came clumsily to the point.

"I was assured, Holy Father, of your friendliness before the election — the Empress —"
Again the Pope cut him short.

"Cardinal Caprarola was not the Vicegerent of Christ, the High Priest of Christendom, as we are now — and those whom Louis of Dendermonde knew, become as nothing before the Pope of Rome, in whose estimate all men are the same."

Balthasar's spirit rose at this haughty speech; his face turned crimson, and he savagely caught at one of his yellow curls.

"Your Holiness can have no object in refusing my alliance," he answered. "Sylvester crowned me with his own hands, and I always lived in friendship with him — he aided me with troops when the Lombards rebelled against their suzerain, and Suabia he placed under an interdict —"

"We are not Sylvester," said the Pope haughtily — —"nor accountable for his doings; as you may show yourself the obedient son of the Church so may we support you — otherwise! — we can denounce as we can uphold, pull down as we can raise up, and it wants but little, Balthasar of Courtrai, to shake your throne from under you."

The Emperor bit his lip, and the scales of his mail gleamed as they rose with his heavy breathing; he knew that if the power of the Vatican was placed on the side of his enemies he was ruined.

"In what way have I offended your Holiness?" he asked, with what humility he could.

The fair young face of Michael II was flushed and proud in expression; the red curls surrounding the tonsure fell across his smooth forehead; his red lips were sternly set and his heavy brows frowned.

"Ye have offended Heaven, for whom we stand," he answered. "And until by penitence ye assoil your soul we must hold you outcast from the mercies of the Church."

"Tell me my sins," said Balthasar hoarsely. "And what I can do to blot them out — masses, money, lands —"

The Pope made a scornful movement with his little hand.

"None of these can make your peace with God and us — one thing only can avail there."

"Tell it me," cried the Emperor eagerly. "If it be a crusade, surely I will go — after Lombardy is subdued."

The Pope flashed a quick glance over him. "We want no knight-errantry in the East; we demand this — that you put away the woman whom you call your wife."

Balthasar stared with dilating eyes.

"Saint Joris guard us!" he muttered; "the woman whom I call my wife!"

"Ysabeau, first wedded to the man whom you succeeded."

Balthasar's hand made an instinctive movement towards his sword.

"I do not understand your Holiness."

The Pope turned in his chair so that the lamplight made his robe one bright purple sheen. "Come here, my lord."

The Emperor advanced to the gold steps; a slim fair hand was held out to him, holding, between finger and thumb, a ring set with a deep red stone.

"Do you know this, my lord?" The Pope's brilliant eyes were fixed on him with an intent and terrible expression.

Balthasar of Courtrai looked at the ring; round the bezel two coats of arms were delicately engraved in the soft red gold.

"Why," he said in a troubled way, "I know the ring — yea, it was made many years ago"

"And given to a woman.

"Certes — yea —"

"It is a wedding ring."

Again the Emperor assented, his blue eyes darkened and questioning.

"The woman to whom in your name it was given still lives."

"Ursula of Rooselaare!" cried Balthasar.

"Yea, Ursula of Rooselaare, your wife."

"My first wife who died before I had seen her, Holiness," stammered the Emperor.

The Pope's strange handsome face was hard and merciless; he held the wedding ring out on his open palm and looked from it to Balthasar.

"She did not die — neither in the convent, as to your shame you know, nor in the house of Master Lukas."

Balthasar could not speak; he saw that this man knew what he had considered was a close secret of his own heart alone.

"Who told you she was dead?" continued the Pope. "A certain youth, who, for his own ends, I think, lied, a wicked youth he was, and he died in Frankfort for compassing the death of the late Emperor — or escaped that end by firing his house, the tale grows faint with years; 'twas he who told you Ursula of Rooselaare was dead; he even showed you her grave — and you were content to take his word — and she was content to be silent."

"Oh, Christus!" cried the Emperor. "Oh, Saint Joris! — — but, holy father — this thing is impossible!" He wrung his hands together and beat his mailed breast. "From whom had you this tale?"

"From Ursula of Rooselaare."

"It cannot be . . . why was she silent all these years? why did she allow me to take Ysabeau to wife?"

A wild expression crossed the Pope's face; he looked beyond the Emperor with deep soft eyes. "Because she loved another man."

A pause fell for a second, then Michael II spoke again.

"I think, too, she something hated you who had failed her, and scorned her — there was her father also, who died shamefully by Ysabeau's command; she meant, I take it, to revenge that upon the Empress, and now, perhaps, her chance has come."

Balthasar gave a dry sob.

"Where is this woman who has so influenced your Holiness against me? An impostor! do not listen to her!"

"She speaks the truth, as God and devils know!" flashed the Pope. "And we, with all the weight of Holy Church, will support her in the maintenance of her just rights; we also have no love for this Eastern woman who slew her lord."

"Nay, that is false" — Balthasar ground his teeth. "I know some said it of her — but it is a lie." "This to me!" cried the Pope. "Beware how ye anger God's Vicegerent."

The Emperor quivered, and put his hand to his brow.

"I bend my neck for your Holiness to step on — so you do not ask me to listen to evil of the Empress."

The Pope rose with a gleam of silk and a sparkle of jewels.

"Ysabeau is not Empress, nor your wife; her son is not your heir, and you must presently part with both of them or suffer the extremity of our wrath — yea, the woman shall ye give into the hands of the executioner to suffer for the death of Melchoir, and the child shall ye turn away from you — and with pains and trouble shall ye search for Ursula of Rooselaare, and finding her, cause her to be acknowledged your wife and Empress of the West. That she lives I know, the rest is for you."

The Emperor drew himself up and folded his arms on his breast.

"This is all I have to say," added the Pope. "And on those terms alone will I secure to you the throne."

"I have but one answer," said Balthasar. "And it would be the same did I deliver it in the face of God — that while I live and have breath to speak, I shall proclaim Ysabeau and none other as my wife, and our son as an Empress's son, and my heir and successor; kingdom and even life may your Holiness despoil me of — but neither the armies of the earth nor the angels of heaven shall take from me these two — this my answer to your Holiness."

The Pope resumed his seat.

"Ye dare to defy me," he said. "Well — ye are a foolish man to set yourself against Heaven; go back and live in sin and wait the judgment."

Balthasar's flesh crept and quivered, but he held his head high, even though the Pope's words opened the prospect of a sure hell.

"Your Holiness has spoken, so also have I," he answered. "I take my leave."

Michael II gazed at him in silence as he bent his head and backed towards the silver door.

No other word passed between Pope and Emperor; the gleaming portals opened; the mail of Balthasar's retinue clinked without, and then soft silence fell on the richly lit room as the door was delicately closed.

"Theirry."

The Pope rose and descended from the dais; the dark arras was lifted cautiously, and Theirry crept into the room.

Michael II stood at the foot of the golden steps; despite his magnificent and flowing draperies, he looked very young and slender.

"Well," he asked, and his eyes were triumphant. "Stand I not in a fair way to cast down the Emperor?"

Theirry moistened his lips.

"Yea — how dared you! — to use the thunderbolts of heaven for such ends!"

The Pope smiled.

"The thunders of heaven may be used to any ends by those who can wield them." "What you said was false?" whispered Theirry, questioning.

The jewelled light flickered over the Pope's face.

"Nay, it was true, Ursula of Rooselaare lives."

"Ye never told me that — in the old days!"

"Maybe I did not know — she lives, and she is in Rome;" he caught hold of the robe across his breast as he spoke, and both voice and eyes were touched with weariness.

"This is a curious tale," answered Theirry in a confused manner. "She must be a strange woman."

"She is a strange woman."

"I would like to see her — who is it that she loves?"

The Pope showed pale; he moved slowly across the room with his head bent.

"A man for whose sake she puts her very life in jeopardy," he said in a low passionate voice. "A man I think, who is unworthy of her."

"She is in Rome?" pondered Theirry.

The Pope lifted an arras that concealed an inner door.

"The first move is made," he said. "Farewell now — I will acquaint you of the progress of your fortunes;" he gave a slight, queer smile; "as for Ursula of Rooselaare, ye have seen her —" "Seen her?"

"Yea; she wears the disguise of a masked dancer in orange."

With that he pointed Theirry to the concealed doorway, and turning, left him.

# Chapter 6

## San Giovanni in Laterano

In the palace on the Aventine, Balthasar stood at a window looking over Rome.

The clouds that had hung for weeks above the city cast a dull yellow glow over marble and stone; the air was hot and sultry, now and then thunder rolled over the Vatican and a flash of lightning revealed the Angel on Castel San Angelo poised above the muddy waters of the Tiber.

A furious, utter dread and terror gripped Balthasar's heart; days had passed since his defiance of the Pope and he had heard no more of his daring, but he was afraid, afraid of Michael II, of the Church, of Heaven behind it — afraid of this woman who had risen from the dead . . .

He knew the number of his enemies and with what difficulty he held Rome, he guessed that the Pope intended his downfall and to put another in his place — but not this almost certain ruin disturbed him day and night, no — the thought that the Church might throw him out and consign his soul to smoky hell.

Bravely enough had he dared the Pope at the time when his heart was hot within him, but in the days that followed his very soul had fainted to think what he had done; he could not sleep nor rest while waiting for outraged Heaven to strike; he darkly believed the continual storm brooding over Rome to be omen of God's wrath with him.

His trouble was the greater because it was secret, the first that, since they had been wedded, he had concealed from Ysabeau. As this touched her, in an infamous and horrible manner, he could neither breathe it to her nor any other, and the loneliness of his miserable apprehension was an added torture.

This morning he had interviewed the envoys from Germany and his chamberlain; tales of anarchy and turmoil in Rome, of rebellion in Germany had further distracted him; now alone in his little marble cabinet, he stared across the gorgeous, storm-wrapt city.

Not long alone; he heard some one quietly enter, and because he knew who it was, he would not turn his head.

She came up to him and laid her hand on his plain brown doublet.

"Balthasar," she said, "will you never tell me what it is that sits so heavily on your heart?" He commanded his voice to answer.

"Nothing, Ysabeau — nothing."

The Empress gave a long, quivering sigh.

"This is the first time you have not trusted me."

He turned his face; white and wan it was of late, with heavy circles under the usually joyous eyes; she winced to see it.

"Oh, my lord!" she cried passionately. "No anguish is so bitter when shared!"

He took her hand and pressed it warmly to his breast; he tried to smile.

"Certes, you know my troubles, Ysabeau, the discontent, the factions — matter enough to make any man grave."

"And the Pope," she said, raising her eyes to his; "most of all it is the Pope."

"His Holiness is no friend to me," said the Emperor in a low voice. "Oh, Ysabeau, we were deceived to aid him to the tiara."

She shuddered.

"I persuaded you . . . blame me . . . I was mad. I set your enemy in authority."

"Nay!" he answered in a great tenderness. "You are to blame for nothing, you, sweet Ysabeau."

He raised the hand he held to his lips; in the thought that he suffered for her sake was a sweet recompense.

She coloured, then paled.

"What will he do?" she asked. "What will he do?"

"Nay — I know not." His fair face overclouded again.

She saw it and terror shook her.

"He said more to you that day than you will tell me!" she cried. "You fear something that you will not reveal to me!"

The Emperor made an attempt at lightness of speech.

"He is a poor knight who tells his lady of his difficulties," he said. "I cannot come crying to you like a child."

She turned to him the soft frail beauty of her face and took his great sword hand between hers. "I am very jealous of you, Balthasar," she said thickly, "jealous that you should shut me out — — from anything."

"You will know soon enough," he answered in a hoarse voice. "But never from me." The tears lay in her violet eyes as she fondled his band.

"Are we not as strong as this man, Balthasar!"

"Nay," he shivered, "for he has the Church behind him — tomorrow, we shall see him again — I dread tomorrow."

"Why?" she asked quickly. "To-morrow is the Feast of the Assumption and we go to the Basilica."

"Yea, and the Pope will be there in his power and I must kneel humbly before him — yet not that alone —"

"Balthasar! what do you fear?"

He breathed heavily.

"Nothing — a folly, an ugly presentiment, of late I have slept so little. — Why is he quiet? — He meditates something."

His blue eyes widened with fear, he put the Empress gently from him.

"Take no heed, sweet, I am only weary and your dear solicitude unnerves me — I must go pray Saint Joris to remember me."

"The Saints!" she cried hotly. "A knife would serve us better could we but thrust it into this Caprarola — who is he, this man who dares menace us?"

The childishly fair face was drawn with anxious love and bitter fury; the purple eyes were wet and brilliant, under her long robe of dull yellow samite her bosom strove painfully with her breath.

The Emperor turned uneasily aside.

"The storm," he said, raising his voice above a whisper with an effort. "I think that it oppresses me and makes me fearful — how many days — how many days, Ysabeau, since we have seen a cloudless sky!"

He moved away from her hastily and left the room with an abrupt step.

The Empress crouched against the marble columns that supported the window, and as her unseeing eyes gazed across the shadowed city a look of cunning calculation, of fierce rage came into her face; it was many years since that sinister expression had marred her loveliness, for, since her second marriage she had met no man who threatened her or menaced her path or the Emperor's as now did his Holiness, Michael II.

She half suspected him of having broken his vile bargain with her, she rightly thought that nothing save the revelation of his first wife's existence could have so subdued and troubled Balthasar's joyous courage and hopeful heart; she cursed herself that she had been a frightened fool to be startled into making a pact she might have known the Cardinal would not keep; she was bitterly furious that she had helped to set him in the position he now turned against her, it had been better had she refused to buy his silence at such a price — better that Cardinal Caprarola should have denounced her than that the Pope should use this knowledge to unseat her husband.

She had never imagined that she had a friend in Michael II, but she had not imagined him so callous, cruel and false as to take her bribe and still betray her — even though the man had revealed himself to her for what he was, as ambitious, unscrupulous and hard; she had not thought he would so shamelessly be false to his word.

Angry scorn filled her heart when she considered the reputation this man had won in his youth — that indeed he still bore with some — yet it could not but stir her admiration to reflect what it must have cost a man of the Pope's nature to play the ascetic saint for so many years. But his piety had been well rewarded — the poor Flemish youth sat in the Vatican now, lord of her husband's fortunes and her own honour.

Then she fell to pondering over the story of Ursula of Rooselaare, wondering where she was, where she had been these years, and how she had met Cardinal Caprarola . . . The Empress dwelt on these things till her head ached; impatiently she thrust wider open the stained glass casement and leant from the window.

But there was no breeze abroad to cool her burning brow, and on all sides the sky was heavy with clouds over which the summer lightning played.

Ysabeau turned her eyes from the threatening prospect, and with a stifled groan began pacing up and down the tesselated floor of the cabinet.

She was interrupted by the entry of a lady tall and fair, leading a beautiful child by the hand. Jacobea of Martzburg and Ysabeau's son.

"We seek for his Grace," smiled the lady. "Wencelaus wishes to say his Latin lesson, and to tell the tale of the three Dukes and the sack of gold that he has lately learnt."

The Empress gave her son a quick glance.

"You shall tell it to me, Wencelaus — my lord is not here."

The boy, golden, large and glorious to look upon, scowled at her.

"Will not tell it you or any woman." Ysabeau answered in a kind of bitter gentleness. "Be not too proud, Wencelaus," and the thought of what his future might be made her eyes fierce.

The Prince tossed his yellow curls. "I want my father." Jacobea, in pity of the Empress's distracted bearing, tried to pacify him.

"His Grace cannot see you now — but presently —" He shook his hand free of hers. "Ye cannot put me off — my father said an hour before the Angelus;" his blue eyes were angry and defiant, but his lips quivered.

The Empress crushed back the wild misery of her thoughts, and caught the child's embroidered yellow sleeve.

"Certes, ye shall see him," she said quietly, "if he promised you — I think he is in the oratory, we will wait at the door until he come forth."

The boy kissed her hand, and, the shadow passed from his lovely face.

Jacobea saw the Empress look down on him with a desperate and heart-broken expression; she wondered at the anguish revealed to her in that second, but she was neither disturbed nor touched; her own heart had been broken so long ago that all emotions were but names to her.

The Empress dismissed her with a glance.

Jacobea left the palace, mounted the little Byzantine chariot with the blue curtains and drove to the church of San Giovanni in Laterano. She went there every day to hear a mass sung for the soul of one who had died long ago.

A large portion of her immense fortune had gone in paying for masses and candles for the repose of Sybilla, one time wife of Sebastian her steward; if gold could send the murdered woman there Jacobea had opened to her the doors of Paradise.

In her quiet monotonous life in a strange land, caring for none, and by none cared for, with a dead heart in her bosom and leaden feet walking heavily the road to the grave, this Sybilla had come to be with Jacobea the most potent thing she knew.

Neither Balthasar nor the Empress, nor any of their Court were so real to her as the steward's dead wife.

She was as certain of her features, her bearing, the manner of her dress, as if she saw her daily; there was no face so familiar to her as the pale countenance of Sybilla with the wide brows and heavy red hair; she saw no ghost, she was not frightened by dreams nor visions, but the thought of Sybilla was continuous.

For ten years she had not spoken her name save in a whisper to the priest, nor had she in any way referred to her; by the people among whom she moved this woman was utterly forgotten, but in Jacobea's bed-chamber stood a samite cushion exquisitely worked with a scarlet lily, and Jacobea looked at it more often than at anything else in the world.

She did not regard this image she had created with terror or dread, with any shuddering remorse or aversion; it was to her a constant companion whom she accepted almost as she accepted herself.

As she stepped from the chariot at the door of San Giovanni in Laterano the gathering thunder rolled round the hills of Rome; she pondered a moment on the ominous clouds that had hung so long over the city that the people began to murmur that they were under God's displeasure, and passed through the dark portals into the dimly illuminated church.

She turned to a little side chapel and knelt on a purple cushion worn by her knees.

Mechanically she listened as the priest murmured over the mass, hurrying it a little that it might not interfere with the Angelus, mechanically she made the responses and rose when it was over with a calm face.

She had done this every day for nine years. There were a few people in the church, kneeling for the Angelus; Jacobea joined them and fixed her eyes on the altar, where a strong purple light glowed and flickered, bringing out points of gold in the moulding of the ancient arches.

A deep hush held the scented stillness; the scattered bent figures were dark and motionless against the mystic clouds of incense and the soft bright lights.

Monks in long brown habits came and stood in the chancel; the bell struck the hour, and young novices entered singing —

"Angelus Domini nuntiavit Mariae, et concepit de Spiritu Sancto."

The monks knelt and folded their hands on their breasts; the response that still seemed very sweet to Jacobea arose.

"Ave Maria, gratia plena —"

A side door near Jacobea opened' softly and a man stepped into the church . . . Now the priest was speaking.

"Ecce ancilla Domini.

fiat mihi secundum verbum tuum."

A strong sense that the new-comer was observing her made Jacobea turn, almost unconsciously, her head towards him as she repeated the "Ave Maria."

A tall richly-dressed man was gazing at her intently; his face was in shadow, but she could see long pearls softly gleam in his ears.

"Et Verbum caro factum est, et habitavit in nobis."

The deep voices of the monks and the subdued tones of the worshippers again answered; Jacobea could distinguish the faltering words of the man near her.

"Ora pro nobs, Sancta Del Genitrix."

Jacobea bent her head in her hands, as she replied —

"Ut digni efficiamur promissionibus Christi."

Priests and novices left the church, the monks filed out and the bent figures rose. The man stepped from the shadows as Jacobea rose to her feet, and their eyes met. "Ah — you!" said Jacobea; she had her hands on her breviary as he had seen them long ago.

She was so little moved by meeting him that she began to clasp the ivory covers, bending her head to do so.

"You remember me?" asked Theirry faintly.

"I have forgotten nothing," she answered calmly. "Why do you seek to recall yourself to me?" "I cannot see you and let you pass."

She looked at him; it was a different face from the one he had known, though little changed in line or colour.

"You must hate me," he faltered.

The words did not touch her.

"Are you free of the devils?" she asked, and crossed herself.

Theirry winced; he remembered that she believed Dirk was dead, that she thought of the Pope as a holy man . . .

"Forgive me," he murmured.

"For what?"

"Ah — that I did not understand you to be always a saintly woman."

Jacobea laughed sadly.

"You must not speak of the past, though you may think of nothing else, even as I do — we might have been friends once, but the Devil was too strong for us."

At that moment Thierry hated Dirk passionately; he felt he could have been happy with this woman, and with her only in the whole world, and he loathed Dirk for making it impossible.

"Well," said Jacobea, in the same unmoved tone, "I must go back — farewell, sir."

Theirry strove with speech in vain; as she moved towards the door he came beside her, his beautiful face white and eager.

Then, by a common impulse, both stopped.

Round one of the dark glittering pillars a brilliant figure flashed into the rich light. The masked dancer in orange.

She stepped up to Theirry and laid her fingers on his scarlet sleeve.

"How does Theirry of Dendermonde keep his word!" she mocked, and her eyes gleamed from their holes; "is your heart of a feather's weight that it flutters this way and that with every breath of air?"

"What does that mean?" asked Jacobea, as the man flushed and shuddered. "And what does she here in this attire?"

The dancer turned to her swiftly

"What of one who drags his weary limbs beneath a Syrian sun in penitence for a deed ye urged him to?" she said in the same tone.

Jacobea stepped back with a quick cry, and Theirry seized the dancer's arm.

"Begone," he said threateningly. "I know you, or who you feign to be."

She answered between laughter and fear.

"Let me go — I have not hurt you; why are you angry, my brave knight?"

At the sound of her voice that she in no way lowered, a monk came forward and sternly ordered her from the church.

"Why?" she asked. "I am masked, holy father, so cannot prove a temptation to the faithful!"

"Leave the church," he commanded, "and if you would worship here come in a fitting spirit and a fitting dress."

The dancer laughed.

"So I am flung out of the house of God — well, sir and sweet lady, will you come to the Mass at the Basilica tomorrow? — nay, do, it will be worth beholding — the Basilica tomorrow! I shall be there."

With that she darted before them and slipped from the church.

Man and woman shuddered and knew not why.

A peal of thunder rolled, the walls of the church shook, and an image of the Virgin was hurled to the marble pavement and shivered into fragments.

# Chapter 7

## The Vengeance of Michael ii

From every church and convent in Rome the bells rang out; it was the Feast of the Assumption and holiday in the city.

Strange, heavy clouds still obscured the sky, and intermittent thunder echoed in the distance. The Basilica of St. Peter was crowded from end to end; the bewildering splendour of walls, ceiling and columns was lit by thousands of wax tapers and coloured lamps; part of the church had been hung with azure and silver; the altar steps were covered in cloth of gold, the altar itself almost hidden with lilies; the various gleaming hues of the marble, orange, rose, pink, mauve, grey and white, the jewel-like sparkle of the mosaic capitals, the ivory carving on the rood screen, the silver arch before the high altar, the silk and satin banners of the church resting here and there before the walls, all combined into one soft yet burning magnificence.

The vast congregation all knelt upon the marble floor, save the Emperor and his wife, who sat under a violet canopy placed opposite the pulpit.

Balthasar wore the imperial purple and buskins; round his brows was the circlet that meant dominion of the Latin world, but his comely face was pale and anxious and his blue eyes troubled. Ysabeau, seated close beside him, sparkled with gems from her throat to her feet; her pale locks, twisted with pearls, hung over her bosom; she wore a high crown of emeralds and her mantle was cloth of silver.

Between them, on a lower step of the dais, stood their little son, gleaming in white satin and overawed by the glitter and the silence.

Surrounding the throne were ladies, courtiers, Frankish knights, members of the Council, German Margraves, Italian nobles, envoys from France, Spain, and resplendent Greeks from the Court of Basil.

Theirry, kneeling in the press, distinguished the calm face of Jacobea of Martzburg among the dames of the Empress's retinue; but he sought in vain through the immense and varied crowd for the dancer in orange.

A faint chant rose from the sacristy, jewelled crosses showed above the heads of the multitude as the monks entered holding them aloft, the fresh voices of the choristers came nearer, acolytes took their places round the altar, and the blue clouds of incense floated over the hushed multitude.

The bells ceased.

The rise and fall of singing filled the Basilica.

Cardinal Orsini, followed by a number of priests, went slowly down the aisle towards the open bronze doors.

His brilliant dalmatica shivered into gleaming light as he moved.

At the door he paused.

The Pontifical train was arriving in a gorgeous dazzle of colour and motion.

Michael II stepped from a gilt car drawn by four white oxen, whose polished horns were wreathed with roses white and red.

Preceded by Cardinals, the vivid tints of whose silk robes burnt in the golden brightness of the Basilica, the Pope passed down the aisle, while the congregation crouched low on their knees and hid their faces.

Emperor and Empress rose; he looked at his son, but she at the Pontiff, who took no heed of either.

Monks, priests and novices moved away from the high altar, where the rows upon rows of candles shone like stars against the sparkling, incense-laden air.

He passed to his gold and ivory seat, and the Cardinals took their places beside him.

Ysabeau, as she resumed her place beside her lord, gazed across the silent, kneeling crowd at Michael II.

His chasuble was alive with the varying hues of jewels, the purple and crimson train of his robes spread to right and left along the altar steps, the triple crown gave forth showers of light from its rubies and diamonds, while the red hair of the wearer caught the candle-glow and shone like a halo round his pale calm face, so curiously delicate of feature to be able to express such resolution, such pride.

His under-garment of white satin was so thickly sewn with pearls that the stuff was hardly visible, his fingers so covered with huge and brilliant rings that they looked of an unnatural slenderness by contrast; he held a crozier encrusted with rubies that darted red fire, and carbuncles flashed on his gold shoes.

The beautiful dark eyes that always held the expression of some passion for ever surging up, for ever held in before reaching expression, were fixed steadily on the bronze doors that now closed the church.

A little tremor of thunder filled the stillness, then the fair, faint chant of the boys arose.

"Gaudeamus omnes in Domino, diem festum celebrantes

Sub honore Beatae

Mariae Virginis, . . . "

Ysabeau murmured the words under her breath; none in the devout multitude with more sincerity.

As the notes quivered into silence Cardinal Orsini murmured a prayer, to which a thousand responses were whispered fervently.

And again the thunder made sombre echo. The Empress put her hand over her eyes; her jewels seemed so heavy they must drag her from the throne, the crown galled her brow; the little Wencelaus stood motionless, a bright colour in his cheeks, his eyes brilliant with excitement; now and then the Emperor looked at him in a secretive, piteous manner.

There was an involuntary stir among the people as the rich voices of the men took up the singing at the end of the epistle, a movement of joy, of pleasure in the triumphant music.

"Alleluia, alleluia.

Assumpta est Maria in Coelum; Gaudet exercitus Angelorum. Alleluia."

Then the Pope moved, descended slowly from the dais and mounted the steps of the high altar, his train upheld by two Archbishops.

Emperor and Empress knelt with the rest as he performed the office of the mass; an intense stillness held the rapt assembly, but as he turned and displayed the Host, before the vast multitude who hid their eyes, as he held it like a captured star above the hushed splendour of the altar, a crash of thunder shook the very foundations of the church, and the walls shivered as if mighty forces beat on them without.

Michael II, the only man erect in the crouching multitude smiled slowly as he replaced the Eucharist; lightning' darted through the high coloured windows and quivered a moment before it was absorbed in the rich lights.

The voices of the choir rose with a melancholy beauty.

"Kyrie eleison, Christe eleison, Kyrie eleison."

The Pope turned to the altar; again the thunder rolled, but his low, steady voice was heard distinctly chanting the "Gloria in excelsis Deo" with the choir.

At the finish Cardinal Orsini took up the prayers, and a half-muffled response came from the crowd.

"Gloria tibi, Domine."

Every head was raised, every right hand made the sacred sign.

"Laus tibi, Christe."

The Pope blessed the multitude and returned to his seat.

Then as Emperor and Empress rose from their knees a soft, bright sound of movement filled the Basilica; Ysabeau put out her hand and caught hold of her husband's.

"Who is this?" she asked in a whisper.

He turned his eyes in the direction of her gaze.

Down the chancel came a tall monk in the robe of the Order of the Black Penitents; his arms were folded, his hands hidden in his sleeves, his deep cowl cast his face into utter shadow.

"I thought Cardinal Colonna preached," whispered Balthasar fearfully, as the monk ascended the pulpit. "I know not this man."

Ysabeau looked at the Pope, who sat motionless in his splendour, his hands resting on the arms of the gold chair, his gaze riveted on the black figure of the monk in the glittering pulpit; a faint smile was on his lips, a faint colour in his cheeks, and Ysabeau's hand tightened on the fingers of her lord.

The monk stood for a moment motionless, evidently contemplating the multitude from the depth of his hood; Balthasar thought he gazed at him, and shivered.

A strange sense of suspense filled the church, even the priests and Cardinals about the altar glanced curiously at the figure in the pulpit; some women began to sob under the influence of nameless and intense excitement.

The monk drew from his sleeve a parchment from which swung a mighty seal, slowly he unfurled it; the Empress crouched closer to Balthasar.

The monk began to speak, and both to Ysabeau and her husband the voice was familiar — a voice long silent in death.

"In the name of Michael II, servant of servants of God and Vicegerent of Christ, I herewith pronounce the anathema over Balthasar of Courtrai, Emperor of the West, over Ysabeau, born Marozia Porphyrogentris, over their son, Wencelaus, over their followers, servants and hosts! I herewith expel them from the pale of Holy Church, and curse them as heretics!

"I forbid any to offer them shelter, food or help, I hurl on their heads the wrath of God and the hatred of man, I forbid any to attend their sick-bed, to receive their confession or to bury their bodies!

"I cut asunder the ties that bind the Latin people in obedience to them, and I lay under an interdict any person, village, town or state that succours or aids them against our wrath! May they and their children and their children's children be blighted and cursed in life and in death, may they taste misery and desolation on the earth before they go to everlasting torment in hell!"

And now the cowled monk caught up one of the candles that lit the pulpit, and held it aloft.

"May their race perish with them and their memories be swallowed in oblivion — thus! As I extinguish this flame may the hand of God extinguish them!"

He cast the candle on to the marble floor beneath the pulpit, the flame was immediately dashed out, a slow smoke curled an instant and vanished.

"For Balthasar of Courtrai cherishes a murderess on the throne, and until he cast her forth and receive his true wife this anathema rests upon his head!"

Emperor and Empress listened, holding each other's hands and staring at the monk; as he ended, and while the awe of utter fear held the assembly numb, Ysabeau rose . . .

But at that same instant the monk tossed back his cowl and revealed the stern, pale features of Melchoir of Brabant, crowned with the imperial diadem . . .

A frenzied shriek broke from the woman, and she fell across the steps of the throne; her crown slipped from her fair head and dazzled on the pavement.

Groaning in anguish Balthasar stooped to raise her up . . . when he again looked at the pulpit it was empty.

Ysabeau's cry had loosened the souls of the multitude, they rose to their feet and began to surge wildly towards the door.

But the Pontiff rose, approached the altar and began calmly to chant the Gratias.

Balthasar gave him a wild and desperate look, staggered and fiercely recovered himself, then took his child by the hand, and supporting with the other the Empress, who struggled back to life, he swept down the aisle, followed by a few of his German knights.

The people shuddered away to right and left to give him passage; the bronze doors were opened and the excommunicated man stepped into the thunder-wrapt streets of the city where he no longer reigned.

# Chapter 8

## Ursula of Rooselaare

"Say I have done well for you — it seems that I must ask your thanks."

The Pope sat at a little table near the window of his private room in the Vatican and rested his face on his hand.

Leaning against the scarlet tapestries that covered the opposite wall was Theirry, clothed in chain mail and heavily armed.

"You think I should be grateful?" he asked in a low voice, his beautiful eyes fixed in a half-frightened, wholly fascinated way on the slim figure of the other.

Michael II wore a straight robe of gold-coloured silk and a skull-cap of crimson and blue; no jewels nor any suggestion of pomp concealed the youthfulness, almost frailty of his appearance; the red hair made his face the paler by contrast; his full lips were highly coloured under the darkened upper lip.

"Grateful?" he repeated, and his voice was mournful. "I think you do not know what I have done — I have dared to cast the Emperor from his throne — lies he not even now without the walls, defying me with a handful of Frankish knights? Is not the excommunication on him?"

"Yea," answered Theirry. "And is it for my sake ye have done this?"

"Must you question it?" returned Michael, with a quick breath. "Yea, for your sake, to make you, as I promised, Emperor of the West — my vengeance had else been more quietly satisfied —" He laughed. "I have not forgot all my magic."

Theirry winced.

"The vision in the Basilica was proof of that — what are you who can bring back the hallowed dead to aid your schemes?"

Michael II answered softly.

"And who are you who take my aid and my friendship, and all the while fear and loathe me?"

He moved his hand from his face and leant forward, showing a deep red mark on his cheek where the palm had pressed.

"Do you think I am not human, Theirry?" He gave a sigh. "If you would believe in me, trust me, be faithful to me — why, our friendship would be the lever to move the universe, and you and I would rule the world between us."

Theirry fingered the arras beside him.

"In what way can I be false to you?"

"You betrayed me once. You are the only man in Rome who knows my secret. But this is truth, if again you forsake me, you bring about your own downfall — stand by me, and I will share with you the dominion of the earth — this, I say, is truth."

Theirry laughed unhappily.

"Sweet devil, there is no God, and I have no soul! — there, do not fear — I shall be very faithful to you — since what is there for man save to glut his desires of pomp and wealth and power?" He moved from the wall and took a quick turn about the room.

"And yet I know not!" he cried. "Can all your magic, all your learning, all your riches, keep you where you are? The clouds hang angrily over Rome, nor have they lifted since Orsini announced you Pope — the people riot in the streets — all beautiful things are dead, many see ghosts and devils walking at twilight across the Maremma . . . Oh, horror! — they say Pan has left his ruined temple to enter Christian churches and laugh in the face of the marble Christ — — can these things be?"

The Pope swept back the hair from his damp brow. "The powers that put me here can keep me here — be you but true to me!"

"Ay, I will be Emperor" — Theirry grasped his sword hilt fiercely — "though the world I rule rot about me, though ghouls and fiends make my Imperial train — I will join hands with Antichrist and see if there be a God or no!"

The Pope rose.

"You must go against Balthasar. You must defeat his hosts and bring to me his Empress, then will I crown you in St. Peter's."

Theirry pressed his hand to his forehead.

"We start tomorrow with the dawn — beneath the banner of God His Church; I, in this mail ye gave me, tempered and forged in Hell!"

"Ye need have no fear of failure; you shall go forth triumphantly and return victoriously. You shall make your dwelling the Golden Palace on the Aventine, and neither Heliogabalus nor Basil, nor Charlemagne shall be more magnificently housed than you . . . "

Michael seemed to check his words suddenly; he turned his face away and looked across the city which lay beneath the heavy pall of clouds.

"Be but true to me," he added in a low voice.

Theirry smiled wildly.

"A curious love have you for me, and but little faith in my strength or constancy — well, you shall see, I go forth tomorrow, with many men and banners, to rout the Emperor utterly."

"Until then, stay in the Vatican," said Michael II suddenly. "My prelates and my nobles know you for their leader now."

"Nay," — Theirry flushed as he answered —"I must go to my own abode in the city." "Jacobea of Martzburg is still in Rome," said the other. "Do you leave me to go to her?" "Nay — I know not even where she lodges," replied Theirry hastily.

Michael smiled bitterly and was silent.

"What is Jacobea to me?" demanded Theirry desperately.

The other gave him a sinister glance.

"Why did you approach her after her devotions in San Giovanni in Laterano — speak to her and recall yourself to her mind?"

Theirry went swiftly pale.

"You know that! — Ah, it was the dancer, your accomplice . . . What mystery is this?" he asked in a distracted way. "Why does not Ursula of Rooselaare come forth under her true name and confound the Emperor? — why does she follow me, and in such a guise?"

Without looking at him Michael answered.

"Maybe because she is very wise — maybe because she is a very fool — let her pass, she has served her turn. You say you do not go to palter with Jacobea, then farewell until tomorrow; I have much to do . . . farewell, Theirry."

He held out his hand with a stately gesture, and, as Theirry took it in his, the curious thought came to him how seldom he had touched so much as Dirk's fingers, even in the old days, so proud a reserve had always encompassed the youth, and, now, the man.

Theirry left the rich-scented chamber and the vast halls of the Vatican and passed into the riotous and lawless streets of Rome.

The storm that had hung so unnaturally long over the city had affected the people; bravoes and assassins crept from their hiding-places in the Catacombs, or the Palatine, and flaunted in the streets; the wine shops were filled with mongrel soldiers of all nations, attracted by the declaration of war from the surrounding towns; blasphemers mocked openly at the processions of monks and pilgrims that traversed the streets chanting the penitential psalms, or scourging themselves in an attempt to avert the wrath of Heaven.

There was no law; crime went unpunished; virtue became a jest; many of the convents were closed and deserted, while their late occupants rejoined the world they suddenly longed for; the poor were despoiled, the rich robbed; ghastly and blasphemous processions nightly paraded the streets in honour of some heathen deity; the priests inspired no respect, the name of God no fear; the plague marched among the people, striking down hundreds; their bodies were flung into the Tiber, and their spirits went to join the devils that nightly danced on the Campagna to the accompaniment of rolling storms.

Witches gathered in the low marches of the Maremma and came at night into the city, trailing grey, fever-laden vapour after them.

The bell-ropes began to rot in the churches, and the bells clattered from the steeples; the gold rusted on the altars, and mice gnawed the garments on the holy images of the Saints.

The people lived with reckless laughter and died with hopeless curses; magicians, warlocks and vile things flourished exceedingly, and all manner of strange and hideous creatures left their caves to prowl the streets at nightfall.

And such under Pope Michael II was Rome, swiftly and in a moment.

Theirry, like all others, went heavily armed; his hand was constantly on his sword hilt as he made his way through the city that was forsaken by God.

With no faltering step or hesitating bearing he passed through the crowds that gathered more thickly as the night came on, and turned towards the Appian Gate.

Here it was gloomy, almost deserted; dark houses bordered the Appian Way, and a few strange figures crept along in their shadow; in the west a sullen glare of crimson showed that the sun was setting behind the thick clouds. Dark began to fall rapidly.

Theirry walked long beyond the Gate and stopped at a low convent building, above the portals of which hung a lamp, its gentle radiance like a star in the heavy, noisome twilight.

The gate, that led into a courtyard, stood half open. Theirry softly pushed it wider and entered. The pure perfume of flowers greeted him; a sense of peace and security, grown strange of late in Rome, filled the square grass court; in the centre was a fountain, almost hidden in white roses; behind their leaves the water dripped pleasantly.

There were no lights in the convent windows, but it was not yet too dark for Theirry to distinguish the slim figure of a lady seated on a wooden bench, her hands passive in her lap. He latched the gate and softly crossed the lawn.

"You said that I might come."

Jacobea turned her head, unsmiling, unsurprised.

"Ay, sir; this place is open to all."

He uncovered before her.

"I cannot hope ye are glad to see me."

"Glad?" She echoed the word as if it sounded in a foreign tongue; then, after a pause, "Yes, I am glad that you have come."

He seated himself beside her, his splendid mail touching her straight grey robe, his full, beautiful face turned towards her worn 'and expressionless features.

"What do you do here?" he asked.

She answered in the same gentle tone; she had a white rose in her hands, and turned it about as she spoke.

"So little — there are two sisters here, and I help them; one can do nothing against the plague, but for the little forsaken children something, rend something for the miserable sick."

"The wretched of Rome are not in your keeping," he said eagerly. "It will mean your life — — why did you not go with the Empress?"

She shook her head.

"I was not needed. I suppose what they said of her was true. I cannot remember clearly, but I think that when Melchoir died I knew it was her doing."

"We must not dwell on the past," cried Theirry. "Have you heard that I lead the Pope's army against Balthasar?"

"Nay;" her eyes were on the white rose.

"Jacobea, I shall be the Emperor."

"The Emperor," she repeated dreamily.

"I shall rule the Latin world — Emperor of the West!"

In the now complete dark they could scarcely see each other; there were no stars, and distant thunder rolled at intervals; Theirry timidly put out his hand and touched the fold of her dress where it lay along the seat.

"I wish you would not stay here — it is so lonely —"

"I think she would wish me to do this."

"She?" he questioned.

Jacobea seemed surprised he did not take her meaning.

"Sybilla."

"O Christus!" shuddered Theirry. "Ye still think of her?"

Jacobea smiled, as he felt rather than saw.

"Think of her? . . . is she not always with me?"

"She is dead."

He saw the blurred outline of the lady's figure stir.

"Yea, she died on a cold morning — it was so cold you could see your breath before you as you rode along, and the road was hard as glass — there was a yellow dawn that day, and the pine trees seemed frozen, they stood so motionless — you would not think it was ten years ago — I wonder how long it seems to her?"

A silence fell upon them for a while, then Theirry broke out desperately —

"Jacobea — — my heart is torn within me — — today I said there was no God — but when I sit by you . . . "

"Yea, there is a God," she answered quietly. "Be very sure of that."

"Then I am past His forgiveness," whispered Theirry.

Again he was mute; he saw before him the regal figure of Dirk — he heard his words —"Be but true to me" — then he thought of Jacobea and Paradise . . . agony ran through his veins.

"Oh, Jacobea!" he cried at last. "I am beyond all measure mean and vile . . . I know not what to do . . . I can be Emperor, yet as I sit here that seems to me as nothing."

"The Pope favours you, you tell me," she said. "He is a priest, and a holy man, and yet — it is strange, what is this talk of Ursula of Rooselaare? — — and yet it is no matter."

His mail clinked in answer to his tremor.

"Tell me what I must do — see, I am in a great confusion; the world is very dark, this way and that show little lights, and I strive to follow hem — but they change and move and blind me — and if I grasp one it is extinguished into greater darkness; I hear whispers, murmurs, threats, I believe them, and believe them not, and all is confusion, confusion!"

Jacobea rose slowly from the bench.

"Why do you come to me?"

"Because ye seem to me nearer heaven than anything I know . . . "

Jacobea pressed the white rose to her bosom. "It is dark now — the flowers smell so sweet — — come into the house."

He followed her dim-seen figure across the grass; she lifted the latch of the convent door and went before him into the building.

For a while she left him in the passage, then returned with a pale lamp in her hand and conducted him into a small, bare chamber, which seemed mean in contrast with the glowing splendour of his appearance.

"The sisters are abroad," said Jacobea. "And I stay here in case any ring the bell for succour." She set the lamp on the wooden table and slowly turned her eyes on Theirry.

"Sir, I am very selfish." She spoke with difficulty, as if she painfully forced expression. "I have thought of myself for so many years — and somehow" — she lightly touched her breast —"I cannot feel, for myself or for others; nothing seems real, save Sybilla; nothing matters save her — — sometimes I cry for little things I find dying alone, for poor unnoticed miseries of animals and children — but for the rest . . . you must not blame me if I do not sympathise; that has gone from me. Nor can I help you; God is far away beyond the stars. I do not think He can stoop to such as you and me — and — and — I do not feel as if I should wake until I die —"

Theirry covered his eyes and moaned.

Jacobea was not looking at him, but at the one bright thing in the room.

A samite cushion worked with a scarlet lily that rested on a chair by the window.

"Each our own way to death," she said. "All we can do is so little compared with that ——

death — see, I think of it as a great crystal light, very cold, that will slowly encompass us, revealing everything, making everything easy to understand — white lilies will not be more beautiful, nor breeze at summer-time more sweet . . . so, sir, must you wait patiently."

She took her gaze from the red flower and turned her tired grey eyes on him.

The blood surged into his face; he clenched his hands and spoke passionately.

"I will renounce the world, I will become a monk . . . "

The words choked in his throat; he looked fearfully round; the lamplight struck his armour into a hundred points of light and cast pale shadows over the whitewashed walls.

"What was that?" asked Jacobea.

One was singing without: Theirry's strained eyes glistened.

"If Love were all!

His perfect servant I would be.

Kissing where his foot might fall, Doing him homage on a lowly knee.

If Love were all!"

Theirry turned and went out into the dark, hot night.

He could see neither roses, nor fountain, nor even the line of the convent wall against the sky; but the light above the gate revealed to him the dancer in orange, who leant against the stone arch of the entrance and sang to a strange long instrument that hung round her neck by a gleaming chain.

At her feet the ape crouched, nodding himself to sleep.

"If Love were all I

But Love is weak.

And Hate oft giveth him a fall.

And Wisdom smites him on the cheek, If Love were all!

Behind Theirry came Jacobea, with the lantern in her hand.

"Who is this?" she asked.

The dancer laughed; the sound of it muffled behind her mask.

Theirry made his way across the dark to her.

"What do you do here?" he demanded fiercely. "The Pope's spy, you!"

"May I not come to worship here as well as another?" she answered.

"You know too much of me!" he cried distractedly. "But I also have some knowledge of you, Ursula of Rooselaare!"

"How does that help you?" she asked, drawing back a little before him.

"I would discover why you follow me — watch me."

He caught her by the arms and held her against the stone gateway.

"Now tell me the meaning of your disguise," he breathed —"and of your league with Michael II."

She said a strange little word underneath her breath; the ape jumped up and tore away the man's hands while the girl bent to a run and sped through the gate.

Theirry gave a cry of pain and rage, and glanced towards the convent; the door was closed; lady and lamp had disappeared in the darkness.

"Shut out!" whispered Theirry. "Shut out!" He turned into the street and saw, by the scattered lanterns along the Appian Way, the figure of the dancer slipping fast towards the city gates. But he gained on her, and at sound of his clattering step she looked round.

"Ah!" she said; "I thought you had stayed with the sweet-faced saint yonder —"

"She wants none of me," he panted —"but I — I mean to see your face to-night . . . " "I am not beautiful," answered the dancer; "and you have seen my face —"

"Seen your face!"

"Certes! in the Basilica on the Fête."

"I knew you not in the press."

"Nevertheless I was there."

"I looked for you."

"I thought ye looked for Jacobea."

"Also I sought you," said Theirry. "Ye madden me."

The ever-gathering tempest was drawing near, with fitful flashes of lightning playing over his jewel-like mail and her orange gown as they made their way through the ruins.

"Do you wander here alone at night?" asked Theirry. "It is a vile place; a man might be afraid." "I have the ape," she said.

"But the storm?"

"In Rome now-a-days we are well used to storms," she answered in a low voice. "Yea."

He did not know what to say to her, but he could not leave her; a strong, a supreme, fascination compelled him to walk beside her, a half-delightful excitement stirred his blood.

"Where are we going?" asked Theirry. The wayside lanterns had ceased; he could see her only by the lightning gleams.

"I know not — why do you follow me?"

"I am mad, I think — the earth rocks beneath me and heaven bends overhead — you lure me and I follow in sheer confusion — Ursula of Rooselaare, why have you lured me? What power is it that you have over me? Wherefore are you disguised?"

She touched his mail in the dark as she answered —

"I am Balthasar's wife."

"Ay," he responded eagerly; "and I do hear ye loved another man —"

"What is that to you?" she asked.

"This — though I have not seen your face — perchance could I love you, Ursula!"

"Ursula!" She laughed on the word.

"Is it not your name?" he cried wildly.

"Yea — but it is long since any used it —"

The hot darkness seemed to twist and writhe about Theirry; he seemed to breathe a nameless and uncontrollable passion in with the storm-laden air.

"Witch or demon," he said, "I have cast in my lot with the Devil and Michael II his servant — I follow the same master as you, Ursula."

He put out his hand through the dark and grasped her arm.

"Who is the man for whose sake ye are silent?" he demanded.

There was no answer; he felt her arm quiver under his hand, and heard the hems of her tunic tinkle against her buskins, as if she trembled.

The air was chokingly hot; Theirry's heart throbbed high.

At last she spoke, in a half-swooning voice.

"I have taken off my mask . . . bend your head and kiss me."

Invisible and potent powers drew him towards her unseen face; his lips touched and kissed its softness . . .

The thunder sounded with such a terrific force and clash that Theirry sprang back; a cry of agony went up from the darkness. He ran blindly forward; her presence had gone from his side, nor could he see or feel her as he moved.

A thousand light shapes danced across the night; witches and warlocks carrying swinging lanterns, imps and fiends.

They gathered round Theirry, shrieking and howling to the accompaniment of the storm.

He ran sobbing down the Appian Way, and his pace was very swift, for all the mail he carried.

# Chapter 9

## Pope and Empress

The Pope walked in the garden of the Vatican, behind him Cardinal Orsini and Cardinal Colonna; the first carried a cluster of daisies, white and yellow, strong in colour and pungent of odour, the second tossed up and down a little ball of gold and blue silk.

Both talked of the horrible state of Rome, of the unending storm hanging over the capital, of the army that had gone forth three days ago to crush the excommunicated Emperor. Michael II was silent.

They went along the marble walks and looked at the goldfish in the basin under the overhanging branches of the yellow rose bushes; they passed the trellis over which the jasmine clustered, and came out on the long terrace, where the peacocks flashed their splendour across the grass.

Oleanders grew here, and lilies; laurel trees rose against the murky heavens that should have shown blue, and curious statues gleamed beside the dark foliage.

Cardinal Colonna dropped his ball and let it roll away across the close grass, and Michael slackened his pace. He wore a white robe, his soft heavy red hair showing a brilliant colour above it; his dark eyes were thoughtful, his pale mouth resolutely set. The Cardinals fell further behind and conversed with the greater ease.

Suddenly the Pope paused and stood waiting, for Paolo Orsini, with a sprig of pink flower at his chin, was coming across the lawn.

Michael II tapped his gold-shod foot on the marble path. "What is it, Orsini?"

The secretary went on one knee.

"Your Holiness, a lady, who will neither unveil nor give her name, has obtained entry to the Vatican and desires to see your Holiness."

The Pope's face darkened.

"I thought ye had brought me news of the return of Theirry of Dendermonde! What can this woman want with us?"

"She says it is a matter of such import it may avert the war, and she prays, for the love of God, not to be denied."

Michael II reflected a moment, his slim fingers pulling at the laurel leaves beside him. "We will see her," he said at length. "Bring her here, Orsini."

The yellow clouds broke over a brief spell of sunshine that fell across the Vatican gardens, though the horizon was dark with a freshly gathering storm; Michael II seated himself on a bench where the sun gleamed.

"Sirs," he said to the two Cardinals, "stand by me and listen to what this woman may say."

And picking a crimson rose from a thorny bush that brushed the seat, he considered it curiously, and only took his eyes from it when Paolo Orsini had returned and led the lady almost to his feet.

Then he looked at her.

She wore a dark rough dress showing marks of ill usage, and over her face a thick veil.

This she loosened as she knelt, and revealed the exceedingly fair, sad face of Ysabeau the Empress.

Michael II went swiftly pale, he fixed large wide eyes on her.

"What do you here, defying us?" he demanded.

She rose.

"I am not here in defiance. I have come to give myself up to punishment for the crime you denounced — the crime for which my lord now suffers."

Michael crushed the rose in his hand and the Cardinals glanced at each other, having never seen him show agitation.

"It did not occur to your Holiness," said Ysabeau, facing him fearlessly, "that I should do this; you thought that he would never give me up and you were right — crown, life, heaven he would forfeit for love of me, but I will not take the sacrifice."

The fitful sunshine touched her great beauty, her fair, soft hair lying loosely on her shoulders, her eyes shadowed and dark, her hollow face.

"Mine was the sin," she continued. "And I who was strong enough to sin alone can take the punishment alone."

At last Michael spoke.

"Ye slew Melchoir of Brabant — ye confess it!"

Her bosom heaved.

"I am here to confess it."

"For love of Balthasar you did it . . . "

"As for love of him I stand here now to take the consequences."

"We have fire on earth and fire in hell for those who do murder," said Michael II; "flames for the body in the market-place, and flames in the pit for the soul, and though the body will not burn long, the soul will burn for eternity."

"I know — do what you will with me."

The Pope cast the crushed rose from him.

"Has Balthasar sent you here?"

She smiled proudly.

"I come without his knowledge." Her voice trembled a little. "I left a writing telling him where I had gone and why —" Her hand crept to her brow. "Enough of that."

Michael II rose.

"Why have you done this?" he cried angrily.

Ysabeau answered swiftly.

"That you may take the curse off him — for my sin you cast him forth, well, if I leave him, if I accept my punishment, if he be free to find the — woman — who can claim him, your Holiness must absolve him of the excommunication."

Michael flushed.

"This comes late — too late;" he turned to the Cardinals. "My lords, is not this love a mad thing? — that she should hope to cheat Heaven so!"

"My hope is not to cheat Heaven but to appease it," said Ysabeau; and the sun, making a pale glimmer in her hair, cast her shadow faintly before her to the Pontiff's feet. "If not for myself, for him."

"This foolish sacrifice," said Michael, "cannot avail Balthasar. Since not of his free will ye are parted from him, how is his sin then lessened?"

She trembled exceedingly.

"Now, perchance he shall loathe me . . . " she said.

"Had you told him to his face of your crime, would he have given you over to our wrath?"

"Nay," she flashed. "It would have been only noble in him to refuse; but since of myself I am come, I pray you, Lord Pope, to send me to death and take the curse off him."

Michael II looked at his hand; the stem of the red rose had scratched his finger, and a tiny drop of blood showed on the white flesh.

"You are a wicked woman, by your own confession," he said, frowning. "Why should I show you any pity?"

"I do not ask pity, but justice for the Emperor. I am the cause of the quarrel, and now ye have me ye can have no bitterness against him."

He gave her a quick sidelong look.

"Do you repent, Ysabeau?"

She shook the clinging hood free of her yellow hair.

"No; the gain was worth the sin, nor am I afraid of you nor of Heaven. I am not of a faltering race, nor of a name easily ashamed. In my own eyes I am not abashed."

Michael raised his head and their eyes met.

"So you would die for him?"

Ysabeau smiled.

"I think I shall. I do not think your Holiness is merciful."

He glanced again at the drop of blood on his finger.

"You show some courage, Ysabeau."

She smiled.

"When I was a child I was taught that they who live as kings and queens must not look for age — the flame soon burns away, leaving the ashes — and gorgeous years are like the flame; why should we taste the dust that follows? I have lived my life."

He answered —

"This shall not save Balthasar, nor take our curse from off him; Theirry of Dendermonde has gone forth with many men and banners, and soon the Roman gates shall open to him and victory lead his charger through the streets! And his reward shall be the Latin world, his badge of triumph the Imperial crown. He is our choice to share with us the dominion of the West, therefore no more of Balthasar — ye might speak until the heavens fell and still our heart be as brass!"

He turned swiftly and caught the arm of Cardinal Orsini.

"Away, my lord, we have given this Greek time enough."

Ysabeau fell on her knees.

"My lord, take off the curse!"

"What shall we do with her?" asked Cardinal Colonna.

She clutched, in her desperation, at the priest's white garments.

"Show some pity; Balthasar dies beneath your wrath —"

Paolo Orsini drew her away, while Michael II stared at her with a touch of fear.

"Cast her without the walls — since the excommunication is upon her we do not need her life." "Oh, sirs!" shrieked Ysabeau, striving after them, "my lord is innocent!"

"Take her away," said Michael. "Cast her from Rome," — he glared at her over his shoulder — —"doubtless the Eastern she-cat will find it worse so to die than as Hugh of Rooselaare perished; come on, my lords."

Leaning on the arm of Cardinal Orsini, he moved away across the Vatican gardens. Paolo Orsini blew a little whistle.

"You must be turned from the city," he said.

Ysabeau rose from the grass.

"This your Christian priest!" she cried hoarsely, staring after the white figure; then, as she saw the guards approaching, she fell into an utter silence.

As Michael II entered the Vatican the sun was again obscured and the thunder rolled; he passed up the silver stairs to his cabinet and closed the door on all.

The storm grew and rioted angrily in the sky; in the height of it came a messenger riding straight to the Vatican.

Blood and dust were smeared on his clothes, and he was weary with swift travel; they brought him to the ebony cabinet and face to face with the Pope.

"From Theirry of Dendermonde?" breathed Michael, his face white as his robe.

"From Theirry of Dendermonde, your Holiness."

"What says he — victory?"

"Balthasar of Courtrai is defeated, his army lies dead, men and horses, in the vale of Tivoli, and his conqueror marches home today."

A shaft of lightning showed the ghastly face of Michael II, and a peal of thunder shook the messenger back against the wall.

# Chapter 10

## The Evening Before the Coronation

The orange marble pillars glowing in the light of a hundred lamps gave the chamber a dazzling brightness; the windows were screened by scarlet silk curtains, and crystal bowls of purple flowers stood on the serpentine floor.

On a low gilt couch against the wall sat Theirry, his gold armour half concealed by a violet and ermine mantle; round his close dark hair was a wreath of red roses, and the long pearls in his ears glimmered with his movements.

Opposite him on a throne supported by basalt lions was Michael II, robed in gold and silver tissues under a dalmatica of orange and crimson brocade.

"It is done," he said in a low eager voice, "and tomorrow I crown you in St. Peter's church; Theirry, it is done."

"Truly our fortunes are marvellous," answered Theirry, "today — when I heard the Princes elect me — an unknown adventurer! — when I heard the mob of Rome shout for me — I thought I had gone mad!"

"It is I who have done this for you," said the Pope softly.

Theirry seemed to shudder in his gorgeous mail.

"Are you afraid of me?" the other asked. "Why do you so seldom look at me?"

Theirry slowly turned his beautiful face.

"I am afraid of my own fortunes — I am not as bold as you," he said fearfully. "You never hesitated to sin."

The Pope moved, and his garments sparkled against the gleaming marble wall.

"I do not sin," he smiled. "I am Sin — I do no evil for I am Evil — but you" — his face became grave, almost sad —"you are very human, better had it been for me never to have met you!" He placed his little hands either side of him on the smooth heads of the basalt lions. "Theirry — for your sake I have risked everything, for your sake maybe I must leave this strange fair life and go back whence I came — so much I care for you, so dearly have I kept the vows we made in Frankfort — cannot you meet with courage the destiny I offer you?" Theirry hid his face in his hands.

The Pope flushed, and a wild light sparkled in his dark eyes.

"Was not your blood warmed by that charge at Tivoli? When knight and horse fell before your spears and your host humbled an Emperor, when Rome rose to greet you and I came to meet you with a kingdom for a gift, did not some fire creep into your veins that might serve to heat you now?"

"A kingdom!" cried Theirry, "the kingdom of Antichrist. The victory was not mine — the cohorts of the Devil galloped beside us and urged us to unholy triumph — Rome is a place of horror, full of witches, ghosts and strange beasts!"

"You said you would be Emperor," answered the Pope. "And I have granted you your wish, if you fail me or betray me now . . . it is over — for both of us."

Theirry rose and paced the chamber.

"Ay, I will be Emperor," he cried feverishly. "Theirry of Dendermonde crowned by the Devil in St. Peter's church — why should I hesitate? I am on the road to hell, to hell . . . " The Pope fixed ardent eyes on him.

"And if ye fail me ye shall go there instantly."

Theirry stopped in his pacing to and fro.

"Why do you say to me so often, 'do not fail me, do not betray me'?"

Michael II answered in a low voice.

"Because I fear it."

Theirry laughed desperately.

"To whom should I betray you! It seems that you have all the world!"

"There is Jacobea of Martzburg."

"Why do you sting me with that name!"

"Belike I thought ye might wish to make her your Empress," said the Pope in sudden mockery. Theirry pressed his hand to his brow.

"She believes in God . . . what is such to me?" he cried.

"The other day you lied to me, saying you knew not where she was — and straightway ye visited her."

"This is your spy's work, Ursula of Rooselaare."

"Maybe," answered the Pope.

Theirry paused before the basalt throne.

"Tell me of her. She follows me — I — I — know not what to think, she has been much in my mind of late, since I —" He broke off, and looked moodily at the ground. "Where has she been these years — what does she mean to do now?"

"She will not trouble you again," answered Michael II, "let her go."

"I cannot — she said I had seen her face —"

"Well, if you have? — take it from me she is not fair."

"I do not think of her fairness," answered Theirry sullenly, "but of the mystery there is behind all of it — — why you never told me of her before, and why she haunts me with witches in her train."

The Pope looked at him curiously.

"For one who has never been an ardent lover ye dwell much on women — I had rather you thought on battles and kingdoms — had I been a — were I you, dancer and nun alike would be nothing to me compared with my coronation on the morrow."

Theirry replied hotly.

"Dancer and nun, as ye term them, are woven in with all I do, I cannot, if I would, forget them. Ah, that I ever came to Rome — would I were still a Chamberlain at Basil's Court or a merchant's clerk in India!"

He covered his face with his trembling hands and turned away across the golden room. The Pope rose in his seat and pressed his jewelled fingers against his breast.

"Would ye had never come my way to be my ruin and your own — would you were not such a sweet fair fool that I must love you! . . . and so, we make ourselves the mock of destiny by these complaints. Oh, if you have the desire to be king show the courage to dare a kingly fate."

Theirry leant against one of the orange marble pillars, the violet mantle falling away from his golden armour, the fainting roses lying slackly in his dark hair.

"You must think me a coward," he said, "and I have been very weak — but that, I think, is passed; I have reached the summit of all the greatness I ever dreamed and it confuses me, but when the Imperial crown is mine you shall find me bold enough."

Michael II flushed and gave a dazzling smile.

"Then are we great indeed! — we shall join hands across the fairest dominion men ever ruled, Suabia is ours, Bohemia and Lombardy, France courts our alliance, Cyprus, the isle of Candy and Malta town, in Rhodes they worship us, and Genoa town owns us master!"

He paused in his speech and stepped down from the throne.

"Do you remember that day in Antwerp, Theirry, when we looked in the mirror?" he said, and his voice was tender and beautiful; "we hardly dared then to think of this."

"We saw a gallows in that mirror," answered Theirry, "a gallows tree beside the triple crown."

"It was for our enemies!" cried Michael; "our enemies whom we have triumphed over; Theirry, think of it, we were very young then, and poor — now I have kings at my footstool, and you will sleep tonight in the Golden Palace of the Aventine!" He laughed joyously. Theirry's face grew gentle at the old memories.

"The house still stands, I wot," he mused, "though the dust be thick over the deserted rooms and the vine chokes the windows — when I was in the East, I have thought with great joy of Antwerp."

The Pope laid his delicate fragrant hand on the glittering vambrace.

"Theirry — do you not value me a little now?"

Theirry smiled, into the ardent eyes.

"You have done more for me than man or God, and above both I do you worship," he answered wildly. "I am not fearful any more, and tomorrow ye shall see me a king indeed."

"Until tomorrow then, farewell. I must attend a Conclave of the Cardinals and show myself unto the multitude in St. Peter's church. You to the palace, on the Aventine, there to sleep soft and dream of gold."

They clasped hands, a hot colour was in the Pope's face.

"The Syrian guards wait below and the Lombard archers who stood beside you at Tivoli — they will attend you to the Imperial Palace."

"What shall I do there?" asked Theirry. "It is early yet, and I do not love to sit alone."

"Then, come to the service in the Basilica — come with a bold bearing and a rich dress to overawe these mongrel crowds of Rome."

To that Theirry made no answer.

"Farewell," he said, and lifted the scarlet curtain that concealed the door, "until to — morrow." The Pope came quickly to his side.

"Do not go to Jacobea to-night," he said earnestly. "Remember, if you fail me now —" "I shall not fail you or myself, again — farewell."

His hand was on the latch when Michael spoke once more —

"I grieve to let you go," he murmured in an agitated tone. "I have not before been fearful, but to-night Theirry smiled.

"You have no cause to dread anything, you with your foot on the neck of the world." He opened the door on to the soft purple light of the stairs and stepped from the room.

In a half-stifled voice the Pope called him. "Theirry! — — be true to me, for on your faith have I staked everything."

Theirry looked over his shoulder and laughed.

"Will you never let me begone?"

The other pressed his hand to his forehead.

"Ay, begone — why should I seek to keep you?"

Theirry descended the stairs and now and then looked up.

Always to see fixed on him the yearning, fierce gaze of the one who stood by the gilded rails and stared down at his glittering figure.

Only when he had completely disappeared in the turn of the stairs did Michael II slowly return to the golden chamber and close the gorgeous doors.

Theirry, splendidly attended, flashed through the riotous streets of Rome to the palace on the Aventine Hill.

There he dismissed the knights.

"I shall not go to the Basilica to-night," he said, "go thou there without me."

He laid aside the golden armour, the purple cloak, and attired himself in a dark habit and a steel corselet; he meant to be Emperor tomorrow, he meant to be faithful to the Pope, but it was in his heart to see Jacobea once more before he accepted the Devil's last gift and sign.

Leaving the palace secretly, when they all thought him in his chamber, he took his way towards the Appian Gate.

Once more, for the last time . . . he would suggest to her that she returned to Martzburg. The plague was rampant in the city; more than once he passed the death-cart attended by friars clanging harsh bells; several houses were sealed and silent; but in the piazzas the people danced and sang, and in the Via Sacra they held a carnival in honour of the victory at Tivoli.

It was nearly dark, starless, and the air heavy with the sense of storm; as he neared the less-frequented part of the city Theirry looked continually behind him to see if the dancer in orange dogged his footsteps — he saw no one.

Very lonely, very silent it was in the Appian Way, the only domestic light he came to the little lamp above the convent gate.

The stillness and gloom of the place chilled his heart, she could not, must not stay here.. He gently pushed the gate and entered.

The hot dusk just revealed to him the dim shapes of the white roses and the dark figure of a lady standing beside them.

"Jacobea," he whispered.

She moved very slowly towards him.

"Ah! you."

"Jacobea — you must not remain in this place! — — where are the nuns?"

She shook her head.

"They are dead of the plague days past, and I have buried them in the garden."

He gave a start of horror.

"You shall go back to Martzburg — you are alone here?"

Her answer came calmly out of the twilight.

"I think there is no one living anywhere near. The plague has been very fierce — you should not come here if you do not wish to die."

"But what of you?" His voice was full of horror.

"Why, what can it matter about me?"

He thought she smiled; he followed her into the house, the chamber where they had sat before. A tall pale candle burnt on the bare table, and by the light of it he saw her face.

"Ye are ill already," he shuddered.

Again she shook her head.

"Why do you come here?" she asked gently. "You are to be Emperor tomorrow."

She crept with a slow sick movement to a bench that stood against the wall and sank down on it; her features showed pinched and wan, her eyes unnaturally blue in the pallor of her face.

"You must return to Martzburg," repeated Theirry distractedly; and thought of her as he had first seen her, bright and gay, in a pale crimson dress . . .

"Nay, I shall return to Martzburg no more," she answered. "He died today."

"He? — who died, Jacobea?"

Very faintly she smiled.

"Sebastian — in Palestine. God let me see him then, because I had never looked on him since that morning on which you saw us, sir . . . he has been a holy man fighting the infidel; they wounded him, I think, and he was sick with fever — he crept into the shade (for it is very hot there, sir), and died."

Theirry stood dumb, and the mad hatred of the devil who had brought about this misery anew possessed him.

Jacobea spoke again.

"Maybe they have met in Paradise — and as for me I hope God may think me fit to die — of late it seemed to me that the fiends were again troubling me" — she clasped her hands tightly on her knees and shivered; "something evil is abroad . . . who is the dancer? . . . last night I saw her crouching by my gate as I was making the grave of Sister Angela, and it seemed, it seemed, that she bewitched me — as the young scholar did, long ago."

Theirry leant heavily against the table.

"She is the Pope's spy and tool," he cried hoarsely, "Ursula of Rooselaare!"

Jacobea's dim eyes were bewildered.

"Ah, Balthasar's wife," she faltered, "but the Pope's tool — how should he meddle with an evil thing?"

Then he told her, in an outburst of wild, unnameable feeling.

"The Pope is Dirk Renswoude — the Pope is Antichrist — do you not understand? And I am to help him rule the kingdom of the Devil!"

Jacobea gave a shuddering cry, half rose in her seat and sank back against the wall. Theirry crossed the room and fell on his knees beside her.

"It is true, true," he sobbed. "And I am damned for ever!"

The lightning darted in from the darkness and thunder crashed above the convent; Theirry laid his head on her lap and her cold fingers touched his hair.

"Since, knowing this, you are his ally," she whispered fearfully.

He answered through clenched teeth.

"Yea, I will be Emperor — and it is too late to turn back."

Jacobea stared across the candle-lit room.

"Dirk Renswoude," she muttered, "and Ursula of Rooselaare — why — was it not to save Hugh of Rooselaare that he rode — that night?"

Theirry lifted his head and looked at her, her utterance was feeble and confused, her eyes glazing in a livid face; he clasped his hands tightly over hers.

"What was Lord Hugh to him?" she asked, "Ursula's father . . . "

"I do not understand," cried Theirry.

"But it is very clear to me — I am dying — she loved you, loves you still — that such things should be . . . "

"Whom do you speak of — Jacobea?" he cried, distracted.

She drooped towards him and he caught her in his arms.

"The city is accursed," she gasped; "give me Christian burial, if ever once you cared for me, and fly, fly!"

She strained and writhed in his frantic embrace. "And you never knew it was a woman," she whispered, "Pope and dancer . . . "

"God!" shrieked Theirry; and staggered to his feet drawing her with him.

She choked her life out against his shoulder, clinging with the desperation of the dying, to him, while he tried to force her into speech.

"Answer me, Jacobea! What authority have you for this hideous thing, in the name of God, Jacobea!"

She slipped from him to the bench.

"Water, a crucifix . . . Oh, I have forgot my prayers." She stretched out her hands towards a wooden crucifix that hung on the wall, caught hold of it, pressed her lips to the feet.. "Sybilla," she said, and died with that name struggling in her throat.

Theirry stepped back from her with a strangled shriek that seemed to tear the breath from his body, and staggered against the table.

The lightning leapt in through the dark window, and appeared to plunge like a sword into the breast of the dead woman.

Dead! — even as she uttered that horror — dead so suddenly. The plague had slain her — he did not wish to die, so he must leave this place — was he not to be Emperor tomorrow?

He fell to laughing.

The candle had burnt almost to the socket; the yellow flame struggling against extinction cast a fantastic leaping light over Jacobea, lying huddled along the bench with her yellow hair across the breast of her rough garment; over Theirry, leaning with slack limbs against the table; it showed his ghastly face, his staring eyes, his dropped jaw — as his laughter died into silence.

Fly! Fly!

He must fly from this Thing that reigned in Rome — he could not face tomorrow, he could not look again into the face of Antichrist . . .

He crawled across the room and stared at Jacobea.

She was not beautiful; he noticed that her hands were torn and stained with earth from making the graves of the nuns . . . she had asked for Christian burial . . . he could not stay to give it her . . .

He fiercely hated her for what she had told him, yet he took up the ends of her yellow hair and kissed them.

Again the thunder and lightning and wild howlings reached him from without, as ghosts and night-hags wandered past to hold court within the accursed city.

The candle shot up a long tongue of flame — and went out.

Theirry staggered across the darkness.

A flash of lightning showed him the door. As the thunder crashed above the city he fled from the convent and from Rome.

## Chapter 11

## The Angels

In a ruined villa, shattered by the barbarians and crumbled by time, sat Ysabeau the Empress looking over the sunless Maremma.

A few olive trees were all that shaded the bare expanse of marshy land, where great pools veiled with unhealthy vapours gleamed faintly under the heavy clouds.

Here and there rose the straight roof of a forsaken convent, or the stately pillars of a deserted palace.

There was no human being in sight.

A few birds flew low over the marshes; sometimes one screamed in through the open roof or darted across the gaping broken doorway.

Then Ysabeau would rise from her sombre silence to spurn them from her with fierce words and stones.

The stained marble was grown with reeds and wild flowers; a straggling vine half twisted round two of the slender columns; and there the Empress sat, huddled in her cloak and gazing over the forlorn marshes.

She had dwelt here for three days; at every sunrise a peasant girl, daring the excommunication, had brought her food, then fled with a frightened face.

Ysabeau saw nothing before her save death, but she did not mean to die by the ignoble way of starvation.

She had not heard of the defeat of Balthasar at Tivoli, nor of the election of Theirry to the crown; day and night she thought on her husband, and pondered how she might still possibly serve him.

She did not hope to see him again; it never occurred to her to return to him; when she had fled his camp she had left a confession behind her — no Greek would have heeded it, but these Saxons, still, to her, foreigners, were different.

And Balthasar had loved Melchoir of Brabant.

It was very hot, with a sullen, close heat; the dreary prospect became hateful to her, and she rose and moved to the inner portion of the villa, where the marigold roots thrust up through the inlaid stone floor, and a remaining portion of the roof cast a shade.

Here she seated herself on the capital of a broken column, and a languid weariness subdued her proud spirit; her head sank back against the stained wall, and she slept.

When she woke the whole landscape was glowing with the soft red of sunset.

She stretched herself, shivered, and looked about her.

Then she suddenly drew herself together and listened.

There were faint voices coming from the outer room, and the sound of a man's tread. Ysabeau held her breath.

But so close a silence followed that she thought she must have been deceived.

For a while she waited, then crept cautiously towards the shattered doorway that led into the other chamber.

She gained it and gazed through.

Sitting where she had just now sat, under the vine-twisted columns, was a huge knight in defaced armour; his back was towards her; by his side his helmet stood, and the great glittering dragon that formed the crest shone in the setting sun.

He was bending over a child that lay asleep on a crimson cloak.

"Balthasar," said Ysabeau.

He gave a little cry, and looked over his shoulder. "Tell me, my lord," she asked in a trembling voice, "as you would tell a stranger, if evil fortune brings you here."

He rose softly, his face flushed.

"I am a ruined man. They have elected another Emperor. Now, I think, it does not matter."
Her eyes travelled in a dazed way to the child.

"Is he sick?"

"Nay, only weary; we have been wandering since Tivoli —"

While he spoke he looked at her, as if the world held nothing else worth gazing on. "I must go," said Ysabeau.

"Must go?"

"I am cast out — I may not share your misfortunes." Balthasar laughed.

"I have been searching for you madly, Ysabeau."

"Searching?"

And now he looked away from her.

"I thought my heart would have burst when I discovered ye had gone to Rome."

"But you found the writing?" she cried.

"Yea —"

"You know — I slew him?"

"I know you went to give your life for me."

"I am accursed!

"You have been faithful to me."

"Oh, Balthasar! — does it make no difference?"

"It cannot," he said, half sadly. "You are my wife — part of me; I have given you my heart to keep, and nothing can alter it."

"You do not mock me?" she questioned, shuddering. "It must be that you mock me — I will go away —"

He stepped before her.

"You shall never leave me again, Ysabeau."

"I had not dared — you have forgiven —"

"I am not your judge —"

"It cannot be that God is so tender!"

"I do not speak for Him," said Balthasar hoarsely —"but for myself —"

She could not answer.

"Ysabeau," he cried jealously, "you — could you have lived apart from me?"

"Nay," she whispered; "I meant to die."

"That I might be forgiven!"

"What else could I do! Would they had slain me and taken the curse from you!"

He put his arm round her bowed shoulders. "There is no curse while we are together, Ysabeau."

Her marvellous hair lay across his dinted mail.

"This is sweeter than our marriage day, Balthasar, for now you know the worst of me —"

"My wife! — my lady and my wife!"

He set her gently on the broken shaft by the door and kissed her hand.

"Wencelaus sleeps," she smiled through tears. "I could not have put him to rest more surely —" "He slept not much last night," said Balthasar, "for the owls and flitter mice — and it was very dark with the moon hidden."

Her hand still lay in his great palm.

"Tell me of yourself," she whispered.

And he told her how they had been defeated at Tivoli, how the remnant of his force had forsaken him, and how Theirry of Dendermonde had been elected Emperor by the wishes of the Pope.

Her eyes grew fierce at that.

"I have ruined you," she said; "made you a beggar."

"If you knew" — he smiled half shyly —"how little I care, for myself — certes, for you."
"Do not shame me," she cried.

"Could I have held a throne without you, Ysabeau?"

Her fingers trembled in his.

"Would I had been a better woman, for your sake, Balthasar."

His swift bright flush dyed his fair face.

"All I grieve for, Ysabeau, is — God."

"God?" she asked, wondering.

"If He should not forgive?" — his blue eyes were troubled —"and we are cursed and cast out —— what think you?"

She drew closer to him.

"Through me! — you grieve, and this is — through me!"

"Nay, our destiny is one — always. Only, I think — of afterwards — yet, if you are — damned, as the priest says, why, I will be so too —"

"Do not fear, Balthasar; if God will not receive me, the little images at Constantinople will forgive me if I pray to them again as I did when I was a child —"

They fell on silence again, while the red colour of the setting sun deepened and cast a glow over their weary faces and the sleeping figure of Wencelaus; the vine leaves fluttered from the ancient marble and the wild-fowl screamed across the marshes.

"Who is this Pope that he should hate us so?" mused Ysabeau. "And who Theirry of Dendermonde that he should be Emperor of the West?"

"He is to be crowned in the Basilica today," said Balthasar.

"While we sit here!"

"I do not understand it. Nor do I now, Ysabeau," — Balthasar looked at her —"greatly care —"

"But you shall care!" she cried. "If I be all to you, I will be that — I must see you again upon the throne; we will to Basil's Court. That this Theirry of Dendermonde should sleep to-night in the golden palace!"

"We have found each other," said the Emperor simply.

She raised his hand, kissed it, and no more was said, while the mists gathered and thickened over the Maremma and the rich hues faded from the sky.

"Who is that?" cried Ysabeau, and pointed across the marsh-land.

A figure, dark against the mists, was running aimlessly, wildly to and fro, winding his way in and out the pools, now and then flinging his arms up in a frantic gesture towards the evening sky.

"A madman," said Balthasar; "see, he runs with no object, round and round, yet always as if pursued —"

Ysabeau drew close to her husband, as they both watched, with a curious fascination, the man being driven hither and thither as by an invisible enemy.

"Is it a ghost?" whispered Ysabeau; "strangely chilled and horror-stricken do I feel —" The Emperor made the sign of the Cross.

"Part of the curse, maybe," he muttered.

Suddenly, as if exhausted, the man stopped and stood still with hanging head and arms; the sun burning to the horizon made a vivid background to his tall dark figure till the heavy noisome vapours rose to the level of the sunset, and the solitary, motionless stranger was blotted from the view of the two watching in the ruined villa.

"Why should we wonder?" said Balthasar. "There must be many men abroad, both Saxon and Roman —"

"Yet, he ran strangely," she murmured; "and I have been here three days and seen no one."

"We must get away," said Balthasar resolutely. "This is a vile spot."

"At dawn a girl comes here with food, enough at least for Wencelaus.

"I have food with me, Ysabeau, given by one who did not know that we were excommunicate."

The Empress looked about her fearfully.

"I heard a step."

Balthasar peered through the mist.

"The man," whispered Ysabeau.

Out of the dreary vapours, the forlorn and foul mists of the marshes, he appeared, stumbling over the stones in his way . . .

He caught hold of the slender pillar by the entrance and stared at the three with distraught eyes. His clothes were dark, wet and soiled, his hair hung lank round a face hollow and pale but of obvious beauty.

"Theirry of Dendermonde!" exclaimed Balthasar. Ysabeau gave a cry that woke the child and sent him frightened into her arms.

"The Emperor," said the new-comer in a feeble voice.

Balthasar answered fiercely — —"Am I still Emperor to you? — you who today were to receive my crown in St. Peter's church?"

Ysabeau clasped Wencelaus tightly to her breast, and her eyes shone with a wrathful triumph. "They have cast him out; Rome rose against such a king!"

Theirry shivered and crouched like one very cold.

"Of my own will I fled from Rome, that city of the Devil!"

Balthasar stared at him.

"Is this the man who broke our ranks at Tivoli?"

"Is this he who would be Emperor of the West?" cried Ysabeau.

"You are the Emperor," said Theirry faintly, "and I pretend no longer to these wrongful honours, nor serve I any longer Antichrist —"

"He is mad!" cried Balthasar.

"Nay," Ysabeau spoke eagerly —"listen to him."

Theirry moaned.

"I have nothing to say — give me a place to rest in."

"Through you we have no place ourselves to rest in," answered Balthasar grimly. "No shelter save these broken walls you see; but since you have returned to your allegiance, we command that you tell us of this Antichrist —"

Theirry straightened himself.

"He who reigns in Rome is Antichrist, Michael, who was Dirk Renswoude — —"

"He perished," said the Emperor, very pale; "and the Pope was Blaise of Dendermonde."

"That was the Devil's work, black magic!" cried Theirry wildly; "the youth Blaise died ten years ago, and Dirk Renswoude took his place."

"It is true!" cried the Empress; "by what he said to me I know it true — now do I see it very clearly."

But Balthasar stared at Theirry in a confused manner.

"I do not understand."

The lightning darted through the broken wall, and a solitary winged thing flapped over the roofless villa.

Theirry began to speak.

He told them, in a thick, expressionless voice, all he knew of Dirk Renswoude.

He did not mention Ursula of Rooselaare. As his tale went on, the storm gathered till all light had vanished from the sky, the lightning rent a starless gloom, and the continual roar of the thunder quivered in the stifling air.

In the pauses between the lightning they could not see each other; Wencelaus sobbed on his mother's breast, and the owls hooted in the crevices of the marble.

Theirry's voice suddenly strengthened.

"Now, turn against Rome, for all men will join you — a force of Lombards marches up from Trastevere, and the Saxons gather without the walls of the accursed city."

A blue flash showed them his face . . . they heard him fall . . .

After a while Balthasar made his way to him through the dark.

"He has fainted," he said fearfully; "is he, belike, mad?"

"He speaks the hideous truth," whispered Ysabeau.

Suddenly, at its very height the storm ceased, the air became cool and fragrant, and a bright moon floated from the clouds.

The silver radiance of it, extraordinarily bright and vivid, illuminated the Maremma, the pools, the tall reeds, the deserted buildings, the ruins that sheltered them; the clouds rolled swiftly from the sky, leaving it clear and blazing with stars.

The first moon and the first stars that had shone since Michael II's reign in the Vatican. Theirry's dark dress and hair, and deathlike face pressed against the marble pavement showed now plainly.

Balthasar looked at his wife; neither dared to speak, but Wencelaus gave a panting sigh of relief at the lifting of the darkness.

"My lord," he said, striving out of his mother's arms, "a goodly company comes across the marsh —"

A great awe and fear held them silent, and the wonderful silver shine of the moon lay over them like a spell.

They saw, slowly approaching them, two knights and two ladies, who seemed to advance without motion across the marsh-land.

The knights wore armour that shone like glass, and long mantles of white samite; the dames were clad in silver tissue, and around their brows were close-pressed wreaths of roses mingled red and white.

Very bright and fair they seemed; the knights came to the fore, carrying silver trumpets; the ladies held each other's hands lovingly, and their gleaming tresses of red and gold wove together as they walked.

They reached the portals of the villa, and the air blew cold and pure.

The lady with the yellow hair who held white violets in her hand, spoke to the other, and her voice was like the echo of the sea in a wide-lipped shell.

They paused; Balthasar drew back before the great light they brought with them, and Ysabeau hid her face, for some of them she knew.

On earth their names had been Melchoir, Sebastian, Jacobea and Sybilla.

"Balthasar," said the foremost Knight, "we are come from the courts of Paradise to bid you march against Rome. In that city reigns Evil, permitted to punish a sinful people, but now her time is come. Go you to Viterbo, there you will find the Cardinal of Narbonne, whom God has ordained Pope, and with him an army; at the head of it storm Rome, and all the people shall join you in destroying Antichrist."

Balthasar fell on his knees.

"And the curse!" he cried.

"'Tis not the curse of God upon you, therefore be comforted, Balthasar of Courtrai, and at the dawn haste to Viterbo."

With that they moved away, and were absorbed into the silver light that transfigured the Maremma.

Balthasar sprang to his feet, shouting —

"I am not excommunicate! I shall be Emperor again. The curse is lifted!"

The moonlight faded, again the clouds rolled up . . .

Balthasar caught Theirry by the shoulder.

"Did you see the vision? — the angels?"

Theirry came shuddering from his swoon.

"I saw nothing — Ursula . . . Ursula . . . "

# Chapter 12

## In the Vatican

In the ebony cabinet in the Vatican sat Michael II; an expression of utter anguish marked his face.

On the gold table were spread books and parchments; the sullen light of a stormy midday filtered through the painted curtains and showed the rich splendours of the chamber, the glittering, closed wings of the shrine, the carved gold arms of the Pope's chair, the threads of silver tissue in his crimson robe.

He sat very still, his elbow resting on the table, his cheek propped on his palm, now and then he looked at the little sand clock.

Presently Paolo Orsini entered; the Pope glanced at him without moving.

"No news?" he asked.

"None of the Lord Theirry, your Holiness." Michael II moistened his lips.

"They have searched — everywhere?"

"Throughout Rome, your Holiness, but —"

"Well?"

"Only this, my lord, a man might easily disappear — there is no law in the city."

"He was armed, they said, when he left the palace; have you sent to the convent I told you of — — St. Angela, beyond the Appian Gate?"

"Yea, your Holiness," answered Orsini, "and they found nought but a dead woman." The Pope averted his eyes.

"What did they with her?" Orsini lifted his brows.

"Cast her into the plague pit, Holiness — that quarter is a charnel-house."

The Pope drew a deep breath.

"Well, he is gone — I do not think him dead," — he flung back his head — "but the game is over, is it not, Orsini? We fling down our pieces and say — good-night!"

His nostrils dilated, his eyes flashed, he brought his open hand softly on to the table. "What does your Holiness mean?" asked Orsini.

"We mean that this puppet Emperor of ours has forsaken us, and that our position becomes perilous," answered the Pope. "Cardinal Narbonne, hurling defiance at us from Viterbo, grows stronger, and the mob — do not seek to deceive me, Orsini, the mob clamours against us?"

"It is true, my lord."

The Pope gave a terrible smile, and his beautiful eyes widened.

"And the soldiers mutiny, the Saxons at Trastevere have joined Balthasar and the Veronese have left me — we have not enough men to hold Rome an hour; well, Orsini, you shall take a summons to the Cardinals and we will hold a conclave, there to decide how we may meet our fortune."

He rose and turned towards the window.

"Hark, do you hear how the factions howl below? — begone, Orsini."

The secretary departed in silence.

Mutterings, murmurings, howlings rose from the accursed city to the Pontiff's chamber; lightning darted from the black heavens, and thunder rolled round the hills of Rome. Michael II walked to and fro in his gorgeous cabinet.

In the three days since Theirry had fled the city, his power had crumbled like a handful of sand; Rome had turned against him, and every hour men fell away from his cause.

The devils, too, had forsaken him; he could not raise the spirits, the magic fires would not burn . . . all was blank darkness and silence.

Up and down he paced, listening to the mob surging in the Piazza of St. Peter.

The day wore on and the storm grew in violence.

Paolo Orsini came again to him, his face pale.

"Half the Cardinals are fled to Viterbo and those remaining refuse to acknowledge your Holiness."

The Pope smiled.

"I had expected it."

"News comes from a Greek runner that Theirry of Dendermonde is with Balthasar's host —" "Also I expected that," said Michael II wildly.

"And they proclaim you," continued Orsini in an agitated manner, "an impostor, one given to evil practices, and by these means incite the people against you; Cardinal Orvieto has led a thousand men across the marshes to the Emperor's army —"

"And Theirry of Dendermonde has denounced me!" said the Pope.

As he spoke one beat for admission on the gilt door. The secretary opened and there entered an Eastern chamberlain.

"Holiness," he cried fearfully, "the people have set fire to your palace on the Palatine Hill, and Cardinal Colonna, with his brother Octavian, have seized Castel San Angelo for the Emperor, and hold it in defiance of your Grace."

As he finished the lightning darted info the now darkening chamber, and the thunder mingled with the howling of the mob that surged beneath the Vatican walls.

"The captain of my guard and those faithful to me," answered the Pope, "will know how to do what may be done — apprise me of the approach of Balthasar's host, and now go."

They left him; he stood for a while listening to those ominous sounds that filled the murky air, then he pressed a spring in one of the mother-of-pearl panels and stepped into the secret chamber that was revealed.

Cautiously he closed the panel by which he had entered, and looked furtively about him.

The small windowless space was lit only by one blood-red lamp, locked cupboards lined the walls, and a huge globe of faint gold, painted with curious and mystic signs, hung from the ceiling.

The Pope's stiff garments made a soft rustling sound as he moved; his quick desperate breathing disturbed the heavy confined air.

In his pallid face his eyes rolled and gleamed.

"Sathanas, Sathanas," he muttered, "is this the end?"

A throbbing shook the red-lit gloom, his last words were echoed mournfully —

"The end."

He clutched his hands into the jewelled embroidery on his breast.

"Now you mock me — by my old allegiance, is this the end?"

Again the echo from the dark walls —

"The end."

The Pope glared in front of him.

"Must I die, Sathanas — must I swiftly die?"

A little confused laughter came before the echo "swiftly die."

He paced up and down the narrow space.

"I staked my fortunes on that man's faith and he has forsaken me, and I have lost, lost!" "Lost! lost!"

The Pope laughed frantically.

"At least she died, Sathanas, her yellow hair rots in the plague pit now; I had some skill left . . . but what was all my skill if I could not keep him faithful to me —"

He clasped his jewelled hand over his eyes; utter silence followed his words now; the globe of pallid gold trembled in the darkness of the domed ceiling, and the mystic characters on it began to writhe and move.

"Long had I lived with the earth beneath my feet had I not met that fair sweet fool, and I go to ruin for his sake who has denounced me —"

The red lamp became dull as a dying coal.

"Ye warned me," breathed the Pope, "that this man would be my bane — you promised on his truth to you and me to halve the world between us; he was false, and you have utterly forsaken me?"

The echo answered —

"Utterly forsaken . . . "

The lamp went out.

The pale luminous globe expanded to a monstrous size, the circle of dark little fiends round it danced and whirled madly..

Then it burst and fell in a thousand fragments at the Pope's feet.

Out of the darkness came a wail as of some thing hurt or dying, then long sighing shook the close air . . .

The Pope felt along the wall, touched the spring and stepped into the ebony cabinet. He looked quite old and small and bowed.

Night had fallen; the chamber was lit by perfumed candles in curious carved sticks of soap-stone; faint veils of incense floated in the air.

Without the thunder rolled and threatened, and the factions of Rome fought in the streets.

The Pope sank into a chair and folded his hands in his lap; his head fell forward on his breast; his lips quivered and two tears rolled down his cheeks.

The Angelus bells rang out over the city, there were not many to ring now; as they quivered away a clock struck, quite near.

The Pope did not move.

Once again Paolo Orsini entered, and Michael II averted his face.

"Holiness, Balthasar marches on Rome," said the secretary, "the mob rush forth to join him, and if the gates were brass, and five times brass, the Vatican could not withstand them." The Pope spoke without looking round.

"Will they storm the Vatican?"

"Ay, that they will, Holiness," answered Orsini.

Now the Pontiff turned his white face.

"What may I do?"

"The captain of the guard suggests that ye come to terms with the Emperor, and by sub-mission save your life."

"That I will not."

"Then it were well if your Holiness would flee; there is a secret way out of the Vatican —"

"And that I will not."

Orsini, too, was very pale.

"Then are you doomed to fall into the hands of Balthasar, and he and his faction say — horrible things."

The Pope rose.

"You think they would lay hands on me?"

"I do fear it!

"It would be a shameful death, Orsini?"

"Surely not that! I cannot think the Emperor would do more than imprison your Holiness."

"Well, you are very faithful, Orsini."

The young Roman shrugged his shoulders.

"Cardinal Narbonne is a Colonna, Holiness, and I have always found you a generous master."

The Pope went to the window. "How they howl!" he said through his teeth, "and Balthasar comes nearer, nearer —"

He checked himself abruptly.

"I will dine here to-night, Orsini, see that everything is done as usual."

The secretary bowed himself out of the gilt door. Michael II went to the table on the dais and took from it a scroll of parchment.

Standing in the centre of the room he unrolled it; some verses were written in a scarlet ink on the smooth surface; in a low voice he read aloud the two last.

"If Love were all!
I had lived glad and meek, Nor heard Ambition call And Valour speak.
If Love were all!"

He smiled bitterly. "But Love is weak.
And often leaves his throne, Among his scattered roses pale To weep and moan.
And I, apostate to his whispered creed.
Shall miss his wings above my pall.
Nor find his face in this my bitter need.
When Love is all!"

"The metre halts," said Michael II, "the metre . . . halts."

He tore the parchment into fragments and scattered them on the floor. Again the gilt doors were opened, this time a chamberlain entered. A herald had brought a fierce and grim message from Balthasar.

It spoke of the Pope as Antichrist, and called on him to submit if he would keep his life.

The Pope read it with haughty eyes; when he had finished he rent it across and cast the pieces down among the others.

"And ye shall hang the herald," he said. "We have so much authority." The chamberlain handed him a second packet, sealed.

"This also the herald brought, Holiness." "From whom?"

"From Theirry of Dendermonde."

"Theirry of — of Dendermonde?"

"Yea, Holiness."

The Pope took the packet.

"Let the herald live," he said, "but cast him into the dungeons."

The chamberlain withdrew.

For a while Michael II stood staring at the packet, while the thunder crashed over Rome. Then he slowly broke the seal.

"What curses have you for me?" he cried wildly. "What curses? You!"

He unfolded the long strip of vellum, and went nearer the candles to read it.

Thus it ran —

"The Emperor's camp, marching on Rome, Theirry of Dendermonde to Michael, Pope of Rome, thus —

"I am approaching madness, I cannot sleep or rest — after days of torment I write to you whom I have twice betrayed. She died on my breast, but I do not care; Balthasar says he saw her walking on the Maremma, but I saw nothing . . . before she died she said something. I think of you and of nothing else, though I have betrayed you, I have never uttered what she said. No one guesses.

"The uncertainty, the horror, gnaw away my heart. So I write this to you."

"This is my message —"

"If you are a devil, be satisfied, for your devil's work is done."

"If you are a man, you have befriended, wronged me, and I have avenged myself."

"If you are that other thing you may be, then I know you love me, and that I kissed you once."

"If this last be true, as I do think it true, have some pity on my long ignorance and believe I have it in me to love even as you have loved."

"Oh, Ursula, I know a city in India where we might live, and you forget you ever ruled in Rome; yonder are other gods who are so old they have forgot to punish, and they would smile on you and me there, Ursula. Balthasar marches on the city, and you must be ruined and discovered — brought to an end so horrible. You have showed me a secret way out of the Vatican, use it now, this night. I am in advance of the host — I shall be without the Appian

Gate tonight, and I have means whereby we may fly to the coast and there take ship to India; until we meet, farewell! and in the name of all the passions you have roused in me — come!"

As the Pope read, all the colour slowly left his face; when he had finished he mechanically rolled up the parchment, then unrolled it again.

Thunder shook the Vatican and the mob howled without.

Again he read the letter.

Then he thrust it into one of the candles and watched it blacken, curl, burst into flame. He flung it on the marble floor and set his gold heel on it, grinding it into ashes.

At the usual hour they served his sumptuous supper; when it was finished and removed, Paolo Orsini came again.

"Will not your Holiness fly, before it is too late?" All traces of anguish and woe had vanished from his master's features; he looked proud and beautiful.

"I shall stay here; but let them who will, seek safety."

He dismissed Orsini and the attendants.

It was now late in the evening — and the thunder unceasing.

The Pope locked the door of the cabinet, then went to the gilt table, and wrote a letter rapidly — — this he folded, sealed with purple wax and stamped with his great thumb ring.

He sat silent a little while after this and stared with great luminous eyes before him, then roused himself and unlocked a drawer in the table.

From this he took some documents, tied together with orange silk, and a ring with a red stone in it.

One by one he burnt the parchments in the candle, and when they were reduced to a little pile of ashes he cast the ring into the midst of it and turned away.

He crossed to the window, drew the curtains and looked out over Rome.

In the black heavens, above the black hills, hung a huge meteor, a blazing globe of fire with a trail of flame . . .

The Pope let the silk fall together again.

He took up one of the candles and went to the gold door that led to his bed-chamber.

Before he opened it he paused a moment; the candle-flame lit his vivid eyes, his haughty face, his glittering vestments..

He turned the handle and entered the dark, spacious room

Through the high, undraped window could clearly be seen the star that seemed to burn away the very sky.

The Pope set the candle on a shelf where it showed dim glimpses of white and gold tapestries, walls of alabaster, a bed of purple and gilt, mysterious, gorgeous luxury..

He returned to the cabinet and took from the bosom of his gown a little bottle of yellow jade; for the stopper a ruby served.

The thunder crashed deafeningly; the lightning seemed to split the room in twain; the Pope stood still, listening.

Then he blew out the candles and returned to his bed-chamber.

Softly he passed into the scented, splendid chamber and closed the door behind him.

In the little pause between two thunder-peals was the sound of a great key turning in a lock.

## Chapter 13

## The Secret

The mob had stormed the Vatican; Octavian Colonna, with a handful of fighting men, ascended the undefended marble staircase.

The papal guards lay slain in the courtyard and in the entrance hall; chamberlains, secretary, pages, and priests, fled or surrendered.

With the Lord Colonna was Theirry of Dendermonde, who had entered Rome that morning by the Appian Gate and headed a faction of the lawless crowd in their wild attack on the Vatican. To himself he kept saying —

"I shall know, she did not come; I shall know, she did not come."

It was early morning; the terrific storm of last night still lingered over Rome; flashes of blue light divided the murky clouds and the thunder hung about the Aventine; the Colonna grew afraid; he waited below in the gorgeous audience-chamber and sent up to the Pope's apartments, demanding his submission and promising him safety.

The overawed crowd retired into the courtyard and the Piazza while Paolo Orsini ascended the silver stairs.

He returned with this message —

"His Holiness's apartments were locked, nor could they make him hear."

"Break down the doors," said the Colonna, but he trembled.

It was a common thought among the knights that Michael II had escaped; a monk offered to show them the secret passage where his Holiness might be even now; many went; but Theirry followed the attendants to the gilt door of the ebony cabinet.

They broke the lock and entered, fearfully.

On the floor torn fragments of parchments, a pile of ashes with a ruby ring lying in the midst . . .

Nothing else.

"His Holiness is in his chamber — we dare not enter."

They had always been afraid of him; even now his name held terror.

"The Colonna waits our news!" cried Theirry wildly, "I — I dare enter."

They tiptoed to the other gilt door; it took them some time to remove the lock.

When at last the door gave and swung open they shrunk away — but Theirry passed into the chamber.

The sombre light of dawn filled it; heavy shadows obscured the rich splendours of golden colours, of gleaming white walls; the men crept after him — it seemed to Theirry as if the world had stopped about them.

On the magnificent purple bed lay the Pope; on his brow the tiara glittered, and on his breast the chasuble; the crozier lay by his side on the samite coverlet, and his feet glittered in their golden shoes; by the crozier was a letter and a jade bottle.

The attendants shrieked and fled.

Theirry crept to the bedside and took up the parchment; his name was over the top; he broke the seal.

He read the fair writing.

"If I be a devil I go whence I came, if a man I lived as one and die as one, if woman I have known Love, conquered it and by it have been vanquished. Whatsoever I am, I perish on the heights, but I do not descend from them. I have known things in their fulness and will not stay to taste the dregs. So, to you greeting, and not for long farewell."

The letter fell from Theirry's hand, fluttered and sank to the floor.

He raised his eyes and saw through the window the meteor, blazing over Rome.

Dead . . .

He looked now at the proud smooth face on the pillow; the gems of the papal crown gleaming above the red locks, the jewelled chasuble sparkling in the strengthening dawn until he was nearly fooled into thinking the bosom heaved beneath.

He was alone.

At least he could know.

The air was like incense sweet and stifling; his blood seemed to beat in his brain with a little foolish sound of melody; a shaft of grey light fell over the splendours of the bed, the roses and dragons, hawks and hounds sewn on the curtains and coverlets; from the Pope's garments rose a subtle and beautiful perfume.

"Ursula," said Theirry; he bent over the bed until the pearls in his ears touched his cheeks. Without the thunder muttered.

To know —

He lifted the dead Pope's arm; there seemed to be neither weight nor substance under the stiff silk. He dropped the sleeve; his cold fingers unclasped the heavy chasuble, underneath lay perfumed samite, white and soft.

An awful sensation crept through his veins; he thought that under these gorgeous vestments was nothing — nothing — ashes.

He did not dare to uncover the bosom that lay, that must lie, under the gleaming samite . . . But he must know.

He lifted up the fair crowned head to peer madly into the proud features . . .

It came away in his hands, like crumbling wood that may preserve, till touched, the semblance of the carving . . . so the Pope's head parted from the trunk.

Theirry smiled with horror and stared at what he held.

Then it disappeared, fell into ashes before his eyes, and the tiara rolled on to the floor. Gone — like an image of smoke.

He sank across the headless thing on the bed.

"Must I follow you to know, follow you to hell?" he whispered.

Now he could open the rich garments.

They were empty of all save dust.

The strange strong perfume was stinging and numbing his brain, his heart; he thought he heard the fiends coming for his soul — at last.

He hid his face in the purple silk robes and felt his blood grow cold.

The room darkened about him, he knew he was being drawn downwards into eternity, he sighed and slipped from the bed on to the floor.

As his last breath hovered on his lips the meteor vanished, the thunder-clouds rolled away from a fair blue sky and a glorious sunrise laughed over the city.

The reign of Antichrist was ended.

Through the Pope's chamber the notes of silver trumpets quivered.

Balthasar's trumpets as his hosts marched triumphantly into Rome.